MIDNIGHT JEWEL

MIDNIGHT JEWEL

RICHELLE MEAD

RAZORBILL®

An Imprint of Penguin Random House

RAZORBILL®

An Imprint of Penguin Random House
Penguin.com

RAZORBILL & colophon is a registered trademark of Penguin Random House LLC.

Copyright © 2017 Richelle Thaler

ISBN: 9781595148438

Printed in the United States of America

1 3 5 7 9 10 8 6 4 2

Interior design by Lindsey Andrews

For all the women and girls out there
who refuse to back down.

CHAPTER 1

"YOU! GIRL! DON'T TAKE ANOTHER STEP, OR I'LL RUN YOU through!"

I froze where I was, halfway up the great stone stairs that led to the cathedral of Kyriel.

The *thump-thump* of boots sounded behind me, and moments later, a young watchman rushed over to block my way. He stood almost a foot taller than me, his dark hair shaved close to the scalp as so many of the watch did. What many of the watch did not do, however, was wield a dagger with such confidence. Most kept the city's peace with heavy clubs.

I met his eyes calmly. "I beg your pardon, sir, but I'm on my way to prayer."

"Don't give me that." His face twisted into a scowl. "Everyone knows you Sims are Alanzan heathens. And I know who *you* are. I remember you and your murderous brother."

A spark of anger kindled inside me, but I kept it hidden. I had a lot of practice ignoring comments like his. "I was actually going to pray for his soul. I'm a faithful devotee of Uros. Do you think the angels would let a heretic step on this holy ground?"

I gestured up to the imposing double doors above us. A great arch, carved into the cathedral's stone, surrounded them and made the entry look even more majestic. A monk of Vaiel, hooded in deep green robes, stepped outside just then, reaffirming the sanctity of where we stood.

The watchman hesitated a moment and then grew stern again. He kept the dagger pointed at me. "Maybe you aren't one of the Alanzans, but I know you're as much of a criminal as everyone else in your family. You just haven't been caught yet. Now tell me where your brother is."

I spread my hands out in helpless confusion, ignoring the impulse to reach for my own knife, which was hidden in a skirt pocket. "I wish I knew. I haven't seen him in over a year."

He pressed the dagger's point to my breastbone. "You're lying."

The heartbreaking part was that I'd actually spoken the truth. Lonzo had sent me one letter when he'd arrived in that land across the sea. And then there'd been silence.

"What's all this?" a new voice asked. A familiar voice.

Another watchman joined us, moving much more casually than his colleague. This man was older, portly, and red-faced. He'd left his thinning hair as it was, probably because there was too little to shave. I kept my eyes fixed serenely ahead, giving no indication that I knew him.

The younger watchman lowered the blade. "Carey, this is the Viana girl. The one whose brother killed Sir Wilhelm last year. That bastard was never brought to justice!"

Watchman Carey stifled a yawn. "Well, I don't see him here. I only see his sister. And no one ever actually proved he did it."

"But you know he did!" spat the other watchman. "We all know it. And she knows where he is! We should be tracking her every move!"

"Into a church? You think her brother is hiding here? Should I go ask that monk if we can conduct a search?"

"Sir—"

"There's nothing here." Watchman Carey managed to sound both bored and irritated. "Only a girl on her way to pray and better her soul—a girl who's done nothing wrong."

The other man's eyes narrowed at me. "She's a Sirminican. They've all done something."

Watchman Carey gestured him away. "Go make yourself useful. Stop a real crime, not one that went cold long ago. And damn it, put that dagger away. You're embarrassing us all."

The young watchman sheathed the blade but held a finger up to my face. I didn't flinch. "Don't think I'll forget this, girl. I'll find your bloody brother, wherever he's hiding."

Once the man had stormed away, Watchman Carey's features sharpened. "Tell me he's not still in the city."

"No," I said, exhaling in relief. "But I really don't know where he is. Just that he's far away."

"You should join him."

A dull ache filled my chest. "I'm trying, sir."

"Try harder. Things like this are going to keep happening. Sir Wilhelm had a lot of friends, and they haven't forgotten." Watchman Carey suddenly looked very weary. "Look, I like you. I really do. You're smart. You know our language. But I'm not a fool. I hear about the girl who stops thieves in the Sirminican district. And that's not a bad thing—but it is something that could get out of hand one day. Just like with your brother."

"Lonzo—"

"Not another word. Sir Wilhelm was as vile as they come, gentry or not. And maybe he deserved what he got, but the less I know, the better."

Watchman Carey's forehead wrinkled up with a frown as a memory held him. He'd been the one to find Isabel, the Sirminican girl Sir Wilhelm had used for his own sick pleasures and then discarded in a river. True, Lonzo had intended to beat him to a pulp, but actually killing Sir Wilhelm? That had been accidental. Most of the watch hadn't cared about that detail—not with a Sirminican involved. Watchman Carey *had* cared and had looked away a number of times as the evidence against Lonzo mounted.

"Get out of here. You can do better." He gave me a wry smile. He was the only member of the watch who'd ever treated me as an equal.

The only one who even attempted my language. "And don't take it amiss when I say I hope we never cross paths again."

He lumbered down the steps without another word, soon disappearing into the crowd on the street. I took a moment to collect myself and continued my journey to the cathedral. The monk remained standing near the door, having observed the whole exchange. He said nothing. The great hood hid his face, but he turned his head and tracked me as I walked inside.

My father had liked conducting clandestine business in churches. No one ever expected it. Only a handful of other people had come inside to pray during the middle of the day in this grand cathedral, one of the biggest in Osfro. They sat solemnly on the glossy wooden pews, heads bowed or eyes fixed on the sculpture of the glorious angel Kyriel that hung before us on the sanctuary wall. A priest in gold and pale green robes quietly lit candles on the altar beneath the angel, and the scent of beeswax and resin filled the air.

I scanned the nave and found the person I sought. I casually made my way over, sitting near him without making eye contact, as though my choice of pew was a coincidence. The wood creaked beneath me, and I nearly sneezed at the man's pretentious herbal cologne.

Bowing my head, I touched my brow first and then my heart. "All praise to Uros, creator of spirit and flesh," I murmured. "All praise to his six glorious angels, defenders of the faithful."

"All praise," the man beside me echoed.

I lifted my head, fixing my eyes on the glorious Kyriel. The angel held a gilded sword and shield, ready to defend mankind from the six wayward angels. My real interest was in the priest as he continued lighting candles in my periphery. When he'd finished with the last one, he retreated to a small alcove and knelt to pray.

Certain he was preoccupied, I reached into my skirt pocket and took out a small, folded piece of paper. I carefully set it on the pew between my companion and me. After several seconds, he took it and slipped it into his own coat pocket.

"Those are the names of ten Alanzans living in Cape Triumph—at least as of last spring," I said softly. "I'm sure there are more. But that's enough to get you connected. You need to memorize them and burn it right away."

He raised his head. "I know that. Give me some credit."

Around the nave, stained-glass windows depicted the other angels in rainbow colors. None of them seemed to care that a heretic was sitting beside me. Kyriel didn't leap forward with his sword. The cathedral's vaulted ceiling didn't come crashing down. Uros didn't hurl lightning from the heavens. *Maybe the Alanzans aren't the heretics*, I mused. *Maybe their way is the right way, and the orthodox who built this church are actually the heretics. Or maybe they're both wrong.*

I finally turned and met my companion's eyes. The dim lighting made them appear more gray than blue, but it couldn't hide their eager sparkle. Cedric Thorn was an extremely handsome man. Not my type—but still nice to look at. I preferred men who were a little rougher around the edges. Men who didn't so obviously deliberate on their clothing each morning.

"I give you a lot of credit. But people's lives are on the line."

His face sobered. "Believe me, I know. Thank you. And here's something for you."

My heart sped up as he reached into his coat, cast a quick glance around, and then produced a rolled sheaf of papers. He set it discreetly between us. "Your contract. Admission to the Glittering Court. A ticket to Adoria."

"Adoria," I repeated, clenching the papers. The Alanzans I knew had sworn he was a man of integrity, but until this moment, I'd had my doubts that he'd uphold his half of the bargain. Plenty of Osfridians had experimented with the Alanzan faith. Plenty had lost interest and happily turned in the real devotees.

"I made a few inquiries," he said, still serious, "but I don't think there's anything I can do to help find your brother once we're over there. They don't always record the names of bond servants. Even when they do, getting those records would require a connection to a customs officer—or enough money to bribe one. I don't have either."

"Maybe my husband will." *Husband.* The word felt strange on my tongue.

"Are you sure that's what you want? A husband?"

I could feel Cedric's gaze on me as I looked down at my hands, still gripping the papers. His polished manners and stylish clothes were deceptive. He might be pretty, but he wasn't stupid.

What did I want? I wanted Adoria. I wanted to find Lonzo. I wanted a life far away from the war and corruption that had engulfed the country of my birth. Could a rich husband and a new land guarantee all those things? No, but I'd have better odds there than I would here, where I was just another hungry refugee packed into a city that hated us.

"I want a husband," I reiterated. It was a small price to pay for all those other benefits. I would honor the contract and accept being a wife. If nothing else, I'd have some sort of choice in who I went to bed with, rather than having it dictated by my father.

As though reading my mind, Cedric remarked, "Your father was a great man. I mean, at least from what I've heard. He saved so many from persecution. He gave his life for it. You must be so proud."

"Yes," I said automatically.

"And I know you want to carry out that legacy. I know you've been protecting people here. It's noble. It's wonderful. But . . . how should I put this . . . well. You need to settle down. Not just with a husband, but in general."

"I know."

"No more sneaking around."

"I know."

"No more alley fights."

"I know."

"No more daggers to throats."

"Cedric, give *me* some credit." If we hadn't been in the cathedral, I would've shouted it. "I'll be the picture of decorum at this finishing school of yours. I'll get cultured and refined. I'll let you show me off at all those parties and wear those beautiful clothes you're always going on about." I glanced down at my worn, stained dress. "Actually, I won't mind that part. Or even the studies." The war back in Sirminica had ended my education there.

Cedric's enthusiasm returned. He really needed to work on discretion. "I know Adoria's your end goal, but try to enjoy the journey too. It won't be that bad."

"Even for a Sirminican?" I asked archly.

The bright smile faltered. I took it as a bad sign that he didn't spout off the pretty assurances and sales pitches that came so naturally to him. "Your first year's still in Osfrid. Even though you'll be at one of our country manors . . . well, you'll face the same bias you see here in the city. Adoria will be a little laxer. Sometimes. But you'll win them over. They'll see who you really are."

After almost two years in Osfrid's capital, I was skeptical, but I didn't let that show as I stood up. The priest had finished and was strolling near our side. "Thank you," I whispered. "This means everything to me."

Cedric tapped his pocket. "So does this."

"Don't come out right after me," I warned. "Wait a while."

"I know, I know. You're not giving me credit again."

I walked out of the cathedral, squinting at the bright afternoon light. The noise of midday Osfro was crushing after the sanctuary's stillness. Before me, the city whirled with life. Wagons and horses clattered down the cobblestone street, and vendors pitched their wares. Pedestrians packed the spaces in between, some headed toward a specific destination while others begged for food and work. Blocky stone buildings loomed over everything, their gloomy solidity a testament to Osfro's history.

Osfro is an old city, I thought. *A city set in its ways. There's no opportunity for me here. Lonzo knew that when he sailed to Adoria. When he left me behind.*

The cathedral doors creaked open, and I stared in surprise as Cedric emerged. "You were supposed to wait," I chastised.

"I forgot to tell you when we're leaving for the manor." He placed a jaunty brown hat atop his auburn hair and tried to block out the sun with his hand. "In four days. Wait at the border of the Sirminican and Bridge districts—by the market. My father and I'll pick you up around the first bell."

"Are you sure your father won't mind me?"

"Not his choice. He let me recruit two girls. I've picked them—sort of. I have to finish the other's paperwork." Cedric sounded unconcerned. Seeing as he'd adopted a religion that often led to death and imprisonment, a father's anger was probably minor by comparison.

"Recruit? Are you leading this girl into a sinful life?"

Cedric and I both spun around at the crotchety voice. The monk of Vaiel was still there, leaning against the arch and clutching a leather-bound copy of *A Testament of Angels*. The shadows had obscured him. Panic shot through me, and then I relaxed as I replayed our brief conversation. We'd said nothing about an outlawed heresy. Cedric and I faced no danger in discussing the Glittering Court.

"No, Brother," said Cedric politely. The monks weren't church leaders like the priests of Uros, but they were treated with the same respect, venerated for their complete immersion into study of the faith. "Quite the opposite, actually. She's joining the Glittering Court."

Even though I couldn't see the monk's face, instinct told me he was staring at me—and scowling. "The Glittering Court? Is that what you call your sordid operation? I may be removed from the world, but I know its ways. Men 'recruit' Sirminican girls all the time, taking advantage of their downtrodden situation and forcing them into despicable deeds. I saw you earlier, girl. I saw the watch interrogating you."

"We were only chatting. I haven't done anything wrong. And the

Glittering Court is very respectable." I tried for calmness and humility. The last thing we needed was for him to draw the city watch's attention back to me. "I'm going to take etiquette classes and then find a husband in Adoria next year."

"And not just any husband," Cedric boasted. "She'll meet only the richest, most elite bachelors of the city. Men who've made their fortunes in the New World want equally elevated wives—and my family's business supplies them." He'd used those exact same words when we met. I wondered if the salesman in him couldn't help it.

A beat of silence followed as the monk contemplated this. Then: "Which city?"

"Cape Triumph. In Denham Colony." Cedric kept smiling, but the shift in his posture betrayed his nervousness. I didn't blame him, with that list in his pocket. Church officials wanted to make an example of native Osfridian converts. Hangings had become common.

When the monk still didn't respond, I crossed my arms and fixed my gaze on his shadowed face. I hoped I was meeting his eyes. "Good Brother, I appreciate your concern. And you're right—desperate girls with no other options *do* turn to desperate means. But I'm not one of those girls."

"Not desperate?" he asked, voice unexpectedly wry for a holy man.

"Not without options. If I don't see any, then I make my own. And no one forces me into anything." My words came out with a bit more fire than I'd intended.

"I can believe that. I'd pity anyone who tried." I could've sworn he was smiling in the depths of that hood. "Good luck to you, miss." He opened the cathedral door and disappeared inside.

Cedric exhaled. "That could have gone a lot worse. I think he must've liked you."

"They don't like anything except their studies."

"He couldn't take his eyes off you," he teased.

"You couldn't even see his eyes! Now go memorize what I gave you. Don't forget to burn it."

Cedric answered with a nod and began descending the great stone steps. "See you in four days."

I stayed where I was and looked down upon the city I'd be leaving behind. I'd come here to escape war, but I felt no loyalty. Learning to be a polished lady in some country manor was a delay in getting to Lonzo, but I was human. I wanted to sleep in a clean bed, instead of on a floor crowded with other refugees. I wanted three meals a day again. I wanted to be around books again.

"Four days." I felt my lips creep into a smile. "Four days, and my new life begins."

CHAPTER 2

I'D MEANT IT WHEN I TOLD CEDRIC I'D BE ON GOOD behavior. I *wanted* to be on good behavior. This opportunity meant too much for both me and Lonzo—I couldn't afford to lose it. And despite all the violence and danger I'd seen in my life, discord wasn't something I relished. I actually longed for order. For peace.

So, it was unfortunate when, six months into my stay with the Glittering Court, I found myself holding a blade to someone's throat.

"Do you hear me?" I cried. "One more word—one more *hint* of this—and you'll regret it for the rest of your life!"

My quarry, Clara Hayes, answered with a defiant smirk, though her eyes revealed uneasiness. It was hard to feel too cocky when you were pressed up against the side of a house with a knife's point resting against your neck. Rain fell steadily around us, but I was too focused on her to care about my soaked hair and nightgown.

"The truth hurts, doesn't it?" she spat.

"It's not the truth, and you know it. *You're* the one who made it up."

"It sure sounds true." Clara tried to shift, ever so slightly, but I kept her pinned in place. "Why else would he let a Sim into this house? I mean, one who's not here to clean it. I guess I can't blame you. He *is* terribly handsome. But I don't think that excuse will hold when his father finds out about this."

I kept my face still. I didn't even blink, which was hard with water running into my eyes. Clara had been my bane since the day I'd arrived at Blue Spring Manor. As Cedric had predicted, some of the

Glittering Court girls carried the same prejudice I'd met in the city. Honestly, though, I didn't think Clara cared one way or another about my background. She was simply a bully. She wanted victims. I'd endured her pranks and taunts with stony resilience, but she'd crossed a line this week when she began spreading rumors that I'd earned my place here by sleeping with Cedric. It had struck too deeply, triggering memories of a time when I'd nearly been forced to trade my body for other favors.

You're a coward, Mira. You have to learn to make tough choices.

"His father's not going to find out," I told Clara. "Especially since there's nothing *to* find out."

"Who do you think he'll believe, you or me? Jasper hates that Cedric recruited you. And when this gets around to him . . . ? Well. There's no way he'll let you stay. It costs him a fortune to get us ready for Adoria. And it costs our suitors even more to pay our marriage fees. For that price, they expect beauty, charm, culture—and virtue."

I leaned forward. "Beauty? You're right. That is important. Here, Adoria, everywhere. I'd hate to see you lose yours."

Her smile vanished. "W-what's that supposed to mean?"

"It means that if you don't stop your lies and start telling everyone the truth, I will ruin you—your face, that is." I slid the blade along her cheek for emphasis. "I will ruin any chance you have of ever getting a husband in Adoria or any other place. A ruined reputation just gets me kicked out. But a ruined face? That'll pretty much turn away any suitor, rich or poor."

She gaped. "You wouldn't dare!"

"If you get me sent away, then what do I have to lose? All I'd have to do is slip into your bedroom with this one night and—" I made a slashing motion with my free hand.

"I'll tell Mistress Masterson about this!"

"Good luck proving it." I released her and backed away. "Now, did you get all of that? I know you have trouble with my accent sometimes."

Clara's response was to jerk open the kitchen door I'd dragged her through earlier and slam it as she stormed inside. But I'd seen her face. I'd scared her.

I took a deep breath and leaned against the house, surprised to find I was shaking. Had I really just threatened to cut up someone's face over gossip? I had no intention of really following through with it, but even the bluff made me feel dirty.

You did what you had to do, Mira, a stern inner voice told me. *You have to get to Lonzo. You can't risk getting thrown out of here because of one petty girl's slander. And you're not the only one with a lot on the line. Cedric needs to get to Adoria too.*

I doubted Jasper Thorn believed every girl in the house was a virgin, but he made sure everyone else believed it. He had a reputation to protect. He wouldn't go easy on anyone he thought had sullied his "merchandise"—not even his own son.

I straightened up and slipped my old knife—which was actually too dull to cut anything, let alone a face—back into its pocket. Now I had to get inside before someone noticed my absence. We weren't even supposed to go out at this hour, and if our housemistress found me drenched, I'd be in even more trouble.

I pulled the kitchen door's handle, and nothing happened. I tugged a few more times, just to make sure it wasn't stuck, and then I groaned.

Clara had locked me out.

"No, no," I muttered, hurrying over to a set of double glass doors also on the manor's backside. They led to a parlor—and they too were locked. I tried a window. Locked. Running back to the kitchen door, I jiggled the handle once again. Nothing. What if I knocked? I had friends here. One might be near the kitchen and let me in. Of course, Mistress Masterson might also be near the kitchen.

"Looks like you could use some help."

I whirled around as a figure emerged from the shadowed yard. It was a man, slightly bent over when he walked, wearing tattered and oversized clothes that were as soaked as mine. At first I thought some vagrant had wandered onto our property, and then I recalled that today was delivery day. I even distantly remembered seeing a man with that same hunched posture among the workers who'd brought groceries to us from the village. Still, I shrank against the door, ready to pound on it and take my chances with Mistress Masterson. My hand moved to the knife.

"Relax," he said in a gravelly voice. His accent reminded me a little of Ingrid's, a girl who'd come here from a southwestern region of Osfrid called the Flatlands. "I'm not going to hurt you. You might take that knife to my face if I did."

"You heard that?" I asked.

I was glad the darkness and rain hid my blush. I hadn't realized I'd had an audience.

Light shining from the windows provided patchy illumination, and a wide-brimmed hat shadowed much of the man's face. I could really only make out a long, scraggly dark beard and a number of scars scattered across rough skin.

"Don't sound so down about it, girl. It was a good threat, and you were pretty convincing. But it's not going to work."

Annoyance pushed my apprehension aside. "What makes you say that? You hear a five-minute talk and think you're some kind of expert?"

"When it comes to this sort of thing? Yes. I *am* an expert. You scared her. But not enough—otherwise she wouldn't have locked that door on you. Once she's had some time to settle down, she's going to try to call your bluff. She'll convince herself you won't really go through with cutting up her face." He paused meaningfully. "Will you?"

"I—I don't know," I lied. I could just barely see his dark eyes in the shadows now. Their gaze seemed to bore right through me.

"Well, you *should* know," he said. "Don't make threats you're not ready to follow through on."

I lifted my chin at his condescending tone. "Thank you for the insight, but now, if you'll excuse me, I need to go inside."

"How? The door—" He paused to cough. "The door's locked."

"That's my problem."

He coughed again. Or maybe it was a laugh. "Yes, it is. And I'm going to help you with it."

From his baggy coat, he pulled out what looked like a small wallet. When he opened it, I saw several thin metal tools of varying lengths. Some were simply straight, and others had curved or hooked ends. He examined a couple in the window's light, angling his face in a way that gave me a glimpse of a star-shaped scar on his left cheek and a small nick on the outer side of his earlobe.

"You're going to pick the lock?" I asked. The rain was lightening, and I pushed back strands of sodden hair.

He didn't look up as he sifted through the tools, but his voice held surprise. "How do you know that?"

"Well . . . because you're holding a lock pick kit."

"That wasn't what I— Never mind. If you're so smart, I guess you don't need me." He started to close the case.

I reached toward his arm and then pulled back. "No, wait. I do need you. I've seen these before, but I don't have my own."

He waited a few moments, maybe to make me worry, and then opened the case again. He selected a tool with a hooked end and inserted it into the handle's keyhole. After a few quick motions, I just barely heard a *click*. He straightened up—as much as his stooped form allowed. "There you go."

"You got it on the first try."

"This is a common kind of lock." He slid the tool back into its holder. "It's not always this easy. Sometimes you've got to listen. Feel out the tumbler inside."

I reached for the handle. "Well, thank you. I appreciate the help."

"Then let me give you a little more. You want that girl to leave you alone? Don't do it with brute force. That has its place, sure, but information is real power."

I let my hand drop back to my side. "What do you mean?"

"Well, that's what she's got over you, right? Information?"

"Not information. Slander. It's not true. I'd never—"

"You're proving my point," he interrupted. "Look how worked up you are—over words. So get some on her. She's got something in her past. Everyone does. Uncover that, and you'll be the one with the power." He held out the pick kit. "Take this. It'll help you get into places you shouldn't. That's where you'll find your answers."

I didn't take it. "I can't accept this."

"I've got three more sets at home." He pushed the kit into my hand and turned around. "Now I've got to go find the other chaps before they head back to the village. Stay out of trouble."

The man trudged off into the darkness, leaving me with the lock picks. I had a sudden urge to call him back, to ask why he would help me without expecting anything in return. And what in the world would he need that many kits for? Instead, I slipped back into the kitchen and up to my room.

Tamsin, one of my roommates, was busy writing a letter and gave my rain-soaked state only a brief glance. "I don't even want to know."

Our other roommate, Adelaide, had been sprawled on her bed with a book and bolted upright. "Well, I do! Six, Mira. What happened to you? You're practically naked."

I glanced down and realized she wasn't entirely wrong. The soaked nightgown clung everywhere. I quickly wrapped a blanket around my body and hoped it had been too dark for the laborer to notice much. "Eh, nothing important. I just accidentally got locked out."

That drew Tamsin's attention back. Little escaped her notice. "Who did it? Clara?"

"It's doesn't matter. Let it go," I said, wringing water out of my black hair. Clara's rumors hadn't reached my roommates yet, and I hoped it stayed that way.

"Of course it bloody matters." Tamsin slipped into her Market District dialect when she got emotional. Mistress Masterson would have been horrified. "Do you know how much trouble you'd get in if you were caught out there? Mistress Masterson would think you'd lost your head for some man and were having secret meetings with him."

Adelaide laughed and flounced back. "I don't think anyone would jump to that."

"Don't treat everything like a joke," Tamsin returned sharply.

"I'm not! But I can't really picture Mira losing her head over anything—especially a man. I mean, good grief, where would she find one? The only men we see are the Thorns and a few instructors. And they're hardly ever here. None of us will even remember how to talk to men by the time we go to Adoria. Mistress Masterson should bring a few around for us to practice with."

Adelaide was joking, but Tamsin took the words seriously. She was always watching out for opportunities. "It *would* be useful to interact with men more often. I'm surprised no one's thought of it. There'll be village men at church tomorrow. Maybe I should try talking to some of them. It might give me an extra edge."

"You're obsessed with your edge," said Adelaide.

"At least I care." Tamsin tossed her brilliant red hair over one shoulder. "Honestly, what good was working in a noble's household all those years if you didn't pick up anything useful? You should be the best of us all."

Adelaide grinned. "You'd smother me in my sleep if I was. This is self-preservation."

"Well, second best, then," Tamsin said huffily.

I smiled as they slipped into familiar roles and forgot about Clara. Somehow, I'd ended up rooming with both the most ambitious girl in the house and the least ambitious one. It had been obvious from our first day here that Tamsin had an agenda and wasn't going to let anyone stop her. She studied and worked more than anyone else. She scrutinized every detail and person around her, assessing how they could further her path to greatness.

And Adelaide? She moved through the world in a different way. She was always quick to smile and find a joke wherever she went. She won everyone over with her easy charm and could talk her way out of any-thing. That turned out to be pretty useful with our instructors, consid-ering Adelaide's performances were all over the place. Sometimes she excelled. Sometimes she failed. None of it ever seemed to bother her.

I loved them both.

Each girl was powerful in her own way, one always burning with drive and the other so light and playful that she practically danced through her days. Me? I was the mediator, the one who kept those extremes balanced.

I woke up with a renewed energy the next morning. Clara's rumors had weighed on me for days, and I was eager to see what would come of last night's "talk." While dressing, Tamsin discovered a spot on her skirt that neither Adelaide nor I could actually see. It drove Tamsin into crisis mode, and Adelaide and I were ready before she was for a change. We left her to her scrubbing and made our way down to the foyer where other girls waited for the carriages that would take us to the village.

Cedric milled around with my housemates and lit up at our ap-proach. He usually stayed in Osfro for school but would occasionally run errands at the manors for his father, now that Charles Thorn—Jasper's brother and the Glittering Court's other owner—had decided to stay in Adoria. I'd grown to like Cedric for the genuine concern he showed for others—and I'd grown to respect him for his continued dedication to the Alanzans.

Adelaide was the other girl he'd recruited—a much better choice than me in Jasper's eyes. I was never jealous of her, but sometimes I felt guilty that Cedric had taken me on, instead of another like her who could give him a higher commission. Despite her inconsistent results, she was the picture of a *real* Osfridian girl—the kind those Adorian men probably truly wanted. Fair skin, blue eyes, golden brown hair. Perfect speech. Endless charm.

"Are you going with us, or just going?" I asked. Cedric would sit through an orthodox church service if his cover required it, though he avoided it when possible. Uros had created twelve angels at the beginning of time, and the orthodox believed six had fallen. The Alanzans still revered all twelve and didn't like listening to sermons that condemned half of those angels as evil.

"Going." He patted the suitcase at his side. "But you know I'll miss you all terribly."

"It's not fair," Adelaide told him, pretending—badly—to be stern. "You get to go back to the city for all sorts of fun while the rest of us have to sit through a dull service."

He attempted an equally serious mien and had about as much success as she did. "It's for the good of your soul."

"My soul's doing just fine, thank you very much. If you *really* cared, you'd tell Mistress Masterson that salvation comes second to us finding husbands and that we should stay home to study instead."

"Salvation comes second to finding husbands?" Cedric put his hands to his chest in horror. "Why, Miss Bailey, that's the most sacrilegious thing I've ever heard. I can't believe you'd even think such a wicked thing."

"I didn't," Adelaide said, finally giving in to the grin she'd been holding back. "Tamsin tells us that every time we go to church."

I laughed with them and then realized that I'd left my gloves in my room—a true sin, as far as Mistress Masterson was concerned. "I've got to go back upstairs. Safe travels, Cedric."

"You too." He patted my arm lightly before returning to his banter with Adelaide. As he did, I heard a gasp the two of them didn't notice.

I turned and saw it had come from Rosamunde, a girl in the house I liked quite a bit. She was huddled by the wall and murmuring something to her roommate, Sylvia. Both girls' eyes widened when they saw me approach.

"What's going on?" I demanded.

"He touched your arm!" said Sylvia.

"It's true then," Rosamunde whispered. "About you and the younger Mister Thorn."

I repressed the urge to roll my eyes. "You know me better! How can you believe that nonsense Clara made up? Just wait. The next time you talk to her, she'll tell you it isn't true."

The two girls exchanged looks. "We were with her earlier today," Rosamunde said. "And she didn't say anything about it not being true."

"Caroline was talking about it," Sylvia said cautiously. "About you and . . . uh, him."

"And Clara was saying it too?" I exclaimed.

Rosamunde frowned. "No . . . Clara didn't really say anything. She just listened and nodded."

"And smiled," added Sylvia. "A lot."

I spun around, searching for Clara, and found her watching me from across the foyer. When we made eye contact, she smirked.

My heart stopped. The stooped man *had* been right. Clara was calling my bluff. Sort of. Maybe she'd stopped repeating the story herself, but it was still going to spread if she did nothing to curb it. She was tacitly confirming it with silence and smiles. It was enough to make me seriously reconsider carving up her face.

Calm down, Mira, I told myself. *She's not a fanatic trying to kill an Alanzan. She's not some alley thug trying to steal coins. She's just a silly girl. Ignore her. You have bigger things to worry about in your life.*

Yes, I did. Things like making it to Adoria and helping Lonzo. Things that could be seriously affected if Clara's lies ran rampant.

Information is real power.

I pondered those words as I continued upstairs. Had the shadowy man been right about that too? Was learning about Clara's past the way to stop her and maintain my goals? Snooping and sneaking had never been my style. I wanted to face problems head-on.

She's got something in her past. Everyone does.

Tamsin was finishing up in our room, bending over to buckle her shoes. I fetched my gloves and then stared at the robe I'd left draped over a chair to dry last night. I'd forgotten about the picks concealed in a pocket. I stared at the robe for several moments, and then, with Tamsin's back to me, I snatched the kit and put it into my skirt's pocket. It was time to see just how powerful information was.

Tamsin smoothed out her dress and then gave an unexpected laugh when she glanced over at me. "Well, well, you sure are serious this morning. You look like you're on a mission."

I managed a strained smile as I walked out the door with her. "I just might be."

CHAPTER 3

THE RUMORS LINGERED IN THE HOUSE FOR A WHILE, but without Clara fueling them, they eventually fizzled away. She still never outright denied them, and I know a few girls continued to believe the worst of me. Others, familiar with Clara's style, figured out that it was all another ploy of hers and let the matter go. The stories never reached Jasper—or my roommates. Tamsin and Adelaide would've confronted Clara, and I didn't want them involved.

But Clara wasn't done with me. Instead of slander, she unleashed a renewed flood of actions to make my life miserable. Stealing my assignments. Tripping me in dance class. Always making little gibes here and there. They were annoying, but I could tolerate them.

And I wasn't done with her either. I began experimenting with the lock picks in secret around the house. Sometimes I did it just to learn the tools and see what I could do. Other times, I actively searched for blackmail material. My boldest act involved breaking into Clara's room and going through her possessions. I didn't uncover any secrets, but I did manage to open a jewelry box with a complicated lock. I felt like I'd passed an exam.

"We have a few changes to our schedule today," Mistress Masterson told us one morning over breakfast. We all stopped eating and stared up at the imposing figure she always made, sharp featured with her gray hair pulled severely back. "Your regular classes are canceled. You'll each have a private meeting with Professor Brewer to determine the most essential language skills you need to improve on and will just focus on them during your language lessons now, in order to speed up their progress. Ah, well, everyone except Adelaide, of course. You won't be meeting with him and can spend the morning studying."

Adelaide brightened, probably because she had no intention of actually studying. Professor Brewer tutored us in speech. I might be the only one here born outside of Osfrid, but many girls had come with local dialects far worse than anything of mine. If the Thorns wanted to prove to our suitors that we could hold our own with the upper class, then we needed to sound like the upper class. After first meeting Professor Brewer, Adelaide had been excused from further lessons. Her refined Osfridian was the only thing she'd perfectly picked up from her time as a fine lady's maid.

"After the assessments," continued Mistress Masterson, "we'll have a special guest over lunch."

We left breakfast in a buzz. Mistress Masterson maintained a strict regimen in our manor. Deviations rarely occurred. Most girls were excited to have a break from classes, but Tamsin was suspicious.

"Something's going on," she told Adelaide and me. "This isn't normal. This is a break from the Glittering Court's routine."

"We have assessments all the time," I reminded her.

Tamsin shook her head. "We already have private sessions with Professor Brewer. What's so special about this one that they'd cancel classes for it? And why suddenly try to speed up linguistics? We have five months left. Plenty of time to fix our core language issues and then work on embellishments that'll *really* impress those Adorian gentlemen. I'm telling you, something weird is happening."

"You aren't actually worried about how you'll do, are you?" asked Adelaide. She put on her mischievous grin. She had a thousand different smiles. "Both of you sound incredible. Just try not to use 'bloody' so much, Tamsin."

Tamsin didn't smile back. She remained thoughtful all morning, barely saying a word to me as we sat outside the office where Professor Brewer conducted the meetings. But even while introspective, Tamsin never missed anything around her—like when Clara attempted a shot at me.

"You must be nervous, Mira. Anyone who looks at you *might* think you're Osfridian. But once you open your mouth? There's no question where you're from. I wonder if the Thorns have ever had a girl without any offers."

"Oh, hush, Clara," Tamsin snapped. "You still sound so much like the butchers' district, I can almost smell the pork rotting. If you haven't shaken *that* by now, you're never going to."

Clara's eyes bugged, but her name was called before she could retort. I grinned, happy to see the return of the feisty Tamsin I knew, but it was short-lived. She grew introspective once more, her sharp mind still trying to puzzle out what was going on.

Professor Brewer beamed when my turn came. I fretted constantly about my accent but knew I was one of his favorites. He'd told me on the first day that he liked new linguistic challenges. "You're much more interesting than curing girls who overuse 'bloody,'" he had said. "Not sure how much more of that I can take."

I sat down opposite him now and smiled back, still a little nervous after all these months. "You're probably going to have a hard time narrowing down my worst problems," I noted.

He scoffed. "Hardly. You're imagining you sound worse than you do. And don't think for an instant that the Adorians—the ones born and raised there—don't have atrocious accents of their own. Just because you're being trained to act like nobility doesn't mean your future husbands are. They sound like Flatlanders, only worse. They stress all the wrong syllables and do unbelievable things with their vowels. Did you know they say *vayse* instead of *vahz*?"

"I still wish I sounded like a native."

"You know the grammatical and phonetic rules by heart—better than most of the girls here. It's all practice now, correcting the sounds imprinted by your first language. Training your mouth to say *sh* and get those short vowels right. Keep up with that, over and over." His wizened face turned thoughtful. He'd once been a professor at the university Cedric attended. "You know, one exercise I've seen that can help people improve their Osfridian is learning the accents of other languages from Evaria."

I appreciated that he always said "Evaria," instead of "the continent," like most Osfridians did. But I was skeptical of his suggestion. "How would that help?"

"When you understand the differences and problems other speakers have, it gives you a greater sense of how your own language fits in. I'll bring you a book on it when I'm back next week." He gave me a wink. "I'm also just curious to see you do it. I think you're better at languages than you realize. It sounds like you picked up Osfridian quickly. They teach you a smattering of Lorandian here, don't they? It uses the same Ruvan roots as Sirminican. I'm sure you'll have an easy time finishing that workbook."

"I already did," I replied.

He laughed and slapped his knee. "See? You're a prodigy."

"More of a cheater. My father traveled in Lorandy when I was little and taught some to my brother and me."

"You should learn the whole language. I'll bring you a Lorandian dictionary too."

"Thank you, sir, but I feel like I should just work on perfecting one language for now."

Professor Brewer's expression turned kind. "You'll do fine over there, Mira. Just fine. Something tells me you were made for a place like that."

Adelaide rejoined us at lunchtime, and more anticipation spread through my housemates as we speculated over our mystery guest. Mistress Masterson waited until we were seated at the dining table before finally revealing the news.

"One of our former girls has sailed back to Osfrid for the summer and will be coming by today to share her experiences. I expect you to be on your best behavior. This is a great opportunity that isn't always offered. I hope you appreciate it."

Jasper, barely able to contain his pride, arrived with our guest soon thereafter. The rest of us had been chattering excitedly but fell into silent awe as she entered the room and took a seat at the table.

Her name was Florence, and she was a wonder, clothed in a wine-colored gown with pink rosettes around the neckline and sleeves. It made our day dresses look shabby, and they were finer than anything I'd ever owned. Her golden hair was arranged in perfect curls. Jewelry decked with brilliant red gems sparkled everywhere. If I had seen her on the street—which seemed improbable, even hypothetically—I would have thought she was Osfridian royalty, not an afternoon guest.

"Florence was the top girl in her year," Jasper told us. "Bid after bid came in. The man she chose had the highest offer. He's one of Denham's wealthiest shipping magnates."

Florence fluttered her lashes and gracefully lifted her teacup. A large diamond ring flashed in the sunlight. "Abner was impossible to resist," she said, her speech *almost* as fine as Adelaide's. "I couldn't help but fall in love."

A few girls clasped their hands, dreamy-eyed. I wondered if Florence's husband's fortune had been equally loveable.

"Achieving that took a lot of work," said Jasper, prompting her to tell us all about how hard she'd applied herself at Swan Ridge Manor. Everyone listened avidly, but not nearly as avidly as when she began to describe the balls and wonders of Adoria. Seeing us so engaged, Jasper rose after finishing his meal and politely excused himself.

"Mistress Masterson and I need to assess some files. But please—enjoy yourselves and ask Florence any questions you like."

Tamsin raised an eyebrow at the mention of our files, and I could only imagine the increase in her paranoia. The opportunity to learn more about Adoria was too strong a lure, however, and her attention shifted back to Florence.

"Is it true we'll get clothes even better than what we have now?" asked Clara, her eyes fixed covetously on the satin gown.

Florence laughed prettily. "Oh, yes. Some like mine. Some even richer. All gorgeous and sparkling. They want us to be a fantasy—to bewitch everyone we meet. And you will—you'll see." Still smiling, she added in a low voice, "Sometimes, those dresses were a little uncomfortable to wear all night. But you can't meet elite men if you don't go to elite events."

After that, everyone wanted to know more about the dresses and if the men were romantic and doting. I was less concerned about romance than finding a man who'd respect me—and be generous enough with his pocketbook to let me pay off Lonzo's bond.

"Is it true everyone can find work? That there are opportunities and education for all?" The question came unexpectedly from Tamsin and was a shift from the lighter topics.

Florence looked a little surprised but was quick to answer. "Oh, yes. Not everyone is rich, of course. There's still crime and poor parts of Cape Triumph. But nothing like you find in some of the Osfro slums. Nothing like that." A small frown was the first break in her bubbly countenance, and I remembered that she too had come from humble roots. "But anyone willing to work hard can find a way to better themselves. Any Osfridian can, that is." As she spoke, her eyes lingered briefly on me. I kept my expression neutral, even as my heart sank. The Adorian colonies, it seemed, would be no different than their motherland.

Adelaide had noticed Florence's gaze. "What about people who aren't Osfridians? Other Evarians come to the colonies, right? And I heard there are even Balanquan settlers."

Florence wrinkled her nose. "Balanquans. They're a strange people."

"What are they like?" exclaimed Caroline.

"They look kind of like Sirminicans." She blatantly stared at me again. "But not exactly the same. You'd know one if you saw one. And they dress so strangely—especially the women. Sometimes in pants."

That elicited a few gasps. "Are they nomads like the Icori?" asked Sylvia, her eyes wide. "Do they wear kilts too?"

"No," Florence admitted. "The Balanquans aren't like that. I hear they have cities and books and laws . . . and other kinds of civilized things. But obviously, not like *our* civilized things. I've only ever seen a couple of Balanquans. They keep to themselves."

"But there is always a need for more people, right?" asked Tamsin, steering us back. "It's all still new. It needs to be built."

"I suppose." Florence seemed uncomfortable at such a serious topic. After several awkward moments, she brightened. "Would you girls like to hear about how amazing Abner is?"

She waxed on about how handsome her husband was, how he catered to her every whim. How he bought her anything she wanted. "Being married to a man like him has been more wonderful than I ever dreamed."

"In all ways?" asked Ingrid. "Even in . . . intimate ways?"

Shock and giggles ran around the table. Florence's cheeks turned a dusky pink, which somehow managed to make her look even prettier. "Well, it wouldn't be proper to go into detail, but I will say it's quite lovely most of the time."

"Most of the time?" I asked pointedly.

Florence looked surprised I'd spoken. "Well . . . what I mean is, some days I'm just so tired, but it *is* a wife's duty. Which I gladly do for him. And as I said—it really can be lovely. And, oh, the sweet things he always says afterward. Pouring out his emotions. Compliment after compliment. Telling me how much he adores me. He's even recited poetry."

I didn't really find "lovely" to be a compelling endorsement, but her words brought more happy sighs from my housemates. It must have stuck with Adelaide too, because later that evening, while we were preparing for bed, she remarked, "I don't remember poetry ever being mentioned in our Female Studies book."

Our Female Studies class was meant to prepare a young lady for her wedding night and other matters not discussed in polite company. Adelaide was fascinated by the whole subject. Its textbook was the only one I ever saw her diligently studying.

"That book is nonsense," Tamsin scoffed. "All cut-and-dried. Its whole focus is on making men happy without ever saying how it can be just as good for women."

Adelaide and I exchanged glances behind Tamsin's back. Neither of us was brave enough to ask how she could speak with such confidence on that matter.

Adelaide finished unbraiding her hair. "I don't need poetry. I just want love. Someone I can look at and feel an instant connection to. Someone who's meant for me, and me for him."

With a wistful sigh, she pulled on a robe and disappeared out the door to go to the washroom. "I hope her expectations lower a little by the time we get there," I said. "I don't want to see her hurt when reality sets in."

"Well, aren't you a ray of sunshine." Tamsin ran a brush through her long hair. "Don't write off her happiness just yet."

"I'm not," I protested. "I want her to be happy. But she's such a romantic, and I don't know if that's realistic. I mean, we have two months to accept an offer. Do you really think we're going to fall madly in love with someone in that time?"

"Stranger things have happened. *I'd* like to." She nodded toward the Female Studies book lying on Adelaide's bed. "It'll make all that business a whole lot better."

"Well, I'm not setting my sights on romance. And don't look at me like that! You've never made any secret about your priorities either. You want the richest, most successful man you can find, and that's what you'll choose, whether love and attraction are involved or not. Me? I don't need the richest. Someone who's established—with a little to splurge—is all I want. That, and respect, of course. Those are my priorities. Maybe he'll be handsome, and maybe I'll like being in bed with him. If not, I'll just deal with it. That's being realistic."

Shock filled Tamsin's brown eyes, and she held the brush in midair, forgotten. "There's realistic and there's depressing, Mira. And that's just . . . I don't even know. Do you hear yourself? You make it sound like a household chore. I can't believe you've already resigned yourself to a cold marriage."

I shrugged. I couldn't explain that I knew for a fact that it usually was pretty easy to turn off your feelings during unwanted advances. I'd done it plenty of times when my father had needed me to distract men for his missions. I'd flirted. I'd let them touch me and kiss me. And . . . I'd felt completely detached. It actually had been like another household chore.

"I just want to go to Adoria," I said at last. Neither Tamsin nor Adelaide knew about Lonzo. I couldn't breathe a word to anyone—not even my beloved roommates—that my brother was a wanted murderer in Osfro.

Tamsin made a face. "Well, I do too, and yes, you're right that I'll choose success over anything else, but I still hope I can snag some love and passion too. You don't know what you're missing out on."

"I do. Well, sort of."

"Oh?"

"I kissed a neighbor boy a few times back in Sirminica, and I liked that." I savored those memories for a moment, the way those kisses had stirred something inside me. "I left for Osfrid before it ever went beyond kissing. But sometimes . . . I wish there had been more. I mean, if I'm going to settle into marriage with someone who feels like a friendly roommate, it'd be nice to have at least known what it was like being with a man . . . just for the pleasure of—"

"Stop, just stop. I don't want to hear any more." Tamsin sank onto her bed and gave up on brushing her hair.

"But you know what I mean. No deep romance. Just a lover to—"

"Yes, yes, I know exactly what you mean, and honestly I don't know what's worse: this likeable 'roommate' husband you'll endure in bed or the illicit lover you don't really care about." Her expression turned affectionate and a little rueful too. "All I know for sure is you've got a lot to learn. Adelaide's not even close to being the most deluded one here."

Adelaide returned right at that last bit. "Deluded about what? You aren't still going on about some conspiracy, are you?"

In the blink of an eye, Tamsin transformed from romantic advisor to the more familiar steely-eyed huntress we knew. "Something *is* happening! I can feel it. And not just the schedule change today. Did you hear Jasper mention that he was going to review files today? I'm telling you, don't let your guard down."

Her words startled me—but not because of the dire fate she foresaw. *Our files.* Mistress Masterson kept all sorts of paperwork in her office. Few of us had ever been in it, but the room had taken on an ominous reputation. Girls were afraid to knock on its door. And no one would dream of breaking into it. But . . .

Files. Files about all of us. Files about Clara.

I waited until I was certain Adelaide and Tamsin were asleep, and then, for extra precaution, I waited a little longer. I lay in the dark, my heart beating frantically as I clutched the pick kit in one hand. Even when I reached a point where I thought everyone in the house should've long since gone to sleep, I still hesitated. What if some insomniac was pacing the halls? What if someone wanted a snack?

But I knew that if I worried about those things much longer, I'd never leave. I'd stay petrified in my bed. I thought about Lonzo's bravery, my father's zealous determination, and even the fantastic deeds of legendary heroes that I still loved to read about in the one book I'd carried with me from Sirminica. I could do this.

Neither girl stirred as I slipped from our room. The hall outside was silent and empty, as was the lower level. I cringed each time the floor squeaked under my feet. It sounded deafening to my ears, and my journey felt like miles. Mistress Masterson's office was in a wing of the house we rarely visited.

When I reached the door, I didn't have a lot of light and had to do most of my work by feel. Many of the house locks I'd experimented with had been common and often straightforward when utilizing the right tool. This lock was new to me, and after some trial and error, I finally had luck with a twisty pick I'd never used before. It took a fair amount of finessing until I finally heard a *click* that I thought must've surely echoed throughout the manor. I opened and shut the door as silently as I could and lit a small lantern once I felt secure.

Sylvia had been called here once and reported back that Mistress Masterson kept her work lair so organized and pristine that it felt eerie. So, I was surprised to see a handful of papers lying haphazardly on the desk. Leaning closer, I spied forceful handwriting scrawled on them that I knew wasn't our housemistress's. This sullying of her sacred space was Jasper's handiwork.

Some of the notes appeared to be directions from him: *Reach out to contacts. Schedule Miss Garrison.* Others were lists of names, including the girls from the other three manors the Glittering Court maintained. Each girl had a number by her name. Mine was *200*, which I assumed would be my marriage fee. It was the minimum for any girl. Adelaide had 250 and a question mark while Tamsin boasted an impressive 350. Another cryptic list displayed fanciful names like *Spirit of Henrietta* and *Good Hope*, with dates written beside them. It was all interesting, but Jasper's leftovers weren't what I needed.

I discovered what I'd been looking for in a wooden filing cabinet—locked, of course—that contained folders bearing each of our names. Clara's immediately jumped out at me, but I reached for my own first. Most of the papers within it were copies of my standing so far, recording the results of all the major tests and assessments. Looking at my progress as a whole, I realized it was pretty respectable. But far more interesting was a document that was essentially my dossier.

It contained my name, my last known address, and a brief biography that simply said I'd come from Sirminica and lived in Osfro for two years. There was no mention of Lonzo. In fact, my family was listed as *NONE*. The contact provided was to an elderly couple I'd lived with in the Sirminican district. Cedric was identified as my recruiter, and the field asking for how I'd been discovered simply said *Referral*. A few other comments in Mistress Masterson's neat writing mentioned my life at the manor thus far and contained a backhanded compliment: *Progressing well for a Sirminican.*

Wright was next to Viana, and swallowing my guilt, I took a peek at Tamsin's folder. Much of it I already knew. She'd worked for her laundress mother and came from a big family. Jasper had recruited her. The comments on her performance were unsurprisingly spectacular. One special note, however, directed a sum of three gold to be delivered monthly from Jasper's own account to Tamsin's mother. There was no explanation.

Adelaide's also held a few surprises. The section covering her progress thus far was lengthier than mine or Tamsin's, mostly because Mistress Masterson was equally perplexed by Adelaide's erratic successes and failures. Her family section said *NONE* like mine, which surprised me. She occasionally mentioned her parents and grandmother, but I hadn't realized they were out of the picture. Her contact field also said *NONE*. She'd served in the home of Lady Elizabeth Witmore, Countess of Rothford, who was a higher ranking noble than I'd expected. How had scattered Adelaide lasted so many years in a household like that?

Ashamed at my snooping, I shoved Adelaide's folder back in the drawer and finally perused Clara's. Much of it was unremarkable. She was Jasper's recruit, born to a butcher's family with seven other daughters. Her reviews were solid, but there, at the bottom of the page, was a special notes section like Tamsin had. Except Clara's was of a very, very different nature than Tamsin's.

I read it twice and then placed it back in the drawer with a smile. "You were right, old man," I murmured to myself. "Information is real power."

CHAPTER 4

I DIDN'T USE THE INFORMATION RIGHT AWAY. I BIDED my time, holding out for exactly the right moment and also working to gather a few more details. My opportunity came almost a month later, when Clara was tormenting another of her favorite targets.

For three days now, poor Theresa had been plagued with an outbreak of red bumps on one of her cheeks. Mistress Masterson hadn't been concerned. "Blemishes happen all the time to girls your age. Either that, or it's a reaction to something new. Perfume. Fabric. You'll have to conduct an inventory yourself. Regardless, it *will* go away." She'd left Theresa with a pot of noxious-smelling ointment and instructions to use a heavy hand with her cosmetics until the skin cleared.

"What if she's wrong?" Clara asked, her voice sweet with faked concern as we filed into the conservatory for a music lesson. "What if it doesn't go away? I've never seen anything like it."

Theresa blanched. "Sh-she said it would. I've been using that cream."

Clara scrutinized Clara's cheek. "It doesn't seem like it's gone to me. I think it's worse."

"It is not," said Adelaide. "You can hardly see it under her makeup."

"Well, you can certainly see all that makeup. Everyone's going to notice it's heavier on one side." Clara pressed a hand to her mouth and gasped. "Oh! I hope it's all cleared up by tomorrow. Mister Thorn is coming, and you know how picky he is. You can worry about these classes all you want, but it's our looks that really matter over there. He won't bring a girl who's . . . well, flawed."

Compared to the rest of the world's problems, Clara's teasing seemed trivial. But Theresa's pained eyes said otherwise. It was the power of words in action again. A small thing could have a big effect.

"Do you have any ideas that might help her, Clara?" I asked mildly. "You used to live over in the Fountain District, didn't you? There are all sorts of apothecaries there. I remember hearing about a really good one on Hightower Street."

The simpering smile on Clara's face froze. It grew tighter and harder, becoming more like a grimace, as she stared at me. Our instructor entered and called us to attention. Clara swallowed and replied in a stiff, quiet voice, "You're mistaken. I lived in the Butchers' District."

I smiled back with a sunniness Adelaide would've envied. I said nothing more about the Fountain District in class. I said nothing about it at dinner. Clara couldn't take her eyes off me all day, and when we were finally released from studies in the evening, she pushed her way toward me as we all meandered up the stairs. I linked my arm through Adelaide's and very loudly invited Sylvia and Rosamunde to study with us. I kept people close until bedtime, never giving Clara the chance to catch me alone.

At breakfast, her face was so ashen that Mistress Masterson asked if she was ill. Clara shook her head, still watching me. I pretended not to notice and made conversation with Tamsin until her expression suddenly filled with alarm. Her gaze lifted to something beyond me, and I turned to see Jasper breezily enter the room. We'd had no warning he was visiting.

"Good morning, girls," he said, more cheerful than I usually heard him. He picked up a few rolls and wrapped them in a cloth. "Forgive me for not joining you, but I've got to eat in my office today. We'll talk more later."

Tamsin's eyes turned from worried to wary, and I could see her thoughts spinning. When nothing noteworthy had happened after our surprise linguistic assessments, she'd finally stopped voicing her fears aloud . . . but I knew she still had them. "This is it," she murmured. "I warned you."

Adelaide patted her on the arm and offered a comforting smile, but it had no effect. "Tamsin, he stops by all the time. It's normal."

Tamsin just shook her head.

Ⓢ

It was the weekend, and classes couldn't shield me from Clara any longer. I didn't mind, though. I'd only wanted to avoid her long enough to build up her paranoia. Now it was time to deliver the blow.

"Why did you ask about the Fountain District?" she hissed, pulling me into a quiet corner later in the day.

"I just thought I'd heard you were over there a lot." My voice mimicked the angelic one she used. "And that you saw an apothecary on Hightower, one you knew very well. But now I realize I must be mixed up. The apothecaries are a few streets over, right? Hightower's all residential. Lots of fine homes. Lots of fine gentlemen—and their families."

Clara grew pale and then bright pink. "I don't know what game you're playing—"

"You know exactly what game I'm playing." I dropped the sweetness. "I know, Clara. I know all about the favor Jasper did for Mister Wakefield, and if you bother me or anyone else in this house again, everyone is going to know about that favor. And I don't just mean gossip anymore. You say or do anything I don't like—if you even *look* any way I don't like—this is all coming out."

"No one will believe—"

"I have proof." That wasn't exactly true, since I couldn't steal the paperwork from Mistress Masterson's office, but my attitude was convincing, as was the mystery of how I knew about this at all. "When they see that proof, they'll all believe—and Jasper is *not* going to be happy. Enjoy the rest of your day."

I left her there gaping and had to stop myself from grinning like an idiot. The special note scrawled in her dossier—in Jasper's own handwriting—had read:

> *Taken on as a favor to Martin Wakefield, following*
> *repeated indiscretions in his Hightower residence.*
> *Upon discovery by Mistress Wakefield, Clara needed*
> *immediate removal. She's pretty and clever and will fit*
> *in well here. She's smart enough to know how lucky*
> *she got, and I doubt the behavior will be repeated.*
> *Still, the sooner she's married, the better.*

A few inquiries to Cedric had provided the rest of the details. He didn't know anything about Clara's backstory, but he'd heard of Martin Wakefield. He was a businessman of some standing and owned apothecary shops in districts all over the city. He couldn't risk a scandal.

I didn't have long to exalt in my victory because a frantic Tamsin found me a few minutes later. She grabbed my arm. "It's happening."

I couldn't bear to tease her when my mood was so good. "Tamsin, you'll worry yourself sick. Take a break, and we'll go find a game and—"

"No!" she exclaimed. "I'm not imagining this. The word just got around—Mistress Masterson wants us all in the ballroom as soon as possible. Where's Adelaide?"

A little of Tamsin's paranoia began to creep into me. "In the kitchen, I think. Today's her chore day."

Tamsin, still clinging to my arm, dragged me forward. "Come on, we can't waste time."

Adelaide, per her way, was doing a haphazard job of washing dishes, and we managed to save her from destroying a copper kettle before finally heading off to the ballroom. We were among the last to arrive and found the vast room's floor covered in blankets. Our housemates sat scattered on them, looking as puzzled as we felt. The three of us found an unoccupied spot and sat down.

When workmen entered and began setting up tables of food—far more than we needed—Tamsin looked ready to hyperventilate. She started rambling about how this must be a surprise quiz on entertaining large groups of posh guests. "No problem. We can do this. We can do this better than the others because none of them have realized what's happening. We've got an edge."

She was still rattling off advice—which seemed to be directed more to herself than to us—when the predicted guests began to enter. They didn't look very posh, but they caused a big reaction. Our housemates began leaping up from their blankets with wild cries, flinging themselves into the arms of those visitors. And in moments, Tamsin was among them, running over to a smiling, tearful cluster of red-haired people.

Adelaide and I sat alone, taking in the sight. "Their families," I murmured. One of the Glittering Court's rules was that during our instruction period, communication with family back in Osfro could only be maintained via letter. We were in our eighth month, which was a long time to go without seeing loved ones.

I watched the reunions with a wistful smile. Adelaide, beside me, did too, and I remembered how her file had also been marked with NONE. Suddenly, two familiar faces walked through the door, and after a moment of shock, I ran forward to embrace Pablo and Fernanda Gagliardi. Lonzo and I had traveled with them from Sirminica, and they'd let us live with them in Osfro. Their small apartment had been only a little bigger than my bedroom at Blue Spring, but they'd been unfailingly generous to those in need.

"What are you doing here?" I exclaimed. The two of them were well into their sixties, and our manor was a long ride from the capital.

"Making sure you're staying out of trouble," said Pablo. More gray streaked his black hair than I recalled. "And I think we're eating. That's all they told us." The sound of my native language was like music.

"Look at you," said Fernanda, tears shining in her eyes as she took me in. I wore a pink voile dress with my hair pulled back and curled.

"Just like a princess."

I immediately led them over to the food. They looked so much skin-nier to me. Had I been that way too? Once their plates were filled, I brought them back to the blanket and sat near Tamsin's family. It was hard not to smile at them. There were three other children, and Tamsin held the youngest on her lap, a girl of two or three, while the others—an older boy and girl—leaned their heads against her. I'd never seen Tamsin's face so full of happiness and free of calculation.

To my astonishment—and Adelaide's—one of her relatives had turned out after all. She was a buxom woman with faded gold hair and a gregarious personality. Adelaide introduced her as Aunt Sally and didn't seem entirely thrilled that this was the relation who'd come to visit.

After introductions and small talk, I switched to Sirminican and asked, "Have there been any letters from Lonzo?" It was my last, des-perate hope—that he'd reestablished communication while I'd been away.

Fernanda shook her head sadly. "No. I'm sorry."

"You'll find him," said Pablo.

I wrung my hands. "What if I've wasted my time with the Glittering Court? A year of not searching for him! I should've become a bond servant and gone over sooner."

"And then what would you have done?" Pablo chided gently. "You'd be bound to an employer for years. You couldn't search for him. But as the wife of some wealthy man, you'll have more freedom and influence."

"And Lonzo never wanted you to become a bondswoman," added Fernanda. "He didn't want you to go there with a debt on your shoulders."

"He didn't want that for himself either," I said.

"He didn't have a choice." Fernanda's kind face grew hard. She'd known Isabel and had helped hide Lonzo from the authorities when he'd accidentally killed her killer. "He had to get out fast. But you?

This is better for you. Only the twelve know what you're meant for, but I know it isn't working endless days on a plantation."

Hearing the twelve angels invoked, as Alanzans did, reminded me that it was Fernanda and Pablo who'd met Cedric and arranged our deal. He had had the power to get me to Adoria, and my father's name had helped me acquire Alanzan contacts in the New World. Like me, Cedric had an agenda in Adoria. He wanted to join up with a newly forming colony called Westhaven that was promoting religious tolerance. Our deal had helped him, and although I knew it was good for me, I still questioned if I'd done the right thing. I barely heard Jasper's fine speeches about all the luxury waiting for us or how he bragged to our families about how cultured and refined we'd become. Would culture and refinement be enough to help me find Lonzo?

I pulled myself from my rumination when word spread that coaches had arrived to take the guests back to Osfro. Time had flown by, and the tears that had flowed upon the guests' arrival now doubled at their departure. A few of the girls looked so devastated that I thought they might very well leave with their loved ones. But this display had clearly impressed everyone's families, and I saw those same distraught girls bolstered with encouraging words from their relatives. While I didn't believe Tamsin would actually leave, she too apparently needed a little motivation. Her face was stricken as she clung to the children, but she nodded along as her mother rested a hand on her cheek and spoke rapidly. I didn't hear what she said, but when I walked by, I caught Tamsin saying," . . . go get you the letters."

I hugged Fernanda and Pablo tightly, wondering if I'd ever see them again. In some ways, they were my last connection to Sirminica. But even as I told them goodbye, my mind was jumping ahead. I found myself thinking like Tamsin. What purpose had this event served? I'd loved it. Everyone had. But it was an uncharacteristic indulgence. A break in the routine. I began to understand why that raised Tamsin's guard so much.

And later, when my housemates and I were called back to the ball-room to assemble around Jasper, I knew for sure that Tamsin had been right all along.

"It was a true delight for me to meet the wonderful people who helped raise you," Jasper began. "But their visit isn't the only surprise you're getting today."

My unease grew.

He grinned. "I hope you're all excited about Adoria, because we're going there—three months earlier than planned." When no one spoke, he added, "As a result, you will also be taking your exams early. They'll start in one week."

The room filled with gasps and the buzz of nervous conversation. Mistress Masterson had to hush everyone so that Jasper could continue. "I know this change in plans is unexpected. But really, it's a reflection of your outstanding progress that we feel confident in bringing you to Adoria early. In just a couple of months, you'll be in a whole new world—adored and coveted like the jewels you are. I know my brother will be overcome when he sees this year's class. I have no doubt you'll all perform excellently in your exams." He smiled more broadly, perhaps hoping that would soothe the anxiety radiating off everyone. "I'd love to stay but must check in on the other manors as well. Cedric, however, will be coming to supervise and offer moral support during your exams."

"Isn't it dangerous?"

The question, spoken boldly and clearly, came from a remarkably serious Adelaide.

"Cedric offering moral support?" Jasper asked.

"No," she said. "Making the crossing in late winter. Isn't that still storm season?" A few girls looked even more anxious, and I got the impression Jasper was trying to hide a scowl.

"I like to think of it more as early spring. And I'd hardly make the journey myself if I thought we'd be in danger. Surely, Adelaide, you haven't gained some sort of nautical knowledge I don't know about, have you? Surpassing mine and that of the ships' captains who agreed to take us?"

Rebuked, Adelaide remained silent, but I could tell she wasn't convinced. After a few more instructions, we were sent back to our rooms, and my friends' reactions were about what I'd expected. Tamsin was already reaching for her books, and Adelaide seemed indifferent—about the tests, at least. Sailing in storm season still bothered her.

Me? I was just restless. I didn't know what to think. Leaving sooner meant I could get to Lonzo sooner. But it also meant my exams, my marriage, and the end of this protected world with my friends would come sooner. Troubled by a tangle of conflicting feelings, I finally left for a walk around the house. I needed space and the chance to clear my head.

I passed a couple of other girls coming and going to the washrooms or kitchen, but most were settling into their rooms for the night. Downstairs, village workers were finishing the last of the picnic's cleanup, and I started to steer clear of them until I saw one who had a familiar stoop and baggy coat.

I approached him quietly as he stacked some crates. "Did they let you in here," I asked, "or did you just pick the locks?"

He jumped and glanced back at me. After giving me a brief, wry look from underneath his floppy hat, he returned to his work. I could see a bit more of his face than that night outside—though still nothing substantial—and it was mostly what I'd observed before. Scraggly beard, scars, dirt. His eyes, dark and sardonic, were the same as well.

"Would you come after me with a knife if I did?" he asked.

"That depends on if you'll tell me what the pick with the double curve is for."

That surprised him again, enough that it warranted a second look. While the hat drooped over part of his face, the chandelier above clearly illuminated the cheek I'd seen before. It had the same weathered surface and same star-like scar. Except . . . was it in a different place? I could've sworn that last time, that scar sat in the center of his cheek. But I saw now that it was much closer to his ear, the one with the nick in its side. I'd obviously been wrong. It'd been dark and rainy that night, and other matters had preoccupied me.

"You tried to use that one?" he asked.

"I've used *all* of them," I replied proudly. "All around the house. Still figuring out how to make a few work. But that one I can't even find a lock for."

"It's for safes," he said after a small coughing fit. "Big safes, the kind banks use. I doubt you've got any around here."

"Have you broken into any safes like that?"

He snorted. "I wouldn't be hauling away your dishes if I had. Looks like you had some sort of fancy affair going on."

"A ballroom picnic—since it's too cold to have one outside. Although I think it was more of a ploy."

He had turned his face from me again but couldn't resist that observation. "How so?"

"Jas—Mister Thorn let us spend time with our families. I think he hoped it would soften the shock of us going early."

He stopped his work. "Early?"

"We're leaving for Adoria in just about a month. Our exams start right away."

"A month," he repeated, staring off in the distance. "That isn't a prime sailing time. It can be done, but it's not pleasant. And sometimes it's, well . . . never mind. Thorn must want to get a jump on other traders. What fool captain did he get to agree to this?"

His keen interest was startling. "I don't know anything about that. Just that I have to be ready in time. Exams. Dress fittings."

The man nodded absentmindedly and seemed to give up on his work altogether. "I have to go."

"What about these?" I gestured to the boxes he'd abandoned.

"Someone else will come for them. Or you can feel free to jump in." He turned toward the door. "Good luck with your tests and dresses."

"Wait," I called as he started to walk away. He paused. "I . . . I did what you said. About information. I used the picks to find out about Clara's past, and you were right. She has a secret, and now I know it. And she knows that I know."

He was angled away from me but seemed to be smiling. "So no more gossip?"

"No more anything. Information is power."

"Well done. You're a natural."

"Do you want your picks back?"

"Keep them. I told you I have extras."

"But why? Why give them to me at all?"

"Because you strike me as a woman who's going to want to go a lot of places that other people say you can't. These will help even the odds." He strode to the door more confidently now, and I knew he'd no longer be delayed. "Thanks for the help," he called back, just before shutting the door. I stared after it, mystified.

"What help?" I asked. The empty room didn't answer back, and after a few more moments, I trudged back up to my room to prepare for the last chapter of my training in the Glittering Court.

CHAPTER 5

I SPENT THE NEXT WEEK WITH MY HEAD IN MY BOOKS. Language remained my top priority, no matter what Professor Brewer said. My accent's implications in daily Adorian life bothered me. I needed a husband with means who'd treat me as an equal. That latter attribute could actually be harder to find, but the more options I had, the better. Likewise, the more Osfridian I appeared while searching for Lonzo, the more influence I'd exert.

Tamsin barely ate or slept. Adelaide existed in her usual way. She gave little thought to her test results and mostly just hoped she'd have a few good choices. Occasionally, she'd practice pronunciation with me, which I found incredibly useful, given her excellent speech. She in turn loved hearing me imitate the accents of other languages. I'd caved to Professor Brewer's suggestion and learned several.

"That's incredible!" laughed Adelaide, the night before exams began. "You sound just like this servant that used to work in our house."

We were supposed to be studying linguistics, but she had talked me into taking a break and imitating someone from Skarsia. A native Osfridian could usually tell I was Sirminican when they heard my natural accent, but my origins were harder to pick out if I masked Osfridian with something else.

"Do a Lorandian one," Adelaide urged, her face alight.

When I did, Adelaide fell over onto her bed giggling, but Tamsin sighed loudly. "If you two don't care about your own studies, at least stop interrupting mine. And I grew up around the corner from a Lorandian baker. You're a little off."

"No, she's not." Adelaide sat back up, still grinning. "They have regional differences just like we do. She's got the northwest perfectly."

Adelaide's smile was infectious, but I did feel bad about bothering Tamsin. She looked so serious surrounded by books. "I'm sorry," I said. "I know how much this means to you."

"Everyone knows," added Adelaide, turning serious. "But you're going to kill yourself. Take a break. At least get a full night's sleep."

Tamsin glanced down at her work with bloodshot eyes and shook her head. "I can't risk it. I can't risk messing up. I have to do the best. I have to be the diamond."

We'd be assigned gemstone ranks based on the order of our scores. It wasn't an exact system. It was more of a fanciful theme the Thorns had come up with to present us in Adoria. They wanted to dress us up in striking colors and embellishments and use the gemstones as a guide to who the more "valuable" girls were. Some jewel ranks were flexible, but the diamond was unquestionably the top one—and girls from the other three manors would be competing for it as well.

"We think you're already the best," Adelaide said loyally.

Tamsin managed an indulgent smile. She fretted about the jewel ranking constantly, and we reassured her each time. "I just need everyone else to think so too. There are forty girls involved now. I at least have to make the top three. I have to meet the best men."

"You will," I said.

"And we'll do anything to help you." Adelaide's sober mien began to turn mischievous. "Including not distracting you with Mira's amazing accents. I guess I'll go read up on Female Studies."

Even Tamsin laughed at that, and although she never broke her studying that night, I noticed she seemed to smile a little more.

But the tension doubled the following morning when our first round of exams began. Even Adelaide felt the heavy mood. Cedric

came to stay with us for the week and offered words of encourage-
ment if we passed in the hall. Mostly, he tried to stay out of our way.

Some exams were written while others required performances and
demonstrations. For Professor Brewer's, we each had to stand in front
of the class and read a passage aloud that we'd never seen before. I
held my paper tightly, trying not to ruin it with my sweaty palms. It
described the wool industry in northern Osfrid and contained several
words I'd never heard. I used what I knew of Osfridian phonetics and
hazarded guesses at their pronunciation. When I finished and looked
up from the paper, Professor Brewer's proud expression told me I'd
done well.

After that, I felt as though a burden had been lifted from my shoulders. I still worked hard on the rest of the tests. I served tea with grace.
I played simple tunes on the piano. I whirled across the ballroom,
counting steps in my head. I wrote essays on Osfridian culture, history, and fashion. When the week finally ended, I knew I hadn't done
everything perfectly, but my scores would be solid. I would pass. The
question would be where I landed in the ranks, but that was mostly a
curiosity. What mattered was getting to Adoria.

The whole house breathed a collective sigh of relief at our hard-
won freedom. Smiles returned, and spirits lifted—especially when
Mistress Masterson told us we could have a party to celebrate Vaiel's
Day. It was the day the orthodox church of Uros honored Vaiel, one of
the six glorious angels, with feasts and parties. It was also the shortest
day of the year and was celebrated by Alanzans with prayers and rituals to Deanziel, one of the six wayward angels, as they contemplated
the return of the light. Both groups treated the day as a major holiday.
Each one thought the other had corrupted it.

Cedric slipped quietly away after sunset, trekking out into the
snowy night to honor all twelve angels in his own manner. He made it
back for dinner and the party that followed, and I let myself truly enjoy the festivities. A few of our instructors celebrated with us, and we
all played games and drank sweet wine after eating. Future husbands

dominated the conversation, and I didn't mind. There was such a feeling of hope and excitement buzzing through us all. It made me believe anything was possible. I'd find Lonzo. Maybe even a husband I liked. And I'd have Tamsin and Adelaide in my life forever, no matter where our marriages took us. After seeing so much darkness over the years, I now had a world opening up before me that was filled with joy and possibility.

Moods stayed cheery in the following days as we waited for results. The exception was Adelaide, which surprised both Tamsin and me. Our friend spoke little and often seemed lost in uncharacteristically dark thoughts. She was also one of the first to race downstairs when the announcement came that our results were in. We all nearly tripped over each other as we crowded into the library, only remembering our manners when we caught sight of Jasper, Mistress Masterson, and a dressmaker named Miss Garrison standing in a line before us. We fell into neat rows, listening in respectful silence as Jasper made one of his inspiring speeches. Then, Mistress Masterson set out the list of scores with a smile, and order broke as we rushed forward.

I found my name and could hardly believe what I saw. Seventh. Seventh of forty. A rush of pleasure and pride swept over me. Apparently I'd learned more than just linguistics. After Tamsin, I had the highest score in our house, though there was a considerable point difference between us. Her score had been nearly perfect. Adelaide had landed right in the middle at nineteen, and Clara—shooting me a scowl—came in at eight.

Adelaide and I hugged, breaking when a familiar voice cut through the din. "How am I ranked third? The girls above me have the same score as me!"

I turned around—along with half the room—to see Tamsin confronting Mistress Masterson. "Yes. You all tied—it was very impressive. Really, what it came down to is aesthetics," Mistress Masterson explained. "Winnifred, the first girl, would look so lovely in the diamond coloring. Ruby's the next most precious stone, and that obviously wouldn't suit you with your hair. So third, as a sapphire, seemed like—"

"Sapphire?" interrupted Tamsin. "*Sapphire?* Everyone knows green is my best color. Isn't an emerald rarer than a sapphire?"

"They're close enough. And my green fabric hasn't arrived yet," said Miss Garrison. Several of her assistants had already entered with bolts of cloth, ready to start taking our measurements. "Isn't likely to show until about a week before you sail."

"And the categories are flexible—it's more of a gemstone *range* we're going for," added Mistress Masterson. "We thought it best just to go forward with sapphire so that she could start on your wardrobe. Otherwise, she'd be working at the last minute."

"Well, maybe she could just sew a little damned faster," snapped Tamsin.

"Tamsin! You are out of line. You will take sapphire and be grateful that you're among the top three. *And* you will watch your language."

Even Tamsin realized she'd gone too far. "Yes, Mistress Masterson. I apologize. But I can retake the exams I did poorly on, right?"

"Yes, of course. Every girl can. Though, I'll be honest, with a ninety-nine percent rating, there's isn't much else to achieve."

Tamsin lifted her chin proudly. "Perfection."

"Poor Tamsin," I murmured. I didn't like seeing my friend upset, but it was hard to feel *too* bad for her. No one could doubt her excellence, and although the top three girls attended more exclusive events, I knew Tamsin would have no difficulty meeting elite men. When Adelaide didn't respond, I glanced over and saw her watching Mistress Masterson with a pensive expression.

"I'm going to ask if I can retake them too," Adelaide finally said.

"Really?" Her face was too earnest for me to suspect her of joking, but I couldn't imagine she'd want to go through all of that stress again. "You scored in the middle. That's not bad."

Adelaide simply shrugged and walked over to get Mistress Masterson's attention. Someone tugged at my sleeve, and I found one of the dressmaker's assistants standing by me. "You're Mirabel, right?" She held up an armful of gold and yellow fabric in all sorts of textures and sheens. "I'm here to measure you. They assigned you topaz."

The fabrics looked so unreal, I was afraid to touch them. I'd been in awe of the clothes we'd worn so far at Blue Spring, but this was a whole new level. A storybook level. The seamstress had just finished measuring my waist when Miss Garrison strolled up and made a click of dismay.

"This won't do. This won't do at all."

Mistress Masterson, overhearing, joined us. "What's the matter?"

Miss Garrison gestured to a swathe of goldenrod velvet I held. "She can't wear these kinds of yellows with an olive complexion. Do you want her to look sick? Her skin is flawless. You need to show it off and change her stone. Give her a deeper color. Or even a brighter one."

After more petitioning, the seamstress convinced Jasper and Mistress Masterson to change me to a garnet and clothe me in reds. Clara, formerly a garnet, hated yellow and regarded me with open contempt. I kept a dignified expression until I heard Jasper say, "Garnet *is* a little more of a common stone, so it might be fitting."

The afternoon became a nonstop whirl. Along with our measurements, Miss Garrison assessed all sorts of details. She'd brought more fabric samples in each color palette than she needed and had to fine-tune which looked best in each girl's set. She draped us in silks and velvets, pairing them with gems and jewelry that made my head swim. She even took notes on our faces and figures, determining what types of necklines and sleeves would be most flattering.

"Well, well," she said, scrutinizing my figure, "aren't you a standout."

"I . . . I'm sorry, what?"

She gestured to my chest with a swatch of red silk. "You can fill out a corset, no question. We've got to push and squeeze some of these girls to make it look like they've got any sort of cleavage at all. But you've got the real thing, and we can show it off. They wear lower necklines over there, you know."

"Er, ah, thank you? But I'm sure there are others . . . that is, I mean everyone knows that Ingrid . . ." I couldn't finish.

"Her over there? Oh, yes. We've actually got to rein her in. Too much, if you can believe it. And she's so short that it makes her look unbalanced—like she's going to fall over. You've got enough here to catch the eye, and you're tall and slim enough that all the proportions work perfectly."

I was too mortified to respond.

"Don't look like that," she said. "We won't do anything indecent, but my job is to make the most of what everyone's got. You'll thank me later."

❧

"What a day," I told my roommates when I was finally allowed the safety of my bedroom. Tamsin had taken comfort in the thought of re-takes and now brimmed with energy. "Didn't all that . . . unsettle you, even a little?" I asked. I couldn't bear to tell them of Miss Garrison's continued analysis of my cleavage. Even recalling it made me cringe.

"I was born for this," Tamsin declared. "The only unsettling part was that I was wearing blue, not green."

Adelaide, stretched out on her bed, gave an exasperated sigh. "Green, blue. It's not life or death."

Tamsin's expression said otherwise. "Easy for you to say, Miss Amethyst. You look ravishing in purple. You're lucky to have landed where you did."

Adelaide didn't respond, and I realized she must not have mentioned her retake plans.

❧

Tamsin soon found out about those plans when she and Adelaide both showed up the following week for retakes, along with a hand-ful of other girls. Tamsin was floored, especially when she found out Adelaide wanted to redo *all* the exams, not just a few subjects. What actually shocked me the most was seeing Adelaide study just as diligently as Tamsin.

During the time that was going on, my only real duties were to show up for my dress fittings. My beautiful red wardrobe increased day by day, and along with being overwhelmed by the opulence, I just couldn't get over the price of it all. One dress would've fed us for months back in Osfro.

"How do they afford all of this?" I asked Miss Garrison at one point. "Do our contract prices really cover the cost of clothes and passage to Adoria?"

"Yes, actually. And then Mister Jasper gets even more back by either selling your dresses or reusing the materials for next year's girls." She looked up from her hemming to study the scarlet velvet gown I wore. It sat off the shoulder and glittered with beaded embellishment. "Although Mister Charles insists that each girl can keep one, if she wants, for her wedding. This would be an excellent one."

"What's Mister Charles like?" We rarely heard about Jasper's brother and partner.

"He has a gentler disposition. I think Mister Jasper would boss him around more, but Mister Charles came into this with much, *much* more money. His late wife was something of an heiress."

"What about Mister Jasper's wife? No one mentions her."

"Mistress Thorn? Living over in Mertonshire, last I heard. They say it's because it's better for her constitution than the city air." Miss Garrison's voice dropped to a conspiratorial whisper. "But between you and me, I believe she and Mister Jasper are simply happier being together . . . when they're not together. I guess some marriages work better that way."

"I suppose so," I murmured, thinking of my own future.

A few days later, the results came back, and Jasper and Mistress Masterson called us to the library again. Both wore stunned expressions.

They didn't even notice when Cedric slipped in late and stood beside them.

"I know some of you have been waiting for your retake results, so you'll be pleased they're in. Most of you showed improvement— for which I'm particularly proud. But there was nothing significant enough to warrant a change in rank or theme." Mistress Masterson paused. "With one exception."

I could hardly believe it. I never doubted Tamsin's determination, but even I'd found it unlikely she could top her ninety-nine percent score.

Mistress Masterson exchanged brief looks with Jasper and then turned back to address us. "Adelaide. The improvement you showed is . . . remarkable, to put it mildly. I've never, ever seen a girl make such a leap in scores. And . . . I've never seen a girl get a perfect over-all score. We rarely have theme changes based on retakes, though of course it happens. And in this case, it's absolutely warranted."

I didn't immediately grasp what had happened. Tamsin, gaping, clearly had.

"Adelaide, my dear, you've replaced Winnifred from Dunford Manor as our diamond," Jasper said. I glanced back and forth be-tween my best friends in disbelief. "Everyone else who scored above your last result will move down a notch. All girls will still keep their gemstone themes, with a few exceptions."

Mistress Masterson took over again and directed her words to Adelaide. "As Mister Thorn said, you'll be our diamond. You and Winnifred are of similar size, and Miss Garrison should have little difficulty fitting you into her clothes. Since her score was so high, it'd hardly seem fair to assign her a semiprecious stone like the amethyst. We think she'll show best as a sapphire, and we've done a couple of other last-minute switches—which means, Tamsin, you can be an emerald after all. Miss Garrison expects the green fabric to arrive next week, and she and her assistants will work around the clock to make sure you're properly outfitted."

Tamsin showed no joy at getting her coveted color. "But . . . if the ranks shifted down, then that means . . . I'm fourth."

"Yes," said Mistress Masterson.

"You'll dazzle them as an emerald," Jasper told Tamsin. "Even if you aren't invited to *all* the elite parties, I know you'll be in high demand. I'm proud of you. I'm proud of all my girls—though it looks like my son managed to find the top jewel this season."

Judging from Cedric's shocked face, it appeared he hadn't been informed of this new ranking ahead of time.

Mistress Masterson dismissed the rest of us but held Adelaide back. Upstairs, all anyone could talk about was the unprecedented switch. I ignored all the questions that rained down on me and steered a visibly distraught Tamsin into the privacy of our room.

She sat on her bed, hands clasped in her lap. She'd always been fair skinned, but the pallor I saw now made me worry she'd faint. "Tamsin—"

"How?" she asked softly, looking up at me with enormous eyes. They glittered with unshed tears. "How is this even possible? I gave it everything, everything that was in me. I worked hard. I studied hard."

I sat beside her. "Of course you did. It's just that Adelaide studied . . ."

I couldn't finish, realizing how foolish I was about to sound.

". . . studied harder than me?" Tamsin supplied. "We both know that's not true. And my dreams are done."

"Of course they aren't!" I found this shaken, downcast Tamsin far more upsetting than the fiery, temperamental one I usually saw.

She took a deep breath. "Mira, for some of these girls, being here has been a dream come true. A roof over their heads. Plenty of food. All those dresses. But none of that really mattered to me. I mean, I liked it all, yes, but it wasn't easy for me to come here. Some days, it's been agonizing. Being away from the city meant—"

Adelaide opened the door, and all trace of the subdued girl beside me evaporated. Tamsin was on her feet in a flash, face full of rage.

"What have you done?" she demanded.

Adelaide winced. "I'm, uh, not sure what you mean."

"The hell you don't! Has this all been some kind of joke? Coast along and then swoop in at the end to crush everyone else?" Tamsin pushed on when Adelaide didn't answer. "How did you do that? How did you score perfectly on everything?"

I could see Adelaide trying to remain calm and put on some semblance of her usual lighthearted manner. But the effort was weak. "I learned a lot of it when I worked in my lady's house. I was around nobility all the time, and I guess I picked up their ways. You know that."

Tamsin clenched her fists at her sides. "Oh yeah? Where were those ways in the last nine months? You've botched things continuously— but not always the same things! You run hot and cold, perfect at some things and then failing at the most basic ones. What kind of game are you playing?"

"It's no game," Adelaide said. "My nerves just got the best of me. Things finally came together during the retakes."

"Impossible. I don't understand how or why you've been doing this, but I know something's going on. And if you think you can just ruin my life and—"

"Oh, come on." Adelaide's composed façade began wearing down. "Your life is far from ruined."

"That's not true. I had it. I was in the top three—the three who get shown the most!—and then *you* came along and pulled that out from under me. You knew how important it was to me but still went ahead and destroyed everything I've worked for."

That was when Adelaide finally lost it. "Tamsin, enough! I've gone along with your theatrics for nine months, but this is going too far. Exactly what in your life has been destroyed? You can converse about current politics, eat a seven-course meal, and play the piano! Maybe you'll miss out on a few parties, but you're still going to marry some rich, prestigious man in the New World. You've come a long way from being a laundress's daughter, and if you were my friend, you'd be happy at how far I've come too."

Tamsin flinched a little at *if you were my friend*, but she didn't back down. "That's the thing. I can't tell how far you've come. I've lived with you all these months but don't know anything about you. The only thing I'm sure of is that you've been lying to us all, and this 'triumph' of yours just proves it!"

I felt sick to my stomach. All the hope I'd joyously built up was crumbling before me. *No, no*, I thought. *I can't lose this. I can't lose this tranquil bubble.* I hated seeing Tamsin so upset. I hated seeing her direct that raw emotion at Adelaide. And I hated the way it changed Adelaide.

"Tamsin." I spoke very cautiously, very lightly. My job was to mediate, as always. "That's not fair. What's wrong with her wanting to do well? It's what we all want. And she told you, nerves always got the best of her—"

"That's the biggest lie of all. She's been fearless from the first day, facing down Clara and traipsing out in the night for holly. The jokes, the carefree air . . . it's all been a cover." Tamsin shifted her glare from me back to Adelaide. "Nerves aren't your problem. I refuse to be sucked into your web of lies, and I will never have anything to do with you again."

I attempted to tell her how extreme that was, but no pleas could sway her. She left in a rage, slamming the door so hard, the floor shook. Adelaide fell apart after that and collapsed to her bed, all of her earlier defiance vanishing. I hurried over and wrapped her in my arms, even though I was on the verge of falling apart myself.

"It's okay," I kept saying. "I'll fix this. She'll come around."

But Tamsin didn't.

At first, I thought she just needed time. We had a week until we sailed to Adoria. Surely, their anger would cool. It did, I suppose, in a way. But it was the kind of cold, seething anger that was almost as deadly as the hot and furious kind. The fact that we all had to sleep in the same room together only worsened it. Tamsin stayed away as much as possible, going to bed late in the hopes that Adelaide would be asleep.

Adelaide, for her part, attempted to make peace a few times. Tamsin wouldn't have it. I tried as well, certain that even stubborn Tamsin would cave. After all, how many times had I seen them and their extreme personalities quarrel? Always, always, they had eventually made up.

But as more time passed, I began to face the awful, horrible realization that this might be unfixable. Everything that had happened to me before—loss, pain, abandonment—was happening again. My parents. Lonzo. Sirminica. The hope I'd had for Adoria grew dark. The ground felt like it was crumbling beneath me. And I was going to fall with it.

On the night before we sailed, I made one last effort, cornering Tamsin in the study. I vowed to stay calm and strong. *I can fix this.*

"Tamsin, please. Hear her out. You've never given her a chance. We sail tomorrow. You two have to forgive each other."

Cold fire flashed in the depths of Tamsin's eyes. "There's no forgiving what she's done. You don't know how badly she's hurt me."

"And neither of *you* understand how badly you're hurting *me*! You two are ripping me in half! I've seen what happens when neither side backs down in a fight. No one wins, Tamsin, and I'm so tired of it. I'm tired of pain. I'm tired of loss. I can't do it anymore—and I can't lose you guys."

Tamsin's face went very still, and after several long moments, she clasped my hands in hers. "Mira, you will never lose me. No matter what else happens or where we go in this world, I will always be there for you." The next words came with a bit of difficulty. "And whatever's happened between Adelaide and me . . . well. I know she'll always be there for you too."

"It won't be the same."

"I'm sorry, Mira. I wish you weren't pulled into this. You're the last person I want to see hurt."

"Then let this go. Please." I had one last, desperate argument. *I can fix this.* "You guys can't go two months, cooped up on the same ship, with this between you."

"You're right," she said, releasing my hands. "We can't."

CHAPTER 6

WE LEFT FROM CULVER, A PORT CITY ON OSFRID'S WEST coast, on a cold and blustery day. Gray water lapped at the docks in front of us, and seagulls screeched and whirled in the sky above. It was so like the city where I'd landed on the other side of the country that I had a brief sense of déjà vu. I'd traveled with my brother that day. This morning, I stood with the two friends who felt like sisters—and who still hadn't made peace with each other.

"Do they really expect us to spend two months in the company of those sailors?" demanded Tamsin, wrinkling her nose as several walked by with loads of cargo. She spoke pointedly to me, even though Adelaide stood right by us.

I studied the passing sailors for several moments before answering. Some of the day laborers that Mistress Masterson frequently hired had been brought on to help, but my Flatlander acquaintance didn't seem to be among them. I turned back to Tamsin and tried to keep my tone light. "Are you saying you didn't run into sailors when you were out delivering laundry?"

"Well, of course I did. But that was then. This is now. I'm at a very different station. I'd hardly associate with the likes of them these days."

"Don't worry," I said. "It's not like you'll have to share a room with them. And someone's got to run the ship."

"Especially since I don't have any sort of nautical knowledge," remarked Adelaide, bitterly recalling Jasper's retort when she'd questioned him about winter storms.

Tamsin nearly responded and then remembered it was Adelaide who'd spoken. Tamsin turned around, putting her back to both of us, and watched as the men continued loading the cargo. Adelaide sighed.

We were taking two ships to Adoria, the *Good Hope* and the *Gray Gull*. Each ship would carry half of the girls, as well as all sorts of goods Jasper planned on selling. A handful of other passengers and commodities were also going with us, so apparently we weren't the only ones willing to risk a winter crossing.

"You'll be in the capable hands of Mistress Culpepper when you arrive," said Mistress Masterson, speaking loudly to be heard over the wind. She tightened her dark shawl around her narrow shoulders. "She runs things on the Adorian side and will look after you."

She and the other manor mistresses stood nearby, all quick to offer advice to us about avoiding sailors and remembering our manners in Adoria. Only some of the houses' mistresses were accompanying us. Mistress Masterson wasn't one of them. Instead, our chaperone aboard the *Good Hope* was the Dunford mistress, Miss Bradley, who seemed nice enough.

Once the cargo was packed away, it was time for us to go aboard. We surprised Mistress Masterson with hugs and then waited for our names to be read. Jasper was calling out for the *Gray Gull*, which would carry the Dunford and Swan Ridge girls, first. When I heard him say Tamsin's name, I thought for sure I must have mixed everything up.

But no, Tamsin separated herself from the Blue Spring Manor girls, handed Mistress Masterson a stack of letters, and then walked down the wharf toward the *Gray Gull*. Her red hair danced in the wind behind her, and she didn't look back.

"Tamsin . . ." I breathed.

Adelaide said nothing, but her blue eyes widened with disbelief. When our turn came to board the *Good Hope*, I whispered, "She'll come around. She has to. This journey will give her a lot of time to think."

But I could hear myself falter and knew that Adelaide didn't believe me. I didn't believe me either. I had to force one foot in front of the other when we started toward the dock. I'd failed. I hadn't fixed things. Several Blue Spring girls shot Adelaide looks of sympathy.

"Can you believe it's that bad?" Clara said to Caroline in a stage whisper. "Tamsin didn't even think she was worth a goodbye."

Tamsin apparently hadn't thought I was worth a goodbye either.

I tried to put on a look of indifference as a sailor led us below the ship's deck and into a narrow corridor that contained our party's cabins. Adelaide came to a startled halt when we entered ours, which was half the size of our former bedroom. The tiny cabin had six bunk beds built into the walls and would hold us, three other Blue Spring girls, and Martha from Swan Ridge—whom Tamsin had swapped places with. Though we'd all come from humble backgrounds, this change from our living conditions at the manors was a shock. Even I had become spoiled, and I sternly reminded myself that when Lonzo and I had sailed from Evaria, we'd had standing room only in a cargo hold packed with other people.

Adelaide still looked glum, so I linked her arm in mine and steered her to the upper deck. I wanted her old smiles back. And she wasn't the only one who needed a distraction. "Come on. They're going to cast off."

This ship dwarfed the little channel-runner I'd sailed on. The *Good Hope* and *Gray Gull* were great beasts of the ocean, vast and powerful and ready to take on the journey ahead. We gathered near the rail with other curious passengers while sailors shouted and scurried around us, each one focused on his task. The mighty ship swayed on the waves—up and down, back and forth—and then slowly pushed away from the wharf as the last line was taken in. Wind filled the billowing sails above, and we were off.

The thrill of it swept up even Adelaide, though I knew she'd spotted Tamsin on the other ship's deck as we departed. The sight of that red hair tore at my heart. *Let her go, Mira*, I scolded myself.

People leave. You've seen it your whole life. Focus on what's to come.
Lonzo. Adoria. The New World. It's finally happening.

Cedric was also traveling on our ship and strolled over as Adelaide
and I discussed cabins. He wore a long, deep red coat of unusual cut—
unusual here, at least. I'd heard it was very fashionable in the Adorian
colonies.

Adelaide gave him the first real smile I'd seen in days. "I suppose
you're staying in a luxury stateroom."

He grinned back. "That would be my father. I'm in a cabin like
yours, bunking with other passengers."

I followed his nod toward a group of people standing at the
opposite railing. After spending the better part of a year in a house
with the same faces each day, I craved new stories and discussions. I
hoped Miss Bradley wouldn't insist on locking us away. Our sailing
companions clearly varied in backgrounds, but all were men—typical,
considering they outnumbered women three to one in the colonies.
Some passengers looked like they'd used every copper they had to
make it aboard this ship. Others, probably merchants and traders,
displayed prosperity in both clothing and manner.

Not enough prosperity, according to Cedric. He was just remarking
on how none of them could afford us when Rosamunde approached.
She joined me in my assessment of our shipmates while Cedric and
Adelaide chatted on my other side. "It sure would save us a lot of trouble if we could just find a respectable match on this trip," Rosamunde
remarked.

"Doesn't sound like anyone here has enough money. Besides, I
assumed you wanted to go to all the parties."

"I do, but sometimes I get nervous thinking about all the pressure
and the crowds." She tilted her head speculatively. "Look at that one
with the blond hair. He's fine looking, don't you think? And his waistcoat is silk. He might have some means."

The man in question had sausage curls above his ears and wore the
rest tied back with a blue silk ribbon. His face was so pale, I couldn't

tell if he was sick or had just overly powdered it. "He looks like he's never been outside before," I said disapprovingly. "And he seems pretty upset about the wind messing up his hair."

"So? Maybe he's a refined gentleman who stays inside reading. All the time. And I think his hair's very elegant." Rosamunde scanned the others. "Okay—what about him? The one with the pipe? He's a little older, but he's dressed well too. And he's very handsome."

I squinted. "He's got a wedding ring on. And he's not *that* handsome."

Rosamunde's face expressed disbelief at my opinion. "Well, that one over there looks pretty good—the one with the long brown coat. Not even you can deny it."

I opened my mouth, ready to protest, and then I did a double take. "Okay," I admitted. "I can't deny it."

Her brow furrowed. "But he needs to be cleaned up. Shaved, for one. And given a haircut. I mean, is he trying to grow it out? Or is he just lazy?"

The young man's glossy black hair did seem confused—too long to lie in the neat, military style favored by older Adorian men but not quite long enough to pull back into the tails that the fashion conscious, like Cedric, wore.

I brushed my own windswept hair back to get a better look. "I don't know. I kind of like the hair and stubble. It makes him . . . rugged."

She rolled her eyes. "Do you think that suit is rugged too? It's actually decently made, but he didn't bother to press it at all. And anyway, he looks comfortable but not rich. We can do better."

As her attention shifted to the other passengers, I kept mine on the black-haired man and took in all those little oddities. Definitely a man of contradictions . . . and a strong, muscled build no one near him could match. My eyes lingered longer than they should have, following the lines of his body, taking note of the broad shoulders and the way his trousers hugged his legs. You didn't get a physique like that from gentlemen's easy pastimes. But there was a vigilant, almost fierce quality to his stance that didn't exactly come from common labor either. I found myself thinking of my scandalous remarks to Tamsin, about the allure of a brief, purely physical affair before settling down with a husband I may or may not love. It was easy to imagine this mysterious man in such a role. Not so easy to imagine ever being able to do it while in the tight grip of the Glittering Court.

And that's when I noticed he was staring at me.

No—I wasn't the one he was looking at. Adelaide was. His eyes, as dark as his hair, rested intently on her as she laughed at some joke of Cedric's, and it was a wonder she couldn't feel that piercing gaze. Or maybe she did. Moments later, she glanced in his direction. Upon being noticed, the man nodded politely and then turned away in a seemingly casual manner—but it wasn't casual. His body crackled with tension, hyperaware of everything surrounding him.

My illicit musings evaporated. Men looked at Adelaide all the time. How couldn't they? She dazzled everyone. But I hadn't read any attraction in his eyes when he watched her. I hadn't read *anything* in his eyes. And that worried me.

I didn't see him as the week progressed, and he gradually slipped my mind. Monotony settled in, as did seasickness. Miss Bradley realized the futility of keeping us all below deck and allowed us freedom of movement, so long as we didn't walk alone or breach any other rules of etiquette. A few girls frequently disregarded the command about traveling in groups. I was one of them.

The ship's motion only bothered Adelaide a little, and me not at all. She took a lot of walks with me in those early days, and we'd chat about what was to come or reminisce about Blue Spring. And Tamsin. We talked about Tamsin all the time. The *Gray Gull* was always in sight. One of my favorite things about being aboard our ship was standing right at the edge of the port or starboard railing. I loved watching the water rush past and feeling the breeze against me, but Adelaide's carefree nature faltered at that.

"Be careful," she told me one day. It was probably the hundredth time she'd said that during our trip.

We were having another deck walk on what was turning into a pleasant afternoon. The sun had broken through the morning haze, and I couldn't stay away from the edge. Adelaide remained a few steps behind me, shaking her head with a smile when I beckoned her forward.

I'd barely turned back to the sun-dappled water when I heard a voice address her: "Your first voyage?"

I spun around, worried I'd have to ward some sailor away from her. Instead, I found myself staring at *him*—the man of contradictions. And he was looking at Adelaide in that same, disconcerting way. I moved swiftly to her side.

"I'm sorry," the man said politely. "We're not supposed to talk without a formal introduction, right?"

"Well, these aren't very formal settings." Adelaide smiled readily, sharing none of my concerns. "I'm Adelaide Bailey, and this is Mira Viana."

He shook our hands. "Grant Elliott. I'd take my hat off if I had one, but I learned long ago that it's not even worth wearing one out in this wind."

"You've been to Adoria before?" I asked.

Grant's eyes flicked briefly to me before returning to her. "Last year. I have a stake in a store that outfits people for exploration and wilderness survival. My partner ran it over the winter, and now I'm coming back."

The idea of exploring Adoria's wilderness almost made me forget my misgivings. One of Adoria's draws was its vast expanse of unknown territory, land that even the Icori and Balanquans hadn't settled. It had always intrigued Lonzo and me. I didn't expect to see much of that wilderness as the pampered wife of some wealthy businessman, but the adventure and romance still beckoned.

"Have you done much exploring yourself, Mister Elliott?" I asked.

Maybe being a frontier adventurer could explain that rugged edge I sensed around an otherwise proper demeanor.

"Here and there. Nothing you'd find interesting." He scratched his chin and focused on Adelaide yet again. He had the same shadow of stubble Rosamunde had noticed, almost as though he purposely maintained it. Not clean cut, not long enough for a beard. "Now, help me understand how your organization works. You're ranked by gemstone, right? And you're the top one?"

"The diamond," she said. "And Mira's a garnet."

"So, that means you'll get to go to all sorts of—"

He was interrupted as an upbeat Cedric walked over to us. "There you are. Looks like the three of you have already met. Mister Elliott is one of the men who shares a cabin with me." The two of them shook hands in greeting. "Adelaide, I need to borrow you for a moment. Mira, will you be able to go back down below with them when they leave?"

Cedric nodded toward a cluster of girls from Guthshire. I could just barely make out one of them describing the virtues of velvet over silk when it came to hair bows.

"Of course," I said, having no intention of joining that gaggle. "And perhaps Mister Elliott could tell me more about his business."

Grant was already backing away. "I'd love to, but I just remembered something I have to follow up on."

He headed off in one direction while Cedric and Adelaide went in another. A couple of the girls in the bow-discussion group watched Grant's departure. I heard one say, "That one needs a woman to look after him."

"Wouldn't matter," remarked another. "He's probably just a common laborer."

"No, I heard he's some kind of merchant," the first girl said. "But a small-time one."

A merchant like that couldn't afford a Glittering Court girl— especially not Adelaide, our diamond. So why had Grant tried so hard to engage her—but not me—in conversation? Was he just trying to see what kind of luck he might have seducing a girl who was out of his league? My gut said no. His behavior was strange but not flirtatious.

As we continued crossing paths in the next few days, I became more and more convinced he was pursuing Adelaide. Whenever she came above deck, he'd materialize like he'd been lying in wait. For her part, she didn't notice. She had other things on her mind, and he never said anything that couldn't have been said in front of Miss Bradley.

I quickly realized he wasn't simply pursuing Adelaide. He was actively avoiding *me*. If he saw me approaching alone, he'd find an excuse to leave. At first, I thought he just didn't want to waste his time on anyone who wasn't her. But when he did happen to catch her in a group, he'd make polite conversation with every other girl. Me? I received as minimal a response as propriety would allow. And I almost never got eye contact.

I then assumed his standoffishness must be because of my background—but Grant never seemed prejudiced toward the handful of other non-Osfridians on board. It was just . . . me.

I didn't tell Adelaide or Cedric about my suspicions, seeing as they were mostly based on instinct. Tamsin might have believed me, which only made me feel worse. Missing her one afternoon, I wandered over to the starboard side of the ship, where the *Gray Gull* sailed perfectly parallel to us. I squinted at the figures moving aboard its deck, hoping to spy a flash of red hair.

"You know she'll have made all sorts of new friends by the time we arrive," a snide voice said behind me.

I closed my eyes a moment before turning to face Clara. "I hope she does," I replied evenly. "It's a long trip."

Clara cocked her head, smiling in that unfriendly way of hers. "You don't get it, do you? She's not going to have anything to do with either of you when we're in Adoria. Adelaide's too much competition . . . and you . . . well, you're you."

"We're friends."

"That's not what it looked like when we left Culver. Come on, Mira. You lived with her. You know how ambitious she is. Having a Sirminican friend isn't going to help her over there, and she's smart enough to know it."

Other people milled about the deck, so I made sure to keep my face pleasant as I said, "Don't you have something else to attend to? Maybe a married man you can get friendly with? I think there are a few on board."

Clara stiffened. Fury flashed in her eyes, but like me, she maintained a cordial façade. "It's always so nice talking to you, Mira. Enjoy the day."

As soon as she was gone, I turned back toward the water and slumped against the rail, resting a hand over my eyes. "Tamsin," I muttered, "why did you have to take it this far?"

"Are you talking to me?"

This new voice was familiar, but unexpected. Grant Elliott. He stood to my left, only a few feet away. He seemed ill at ease, as though he had to force himself to speak.

"No," I said, not even caring that I finally had his attention. My mood was too dark for that or even tact. "And I have a feeling you know that, Mister Elliott. You seem like you're an observant man."

"You think so, huh?" His voice held amusement, though his expression stayed serious. He leaned against the rail beside me and watched the *Gray Gull*. "Are you . . ." A deep breath. "Are you okay? Your face after that girl—"

"That girl is no one," I snapped. "Or any of your business."

He straightened up. "Okay. I'll leave you alone."

"No, wait." I shook off my gloom, suddenly aware of the opportunity before me. "I'm being rude. I'm sorry. Don't go."

He wavered, even shifting from foot to foot, and I thought I'd lost him. After a little more hesitancy, he settled against the rail but pointedly looked away from me. "No need to apologize. We all have our days."

My mind raced, and I tried to slow it down. I had him. At last. Now I needed to keep him. "Are you . . . are you excited to return to Adoria?"

"I wouldn't say 'excited.' But I've got work to do in Cape Triumph. And a couple of people I'd like to see."

As I started to reply, I had a weird sense of familiarity. Like I should know him. But it wasn't possible. "You're lucky. Going home to people who care about you." Images of Lonzo and Tamsin flashed through my mind.

"I'm not sure I think of Cape Triumph as home."

"I've always thought people are what make a place home."

"People complicate things. They can be dangerous if you get attached to them."

He still wouldn't look at me, but I realized he'd dropped that overly proper air he usually projected. He was almost candid now, revealing a slight shift in the way he spoke. I always used my best Osfridian in public, but when I relaxed among friends, my natural accent slipped back in. I felt like that was happening to him now, but I just couldn't figure out what I was hearing in his voice. It was maddening. As a student of linguistics, I needed to unravel it. And as Adelaide's best friend, I needed to unravel him.

"Thinking that way sounds like it'd be . . . lonely."

He only shrugged. I was in grasping distance of figuring out that cadence in his voice.

"Is your voyage going well?"

"Any voyage where you're still afloat is going well."

Silence again. I had it. Almost. I'd heard enough colonial accents on board to recognize them now, even carefully hidden under the proper Osfridian pronunciation he managed so well. But something still felt off about his. "Mister Elliott . . . which part of Adoria were you born in?"

His whole posture changed, growing stiff. Wary. "What makes you think I was born there at all?"

"It's in your voice, your accent. I mean, it's hard to pick up—but it's there. The way you stress your vowels, I think."

I finally received eye contact, and it was filled with suspicion. "And how in the world would you—" He stopped and averted his gaze once more. "I've traveled around. I've probably picked up some of the local sounds."

"Were you outside the central colonies? I haven't heard many Adorians from the edges, but there must be regional differences."

"Are you a linguistics professor in your free time, Miss Viana?"

"No, but I worked with one back in Osfrid." I noted how he'd dodged my question. "I've been trying to get rid of my Sirminican accent."

"Why?"

I thought he must be joking, but he seemed legitimately puzzled. "Most people think I'll make a better match if my accent isn't so noticeable."

His eyes traveled over my body, studying me from head to toe. "Unless you're marrying a blind man, no husband's going to care about your accent."

Heat flooded my face. I had no reason to feel offended, seeing as I'd sized him up in exactly the same manner that first day. "Well, I should hope he'd care about more than just my looks," I shot back.

"Did I say anything about your looks?" He was watching the waves again, but I could see a wry smile playing at his lips.

"You didn't have to."

"I meant no offense, which I think you know—because you seem like you're pretty observant too." Decorous Grant returned as he gave me a small bow and turned in the direction of the door that led below. "Thank you for your time, Miss Viana."

He walked away, and that was when I spotted something I'd never noticed before—probably because the wind was always blowing his hair around.

A nick in his left ear.

My jaw dropped. I'd seen that nick before, twice—in the laborer who'd been at Blue Spring. A coincidence, I started to tell myself. That was all it could be. The Flatlander had been older, scarred, and stooped. Not to mention prone to coughing. Grant, while a little untidy sometimes, was a striking man and not much older than me. He was educated. He talked easily to the middle- and upper-class passengers on board. The two men had nothing in common, except that ear.

And their voices, I realized. The laborer had had a heavy Flatlander accent, similar to Ingrid's, but there'd always been a slight twang in his that differed from hers. Something I couldn't identify then, just as I couldn't identify it in Grant's voice now.

How was this possible? How could one man pull off two completely different people? An accent change was the first way, I supposed. I could imitate any number of them—why not Grant? And how hard was it to fake a hunched back and coughing fits? I'd never been able to study his entire face back at Blue Spring. Mostly I'd just seen his eyes—dark, cynical eyes. Eyes that didn't miss anything.

I gripped the rail tightly. Okay. They *could* be the same person. But to what end? Why had he been at Blue Spring, and why was he on our ship now?

And most importantly, why was he so focused on Adelaide?

I had no idea what he'd want with my friend, but it couldn't be good if it involved disguises and fake identities. I felt a tightness in my chest as I scurried downstairs to check on Adelaide. I would protect her. I would learn what Grant was doing and stop him.

I just had to figure out how.

CHAPTER 7

MY CHANCE CAME A FEW DAYS LATER DURING A WALK with Adelaide and Cedric. Another passenger passed by and offered Cedric an invitation to a card game that night, which Cedric accepted. After the other man left, Adelaide and I demanded more information.

"It's a thing the men do around here a couple of times a week," Cedric explained. "The passengers—not the sailors. My father's not that good at it, but he keeps going back, convinced he'll get his lucky break."

"And I'm sure you fleece them all each time," said Adelaide.

"I'm worse than some, better than most."

"Do all the men you room with play?" I asked.

"Yes, everyone in my room goes. Some shouldn't," he said with a laugh. "Jeb Carson? The old man with the white mustache? He's even worse than Father. But Grant Elliott's the one doing the fleecing. He's a great bluffer."

"No surprise," I muttered.

When the card game came that evening, I sneaked out of our wing, evading both Adelaide and Miss Bradley. I found Agostino, the Sirminican sailor, and convinced him to take me to Cedric and Grant's cabin. "I don't want to get in trouble if they catch you stealing," he said. He liked having someone to converse with in Sirminican, but we weren't exactly best friends. "And why do you need to steal anyway if you're going to be some rich man's wife?"

"I'm not stealing. And I won't say a word about you if I'm caught."

He dubiously handed over a lantern and closed the door behind me. I stared around the empty cabin, unsure where to start. Cedric's bed and belongings were easy to spot. Others were less obvious. A couple of trunks were unlocked, and a quick perusal of their contents let me rule them out as Grant's. Then, I spotted a familiar coat lying on a bunk. It was cut long in the Adorian fashion, made of dark brown worsted wool, and I'd seen it on Grant many times. Under the bunk was a worn black leather trunk. I slid it out, unsurprised to find it locked.

I produced my pick kit from a pocket in my dress. The irony of using Grant's gift to break into his possessions wasn't lost on me. The trunk possessed a type of lock I'd never seen, but after some experimentation, I finally clicked it open.

The contents proved disappointing. Clothes, mostly, and ordinary ones at that. A couple of books—high Osfridian literature. A brush. A razor that he apparently rarely used. I sat back on my heels, deflated. I'd been certain I'd get some big revelation here, something that would explain the mystery behind Grant Elliott and—

The trunk itself. There was something wrong with it. I examined it from where I sat on the floor, and then I leaned forward to look inside. The interior and exterior sizes didn't match. I pulled everything out and piled it up behind me. Once the trunk was empty, I could tell for sure that I was looking at a false bottom. The trunk held more; it was just concealed.

I ran my fingers along the edges of the wooden bottom, searching for some catch. At last, I located a small metal piece that popped up as though it might be used to pull that board out. But there was a keyhole in it, and the false bottom still didn't budge. I took out the lock picks again, selecting the tiniest one.

Figuring out how to maneuver such a delicate tool took even longer than my first attempt. In the back of my mind, I worried constantly about someone walking through the door. How long did card games go? At last, I heard a pop, and when I tugged on the metal lever, the false bottom lifted to reveal the rest of the trunk's interior.

The first thing I saw was a gun.

That was a bad start. I gingerly pushed it to the side. A lock pick kit sat beside it, and I recalled Grant boasting he had three more sets. What had he done with the rest? Given them to other vengeful girls? There was a money bag too—a heavy one—but I didn't count it. Beneath that sat a pile of matted hair, and I wondered if he'd stored some dead animal in there. But when I lifted it out, I recognized it as a false beard—the same beard my "friend" had worn at Blue Spring. A few other wigs and fake mustaches accompanied the beard. There was also a cosmetics set. Some of the creams and pigments were akin to what we'd been trained to use at Blue Spring. Other substances were more mysterious and had strange textures. Textures that might very well look like scars when painted on the skin, I realized.

"Okay," I murmured. "I know the how. But what's the why?"

A leather-bound journal hinted at answers. I opened it eagerly, only to be faced with blank pages. As I started to shut the book, the faint scent of citrus wafted through the air. I double-checked for any missed writing but only noticed that many pages had been ripped from the beginning.

An old memory came back to me, my father sending and receiving messages from secret sources in his network. I uncovered the lantern and held the first page up to the flame, as close as I could without burning the paper.

Words slowly appeared.

These had been written with so-called invisible ink, made with lemon juice or some other acidic substance. It didn't show up until exposed to heat. Triumphant, I turned the page and positioned the second one by the fire. Words appeared on that and on a third, but no more. I now had a letter and a list of names.

Mister Silas Garrett
Percival & Sons Tailoring
Cape Triumph
Denham Colony

My dearest Silas,

It was a delight to receive your letter. You're as blunt as ever, a trait I see you've passed on to your protégé. I've enjoyed having him as a guest this winter, and I believe you'll find him more polished. As much as it pains me to admit when you're right, I agree that he's been an excellent student of espionage. He easily learned all the old tricks—and a few new ones.

Our spies on this side of the water have continued investigating the conspiracy you and I communicated about last fall. Evidence suggests there's still dissent brewing among some colonials. What makes them more dangerous is that they're now receiving aid from the Lorandians in the form of supplies, both smuggled from the continent and stolen locally. Guns and rations can turn grumblers and whiners into a serious army. Lorandy has always eyed our territory; we can't let this situation give them a foothold.

Cutting off the rebels' resources is now our main objective. It will set back any other treasonous plans, and then we can chase those down as well. The attached list contains the names of individuals who are in positions capable of aiding the conspiracy, men with power or critical jobs. We also believe there is a Lorandian nobleman at work in the colonies who's

directly giving a substantial amount of gold to the
traitors. Tracing that money will help find them.

   Your protégé can fill you in on the rest of the
mission's details, as well as a unique opportunity. He's
also in possession of the Adorian McGraw branch's
annual stipend. This matter is of such urgency that
His Majesty is offering an additional five-hundred-
gold reward if the conspiracy can be stamped out by
autumn. You may distribute that bonus as you like,
either among your agents or perhaps to move your
office out of a tailor's shop.

                              Sincerely yours,
                              Sir Ronald Aspen

I had to steady my trembling hands as I read the letter again. *The McGraw Agency!* It was almost like something from the heroic stories I loved to read. Everyone knew about the McGraw Agency in Osfro, but few people knew anyone *in* the agency. They worked in law enforcement but not in the way the soldiers or watches did. Their cases were bigger. Osfrid's elite hired them to investigate private matters. And the crown hired them for matters of national security. Some agents worked openly while conducting investigations and gathering intelligence. But others worked in secret, without anyone knowing their identities. *Shadowmen,* I'd once heard them called. That was where their mystique came from—that and alleged stories of death-defying heroics.

A rattling of the cabin's door handle jerked me from my daydreams and brought me to my feet. I offered a prayer to any number of angels—six or twelve—that Cedric would walk through. He didn't.

Grant moved faster than I could've imagined. He slammed the door and closed the distance between us in moments. In one swift motion, he grabbed hold of me and pushed me against the wall.

"What are you doing in here?" he demanded. "Who sent you?"

His hands gripped my wrists tightly, and his face was inches from mine. But even after a year of disuse, all of the old defense lessons tumbled back into my brain.

Avoid a fight if you can, my father would say. *And if you can't, then you put everything you've got into it.* And then Lonzo: *Don't let their size fool you. The bigger they are, the easier of a target.*

I kneed Grant in the leg, not enough to make him fall, but it surprised him so much that he eased up his hold. I yanked my arms free, swiped at his face with my nails, and then, when he took a step back, I followed through with an upward jab to the side of his neck. *Heads are hard, little sister. Go for the stomach. Go for the neck.*

Grant made a startled choking sound, and I sprang away, heading for the door. I made it halfway across the cabin before he tackled me from behind. I landed stomach first, the fall knocking the wind out of me. He threw himself onto my back, pinning me in place with his greater weight.

"Let me go!" I yelled, trying to crane my neck and look up at him.

"Hush, I don't want to hurt you!"

"You slammed me against the wall!"

"I *restrained* you so I could find out why you're robbing me! Who sent you?"

"No one sent me! I was trying to find out why you were stalking my best friend."

That gave him pause, but he didn't let up on me. "Stalking her?"

"Don't think I haven't noticed."

Another pause. "We need to talk. If I let you go, are you going to run? Or claw up what's left of my face?"

"What are my alternatives? Enjoying your pleasant company?"

"I want you to explain yourself. If you aren't here to rob me, why are you here?"

"I'm the one who has to explain myself?" I struggled, hoping I could maybe get in an elbow jab. No luck.

"Fine. We'll both explain. And I mean it, I don't want to hurt you. I *won't* hurt you. I'll swear it by your favorite angel."

Blood pounded through me, battle rage squashing my fear. "I'll stay if I can stand by the door."

"Fair enough."

He stood up, and I scrambled to the door, putting one hand on its knob. He held up his palms and backed up to the cabin's other side. I really had scratched up his face. His rugged good looks were now *very* rugged.

The polite, pleasant façade he showed in public was gone. Even the sardonic persona from the deck had vanished. Someone sharp and deadly now stood before me. "So. Let's talk. Why are—" He did a double take, suddenly noticing now that the trunk's false bottom was out. "How did you open that?"

I held up the lock pick kit from a pocket in my dress's skirt. "With your assistance."

His incredulity grew. "I was an idiot to give you that! Next time I try to help someone, I'll have to remember to ask if she's a spy first."

"I'm not a spy." I slipped the picks back into the pocket where I kept my knife and wrapped my hand around the hilt.

Grant pointed at the open journal, its words plain to see. "Then how did you know to do that?"

"My father taught me. He was . . ."

"Don't tell me. A spy?"

"No! What he was isn't important right now." My hand was sweaty, and I had to adjust my grip on the knife. "I came here to make sure you don't hurt my friend."

"Hurt her? Why in Ozhiel's hell would I do that?"

"You tell me! You're the one pursuing her. I should've just gone straight to Cedric or Jasper and let them know that there's a con man obsessed with getting his hands on—"

"Stop right there. Let's get some things straight." He held up a finger. "First, you need to stop saying 'obsessed.' It makes me sound unstable." Another finger. "Second, I have no intention of 'getting my hands' on her. I wouldn't even know where to start with all those dress layers." Up went the third finger. "And finally . . . 'con man'?"

"How else would you describe a man who snoops around someone's house in disguise and then follows them onto a ship under another false identity?"

"This *is* my real identity," he snapped. "Mostly. And if you actually read that letter, you'd have your answer."

His voice held a query, trying to determine how much I knew. "Yes. I read it all. I know about the McGraw Agency. About your mission. Do you think we're traitors? That Adelaide is?"

His ensuing silence came from uncertainty, not anger. I realized then that he was afraid to say anything or give up any more of the conspiracy he was enmeshed in.

"I already know plenty," I boasted. "You might as well trust me with the rest."

"I can't trust anyone. Especially a woman who broke into my room."

"I told you, it was to protect Adelaide! What would you do if someone was stalking your best friend?"

"I wouldn't have to do anything. As soon as she noticed some guy sneaking around, she'd beat him to a pulp."

I considered that for a moment, fascinated by the idea that someone who thought caring about people was dangerous actually had a best friend—a female one who could apparently beat someone "to a pulp."

"Just tell me." Hopefully, if I tried for a civil attitude, he might do the same. "Please. I've already read everything. What else is there to do?"

"I could hand you over to the authorities for treason. Maybe you can find a husband in prison."

So much for civility. "I haven't done anything treasonous! I'm just trying to save my friend."

He raked a hand through his hair and began pacing the room. "You read the letter. You saw the part about how the leaders of this conspiracy are most likely men of power and influence—men a humble shopkeeper like me can't get easy access to."

"*Are* you a humble shopkeeper? Or are you a McGraw agent? Or are you a laborer with a bad back?"

"I'm all of those. Except my back is just fine." He paused. "How did you recognize me?"

"Your ear," I said. "And then that made me think of other things. Like that inflection I keep hearing in your voice. And how your scars were in different places when I saw you at Blue Spring. Not by much. But enough."

I didn't catch what Grant muttered next. The language was none I knew. But I'd apparently passed some sort of test. "I won't cross paths with many of those powerful men," he finally said. "But you girls will. And if what everyone says is true, your friend will cross paths with most of them."

"You want . . . you want Adelaide to be a spy?"

"The correct term is 'asset,'" he said. "Someone who gathers information for a spy. Can you talk to her for me?"

"No. I don't want Adelaide involved in anything dangerous."

"All she has to do is watch and listen at all those fancy balls and dinners."

"No."

He let out a long-suffering sigh. "Fine, then why don't we just forget about all this and be on our respective ways. I'm sure we each have important things to do—some of us more so than others." I didn't believe he'd give up on her so easily, but before I could call him out, he asked, "And how much money will it take to keep you quiet?"

I froze. "Money? How . . . much are you offering?"

"Now we're getting somewhere. Two gold."

A crazy idea began forming in the back of my mind. "I need two hundred."

"Two hundred? I barely have five to my name. And if I did have two hundred, I wouldn't give it to you."

I pointed at the journal. "But you'll get that huge reward for solving the case."

"*I* won't get it. Silas controls it. Then there'll be other expenses to compensate. But a little silence isn't worth two hundred. Not even an asset is."

"Were you going to pay Adelaide? How much?"

"To be determined," he said flatly.

"Look, you're right about her being the best at the Glittering Court. She earned that diamond title. But this—this sneaking around? Subterfuge, gathering information, and all that? It's not in her nature. *I'm* the one you want."

I braced myself for one of his biting remarks, but when he spoke, his tone held . . . well, not respect, exactly. But a little less sarcasm. "I'll give you points for subterfuge. And you're resourceful. You've certainly taught me a lesson about not using heat-sensitive inks." He touched one of the scratches on his face and winced. "And to take your threats seriously. I can't imagine if you'd had the knife."

I pulled the blade out. "I do have it."

He stepped forward to study it more closely. "Can it even cut anything?"

"Come closer and find out."

That brought a smile. Not a trusting one, by any means. But it was appreciative. "Her scores will get her into places you can't go."

"I don't need good scores to get into places," I said, looking around the cabin meaningfully. "I've got skills no other girl here has."

"And you've also got a Sirminican name. None of the others belong to a group that most Osfridians see as deceitful, dark-skinned heretics that are filling the capital's streets and stealing everything they can get their dirty hands on."

The breath seemed to leave my body, and I took a threatening step forward. "You don't know anything about us!"

"Don't hit me again," he said, and I realized I'd started to raise my hand. "I didn't say *I* see it that way. But I'm telling you how others will. And don't act like you haven't already felt it."

A little of my rage faded. "Yes."

"You'll see it again. It's how a lot of them are—especially anyone in Cape Triumph who was born in Osfrid. Trust me, I know firsthand how this works." He studied me even more intently this time. "But you *are* scrappy. And maybe you could make headway with some of the longtime colonials. They aren't always so small-minded, not after surviving there that long."

Now I studied him, trying to read his intentions. "Does that mean . . . are you giving me the asset job?"

"I'm *considering* it. And that's mostly because I'm tired, and you've worn me down." Grudgingly, he added, "And . . . it might be useful if you could pick a few locks at those parties you'll be at."

Excitement surged in me—and not just for the money. There was an allure to being part of the fabled McGraw Agency. Not part of it, I supposed. More like . . . a hired contractor. But still. I'd be doing something greater than dressing up for parties. I'd be continuing the family legacy of fighting injustice—but it'd be on my terms, not my father's.

And Lonzo . . . if I could earn some gold of my own, I wouldn't have to stress about my husband paying the bond. And if I could earn *a lot* of gold, I could pay off my own contract. I wouldn't need a husband at all. The thought made me giddy.

But those were big "ifs." And I didn't have any gold yet.

"I can do more than spy," I said. "All my accents are good. You can teach me to disguise myself, and you've seen how I fight. I've used a sword and—"

"Whoa, whoa." He held up his hands. "Slow down, buccaneer. I don't need to teach you any of that. *I* do that. Well, not the sword part. I need you to observe. I need you to distract men so that they say stupid things and give in to what you want. Can you do that?"

A little of my enthusiasm dimmed, and suddenly, it was like working for my father again. Fighting injustice by being a pretty face. By distracting. By offering myself.

But, Lonzo . . .

"If that's what you want? Yes. But I'm serious—don't underestimate the rest of what I can do. I got in here by learning your habits. And then I broke through your letter's protection. Sounds a lot like what you need an asset to do."

"Protection? Hardly. Lemon juice is a rookie's trick. But Aspen didn't know what reagents Silas was using these days."

I didn't know what a reagent was, so I pushed what I did know. "My father used ciphers and codes and masks and—"

"Yes, yes, I get that. What I don't get is why he did all that if he wasn't a spy."

Grant looked at me expectantly, and I realized this was the last thing that stood between me and the job. No one in this new life of mine, except Cedric, knew about my father's past. How would Grant take that knowledge? Deny me? Share it with others? I might not be an Alanzan, but no one would believe it. On the other hand, my gut told me that if I lied to Grant, he'd know.

"My father was a crusader of sorts. He was known best for smuggling Alanzans out of Sirminica. Before the war . . . well, the king and the church did horrible things to them. My father couldn't stand aside and let that happen, even if we didn't share their faith. He used every resource he had to help them—and that included his family."

"Where is he now?"

"Dead."

Grant's expression didn't change. "Okay, Mirabel," he said at last. "I'll sign on to this plan, fool that I am. What is there to lose? Aside from the entirety of Osfrid's colonial holdings. And my future. But don't trouble yourself over that."

"You know, you make it a little hard for people to like you."

"You don't have to like me, Mirabel. You just have to work with me."

"Most people call me Mira."

"And I call you Mirabel. Now get out of here before someone finds you. I have enough to worry about without the Thorns coming after me." He began replacing the trunk's contents.

"Not yet. We haven't talked about money. You said assets get paid."

"You're not getting two hundred. I'll give you . . . twenty."

"Fifty."

"Thirty."

"Fifty."

He threw up his hands. "That's not how negotiation works. You're supposed to come back with forty, and then we settle on thirty-five."

"Fifty," I repeated.

"You're a little short of your contract price, you know."

I let him think that paying my Glittering Court contract was my primary goal. "I'll worry about that other one hundred fifty."

"You're going to have to worry about one hundred sixty. Because I can't go over forty. I'm already giving away money that isn't mine to give."

I bit off a protest and asked instead, "Could you use your resources—the agency's resources—to track a bond servant who came into Cape Triumph last year?"

He crossed his arms and leaned against the bunk. "Ah. Got someone else in mind for a husband?"

"Nothing like that. He's—a family friend." Even across the sea, I couldn't reveal Lonzo's identity. "I know the company he signed on with, but I don't know who bought the bond or where they went. Just somewhere in the outer colonies."

"No."

"You didn't think about that for very long."

"I don't have to. Even if I got Silas to sign off on using our connections, it's nearly impossible to track a poorly documented bondsman. And I've just got too much other stuff going on to waste my time with that."

"But—"

"No, Mirabel."

I kept the disappointment off my face. "If you can't help with that, then I'm not budging on fifty."

"Come on!"

"Fifty—or no deal. You'll regret it if you lose me."

"I have a feeling I'll regret this no matter what." Grant held out his hand to me. "Fifty it is."

CHAPTER 8

I NEVER LOOKED AT GRANT THE SAME WAY AGAIN.

Or at least, I never looked at his public persona the same way again. As our journey went on, I continually felt like I was at the theater. Whenever I ran into him in the company of others, he'd behave as the paragon of etiquette. I couldn't take it seriously, not when I'd seen his true nature: gruff, sarcastic, and blunt. He looked the same but might as well have been putting on another disguise.

"You know how to be nice," I told him one day as we stood at the upper deck's railing, a few weeks into the journey. "You know how to be genteel. Why not just do it all the time? You'd make more friends."

"What makes you think I don't already have legions of friends? And just because I know how to do it doesn't mean it feels natural. I know how to wear a suit, and I don't really like that either." He tugged at his collar.

"There's wearing it, and there's *wearing* it. And yours don't fit. A little tailoring would do wonders. Didn't that letter say your mentor's office is in a tailor's shop? Maybe you can get a discount when we arrive."

Grant shook his head in exasperation. "Congratulations on your amazing memory. Now tell me how you used it to learn something."

This had become a game of ours. Every day, I'd try to discover something new about one of the passengers, either by outright eavesdropping or coaxing them into conversation. It wasn't always easy. I could find a reason to talk to girls from the other manor, but propriety frowned on my striking up a conversation with a sailor or even an unknown male passenger. I'd started to enjoy these tests. Adelaide rarely wanted to come above deck anymore, and Grant—frustrating or not—was a good diversion.

"I spoke to Mister Kent and Mister Robertson today. Mister Kent's a paper merchant. He's been in Adoria for a while." I tried to stick to facts and edit out any personal opinions that weren't based on solid evidence. "Mister Robertson's never been there. He's pretty dismissive of anyone who's not of Osfridian descent. Icori and Lorandians. Balanquans. And me, for that matter."

Grant stayed silent, his eyes on the horizon.

"Mister Robertson doesn't have anything established in Adoria yet, but he's certain he'll make his fortune there," I continued. "Mister Kent is doing well, but some of his caravans have been raided by pirates, so he's looking to hire extra security. I struck up conversation with them by 'accidentally' dropping my bracelet nearby and claiming the clasp was broken. I told them it was my grandmother's and that we'd been minor nobility before the revolution drove us out. Mister Kent retrieved it for me and gave me the name of a jeweler in Cape Triumph. Oh. And he also offered me a discount on paper."

When I fell into silence, Grant turned back to me. "That's it?"

"That's a lot."

"Discount paper and a jeweler? Tell me how that could be useful." I knew the tone in his voice. This was a test too.

"A jeweler will have contact with wealthy citizens. Walking in with a referral is less suspicious than coming in off the street and fishing for information. And if I ever need to talk to Mister Kent again, I've got easy openings. I can say I forgot the jeweler's name. Or I can come to buy the paper."

"That may be true." From Grant, that was high praise. "But if you were really charming, you'd have gotten the paper for free. You didn't flirt."

"How do you know that?"

"Because you never flirt. Do you know how?"

"You never flirt either."

"I don't need to."

"Maybe you would've recruited Adelaide if you'd flirted with her instead of putting on all your stiff-suited politeness."

He made a grunt of amusement. "I doubt it. She's too focused on a larger prize to have her head turned by me."

"Maybe you're just no good at it." He dished out so much critique that it was nice to jab back.

"Your bit about being minor nobility is good. Most Osfridians only think of Sirminicans as the poor refugees they see out in the streets. But Sirminica has an iconic past—more so than Osfrid, really. You're the descendants of Ruva, the civilization that brought peace and culture to Evaria. Remind your marks about that. And your actual suitors."

"You're dodging my question."

"Because you're not asking the right one. Why is Kent hiring security? It's important."

His avoidance irritated me, but after a moment, I recognized what he was hinting at. "Because *pirates* are raiding his caravans . . . that's weird, isn't it? His caravans travel by land . . . so why would he mention pirates?"

"Exactly. You need to understand how this works in Cape Triumph. Pirates were an early problem in all the Adorian colonies. Most of the military sent over was used for ground campaigns against the Icori. The ocean was left wide open. And once trade really started booming between the colonies and Osfrid, all these fat ships full of treasure were just waiting for some enterprising man to snatch. And there are *always* men like that."

"You said it was an early problem. Doesn't it still happen?"

"Sure. But the royal navy has more of a presence now. They patrol the coasts. Lots of merchant ships arm themselves or hire mercenary escorts. The pirate trade dwindled, so some of them moved to land."

"Wouldn't they be called brigands then?" I asked. "Thieves? Bandits?"

"You'd think so. But they still claim piracy as part of their identity. And there's more to that. Some of them have become local celebrities. They wear masks and take on flamboyant personas. Everyone knows their names and tells stories of their courage and cunning."

"Theft is courageous and cunning?"

He rolled his eyes. "It is by the time these stories get around. Most of their raids are done against native Osfridians, the fat and the rich ones. Your average working colonial won't get too upset by that. They don't really see those kinds of people as 'real' people, and everyone likes a little challenge to authority now and then. From there, all it takes is these so-called pirates tossing a few coins someone's way—to a sick old man, a hungry kid—and suddenly they're heroes. No one's going to turn them in."

"But their victims *are* real people. Just look at Mister Kent," I said indignantly. "He's very real."

Grant returned to gazing at the sea. "Not to them. He's just another payday to them. Law enforcement's sketchy there. The militia does some of it, but for a lot of people, these pirates are the closest they've got to justice. And if that wasn't enough, Sir Ronald's certain the traitors are buying stolen goods from them, making the trail harder to follow." Grant returned to gazing at the sea. "I'm sure Silas would kill to have eyes and ears hidden in that circle."

"Any chance the pirates will come to Glittering Court parties?"

"I wish. I'm sure they'd be impressed by your knife."

A few other Glittering Court girls had emerged for strolls, and I took a few steps back. "Time for me to go. You know, they all think you're a brawler after they saw what I did to your face." It had long since healed, but I felt he deserved a reminder every once in a while. Even scratched, his face had maintained the rough-edged good looks I'd found so enticing when we'd set sail. But the more I dealt with his trying personality, the harder it was to imagine him as the hero of some passionate whirlwind affair.

"Wait. Mirabel. Before you go . . ." Grant didn't turn around, and

I heard an uncharacteristic strain in his voice. "You're right. Sort of. I can talk to women without offending them. Sometimes I can make them like me. Am I the best at flirting? No, but I don't have to flirt. You do."

"That sounds a little hypocritical."

"Because it's a lot hypocritical."

"You're honest, I'll give you that."

He turned and met my eyes. "I have to lie for a living to complete my jobs—and to stay alive. But if we're working together, and you're around me—the *real* me—then I will always tell you the truth. I don't like to waste words. If there's nothing to say, I usually won't say it. If there's something to say, then I'll tell you what I'm thinking. Often with no filter. But it will be the truth."

"Okay," I said, a bit taken aback by his intensity.

"And I'm telling you, for this case, there'll be times you'll have to do a little more than rely on your looks. I'm not asking you to go to bed with anyone. But make sure you know how to use those looks. These traitors we're dealing with may be crafty, but even a brilliant man will get stupid with a pretty girl. And almost all of them will underestimate you. If you let them have a few drinks, boost their egos, smile in the right way . . . well, you increase the odds that they'll start thinking more about how they want to sleep with you than about the information they shouldn't let slip. That's what flirting's for." When I didn't respond, he asked, "Do you get what I'm saying?"

"Of course."

"Of course?"

I couldn't take pleasure in his surprise. I was lost in the past, lost in memories of conversations I rarely let surface. Conversations very similar to this one.

First: *It's a little skin, Mira. Just enough to throw him off so we can learn their plans.*

Later: *He'll put his arm around you, maybe kiss you, but don't think about it. Turn off your feelings. Remember this is for the greater good.*

And then: *Men can say careless things when they're in bed. I know it's asking a lot, but think of it as using a tool. A weapon, even. It might be uncomfortable, but you won't be in any danger. People are giving up their lives for this cause. Can't you give up your body—just for a short time?*

Finally: *You're a coward, Mira. You have to learn to make tough choices.* My mind dragged itself back to the present. To finding my brother. I met Grant squarely in the eye. "I'm not stupid. We talk about locks and codes, but I know that's not what you hired me for."

"I've never, for one second, thought you were stupid."

"If you need me to flirt, I can flirt. I know how to get favors from men. I've done it before."

I couldn't read the pause that followed. Did he doubt me? "Then refresh your skills, Mirabel. Get some man on this ship to go out of his way to do something for you. Something that's an inconvenience. More than discounted paper."

"Easy," I told him. "But I want something from you in return."

"More than fifty gold? You want my share of the reward too?"

It certainly was tempting, but I knew his limits by now. "If I pull off getting a big favor, then I want you to tell me where you're from. What that thing in your voice is that I can't figure out."

I couldn't see his face, but I knew he was smiling. "It had better be a really, really good favor."

Grant never mentioned flirting again. He didn't push me for a deadline. When we had our clandestine meetings throughout that week, we'd talk about other things. He'd elaborate on Denham's political climate. I worked on memorizing the list of suspect names and each one's history. He kept saying I didn't need to know any other tricks of the espionage trade, but he taught them anyway.

I stood by my claim that I could charm men, but when I used to do it for my father's causes, it was usually with men who would take the lead. I just had to show up and play along. A party of Adorian suitors might be that way too, but here, on a ship where all the men knew to be cautious with us, it could be more difficult.

"How do you flirt?"

Adelaide looked up from the dress she was buttoning. Our cabin mates were away, and I decided to get an outside opinion. "Do you mean me in particular?" she asked. "Or just a general method to flirting?"

"Either." I leaned back against the wall, feeling the gentle rocking of the ship. "And I guess it's not just flirting. You can get anyone to talk to you. Everyone likes you."

"Oh, Mira. Plenty of people like you."

"That's not what I'm— Look, I know it's weird. I just want to know how you do it. How you get them to open up to you."

She returned to her dress. "I don't know how I do it. I don't even really think I'm flirting that much. But I mean, common ground is a place to start. Find a connection over something you both relate to. Be interested. Make them feel special."

"That's it? Just those things?"

"It's more in how you do them. You can't overthink it." She straightened up and smoothed her skirts. "Oh, and confidence. I mean, sometimes you need to be demure. But if you're ever in some situation that needs a crazy solution, just be confident. If you act like you're completely convinced about something, people will go along with it."

I nodded, running through a mental list of passengers and what interests we might share. "Wow, you look great," I said, suddenly noticing what she had on. It was one of her nicer Adorian dresses, certainly not a ball gown, but a few steps up from the day frocks we wore on the ship.

"We've got that dinner tonight—the one with other passengers?"

I groaned. Miss Bradley had decided we needed to stay up to date on our lessons, so she'd arranged to have some of "the more respectable passengers" dine with us in our common room. She'd instructed us to put on our most formal manners—and elegant clothes. The bulk of our wardrobe, especially the truly grand pieces, was in storage. I sifted through what I had in my trunk and produced a burgundy, embossed velvet dress meant to be worn over a frilly white chemise. The velvet pattern hid the wrinkles acquired from being kept folded for so long.

"Watch that shoulder," Adelaide teased as I searched for hairpins. "Miss Bradley'll have a fit over such indecency."

I glanced up from the hairpins and realized what she meant. The dress's wide, scooped neckline—cut low, in the Adorian style—had slipped off my left shoulder. Hardly indecent, but Miss Bradley *would* chastise me for sloppiness. I tugged it back up. "I don't remember this being so loose."

"It's the food around here. We're all losing weight. When we get there, you'll have to make up for it in Adorian pastries or get your wardrobe altered."

"Ugh, don't mention pastries. I wonder if Miss Bradley's going to dress up tonight's food too."

Adelaide grinned. "Sure. Maybe a nice butter and wine sauce to go over the hardtack?"

We arrived in the common room early and found a few of the guests already seated, including my acquaintance Mister Kent. I was pondering whether to use tonight as my big flirting opportunity when a fretful Miss Bradley said, "Mira? Will you go round up the others? They should be here by now." We had a half hour until dinner, but she was treating this like a royal banquet.

I knocked on a few cabin doors and passed on her message. Sylvia and Rosamunde were still unaccounted for, which meant they'd probably lost track of time above deck. I headed for the end of our corridor, and as I turned toward the steps that would lead up, I nearly ran into Grant coming from his section of the ship. I froze a moment, surprised to see him over here at all *and* dressed up. He had on the fine suit he'd worn at our departure, with the linen shirt and suede vest, but it had been further embellished with a dinner coat and black cravat.

"*You're* one of the better passengers?" I blurted out.

"What?" He looked equally rattled.

"Miss Bradley said she was only inviting the, uh, elite passengers tonight. I didn't expect you to see you."

His face settled into its characteristic wryness as he leaned against the ladder. "She must have been desperate to fill those seats with whatever vagabonds she could find."

I crossed my arms over my chest and immediately felt the dress slip again. Grant's posture didn't change, but his eyes tracked the fabric's movement as it bared the top of my shoulder. It didn't surprise me that he noticed it; he noticed everything. But it seemed to me he studied it more intently than he needed to. And he certainly didn't need to examine the rest of the dress's lacy neckline as it ran along my cleavage—but he did anyway. I left the rebellious sleeve where it was and took a step closer.

Even a brilliant man will get stupid with a pretty girl.

"They *are* going to think you're a vagabond if you don't neaten yourself up," I scolded. He practically jumped when I lifted his collar and began retying the cravat. Aside from our fight in his cabin, we'd never touched before. "Wasn't the whole point of you going to Osfro to get some polish? You should know how to do this."

"I do know how to do it. I just don't like taking the time with the details."

"You took the time with your Flatlander disguise."

"That's different. That was a riskier job. But a comfortable shopkeeper? A few wrinkles aren't going to raise anyone's suspicions."

I finished the cravat and tucked it down under the vest, making sure my fingers also grazed the skin on his neck. "A few?" I let my hands run slowly down his chest as I smoothed out the soft fabric.

"You'd better brush up on your counting skills before we arrive. Seems like a necessary ability for a spy who's supposed to be collecting information."

"I . . ." He watched my hands for a few seconds and then cleared his throat. "I count just fine."

I stopped fixing the wrinkles but left my hands pressed against him, as though some unexpected thought had suddenly distracted me into forgetting they were there. "Look . . . seriously, I'm sure you really will be busy with all sorts of things once we're in Cape Triumph, and I know what you said, but . . ."

He cocked his head. "But what?"

I sighed, gave his coat one last tug to straighten it, and then clasped my hands before me. In doing so, I leaned forward ever so slightly, exposing just a whisper more of what lay underneath the dress's top. I could imagine Miss Garrison nodding in approval. *My job is to make the most of what everyone's got. You'll thank me later.*

"Are you sure you won't have time to look into where my friend with the bond went?" I asked.

"Oh." He didn't immediately reject me, so that was promising. "Well, I meant what I said. It's not as easy as it sounds."

"I know, but—" I looked up and feigned shock. "Don't you own a comb?"

"Wha—"

I stood on my tiptoes, bringing us closer, and tried to smooth down the flyaway pieces of his rebellious hair. It was softer and silkier than I expected. "Your hair's actually manageable when it's not out in the wind. You have no excuse."

My fingers trailed idly through the strands of his hair, my face was only a couple of inches from his, and . . . was he breathing faster? Yes. Yes, he was. Against all odds, I'd sidetracked shrewd, no-nonsense Grant Elliott with feminine wiles. Maybe even flustered him?

I hadn't known if my impulsive idea to make him the object of the flirting challenge would work. He wasn't the type to get easily distracted. He lived and breathed his mission. He should've noticed my act right away, especially since he was so good at spotting subterfuge.

Except it wasn't subterfuge. Not exactly. Maybe I didn't always like him, but his infuriating personality didn't seem like such a deterrent just then, not when an unexpected thrill was slowly uncoiling and spreading throughout my body. I wanted to stand closer. I wanted to touch more than his hair. I wanted him to touch me back.

And maybe Grant didn't always like me either, but I could tell, at least in this moment, he liked being close to me too. He liked looking at me. He liked me touching him. It turned out we had common ground after all.

"Now," I said, forcing myself back to cool calculation, "about my friend."

"Your . . . ? Right. Finding where he is." Grant was having trouble deciding where to focus. Looking into my eyes seemed to unsettle him. So he'd let his eyes stray to my bodice and linger there until he remembered he wasn't supposed to. "There should be a ship manifest on file with the port, and maybe a record of who he signed on with. But if they left Denham for some unknown colony, that gets a lot more complicated."

"But it's not impossible."

"No. It just means sending out feelers to a lot of different places."

"Don't you have friends everywhere?"

"Silas does."

I finished taming his hair—it really did look better, not that I minded the tousled look—and let my hands drop to my side. But I stayed where I was and looked up at him with wide-eyed pleading that wasn't faked.

"Please, Grant? Can't you just make a few inquiries?"

Silence hung between us. And more. The space between us smoldered.

He exhaled. "I . . . There are a couple of people I can check with."

"Only a couple? After I went to all that work so that you're fit to be seen in polite company?"

A little of his old sardonic smile came out, but his eyes still betrayed other thoughts in his mind. He reached toward the fallen sleeve and pushed it up. And just with that, his fingertips against my skin, I inhaled sharply and forgot all about my scheming.

"You have no reason to talk," he said. "You're just as negligent—"

The door to the upper deck suddenly opened, and we sprang apart as Sylvia and Rosamunde came scurrying down, faces frantic. "Are we late?" Sylvia exclaimed. "We almost forgot about dinner."

I swallowed. Increasing the space between Grant and me made me realize just how little there'd been moments ago. "No, you're fine. But we should get to dinner."

Grant gestured toward our hall. "After you, ladies."

Sylvia smiled as she passed him. "You look very nice tonight, Mister Elliott. Is there something different about your hair?"

At dinner, Grant and I sat at opposite ends of the table. He barely glanced in my direction and made his typically flawless conversation with those near him. That distance cleared my head. I relaxed. That craving to touch and be touched faded, and I felt more in control— and exultant. My plan had worked.

Now I had to wait and see how long it took him to notice.

The next morning, as I was watching the sunrise at the stern, I heard footsteps behind me. Then: "What you hear, what no one else ever seems to hear, isn't some regional colonial accent. What you're hearing is that I didn't start speaking Osfridian until I was eight."

I turned to find Grant standing with his arms crossed. "Of course!" I exclaimed. "It's not your first language. I considered that, but I know how most Evarian speakers sound when they learn Osfridian."

"I didn't grow up speaking any language from Evaria."

I stared, confused, for several moments. Then, I couldn't help a slow smile spreading over my face. "You're Balanquan."

"*Half*-Balanquan."

"You don't look . . . I mean. I haven't actually met one of them. But I never would have guessed you weren't . . ." I nearly said "one of us" and then felt stupid. I'd often complained about "us" and "them" hostilities between Osfridians and Sirminicans, yet here I was doing it with another group of people.

"What I am is more obvious to Balanquans than Osfridians."

"Do they know? Here? Or in Cape Triumph?"

He shook his head. "Most don't. It's simpler that way."

"So you get to blend in."

"Is that what you want to do?"

I had to think about that question for a long time. "I'll always think of myself as Sirminican—and I'm proud of that. But I'm trying to survive in an Osfridian world. I'm trying to earn its respect. I don't know if that makes sense."

"It makes perfect sense." His gaze turned briefly inward. "When others so easily dismiss you, you want—no, need—to prove them wrong. To demand that respect."

I tilted my head, putting myself more in his line of vision. "Are we still talking about me?"

He blinked and focused back on me. "You're feeling very clever today, aren't you?"

"Well, you're not the only one who's good at reading people."

"Apparently not that good," he said with a scoff. "Even I get fooled sometimes."

There it was. Acknowledgment of my accomplishment. "You told me to practice. You didn't say on whom."

"Hey, I'm not chastising you. You did a good job." He paused, his thoughts again straying away from me. Or to me? To last night? "You did what you needed to do. But why should I be surprised? If you don't see any options, you make your own. At least, that's what I've heard."

His dark eyes were locked back on my face, eagerly waiting to catch every bit of my reaction. My smile faded. Why did those words sound familiar? Why did he seem so smug?

Good Brother, I appreciate your concern. And you're right— desperate girls with no other options turn to desperate means. But I'm not one of those girls.

Not desperate?

Not without options. If I don't see any, then I make my own.

I gasped. "That . . . was you! Almost a year ago! The monk on the church steps with Cedric."

I'd never seen such a big smile on Grant's face. "How do you think I got the idea to investigate your manor? Sir Ronald had me practicing disguises that day, and then fate delivered the perfect way to spy in Adoria. I'd heard of the Glittering Court before I left but hadn't un- derstood its full potential until then."

"Unbelievable." I shook my head. "I bet you've just been waiting for the perfect time to tell me this. I *knew* there was something weird going on then. Monks always keep their eyes down, but you were staring right at me."

"Hard not to. I was just trying to eavesdrop on churchgoers, and then you two came out, a smooth-talking student and this fearless girl who . . ."

"Who what?" I prompted.

The smile disappeared. He shoved his hands in his pockets and put his back to me. "Who had better not use me for practice again. See you tomorrow, Mirabel."

CHAPTER 9

ONWARD AND ONWARD WE WENT, EVERY DAY BRINGING us closer to Adoria. The days felt short now, and Grant was growing restless—nervous, even. He was quieter, often lost in his own thoughts. When he did talk to me, he'd usually end up repeating past lessons about Adoria. His sarcasm had lessened too.

"Everything's important," he told me one gloomy afternoon. Few people were out, though the captain expected us to sight land sometime this week. "Pay attention to who else these men talk to. Make note of any favorite pubs or businesses they mention. No one's going to openly come out as a traitor, but they might tell you something useful without realizing it. You've just got to make sure *you* realize it."

"I know. And I'm ready. I learned your codes. I memorized all the names, all the history. I can do this."

He leaned against the ship's rail and faced me, his elbow resting on the top of the wood. It was one of those rare days when the wind was still, letting his black hair rest around his face. I didn't often get such a clear view of him. "I know you can. I just don't want to miss anything."

Such earnestness from him was rare, and I found myself in an equally unexpected role of reassurance. "You won't. You're going to do this. You'll find these traitors and cut off their resources. You'll be a hero."

A glimmer of his dry humor surfaced. "You've got a lot of faith in me. How do you know I'm not actually a terrible spy? You've barely known me two months."

"I've known you for almost a year," I corrected. "Anyone who can pull off being a monk, a Flatlander, and . . . whatever you are now won't have any trouble rooting out a handful of disgruntled men."

"I hope you're right. A handful of disgruntled men can do a lot of damage, especially men who are used to power and entitlement."

"I know. Because they're not the ones who actually have to deal with the consequences." A coldness settled in the pit of my stomach as images of the past played through my mind. "The innocents do, people who don't even want to be involved."

"Adoria won't become Sirminica, Mirabel."

The gentleness of his tone startled me as much as shouting would have. "How did you know that's what I was thinking?"

"Because I pay attention. Because I can tell you're not just running to a new place—you're running from an old one. You wear your ghosts."

I shivered. "What's that supposed to mean?"

"It's what the Balanquans say when you keep the spirits of your loved ones close. That your pull is too strong to let them go on to the next world." He gave me a pointed look. "And sometimes *their* pull is too strong. Like your father's on you."

I just stared at him.

Grant shrugged and said, "I told you, I pay attention."

"My father was a hero. He saved countless lives." I grew angry, seeing Grant's blasé expression. "I don't owe you my life history! And I don't see you bursting with stories about your father either."

"You want to know about him?"

"Like you'd really tell me."

Grant shifted his stance against the rail, leaning over it and crossing his arms so that I only saw his profile now. He stayed silent for so long that I thought he'd relinquished the topic until he said, "He was Osfridian. My mother met him when she came to Cape Triumph with a trading group. They never married, and she never saw him again after she left. The Balanquans believe fathers should be in charge of teaching sons. If your father can't, another male relative does. My uncle did for me, but he hated it. He hated me. And when I was ten, he finally claimed it wasn't right to deny me my 'real' heritage. He sent me back to Cape Triumph to find my father, but he wasn't there. Hadn't been for years."

"What did you do?" I was reluctant to speak, fearful he'd stop if he actually noticed he was opening up for once.

"This couple felt sorry for me and took me in—clothed me, fed me. They didn't have any children of their own. They were good people, but they weren't my parents, and I was angry about that. I got angrier and angrier as the years went by. I only wanted my father. Then, one day . . . he came back. And he was not a good person. Do you want to go inside?"

The abrupt question startled me, and I realized he'd noticed me trying to pull my cloak closer against the chill in the air. "I'm fine. Keep going. Why wasn't he a good person?"

Grant hesitated, and I thought for sure I'd lost the moment. "Because he was an outlaw of sorts, not that I knew that at the time. I didn't know anything about him, really, but when he offered to take me with him, I didn't look back. I was fourteen. We went south—to the lands the Sirminicans abandoned when the war came. And I lived a life—and did things in that life—that are going to haunt me for the rest of this one. I thought I wanted it. I thought following my father's path was the right thing. But after almost three years, I woke up one morning and realized I didn't want that path. I needed to get out of that life before I turned into something that couldn't be undone— what my father had already become. And so I left. I let him go."

I shivered, though it had nothing to do with the cold. Grant's past shared a lot of traits with mine, but I couldn't bear to admit it.

"I told you mine. Are you going to tell me yours now?"

"Why do you care so much?"

He shifted his stance, rearranging the way he leaned on the rail. "Because . . . because I'd like to understand why you're you."

"My father was a hero," I repeated. "Fighting to protect others is a noble thing."

"I'm not denying any of that." His tone was actually mild, but he had that look in his eyes, the one that could penetrate right into a person's soul. "And I can see that drive in you. You're ready to take on the world for the sake of justice. But I also see this look you get when your father comes up. Something about him bothers you."

I suddenly felt stifled and trapped, despite the wide-open deck. "Your interrogation bothers me!"

"I'm trying to be nice."

"Well, you aren't very good at it."

Anger kindled in his eyes. "I can't believe you once accused *me* of being hard to like."

"You don't have to like me," I reminded him. "We just have to work together."

His response was to take off his long coat and toss it to me. "Put this on."

"Why?"

"Because it's freezing out here. And I do like you." He sounded as though it annoyed him to admit it.

I clutched the coat to my chest, the heavy brown wool still warm from the heat of his body. The ire faded from me, and I looked down. "I just don't want to talk about my father, that's all."

"Yes, I've gathered that. Now put the damned coat on. Or, no— forget it. Let's just go inside. No one else is stupid enough to be out in this wind."

Slowly, I lifted my head and gazed around. The sea roiled with angry waves, so dark they almost looked black. I'd been steadying myself and adjusting to the ship's increased rocking without even realizing it.

"How did it get so windy so quickly?" I asked. "It was calm when we came out. I couldn't believe how well your hair was staying in place."

"You were studying my hair?"

"You tell me to study everything."

But I didn't feel nearly as flippant as I sounded. My skin crawled. The change in weather really had come on too suddenly. Lightning forked above us, and a huge wave hit the boat with such force that we—and some nearby sailors—had to scramble for footing. Grant caught me, keeping an arm around me until the deck steadied again.

Agostino ran up to us and said in Sirminican, "The captain wants all the passengers back in their cabins."

"But it's just another storm, right?" I asked. Rain began to fall. "You deal with these all the time."

"Just get back to your room." He scurried off to the other side of the ship.

"I don't need to know Sirminican to understand that," Grant said. "Let's go."

The rain came in sheets now, and the wind was so fierce that Grant had to fight to open the door that would let us climb below. It slammed shut as soon as he released it inside, but I could still hear the howling on the other side of the thick wood.

"I'm going to try to find out just how bad this is," Grant said. "But I'd get ready for a long night if I were you."

"Wait," I called as he began heading for his corridor. "Grant, I . . ." He paused and glanced back. He didn't look mad anymore. I couldn't tell what he was. And I didn't even know what I wanted to say. I simply handed him the coat.

"Be careful, Mirabel." He vanished around a corner.

Back in my wing, I found my cabin empty and discovered that most of the girls had congregated in our common room. "Now, now, it's just a little rough water," Miss Bradley was telling them. The ship was heaving wildly now, and at least one girl gasped or screamed each time we rocked. "It'll smooth out soon."

"Where's Adelaide?" I demanded.

Caroline glanced around. "Maybe she's in your cabin."

"No, I was just there."

"Just wait. I'm sure she'll be back soon," said Miss Bradley.

But I slipped out of the door as soon as her back was turned, just in case Adelaide and I had unknowingly crossed paths. No luck. My room was still empty. I headed up to the deck again, making slow progress as the ship lurched. Even knowing what to expect outside, it was still a shock to fight my way out the door and immediately be slammed back by the gale. The storm had escalated far more than I'd expected, the rain now lashing my face. Wiping water out of my eyes, I stepped into the deluge on shaky legs and crept across the deck.

No one would have guessed it was only late afternoon. Dark, menacing clouds churned above, and it was hard to tell where they ended and the sea began. The rain obscured vision even more, and the only things I could clearly see were bolts of lightning that were almost instantly chased by thunder.

I squinted around, trying to find Adelaide. The lavender dress she'd worn this morning would have normally made her stand out. But everyone's clothes were soaked and stuck to their body, making color difficult to discern. And everyone on deck was in motion. It was all crew as far as I could tell, and they frantically went about their work, hurrying to secure the ship as the captain and first mate struggled to be heard above the noise.

I moved among them, barely noticed by the panicked sailors, and kept searching for Adelaide. My shoes slipped on the wet wood, and the wind made movement even more difficult as I completed an unwieldy circuit of the deck. No sign of Adelaide. No sign of any passengers. Only I was foolish enough to face the elements, and it was time I got out of everyone's way.

As I turned toward one of the doors leading below, I heard a cry off to my left. A sailor—practically a boy, younger than me—had just lost his grip on a rope that connected to one of the sails. The wind snatched the rope away, causing it to flutter wildly as the sail above us unfurled. He strained to reach the dancing line but wasn't quite tall enough. I hurried to his side and tried my luck. I was the right height, but the rope's wild movement made it hard to catch. It slipped through my fingers several times before I was finally able to grasp its end.

The mast above us was one of the smaller ones, but I could see it bending as the wind filled its sails. Other sails were being reefed, and if this one wasn't brought in soon, the mast would snap from the force of the storm. I handed the rope to the boy, who began pulling at it to no avail. I heard a crack from above, but the mast stayed put. Grabbing hold of the rope, I tried to add my weight, but the wet fibers kept slipping through my fingers.

"Out of the way," a voice barked. A large, burly sailor had stridden up to us and snatched the rope away. It slipped in his hands too, but his grip was surer, his muscles stronger. As he drew the sail in, the strain on the mast eased up. When he'd reeled in enough, he tied the rope up securely and hurried off to his next task without a word to us.

The young sailor gave me a quick nod of thanks and started to follow the other man when we both heard the cracking sound again. A yard broke free of the mast and began to fall. I pushed my young companion out of the way but wasn't quite fast enough. I slipped and fell backward on the deck, near its edge. The beam came down on my foot, and it was only through the most incredible luck that the part that landed on me was slightly hollowed out—big enough to save my foot and ankle from being crushed by the beam's full force, but not big enough to let my leg slide out. I was trapped.

The sailor jumped down beside me and tried to push the beam off but didn't even budge it. "I'll get help," he shouted. He disappeared into the haze of rain, and judging from the frantic way everyone was hustling about, I doubted help would be coming anytime soon. No sailor would halt work that could save this ship in order to rescue one unwary passenger.

I tried tugging my leg again, but the yard held fast. It was so heavy that it didn't roll around as many other loose items did on the rocking ship, so that was something. Pinned in place, I was able to focus more on what was happening. Most of the sails had been secured. Waves broke over the ship's deck when we tipped too far, making me feel certain we'd go all the way over. We righted each time, but part of me kept thinking it was just a matter of time before our luck ended.

Through the wind, I heard a crotchety voice yell at someone, "What are you doing, girl? Get below!"

And a familiar voice answered: "Get help! You have to get it off her!"

Astonished, I looked up as Adelaide came toward me, fear on her pale face. An old sailor was hurrying past her. "*You* get it off her. We've got to keep this ship from sinking."

Adelaide knelt beside me and attempted to pull the beam away. A new panic set in, not for me, but for my friend. The wind and waves were too powerful, and we were dangerously close to the edge.

"It's too heavy! Leave me, and get back below."

Adelaide's face hardened as she tried again. "Never."

I could see the effort it cost her, the pain she endured. As I tried to urge her away again, Grant suddenly crouched down beside her. His flyaway hair was now slicked down against his head. "Pull with me," he ordered Adelaide. When their efforts proved fruitless, he shot her a glare. "Damn it. Are you even trying, girl?"

If Adelaide was shocked at the difference between real-Grant and public-Grant, she didn't show it. She was too worked up over me, too scared and frustrated. "Of course I am!"

I couldn't stand the risk they were taking. "You both need to go—"

"Be quiet," Grant told me. He glanced back at Adelaide. "We'll do it on the count of three. Put all the strength you've got into it, and then dig up some you didn't even know you had. One—two—three!"

They worked together, pushing their muscles as far as they would go. At first, it looked as though this attempt too would fail, and then I felt the slightest change of pressure above my ankle. It wasn't much, but the beam shifted just enough for me to slide my foot out before they released their load. Grant shot over to my side and slid an arm around my waist to help me up. I wobbled a bit but managed to stand and put weight on my foot.

"Can you walk?" he asked.

I nodded, but with each step, I felt a shooting pain in my ankle. Adelaide quickly supported me on my other side, and the three of us hobbled across the deck, fighting our way through the lashing wind and rain. A streak of lightning drew my eye toward the sea, and I did a double take at what I saw. Off in the distance, through the murky light and haze of rain, I could see the *Gray Gull* fighting its own battle on the ocean. Wind and waves tossed it around effortlessly. I knew the ship was as heavy and hulking as ours, but in that moment, it appeared so fragile.

"Adelaide," I said, pointing.

She came to a stop and looked where I indicated. Her eyes widened, and I knew she was thinking of Tamsin.

Grant nudged us both. "Stop gaping! Go! Hurry!"

We made it inside and back down to our hallway. "Where are you going?" I asked when Grant immediately began heading back in the direction we'd come.

"To see if any other fools need help."

"Men get to do everything," I grumbled after him.

"You want to go back out there?" Adelaide asked, pushing a tangle of dripping hair out of her face.

"I'd rather do something useful than sit around and worry about my dress being wet."

"Girls!" Miss Bradley called from the common room. "Get in here! Thank Uros you're safe."

The rest of our cohort was still inside, many weeping and clinging to each other for comfort. I didn't think I'd broken any bones, but it felt good to sit and rest my foot and ankle. They'd probably hurt for a few days, but I didn't expect to be doing anything particularly athletic in the near future. I could see pale faces and wide eyes throughout the room. We were all scared. Everyone on the *Gray Gull* had to be scared too. But at least Adelaide and I had each other for comfort. Who was there for Tamsin?

On and on that night went. I grew so used to the constant rocking that even when we hit small lulls, the room still seemed to spin. And those lulls provided illusory hope that soon gave way to heaving even worse than what we'd experienced before. If it wasn't for Adelaide, I probably would've gone back up to the deck. To do what, I couldn't say. Probably just cause more hassle for someone. But it was hard for me to think of the sailors working to save our lives while we sat safely down here, doing nothing.

Grant was up there too. He'd grumbled and snapped at us, but I'd seen the concern in his eyes when he looked me over. And for someone who could put on such an arrogant air and talk about staying unattached from others, he'd headed back into the storm without hesitation.

It wasn't until the night's end that I dared believe the worst was over. The waters calmed, and the ship steadied. Girls fell into restful sleep, and Adelaide and I exchanged wondering looks, neither having the courage to voice what we both hoped. Cedric finally stopped by the room, just long enough to give an update.

"My father talked to the captain, and we're out of it," he said. Adelaide sighed happily against me as he continued. "Amazingly, no one was lost, and there was no damage to the ship. It's unclear how the cargo fared, but we'll figure that out later. It's still night, and as soon as the clouds clear, the captain can assess our position. In the meantime, get what rest you can."

"No more sea voyages for me," Adelaide said when he was gone. "If my husband wants to go visit his family in Osfrid, he'll have to go alone."

"Make sure you state that up front when the suitors come calling."

She laughed, and it felt like years since I'd heard that sound. I grinned back, feeling a thousand times lighter. We'd made it. Somehow, against all odds, we'd made it. Adelaide drifted in and out of a restless sleep as the night wound down, but all I could do was count the minutes until morning. I needed to go outside and see for myself that it was really over. When I was certain the time was right, I be-seeched Miss Bradley for permission to go up.

Others followed, uncertain of what awaited us. We emerged to a pale, misty morning. A little sun shone, feeling as though it too had taken a beating in the stormy fray. Pieces of debris littered the deck, and every part of the ship was soaked. The sailors and a few pas-sengers, like Adelaide and me, had clearly been drenched as well. I'd mostly dried off overnight, though it left my dress stiff and wrinkled.

We all stared in awe, and it was hard to say what was more won-drous. That we'd survived? That the waters could be so calm now after last night's fury?

I felt a familiar presence next to me and almost wilted with relief. Grant. "Look," he said. I followed where he pointed, off toward the western horizon. Usually, we could expect to see the sky and sea meet-ing in a faint gray seam. Today, they were separated by a swath of dark green and brown.

Land.

"I could've sworn that storm blew us to the ninth hell—but if so, it apparently blew us back. That's Cape Triumph."

I gave Grant an incredulous look and earned a smile back. I turned my hungry gaze back to the west. I'd expected to be at the bottom of the sea, and here we were, facing our future instead.

"Adoria," Adelaide murmured, joy filling her face. "Adoria!"

An excited titter ran through some of the passengers, but not ev-eryone shared our enthusiasm. Cedric and Jasper stood together with matching, somber expressions. It was the most alike they'd ever looked.

Adelaide noticed them too. "What's wrong?" she asked.

I saw the sailor before she did. He'd come up beside Cedric and held a piece of splintered wood carved into the shape of a woman's face. I heard Grant swear softly in Balanquan. Or maybe it was a prayer. Adelaide leaned toward the sailor and blanched when she recognized what I'd already identified. *The Gray Gull*'s figurehead. I'd seen it up close when we'd boarded in Osfrid and from a distance throughout our journey, barely discernible on our sister ship.

But the *Gray Gull* wasn't beside us anymore—at least, not as we'd known it. All I could see of it now were fragments floating in the water.

CHAPTER 10

THE FACE THAT STARED BACK AT ME IN THE MIRROR couldn't be mine. And it wasn't because of the carefully applied makeup or elegant chignon. It wasn't the glittering garnets on my throat and ears. It wasn't the red satin dress embroidered with gold.

It was the look on my face—the look of someone who felt nothing. That couldn't be me. It wasn't possible that I'd just lost one of my best friends and was now about to parade through Cape Triumph as though I had no care in the world. That couldn't be me.

I envied Adelaide. When Jasper had told us we'd still carry on with the Glittering Court's procession into Cape Triumph, she hadn't concealed her emotions. She'd raged at him and then run off with tears spilling from her eyes. I'd nearly gone after her, but Cedric had been faster. "I'll take care of it," he'd said as he rushed by me.

Adelaide hadn't been afraid to let her grief show. I was. I knew that if I allowed even a tiny piece of it out, there'd be no stopping the rest. It was all or nothing. And I couldn't let the others see that. I couldn't let them see that tough, levelheaded Mira was falling apart inside. That I was disintegrating.

Mira, you will never lose me. No matter what else happens or where we go in this world, I will always be there for you.

So Tamsin had said. But she was no longer in this world.

And for a short time, I worried I might lose Adelaide as well. When she'd stormed away, she'd threatened to return to Osfrid and fulfill her contract in a workhouse. She took so long to return to our cabin that

I began to wonder if she'd been sincere. Finally, she crept through the doorway, and I swiftly pulled her into a hug.

"I don't want to go back," she assured me, a catch in her throat. "But it's just . . . I don't know how I'm supposed to . . . we can't possibly . . . I don't know. You have no problem doing this?"

I had a lot of problems doing this. I wanted to curl into a ball and cry until I had no tears left. I didn't want to mark Tamsin's death by dressing up. I didn't want to smile and flutter my lashes at our admirers. But this was what we were stuck with, and I had to take care of Adelaide now.

"Of course I do," I said, trying to sound brisk and pragmatic. "But getting shipped back to Osfrid isn't going to accomplish anything. I need to go forward, get to the next stage. And you do too."

"I know. And I mean . . . I really do understand what I signed on for. I *want* to do it. But Tamsin . . ."

I knew what she couldn't say. She felt guilty. She thought she was responsible for Tamsin being on the other ship. But I had failed them both. I should have been the peacemaker.

"I know," I told her. "I feel the same way. But it's not your fault."

Miss Bradley was calling for everyone to assemble, and I quickly helped Adelaide change into her gray and silver gown. I painted kohl around her bloodshot eyes and arranged curling tendrils to perfectly frame her face. When we were finished, she looked as flawless as I did—except that grief still filled her face.

"We can do this, Adelaide."

"You're so strong," she said.

Then why was I the one too afraid to show how I felt?

We gathered on deck with the other passengers, and Miss Bradley gave us a brief reminder of what to expect. The captain had already raised a flag as we neared Cape Triumph, one that residents would recognize as the Glittering Court's. Every year, potential suitors and curious gawkers would gather at the piers to watch us disembark. Jasper, ever the showman, turned it into a big procession, building up the drama and glamour to make sure we were a sensation the moment we literally set foot in Adoria. I hated him for making us do it, and yet, some small, detached part of me understood his reasoning. He was here to conduct business. My companions and I were here to find advantageous marriages. Trudging off the ship in black, with heads hung low, wasn't really a promising start to that venture.

The shore grew closer and closer. Cape Triumph sat just inside the tip of a piece of land that curled around Denham Bay. Its inner location offered the port city some protection from storms but still kept it easily accessible to ships sailing in from across the sea or along the coast. It was one of the oldest and most important ports in the Osfridian colonies, but the collection of houses, churches, and commercial buildings coming into view seemed like they'd hardly made a dent in that wild coastline. Great forests surrounded it, both towering evergreens and deciduous trees still leafless from the winter. It reminded me of the mountain ranges in northern Sirminica: miles and miles of nature in its purest, hardiest form. This wilderness looked invincible, as though no human hands could ever tame it. But, I supposed, Osfrid had once looked that way too.

I wasn't surprised when Grant materialized beside me in that way he had. With everyone in the crowd so transfixed by Adoria, no one noticed him seeking me out.

"Mirabel—"

"I know, I know," I said quietly, keeping my eyes on the coastline. "And don't worry. This doesn't change anything. I'll still do what you need me to."

He stayed quiet for so long that I had to glance over and make sure he hadn't left. "That's not why I'm here. I just wanted to say . . . I'm sorry. And to tell you to be careful about carrying another ghost."

"You think I should forget my friend?"

"No. I think you shouldn't forget that *you're* still alive."

He melted into the other passengers, and I felt a brief pang of envy. *People complicate things. They can be dangerous if you get attached to them.* He'd told me that in our first real talk, and I'd been dismissive. Now, I understood what he meant. Losing Lonzo and Tamsin wouldn't hurt as much if I didn't love them. But my life would be so much emptier without that love.

Miss Bradley strode up, clapping her hands for emphasis. "Girls, girls. Let's get ready. We'll be the first ones off once the ship is secured."

The *Good Hope* glided nearer the pier. This side of Denham Bay boasted smooth, easy waters for ships to dock, again adding to Cape Triumph's ideal placement. The bay's far side flanked other colonial territories and was much less hospitable. Its shallow and rocky water allowed smaller boats to get in but nothing like our ship.

I found myself squeezing Adelaide's hand again as the sailors carefully maneuvered the ship and began throwing ropes to the wharf. I'd spent so much of the past few years trying to blend in that the sight of all those people watching and waiting for us on shore was more intimidating than the untamed city and wilderness behind them. Once securely tied, we had to wait for port officials to come aboard and talk to the captain. Customs officers followed them to begin their arduous inventorying, and before I knew it, we were ushered off to the shore and lined up.

After so much time at sea, solid ground felt nearly as disorienting as the rocking deck once had. Miss Bradley lined us up by rank, and Adelaide went first, bravely taking up that conspicuous position. Amelia, a girl from the other manor, came after her. And then Miss Bradley summoned me.

"Why are you putting me third?" I asked.

Her face was grim. "Because you *are* third now. Nearly everyone else above you was on the *Gray Gull*."

The top three. What Tamsin had most coveted. I met Adelaide's eyes and had to look away from the anguish I saw in them. Because if I looked at her too long, I was going to have to acknowledge my own pain. And if I did, I didn't know how long I could keep my hardened façade.

"Adelaide, you need to go now," said Miss Bradley, not unkindly.

Adelaide threw her shoulders back and lifted her head high as she stepped forward. The transformation was remarkable. One would never have guessed that her heart was broken or that she was being paraded off like some prize animal at market. She walked—no, glided—with a regality that seemed to embody the new nobility the Thorns were always going on and on about. She acted as though this type of display was nothing to her, like she'd done it her entire life.

Inspired by Adelaide's example, I fell into step behind Amelia. It was hard to keep looking straight ahead—not so much out of fear as curiosity. I wanted to study this new world and its people. The glimpses I stole showed a variety far surpassing everything I'd expected. Dignified citizens in velvet and silk. Rough-and-tumble folk in worn jackets and beaver hats. Men, women, children. I'd seen hangings in Osfro that drew less attention than we did—and those were pretty popular spectacles.

And a few in this group—the less mannered, at least—didn't hesitate to share their thoughts about us. Leers, vulgar remarks. Propositions. Some comments were directed toward our group as a whole. One woman referred to us as the "Glittering Harlots." Other onlookers singled us out. Amelia, ahead of me, was easily visible with her auburn hair, and I saw her flinch over one particularly lewd comment about "that ginger." I, of course, was also conspicuous as the "Sirminican girl"—though "girl" wasn't always the word they used.

The hecklers were by far and away a minority. Most of the crowd simply regarded us as a novelty. Children looked at us with awe. And some men, the obvious elite, were sizing us up in a more professional way and would probably make inquiries later.

The procession ended in a cluster of coaches hired by Jasper, surrounded by burly bodyguards he also employed. "Only a fool leaves treasure unguarded," I heard him say as Adelaide and I were directed to a carriage. His eyes surveyed the crowd. "Excellent, excellent. I can already see the potential buyers. I suppose having half the set might drive up the prices."

I bit my lip so hard that I nearly drew blood. Anger and grief burned in my chest, and I fought to keep my calm as I walked past him and climbed into the carriage. It jerked to a start, and we got our first real view of Cape Triumph. I settled back in the seat and rubbed my ankle, which ached from my adventures in the storm. Walking on it in the procession had actually been more painful than dealing with the crowd.

Grant had explained enough of the city's geography for me to understand that the docks were on its southern side. We skimmed the city's outskirts, never passing through its busy, commercial heart. I wondered how long that business district would stay contained. Cape Triumph was expanding quickly, and we passed many in-progress or only recently completed buildings. They were all rough and more utilitarian than aesthetic at this point. They hadn't had the centuries of polishing and remodeling that cities across the sea had. I'd seen villages of this style on my journeys, but I could tell the ragtag structures were foreign to Adelaide, who'd spent most of her life in Osfro's regal, historic districts.

A muddy road led us out through the vast rural lands surrounding the city, which were stark and foreboding. Spring buds were fighting their way through, but winter had yet to relinquish its hold.

Our new home, Wisteria Hollow, was a pretty white house with black shutters. Although smaller than Blue Spring, it was far nicer than anything we'd passed in our brief trip through the edge of Cape Triumph. The hired men helped us down from the coaches and then set to work unloading luggage. Inside, we were greeted by Charles Thorn and the house's stern-faced caretaker, Mistress Culpepper. I could immediately tell Charles had a kinder disposition than his brother; he expressed true sorrow when he heard about the *Gray Gull*'s loss. He quickly agreed to Cedric's suggestion that we delay our social season.

"Yes, yes, certainly. My poor jewels—of course you must recover. But then you will have such fun once the season begins! Your promenade was only a taste of the delights to come." Charles pushed up his spectacles and smiled at all of us.

"Promenade" was hardly the word I would have chosen to describe our earlier procession, but he seemed sincere in his good intentions.

Mistress Culpepper proved a bit cooler in her reception. She made Mistress Masterson seem indulgent. "No doubt many of you think the New World is a looser place, where you will be allowed to run wild. But not while I am in charge of this house. You will follow all rules I set and adhere to their every detail. There will be no inappropriate or uncouth behavior under my roof." Her eyes rested on me.

Adelaide and I had a room all to ourselves, but it was a bittersweet luxury. It had two extra beds, meant to accommodate more girls— girls who wouldn't be joining us. I stared at one of the empty beds, pushed up by the window, and felt a lump in my throat as I recalled the first day I'd met Tamsin. She'd refused the window bed in our room, lecturing us about sunlight and freckles.

Once we'd settled in and understood the rules of our new home, we were left alone to mourn, as promised. There seemed to be some debate among the Thorns on how many days that mourning would last, but for now, we had nothing to do but rest and adjust. After all the activity of the last day or so, that stillness came as a shock.

Adelaide just wanted to lie down and seize a moment of peace, and I didn't challenge her on that or her plea that I not worry about her. She needed to process what had happened. No words of mine could change the responsibility she felt for Tamsin's death, and I could only hope my friend wouldn't let herself be burdened with undeserved guilt.

Desperate for distraction, I "processed" my grief by exploring the house. Wisteria Hollow had two main stories, with a cellar below and a small attic above. Although the house was set on vast acreage, the rugged land wasn't manicured or designed for recreational strolling.

Going outdoors was discouraged and only allowed upon the front porch, under the mercenaries' watchful eyes.

Wisteria Hollow also didn't have the excess of rooms that Blue Spring did. No ballroom, no conservatory, no drawing room. Nearly every space here served a utilitarian function, the exception being an ornate parlor. Even that, I was given to understand, would be busy once our suitors came calling. A railed landing looked down upon the parlor from the second floor and offered precious privacy. I settled in that nook once I'd explored everything else, curling up against the wall to make myself as small as I could.

Tamsin is dead.

I expected to burst into sobs or scream my outrage to the world. But the blaze of emotions in my chest had gone cold. I felt hollow now, with only the ache of loss to fill that space. Grant had said I carried ghosts, but he was wrong. I felt like one. Insubstantial. Lost.

The floor creaked, and someone sat beside me. Glad I hadn't cried, I looked up to see which of my housemates had discovered this spot.

But it was no one from the Glittering Court. The woman beside me wore wide-legged trousers, and a loose, untucked blouse with deep blue embroidery at the collar and bell sleeves. A long necklace of pearls and intricately fashioned gold leaves hung around her neck. Her long black hair rested over her shoulder in a loose braid that made me envious of easier days. And her skin . . . was the same color as mine. For a heartbeat, I thought I'd found another Sirminican. But no.

"You're Balanquan," I exclaimed.

Amusement filled her beautiful features, which boasted lively dark eyes and high cheekbones that half the girls in the house would've killed for. "And you're Mirabel."

"I'm sorry." I felt myself blushing. "That was rude of me to say."

"Compared to some greetings I get? Hardly."

The cadence of her voice captivated me. The accent was a heavier, purer version of what underscored Grant's words. It was so different

from anything Evarian, and I wished I could understand the language's dynamics.

"You can call me Mira," I told her. "And it's very nice to meet
you . . . ?"

"Aiana." She extended her hand, and I shook it. Silver rings adorned
almost every finger. "I know you're mourning your friends. I won't
bother you for long."

"Mostly just one friend." I looked away, the novelty of meeting
Aiana suddenly replaced by a stab to my heart. "And I don't know
how I'm going to get by without her."

"Don't your people believe the dead are guided to a paradise by
angels? Floating off on a sea of light?"

"I don't know what I believe." I rubbed the bridge of my nose and
tried to force my mind from Tamsin. "You're Grant's contact, aren't
you? The one who'll take my messages to him. How are you going to
do that?"

"I work here," she said, smiling again. "For the Thorns. We aren't
supposed to have met yet, but I wanted you to know who I am."

"What kind of work do you do for the Thorns?"

Aiana spread out her hands. "Everything. Sometimes I chaperone
parties. Sometimes I work as a bodyguard. Between seasons, I check
up on married girls to see if they're happy and are being treated well
by their husbands. I make sure everything is going well, really."

"And what happens if everything isn't going well?"

"Then I deal with it," she said after several moments. "Usually
through reasonable means. Some marriages have been dissolved, but
that's rare."

"And if . . . if things can't be resolved through reasonable means?"

"Then I deal with it," she repeated.

She was half a foot taller than me, and even in the loose clothing, I
could see a lean, muscled body. Something in her tone gave me a few
ideas as to how exactly she might deal with such problems.

"Grant gave me the impression that most Balanquans stay away from us—people from Evaria and Osfrid." It was another bold thing to say, but there was an easiness about her that made me feel comfortable about speaking bluntly. "That . . . they . . . you think we're primitive."

She laughed. "Not primitive. More like . . . uncouth. Most Balanquans think your people have little to offer and that your ambition is dangerous."

"And you don't?"

"I think you have something to offer." She didn't acknowledge the dangerous assertion. "There's something fascinating about all of you. Uncouth, yes. But never boring. I didn't plan on staying here—but then, I didn't really have any plans at all when I arrived. Before I knew it, I'd connected with the Thorns and found I was content. And I get to keep an eye on Iyitsi."

"Who's I-yit-si?" I stumbled over the word.

"Who do you think?"

"Grant?"

"Yes." Her earlier amusement faded. "I don't like him using you, but he's never listened to me before. Why should he start now?"

"Is it hard for you here? Being Balanquan?" I faced enough prejudice, and I had much more in common with the locals than she did.

"In some ways. Not in others. I don't make any secret of who I am, and that's easier than trying to dress or behave like one of you. If I did, I'd always be lacking. It's better being true to myself and openly Balanquan. People don't question my identity. Now, how they feel about Balanquans personally? That's always a surprise."

"Grant says things are simpler when he plays up his Osfridian side."

"Simpler for others, maybe. As for him? Well, nothing is simple with him. But yes, he speaks like a local and shows enough of his father's side that no one gives him a second glance. I don't even think the benefits of seeming fully Osfridian matter as much as just proving he can transform into whoever he wants. As long as he can do that, he doesn't have to figure out who he is." Her gaze turned inward a moment as she pondered her own words. A few moments later, she shook off the mood and became stern. "Well. Don't let his goals interfere with yours, Mira. You didn't come here to chase conspiracies, and the instant you want free of that, let me know."

Something in her words triggered a question that had long bugged me. "You just called me Mira. He always calls me Mirabel. Is there any reason for that? Or just his own quirk?"

That smile returned. "Names have meaning. Power. Mirabel is your birth name, right? The one your parents gave you? It defines you. Shortening it or making a nickname out of it diminishes that importance. So, we give other names if needed. Those who take on new status—a military leader, for example—can choose another name for that role. A person who's been shunned may also choose something different. And in affectionate relationships—friend, family, husband, wife—we usually end up calling them something different too. A name just between two people. It signifies a bond. It could be something as simple as 'brother' or 'sister.' It could be something descriptive. The best translation for this is . . . a 'close name.'"

"But you don't keep that custom if you call me Mira."

"I keep it among my people. With you, I feel it's more important to adhere to your customs."

I pondered all of that. "Is I-yi-yitsi Grant's birth name?"

"Iyitsi," she corrected. "It's what I call him. He never told me his Balanquan birth name."

"Does it mean anything?"

"Iyitsi is one of our gods. A trickster. The masked god. The god with many faces." Her eyes sparkled again. "He hates it, but I think it fits him perfectly."

Mulling over what I knew of Grant, I said, "I couldn't agree more."

CHAPTER 11

I HAD MIXED FEELINGS ONCE THE REAL BUSINESS OF the Glittering Court began. On the one hand, I welcomed a break in the doldrums we'd fallen into. But it also meant I had to face up to the future I'd been trying to escape. I could no longer let Tamsin's loss be the center of my thoughts.

Technically, we were still in mourning when potential suitors started showing up. Jasper and Charles had made it publicly clear that we weren't officially "on the market" until after our opening ball, but they also didn't turn away men who claimed they only wanted to make polite inquiries. Some of these men really did stop by out of general curiosity—wanting to know prices, what qualities to expect in us, etc. Other men, however, had been present at our arrival and had already spotted specific girls of interest.

My hideaway on the landing had been compromised when my housemates realized it looked down on the parlor where the Thorns received their visitors. Unable to resist, we would all gather in an excited huddle to eavesdrop on the conversations below. Each girl hoped to hear her name mentioned and also wanted to check out everyone else's prospects. They cooed over who seemed the handsomest, the most romantic. Me? I assessed the suitors in a much cooler way, trying to determine which one might give me the least hassle and most freedom.

I was also enthralled at seeing the Thorns at work. Selling and pitching ran in their blood, even docile Charles. The three of them took turns managing these meetings, though sometimes, more than one Thorn would greet a man. I loved those meetings best because the suitors never stood a chance.

One man who had the bad luck of facing down both Cedric and Jasper especially made me pay attention—because he was on Grant's list.

His name was Theodore Craft. He'd made his fortune by operating a number of distilleries in Denham and adjacent colonies. Grant's mentor, Silas Garrett, had begun investigating him just before Grant left. Apparently, Craft made oddly timed—and suspicious—trips to visit his holdings, trips someone of his means didn't even probably need to make in person.

I leaned forward as Cedric urged him to sit. Theodore was a stout man, balding at the temples, and dressed to impress. He was interested in Beatrice, a girl from Guthshire, and made no pretense about why he wanted her.

"I like blondes," he stated. Since no one knew anything about us except our looks, attraction was pretty much the only reason a man might be drawn to one of us. A lot of them would try to make up deeper reasons, saying things like "She looks like she's a hard worker." But we knew the truth.

"Well, we have a number of them," said Cedric, cheerful as ever. "All talented and lovely."

"I liked the looks of that one." Beatrice beamed at that until Theodore added, "But I'm open to others if there's a big enough price difference. I'm overdue for a wife, you see, and I intend to make sure I choose one worthy of my station. I make the finest rum and whiskey in all the colonies, you know."

"Oh, yes," said Jasper. "I'm well aware. Everyone knows your exceptional business."

I believed Jasper. In fact, I believed he probably had a good idea of how much Theodore earned, down to the last coin. He spent a lot of time researching Cape Triumph's well-to-do citizens.

"A respectable businessman needs a respectable wife," added

Cedric. It was a line he used all the time. "And it's a good thing you've come to speak to us early. I mean, we aren't brokering any deals yet, but we've had many, *many* inquiries."

Jasper nodded along with his son. "I expect most of these girls to be spoken for before the opening ball is even over. We have fewer this year, you know. So unfortunately, some men are going to be disappointed."

A small frown was the only sign of Cedric's displeasure at the subtle reference to the *Gray Gull*, but he was still quick to play off his father's lead. "That's why making an early decision is going to be so critical. Those who delay are going to miss their chance. Why, we've even heard of men already moving assets and taking loans for their fees—isn't that right, Father?"

"Absolutely. Of course, the girls have all season to choose, but if presented with an early, respectable proposal at our debut gala? Especially with surety money involved?" Jasper shrugged eloquently. "Well. I doubt these jewels are going to wait around."

The Thorns would often try to upsell callers on a more expensive girl, but a line of delicate questioning soon revealed that Beatrice was right at the top of Theodore's price range. So Jasper and Cedric went to work, pitching her hard and extolling her virtues and—of course—beauty.

"When is your opening ball?" he asked nervously. "I have an important trip to make to Bakerston in the morning. One that I can't reschedule. I'll be there for two days."

"The announcement isn't official yet, but I can say that you'll have just enough time," Jasper told him conspiratorially. "But don't extend your trip."

Theodore lit up. "I won't, I won't. And I'll start looking into my accounts today."

A trip to Bakerston. One he couldn't reschedule.

My heartbeat quickened. It was exactly the kind of information Grant wanted: movement from a man under suspicion because of mysterious trips.

With everyone in the house so preoccupied watching our suitors, it was easy to slip off later on and sneak outside to the porch. "Hey," I said, beckoning one of the mercenaries. "Do you know where Aiana is?" I didn't know how else to locate her, especially since we weren't supposed to have met yet.

The man hesitated, knowing the rules about talking to us. "No. It's her day off. Now get back inside."

My heart sank. I couldn't expect Aiana to be at my constant beck and call, but it made using her as a go-between with Grant difficult. How critical was the information about Theodore Craft? Pretty critical, if he was leaving in the morning.

Before I could really ponder what to do with this problem, high drama swept the house when Warren Doyle, the governor of Denham's son, arrived. Every girl in the house crowded close to the railing, trying to get a better look at the parlor meeting below. I could understand the buzz. Warren was handsome, polite, and quick to inform the Thorns that he'd actually just been appointed governor of his own new colony, Hadisen. Several girls near me clasped their hands in excitement. One offered up a prayer.

But it was in vain because Warren had already decided on one girl and one girl only: Adelaide. A visibly eager Jasper snatched the pitch from Cedric, rather than engaging in their usual volley.

"She is certainly incomparable," Jasper said. Warren hadn't just admired her from the decks; he'd also quickly learned about her excelling at every subject. Jasper again hinted that the ball was close and that Warren wouldn't have long to wait before meeting her. Warren's reaction was a little different than Theodore's.

"I don't really need to meet her," said Warren. "I'm sure she's exceptional. And I'd like to seal a marriage contract now."

Cedric, who'd said little in the exchange, flinched. "That's not . . . how it works. The girls meet all potential suitors in our social season. Then they choose."

"I don't want to risk losing her to someone who might woo her with a lot of flash and no substance," Warren told him. "I'll put out a price to make it worth your while for removing her early—one I might not be willing to match if I have to wait. One thousand gold if you do the deal right now."

It was an unheard-of price. I heard gasps around me. Adelaide remained silent, but that was because she was holding her breath. Or maybe she just couldn't breathe at all. I think there was a very good possibility Jasper might have changed the Glittering Court's rules then and there if Cedric hadn't been so adamant in his stance.

"It would be a breach of our normal policy," admitted Jasper. "But I'm sure, given the circumstance, there'd be no harm in her at least meeting him now and—"

"She gets to see her options and choose," said Cedric. "It's in her contract. No preemptive deals."

The two went back and forth, even though the commission from such a match would have gone to Cedric. I wasn't surprised at this honorable attitude. He'd made it clear at our first meeting and his visits to the manor that he wanted us to be more than commodities. He finally prevailed, though we all knew father and son would have a heated discussion later. Warren reluctantly departed—defeated, for now.

His offer was the talk of the house that night. Many thought Cedric was foolish for turning it down. And many thought Adelaide should've run downstairs and accepted it herself.

For her part, Adelaide was conflicted. She too wondered if she should've jumped on such an offer to such a powerful man. At the same time, she respected Cedric's insistence that she meet all her choices. She paced our room, ruminating and weighing each side. I had little to offer except an attentive ear.

"Tamsin would've taken the deal," Adelaide finally declared.

I couldn't help a small smile. "Tamsin would've called for a priest and offered to marry him on the spot."

Adelaide didn't return my smile. Her face remained bleak. "Tamsin should have been the one getting the offer. She should have been the diamond."

I hurried forward and wrapped my arms around her. "Don't think like that."

"I just don't feel like I deserve this."

"Tamsin loved you. You earned your place here." Grant's words on the ship echoed back to me, suddenly more meaningful. "And don't forget that *you're* still alive."

Warren's proposal continued to trouble her, but at least guilt no longer factored into it. As for me, I had my own dilemma to deal with that night. What to do about Theodore Craft? It weighed on me through dinner and while preparing for bed. Adelaide went to sleep early, which was a relief. Distracted or not, she would've eventually noticed my inner conflict.

A risky option suddenly presented itself while I was returning from the washroom. A maid carrying an armful of boxes passed me as she walked toward the attic door at the end of my hall. I paused and watched as she disappeared up a small set of stairs. I'd explored that area in my first few days, finding little more than storage. As soon as she returned and headed back to the main floor, I darted forward and made my own climb to the attic. Sure enough—I'd remembered correctly. A large, square window overlooked the house's sparse rear grounds. The bodyguards rarely patrolled this side of the house, as there were no first-floor windows. They stayed near the front and sides, close to the doors. And since this window was on the third floor, it was even more neglected since there was no way to—

I moved closer and squinted at the darkness outside. A wooden trellis leaned against the house—a delicate one, but one that might very well hold a girl's weight. I stared at it, my mind spinning. Waiting until I saw Aiana again was the smart thing. The safe thing. But for all I knew, she had tomorrow off as well. And the next day. When would I ever get this news to Grant? No one had told me what to do in this situation.

Decision made, I crept back to my room. Fumbling in the dark, I slipped into a light wool dress and pinned my hair back out of my face. On my way out of the room, I wrapped a robe around me, in case I encountered anyone in the hall who wanted to know why I was dressed and still awake. But there was no need. Everyone on this floor was asleep, or soon would be.

I opened the attic door without a sound. Moonlight shone from above, illuminating the stairs like a magic pathway. I made my way up and forced open the window's latch to get a better look at the trellis. Old, but definitely sturdy enough to get me down. No guards in the backyard. This was my chance. I took off the robe and put my foot on the window's ledge, ready to take the plunge. A cold wind made me shiver, reminding me spring wasn't here yet. In my haste, I hadn't grabbed any outerwear.

Luckily, I had stacks and stacks of extra clothing and accessories behind me. I recalled Mistress Culpepper ordering some of our seafaring attire put into storage. Had those heavy cloaks ended up here? One by one, I opened each box, finding hair combs and shoes and bracelets—but no cloaks. I was nearly at the end when I came across a box of wigs. I started to close it as well and then found myself thinking of Grant dressed up as a stooped and grizzled laborer.

What risks did I face by sneaking out? Being caught, obviously. Either by the Glittering Court's people or some brigand on the road to Cape Triumph. Even if I made it without being detained, I might still be recognized. I'd have a lot of explaining to do and could jeopardize my position.

I looked down and saw only fantastic pieces. Purple wigs. Orange wigs. Pink wigs. Hardly what I'd want to remain inconspicuous. But then, among the showy wigs, I spotted a long blonde one, a very realistic one—and one very different from my own hair. I seized it and went on to the other boxes.

At last, I found the one holding cloaks and other outwear. These might be "everyday" to us, but they were probably richer than what most Cape Triumph citizens owned. Nice clothes could make you a target alone on the road, but I had to hope the fur-trimmed black wool cloak I grabbed would be better than silk. Leather gloves and a cold-weather mask of black velvet completed the set. These masks covered the upper half of the face and were common on both sides of the ocean. Some people treated them as a fashion item. Mistress Culpepper disliked them because they could smear eye makeup, but she also said they were occasionally a necessary evil against icy winds that might chap a young girl's skin.

By the time I'd scaled down the trellis and stood in the yard below, I was no longer Mira Viana. I was a masked blonde woman, clothed in black, ready to plunge forward into the night.

CHAPTER 12

I MOVED SLOWLY OVER THE GROUNDS, KEEPING TO THE shadows and patiently waiting for times when the watchmen weren't looking in my direction. Although their job was to scan everything, their biggest priority was to stop any rampaging man from busting through the door and taking advantage of the delicate women within.

The dirt road to Cape Triumph lay right in front of the house, easy to follow to town. Easy for anyone to follow—that was the problem. Masked or not, I was alone at night and armed only with my battered knife. And although it was the preferred road for those traveling from remote parts of Denham, it wasn't actually a direct route to Cape Triumph. It was as direct as man's engineering could manage, however. I'd heard the hired guards grumbling about it. All around us in this part of Denham, the land lay like a patchwork quilt. Some areas were cleared, either for future or past plantings. Larger tracts of forest surrounded those, comprised of all sorts of vegetation. One such wooded region stood between Wisteria Hollow and the outskirts of Cape Triumph. Cutting directly across it, the men said, would chop off a third of the travel time. But the land was overgrown and, worse, parts were marshy. Even if anyone managed to clear some of it, it'd be too risky to bring wagons and carriages through.

But someone on foot might be able to navigate it just fine. And if that someone happened to run into another traveler, it would be easier to hide among the trees than on an open road.

I plunged into the woods, immediately snagging my cloak and skirt on brambles. The vines had dried up in winter, but their thorns had stayed sharp. They didn't hurt so much as slow me down—as did stepping over falling branches and other forest debris. It made stealth impossible.

When I reached the section near the marsh, I found the mud frozen solid. That was one benefit of the cold, I supposed, but the ground was still rough and uneven. A rudimentary trail finally offered some relief, though it was so narrow that I couldn't place my feet side by side on it.

I emerged onto another road about half an hour after my trek had begun, torn and dirty, my ankle aching. To the north, less than a mile away, the city's lights offered a faint glow, and renewed energy surged through me. Packed earth and wheel tracks confirmed this was a busy road, and two men on horseback thundered by me without a second glance. I followed eagerly, almost as excited about going into the city as I was to deliver my news. A wagon passed me too, and soon, my road joined into an even wider one with more foot traffic. By then, Cape Triumph's great fort loomed over us, and I realized I'd come to the city's main entrance. Only two soldiers stood watch atop the barracks. One looked like he was busy cleaning his gun. Or maybe whittling.

I had to force myself to keep moving once I stepped through the gates. I wanted to stand there and memorize every detail around me. I'd been in cities before—old cities like Santa Luz and Osfro. Cities steeped in history, whose very stones had pedigrees and whose districts were neatly portioned off between the rich and the poor. Here, the lines were more blurred. I knew the history of Cape Triumph's layout, and I could see it all as I walked the streets and hoped I didn't look too much like an outsider. The oldest areas of the city bore the signs of early colonization, where settlers had put up whatever buildings and businesses they could defend, with little regard to any cohesive plan. Farther out, the streets had been constructed with greater thought and apportioned into residential and commercial areas. But even among these, the old rules had been broken. A jeweler's shop next to a tanner's. An elegant millinery store beside a tavern.

I suspected the city's residential areas would have stronger divides between rich and poor, but here, in the heart of commerce, everything was a delightful jumble. Its people were too, showing the same range of class and wardrobe I'd observed at the docks. Most were out for entertainment at this hour, and most were men. I made a point to walk with purpose, as I'd long discovered that attracted the least amount of attention.

I passed an older couple closing up a late-night pastry stand and asked if they knew where Grant's store was. I used a Belsian accent. It hid my Sirminican one but was easy for Osfridians to understand.

"Lots of those stores these days," the old woman told me. "Everyone wants to go off into the wilderness and strike it rich."

"One of the proprietors is Elliott," I said.

Her husband scratched his head. "Oh. Winslow and Elliott. Over on Broad Street. Are they still alive?"

"Well, their store's still open," the woman replied.

"I haven't seen a Winslow or Elliott there in years," he argued. "I don't think there's ever even been an Elliott."

"There's an Elliott there now," I said. "Just returned from Osfro." Grant had told me a little of the cover story. It was a legitimate business, and Winslow, the original founder, had retired and managed it from afar through proxies. As a loyal subject and friend to the Mc-Graw Agency, he'd made an arrangement with Silas to set up Grant as a faux co-owner.

"Well, there you have it," said the wife. "Now just take Central over there two blocks to Broad and turn right. You can't miss it."

"They're probably closed," her husband pointed out.

I repressed a groan. There was a good chance he was right, and if so, how would I find Grant? I thought back to Silas Garrett's letter. "What about Percival and Son's Clothiers? Do you know where that is?"

The man brightened. "You mean Percy the tailor? Oh, sure."

They gave me those directions too, but I stopped by Grant's store

first, just in case he worked late hours. The stenciled WINSLOW & EL-
LIOTT sign stood out prominently—as did another reading CLOSED.
Feeling a little less sure of myself, I took the street to the tailor's shop
and hoped for better luck.

But it too was closed. I sighed. Either Silas didn't really live there or
he was out on the town. Looking up, I saw that all of the businesses
had second floors. A few windows were dark, but most were lit up.
Like the one above the tailor's. Mundane businesses open this late?
No, I realized, spying a narrow staircase that led up to a walkway
around the second story. The lower floor was commercial space, the
upper one residential. I followed the stairs up and knocked on the
door directly above the tailor's shop.

An older man opened it, his hair streaked with gray and skin wizened from the sun. He raised one bushy eyebrow upon seeing me, and
I suddenly wondered what I would do if my hunch had been wrong.
An outcry from behind the man, however, told me I had found the
right place.

"You have *got* to be kidding me. Get her in before somebody sees
her."

The older man grunted and stepped aside, his eyes watchful and
shrewd. Grant strode toward me with an expression I knew well. In
work trousers and a barely tucked-in shirt, he was a much more casual
version of the proper passenger aboard the *Good Hope*. His hair was
about the same.

"Too late," I said, as the door shut behind me. "Plenty of people
saw me. But no one recognized me."

"I recognized you in two seconds. Take that off. You're a terrible
blonde."

The other man strolled over, hands stuffed in his pockets. "Always
so genteel, Grant. Glad to see Osfro didn't change you. Aren't you
going to introduce me to your friend?"

Grant waved vaguely in my direction. "Yes, yes. Mirabel Viana,
Silas Garrett. Silas, Mirabel."

A small mirror on the wall showed that I didn't make a terrible blonde. I could pass for an Osfridian—or a Belsian—more than I'd expected.

I took the wig and mask off and shook Silas's hand. "It's nice to meet you. And you can call me Mira."

Silas's expression didn't change much, but that eyebrow rose once more as he studied my face. In a mild tone, he remarked, "The boy's right for once. That wig is holding you back."

"What do you mean, 'for once'?"

"What is she doing here?" Silas asked in return.

"Good question." Grant's gaze swiveled back to me. "You know the asset arrangement. You aren't supposed to come to me."

"Asset?" Silas's other eyebrow rose. "Since when are *you* running assets?"

I shot him a nervous glance before answering Grant. "Aiana wasn't around."

"Are you one of those Glittering Court girls?" Silas's incredulity grew as he kept looking between Grant and me. "Do you have her *and* Aiana both involved in this? Are you out of your mind?"

It was the first time I'd ever seen Grant look even a little intimidated. "She'll run into most of our suspects. She gets the info, Aiana brings it to us. It's perfect."

"Nothing about this is perfect," said Silas.

"And she wouldn't be here if there wasn't a good reason," added Grant pointedly. Almost hopefully.

I swallowed, a bit taken aback as both men turned their attention on me. Silas had a different type of forcefulness than Grant did. A lot of Grant's just came from his own self-assurance and disregard for social niceties. Silas radiated authority, despite his deceivingly mild exterior. His presence filled up a room. I could understand how he ran the McGraw Agency in the colonies.

I steeled myself as I met his eyes. "Theodore Craft was in our house today and mentioned that he was going to Bakerston tomorrow. That it was important and couldn't be rescheduled."

Silence fell. Neither man said or did anything, and I began to feel stupid. The words I'd just uttered seemed so trite. So insignificant. I'd just delivered a meaningless piece of trivia.

At last, Silas threw his arms up in the air and stalked away from us. "Damn it!"

I looked uneasily at Grant, who was . . . glowing. "Don't worry," he said. "Silas is just mad because I *was* right."

Silas spun back around. "I never said that."

"You're thinking it." The humor faded from Grant's expression, replaced by something more serious. Intense. "But you were right too. You thought Craft was smuggling out the contraband. And I heard two merchant ships came in yesterday."

"Then it seems like *I* was right to bring you this," I said.

Grant regarded me with something shockingly similar to pride. "Yes, you were."

Silas began pacing the room. "We've got to send word to Crenshaw. Immediately. He can find out who's meeting with Craft."

"I can leave right now," said Grant. He reached for a heavy leather coat draped over a chair.

"No, I'll go," said Silas. "I can leave tonight. My joints aren't what they used to be, but I'm still as fast a rider as you. Crenshaw knows me better, and I don't want your cover questioned. You need to get established here. See if you can learn what Craft's public reason is for going. And find out if Abraham Miller was the customs inspector on duty. We really need to search his place one of these days, if we can ever get a safe chance."

"And what should I do?" I asked.

"Go back to finding a husband." Silas came to a halt and turned to Grant. "And you're going to make sure she gets home tonight. But first—a word in private. Please, have a seat and make yourself comfortable, Miss Viana."

Silas jerked his head toward what appeared to be a bedroom.

Grimacing, Grant followed obediently. Silas shut the door.

I settled down on the chair that held Grant's coat and looked around as I propped up my leg. A tidy kitchen sat off to one side, and the loft's main space appeared to be a mix of living room and office. From the bedroom, I could just barely hear muffled voices—angry ones. I stared at the door avidly, wondering if my spy career was at an end. Tossing ethics aside, I jumped up and pressed my ear to the oak.

"—know anything about the Glittering Court?" Silas was saying. "They consider those girls valuable merchandise! The Thorns hire thugs to guard them. It's not going to go well for you if you're caught dragging her around at night!"

"Her position—"

"Damn her position. Magic isn't going to happen just because she's pretty and well placed. Of all the times for you to— Argh. I can't believe this." I heard the floor creak and wondered if Silas was pacing again.

"She isn't some hapless girl." Grant sounded remarkably calm. "She already knew a lot of our methods, and she picked up on everything else I knew in a matter of weeks."

"I'm surprised it took that long," grumbled Silas.

"*And*, she even memorized the entire cipher."

"You showed her the cipher? Yes. Yes, of course you did."

"How else was she going to safely pass written notes?"

"Well, apparently by putting on a mask and sneaking off in the middle of the night! You're lucky she's alive, alone and defenseless."

"She's not defenseless. She carries a knife. She knows how to fight."

I could hardly believe what I was hearing. On the ship, Grant had always kept his praise at a minimum.

"Her coming here wasn't the plan," Grant continued, "but given the circumstances with Aiana—"

"Aiana shouldn't be involved with this either. People already mistrust Balanquans. She'll get in a lot of trouble if she's caught sneaking around."

"Aiana can take care of herself. Don't worry about her."

"She's not the biggest problem. You are. You don't know how to run spies, so don't start now. *If* you were doing this the right way, no one in your ring would talk to each other. They wouldn't know each either. They wouldn't know how to get here! Your prodigy should have used her cipher skills to leave a message in a dead drop for Aiana on the Thorn property, which then would've been passed on to you in another drop."

"Mirabel knew the news was important and had to get it to me," Grant argued. "This was pretty resourceful."

"This is how spies get made—and killed. She's not doing this again. She's out. She needs to go back to her parties and dresses."

I closed my eyes. *No, no.* I needed this. I needed the money to help Lonzo. And I needed it for myself, to prove I was capable and resourceful.

"Silas, you'd be wasting a huge opportunity. Let her do this. She's smart. She's got the right connections. She can distract men."

"Yes, I can tell."

"What's that supposed to mean?"

"You know what it means. Are you sleeping with this girl?"

A beat of silence. I opened my eyes.

"Of course not."

"Do you want to?" pushed Silas.

Another hesitation. "You're wasting time. This is irrelevant and ridiculous."

"You being ridiculous *is* relevant." When Silas spoke again, he was calmer. Wearier. "Look, this is the biggest case we've ever had. It's bigger than us. The colonies are in danger. As is your future. Have you changed your mind? Have you forgotten what's at stake for you?"

"I haven't forgotten."

"Then cut her off, Grant."

When neither man said anything else, I realized they were probably about to come out. I scrambled back to my chair and pretended to be focused on my ankle as the door opened.

"Thank you for your assistance tonight," Silas told me, his tone far more cordial than it had been a minute ago. He picked up a coat and a satchel. "Grant will get you back. I'm off to Bakerston."

He left without another word. I looked up at Grant expectantly, ready to hear him say my work with the McGraw Agency was over. Instead, he asked, "What's wrong with your foot?"

"Hmm? Oh. The ankle's hurt ever since the storm. And now my calf does too."

"Does it?" He knelt in front of me and reached toward my leg, then stopped and glanced up expectantly. I realized he was waiting for permission.

"Go ahead," I said, still mystified that he hadn't said a word about Silas's orders yet.

Gingerly, Grant pushed my skirt up to my knee. "Hold it there." He then took off my muddy shoe and gently probed around my ankle and foot, gauging my reaction. After that, he moved up to my calf. When he pressed on its inner side, I gave a sharp intake of breath and winced.

"Your ankle's okay," he said. "But you've been walking on it funny—putting your weight on the ball and the side? Probably trying to spare the ankle at the expense of the rest. That stresses the muscles and probably gave you a nice spasm getting over here. I can help." When he poked the ankle again, I yelped and swatted his hand aside.

"That's helping?"

"Part of the process. It'll release, but yes, it's going to get worse before it gets better. Up to you. I'm not the one who has to dance in strappy little shoes for the next few weeks."

"Fine. Do what you've got to— Ow!"

He wasn't kidding about it getting worse. I'd known all the muscles were sore in that part of my leg, but I hadn't realized what a hard knot I had in my calf until he started digging his fingers into it.

"Relax this," he ordered, straightening my leg. "No—you just tensed it more. *Relax*. Let it drop. Don't try to do anything with it. Don't even hold it up."

I relaxed my leg as best I could and tried not to cry out as the brutal massage continued. I gritted my teeth. "What happened with Silas?"

"About what I expected." Grant didn't look up. "A lot of grumbling."

"He—he didn't seem very happy about me being here. I figured he'd end the deal. Tell me to go away and refuse to pay me."

"No one's getting rid of you. Not after you got such good information. He caught me up on the situation when I got into town. There haven't been many ships coming in yet, but Craft's trips always coincide with when one arrives. This is the first time Silas has gotten a heads-up before he left. And it's all thanks to you and your brilliance."

"Stop it. You've never been this nice to me. It's unsettling." That, and I still couldn't believe he was lying to me. Or was he? Nothing he'd said was untrue. He just wasn't telling me the whole truth.

I felt even more rattled when he looked up and smiled at me. Really smiled. It even reached his eyes, and it made something in my chest tighten. I'd never seen Grant so . . . happy. Like a normal, easygoing person—not some tense cynic who was always hyperfocused on his work.

"You, Mirabel, have just proven you're worth fifty gold. But don't think you'll get a copper more."

"I wouldn't dream of it," I murmured, watching as he returned to his work. "So what do I do now? Go on with life at the Glittering Court? Get ready to charm and dance with all the men I can manage?"

He paused, his hands resting on either side of my calf. I couldn't see his face so well from this angle, but it looked like that smile had faded a bit. "I suppose so. That's what you're here for. How's the leg now?"

I tentatively pressed against the side of my calf. The knot hadn't entirely released, but it was smaller and softer. The whole muscle had relaxed. Freed from the worst of the pain, I suddenly realized what a scandalous situation I was in. A man at my feet. My skirt hiked up. His hands on my leg.

But I wasn't scandalized. Through some unspoken agreement, he and I had never mentioned the time I'd tricked the favor from him. We'd behaved as properly as male and female acquaintances should, only lapsing into informality when our lessons segued into banter or one of us outraged the other. I still studied those sculpted features sometimes, still thought back to when I'd run my hands over his hair and chest. But it was easy to shelve any lingering desire when I was focused on my larger goals in Adoria. It was very easy when I no longer saw him every day.

But here he was in front of me now, holding my leg in his hands. His skin felt warm against mine, and every place his fingers had traveled along my body had come to life. And places that hadn't been touched hoped they would be.

Get a grip, I told myself. *Turn this off, just like you have before. You have more important things to worry about. Remember when you talked to Tamsin? When you made going to bed with a man sound like something you could take or leave with ease? Leave this one.*

But when I'd so flippantly told Tamsin that, I hadn't been faced with a man who was so frustratingly attractive—and just frustrating in general. A man who was looking at me as though he too had suddenly realized the nature of our current situation.

I hastily released the skirt. His hands dropped almost as quickly. "Better," I said. "Still sore, but the regular kind of active sore."

"Good."

An awkward moment seized us, and I wished I knew what he was thinking. He had his inscrutable mask back on. "How . . . how'd you know what to do?" I asked at last.

"Because once, in another life, I was apprenticed to a healer."

"Really? When?"

"With my uncle. But like I said, that was another life." Grant got to his feet and handed me my shoe. "This'll all get better if you stop

trying to spare your ankle when you walk. Let it do a little work sometimes, and then just rest when you can. Dancing's not going to do you
any favors."

"It can't be helped." I stood up as well and tentatively put weight
on the afflicted leg. "Much better."

"Silas took the only horse I have easy access to, but I can hunt
down another one."

"No need. I can make it back. And you don't have to walk with
me. I'll be fine."

"Probably. But dark streets and country highways are dangerous
for anyone alone."

"I actually wasn't on the highway that much. I cut through some
woods by Wisteria Hollow."

"Keeler's Pond Woods? You walked through a bog in the dark?"

"It was frozen. And there was a path."

"Mirabel."

It was all he said before disappearing into the bedroom. When he
returned, he was a less-scarred version of his laborer self from Osfrid,
complete with scraggly wig and too-big coat. "Why the disguise?" I
asked as I put on my own.

"Grant Elliott shouldn't be linked to much more than his shop. An
occasional night out, a quick drink at a tavern? Not a big deal. Nightly
outings might raise questions."

Plenty of revelers were still out on the town when we left, and
Grant led us around the more crowded spots. I eyed those raucous
streets with longing, hoping I'd get to explore them one day. Maybe I
could marry a tavern owner.

Grant and I spoke little as we passed through the main gates and
onto the highway. We didn't touch, but I was acutely aware of every
inch between us. I finally stopped and pointed to a wooded area along
the side of the road. I'd made note of an oddly shaped stump when I'd
emerged from the brush earlier. "This is the path back."

Grant cocked his head as he stared at it. "You really are reckless."

"I think you meant to say 'fearless.' And seriously—let me go on my own at this point. The trail's tight, and if I'm caught on the other side, it'll be better if you aren't with me."

He studied the dark trees a little longer and finally turned back to me. "Be careful. If you hear anyone—anything—stop and hide."

"I will." But I stayed put. I had to try one more time. "Grant . . . are you sure I'm not in trouble with Silas? Are you sure *you're* not in trouble?"

"Me? In trouble? Hardly."

"He seemed so angry."

"It's the eyebrows. They make him look scarier than he really is."

"I'm serious."

"So am I." Grant kicked at the dirt road. "You were right on the ship. I would've regretted not having you on this case."

And that was it. No hint of cutting me off.

"Okay." I turned toward the woods. "I'll see you . . . sometime."

"Be careful," he repeated. "Don't get lost out there."

I pointed to the sky. "I've got help. The constellations are the same here as in Evaria. I know where they move during the seasons. And I know that Ariniel's star doesn't move at all."

He looked up with me. "For Balanquans, Ariniel's star is the way-farers' star—the star that always brings you home, no matter how lost you are. The only thing a wanderer can count on."

"You must know it well," I teased, thinking of the stories about his past.

"It guides me. But it's never brought me home. Good night, Mirabel."

CHAPTER 13

IN THE DAYS THAT FOLLOWED, I LONGED TO KNOW WHAT
Silas and Grant were doing and if my tip had helped. But that wasn't
how the asset arrangement worked. I provided Grant with information. He didn't pass it back. If I had nothing to give, there was no
reason for contact.

The approach of our opening ball ensured no one sat still at Wisteria Hollow. Mistress Culpepper and Miss Bradley had us endlessly
trying on dresses and experimenting with hairstyles. No alteration was
too small, not if it led to perfection. The designers in Osfrid had out-
done themselves with my fiery debut dress. The silk caught the light
at every angle, blazing into a hundred shades of red. They'd trimmed
the dress with black accents, which Mistress Culpepper didn't like. She
thought it was gloomy.

"You're a ruby," she told me, frowning at the glittering jet beds
along my neckline and sleeves. "You need to look the part."

"I'm a garnet."

"No, a ruby. You jumped up to the third position. We couldn't
leave you as a lesser stone."

She attempted a few modifications to the dress that week, swap-
ping out the ruffled black petticoats for other colors or covering up
the beads with ribbons. But in the end, she conceded that the original
design was best.

I liked the black. It seemed daring to me. Dangerous. It reminded
me of my masked escapade.

When the big night finally came, the Thorns had to hire a fleet of carriages to transport us all. Mistress Culpepper would only let us ride two to a coach—one in each seat—to keep our ensembles as pristine as possible. There'd be no unnecessary wrinkles or tears on her watch. I rode with Adelaide, of course, who sat across from me in crystals and white silk. I envied that they hadn't altered her natural hair and had simply arranged it in a partial updo. I'd been able to wear my hair down, which I liked, but Mistress Culpepper had "enhanced" it with clipped-in strands of deep red. Other girls had been weighted down with heavy, elaborate wigs, so it could have been worse.

Our journey took us through the heart of Cape Triumph, and I leaned eagerly toward the window, taking in details that hadn't been as obvious at night. The ordinary businesses were still open, and the people moving on the streets did so for work and mundane affairs, not pleasure and nightlife. Even so, Cape Triumph's medley of residents continued to enthrall me. One group of men crossing the street near our carriage wore masks and flamboyant clothing, sporting brightly colored coats and plumed hats. I wondered if I was seeing the city's famed pirates, but a little more scrutiny made me decide that even pirates with a flair for the dramatic had to get their hands dirty. This group's clothes were spotless, like they'd never even come close to wear and tear. The men were all young, too, almost desperately hoping to be noticed as they strutted down the road. These were the ones who *wanted* to be pirates.

A great hall on the city's far side hosted the event. At its front entrance, Cape Triumph's high society was also arriving—not just suitors, but also those who wanted to see and be seen. Our carriages traveled to the back so that we could be taken in a private door and led to a concealed holding area, away from the main room. It gave Mistress Culpepper and Miss Bradley more time to fuss over us while Jasper delivered last-minute instructions.

Cedric, looking very splendid in a grayish-blue dress coat, strolled over and stood with Adelaide and me, offering occasional comments as we watched the flurry in the room. He explained how suitors interested in us would have to speak to our "representatives" to schedule a dance tonight. It was both an attempt at organization and a means of making sure high-status suitors received preferential treatment. I wasn't surprised to hear Cedric would manage Adelaide's dance card. I was surprised, however, when he pointed at Aiana and said she'd be in charge of me.

She stood across the room, speaking with Charles. Her outfit still consisted of a split skirt and blouse ensemble, but the fabric was dressier and the embellishment more elaborate. Realizing I wasn't supposed to have met her yet, I tried to mirror Adelaide's surprise.

"Who is she?" I asked.

"She's Balanquan. Does various jobs for us," Cedric said.

More jobs than you know, I thought.

Our procession into the hall started before I had a chance to talk to her. It was a more formal, more civilized version of our arrival at the docks. We entered one by one, paused as we were announced, and then walked down a long aisle toward a dais on the room's opposite side. Adelaide set the pace, as elegant and poised as ever, acting as though the posh onlookers and richly decorated hall were nothing to her. The party guests regarded her with wonder and awed murmurs.

I received a few more whispers and astonished looks than she did, which didn't surprise me. What did surprise me was that I too earned plenty of admiration. There were no slurs as there had been at the docks. I was so used to being "the Sirminican" and treated as an add-on to the other girls that it felt strange to be regarded as their equal.

Well, some thought I was their equal. Others . . . not so much.

"Are you really for sale?" one man asked me during my first waltz.

I hated that word choice and tried to maintain a pleasant smile as I composed a diplomatic response. "I'm available for marriage, so long as a prospective husband can pay off my contract fee."

He studied me skeptically. "Oh. I thought maybe the Thorns were expanding their business."

"Expanding it?"

"Well. They've never brought a Sirminican before. Why start when there must be hundreds of Osfridian girls who'd gladly come over? I thought perhaps . . . well, that putting you with the girls who are actually eligible was a front. That maybe the Thorns were now selling services to men who don't want a wife but are still, ah, interested in female company. There's a huge demand for that, you know."

He went on to elaborate on what a great business idea that'd be, even though I assured him multiple times that the Thorns weren't conducting anything like that. I gripped his hand tightly as we danced, so that I wouldn't be tempted to slap him.

"Think about it," the man told me when the music ended. "It might pay better than marriage."

I couldn't even utter a word, and simply let Aiana lead me to my next partner.

"Are you okay?" she asked. "You look . . . displeased."

Displeased? That was an understatement. "Aiana, do you think it would ruin the party if I choked someone?"

Her lips twitched with a smile. "I think the Thorns might frown upon that, yes."

Some men behaved quite nicely to me and seemed genuinely open to a Sirminican wife. But that didn't mean they were nice men.

One such was a judge named Abel Mathers. He was charmed by the vague suggestion of ruined nobility in my past and sympathetic to the plight of Sirminicans in general. "Can't blame them for wanting to leave. It's terrible what's happened."

"It is. But it's hard getting out—and then almost harder finding a place to go."

He nodded along. "They should all come here."

"It's an expensive trip."

"As bondsmen. Bondswomen. The trip is paid for. They get food, lodging. It's better than what a lot of other people have. And they actually have a chance to pay off their freedom in a reasonable amount of time."

I nearly debated "reasonable" with him, but another word held me up. "They *actually* have a chance? Compared to what else?"

"Penal workers, of course."

"What are they?"

"Well, they're similar. They too are bound to a master and a work contract, but they do so because they're fulfilling a sentence for a crime—a petty one. Something like theft, not murder. It's a more useful punishment than locking someone away. They aren't paid like bondsmen, of course."

I frowned. "Then how do they earn their freedom?"

"By putting in their time, which depends on the length of their contract. The judge sets the time frame when the criminal is sentenced in court."

"Are there standards or rules? Or is it just up to the judge?"

"There are guidelines," he said with a wink. "But ultimately, the judge decides how long they have to serve—and who they serve. People who want penal laborers or servants can apply to the court to get one."

I was growing increasingly dumbfounded. "They can just ask for a worker they don't have to pay? There must be a lot of demand for that."

"Oh, there is. More demand than available prisoners, actually." He was smiling too much for a topic that didn't seem so cheerful. He had a golden tooth I hadn't noticed earlier.

"And you said the judges decide who gets these workers?"

"Yes, based on who we think is the best fit. Interested petitioners go out of their way to meet with judges and make their cases for why they need workers, what kind, for how long. That sort of thing. And depending on the extent of their motivation, we go from there."

"The extent of their motivation . . ." I noted the gold tooth again, as well as his overall presentation. Velvet suitcoat. Sapphire broach. A judge could make enough to afford a Glittering Court girl, but this judge was doing very, very well. "People give you bribes if you grant them penal workers."

"I like to think of them as incentives, not bribes." He didn't seem ashamed in the least. "There's no harm, really. The extra labor improves our society. An extended sentence keeps those elements off the streets. And if I make a little on the side? Well, it keeps me in a lifestyle a pretty young wife would certainly enjoy."

He took my silence as agreement. Really, I was pondering the endless ways that system could be abused. It sickened me, and I couldn't stop thinking about it when I was sent to my next partner.

"Are you feeling well, Miss Viana?" he asked politely.

I forced a smile. My new partner wasn't much older than me and looked sincerely friendly. "Yes, I'm sorry. Just getting tired."

"I can only imagine. They put you through a lot."

"You're the first to acknowledge that. Were you born in Cape Triumph, Mister Chambers?" He spoke like many of the men here, a solidly Adorian accent that bore the inflections of tutoring from an Osfridian.

"I hope you'll call me Cornelius. Hearing 'Mister Chambers' makes me think of my father," he said with a chuckle. "And yes, I was born here. My father came over almost forty years ago, back when we were still battling the Icori and claiming our rights. Our family is one of the oldest in Adoria. We have tobacco and indigo plantations in both Denham and North Joyce. Our goods are sold all over the world, and true connoisseurs know the quality of our merchandise."

"That's very impressive."

He turned sheepish. "Maybe too impressive. Forgive me—I'm overselling to the point of bragging. I'm just anxious to make it clear what a good position you—or anyone marrying into our family—would have."

"I think it's obvious how good it would be," I said, charmed by his fluster. "And I'm flattered that you're even considering me. I haven't seen a lot of that tonight."

He looked genuinely surprised. "What do you mean?"

"Just that a lot of the men here would prefer Osfridian brides, not Sirminican ones."

"Fools. Caught up in ignorance and blind prejudice," he spat. "This isn't a land that can be governed by antiquated beliefs and rigid policies. We call this a new world for a reason—a world where anyone, of any background, can make something of themselves. That's what we must be going forward. Those who don't will be left behind. And considering half of the men in this room started with nothing, they're hypocrites as well as fools if they think otherwise."

"Mister Chambers—Cornelius—you can't imagine how inspiring it is to—" I stopped as my gaze landed on where his fingers wrapped around my hand. "Is that . . . a wedding ring?"

"Oh, yes. I was married last autumn. She's wonderful. I can scarcely believe that—" His eyes widened. "What a babbling idiot I am! I should've explained right away. I'm not here tonight for a bride."

I looked up from the ring. "So I see."

"I'm here to find a bride for my father."

"Your . . . father?"

"Rupert Chambers. He's looking for a new wife. It's a long journey from our estate into town, so I came to search on his behalf and save him the trip. He was quite the traveler once, you know. Loves Evaria. Loves Sirminica. So when I saw you, I realized what a great opportunity we had. You've seen so much of the world, you're so refined . . . you'd get along beautifully. He loves a good conversation."

I kept the smile plastered on my face and thought back to him saying his father had arrived here forty years ago. "That's so kind of you. And how fascinating that he's traveled so much. Was your father a, uh, child when he came to Adoria?"

"In his twenties. But he went back across the Sunset Sea a number of times. He's a very cultured man."

And an old man, I thought, doing the math. At least sixty.

"Yes," said Cornelius, who seemed to guess what I was thinking, "there'd be an age difference, but as I said, marrying into our family would give you every luxury you've ever desired. And my father shares my views on the future of this land. No outdated prejudice in our home. We won't allow any slight to fall your way. All that matters is what a wise and enterprising girl you are—and a beautiful one."

"I honestly don't know what to say."

"At least tell me you'll meet him," Cornelius pushed. "Add one of our parties to your schedule and talk to him. If it doesn't work out, then that's all there is to it, and you'll be off to some other lavish offer."

His face was so earnest, his eyes so big that I couldn't deny him. "I'd love to meet your father," I said.

He spent the rest of our dance lauding his father and their family's virtues, right up until the moment Aiana sent me on to the next man. By this point, I was exhausted with conversation.

"Did I see you dancing with Cornelius Chambers?" he asked. This new partner also had a colonial accent, stronger and less refined than Cornelius's. "He's a good pal of mine."

"He seems very nice," I said automatically. "I think I'll be attending a party at his home at some point."

"I'll be attending one there tonight." His expression turned sly. "But it'll probably be a lot different than the one you'll go to."

"How so, Mister— I'm so sorry. I missed your name." I'd been too distracted when Aiana introduced us.

"Miller. Abraham Miller. Cornelius hosts the best poker games in this colony. Maybe any colony. A bunch of us are heading way out to his place as soon as this lets out. Should be fun. We'll have a lot to talk about after this, and maybe I'll make some coin on the side."

Abraham Miller.

I knew that name. I'd heard it just a few nights ago when I'd told Silas and Grant about Theodore Craft. Abraham Miller worked in the port's customs office and was suspected of forging ship manifests for the conspirators. *And find out if Abraham Miller was the customs inspector on duty. We really need to search his place one of these days, if we can ever get a safe chance.*

"I wish you good luck then, Mister Miller," I said. "Isn't the Chambers plantation well outside of town? Seems like you'll have a late night."

His lips flattened into a straight line. "Yes, that's the one downside about his games. Takes over an hour to get there, even by horse. Their family used to keep a town house here in the city but sold it over the winter. No idea why."

When that dance ended, Aiana told me I could have a short break. As we walked toward the dais, I whispered, "I have some information that Grant might want. Do you think you could get a message to him tonight?"

She turned, puzzled. "I thought you were done with all of that."

"Why?"

"Because I spoke to Silas the other day. He told me about your trip to see him." She didn't elaborate on my illicit excursion, but her expression conveyed exactly what she thought of it. "He also said it was a bad idea having you involved and that you'd been cut out."

"He changed his mind. I think Grant talked him around." I hoped she wouldn't read the lie in me, that Grant simply hadn't followed Silas's instructions.

"I wish he hadn't." Her frown deepened. "I can't get anything to Grant tonight—not with all of this going on—but I'll take a message in the morning."

"But—"

"It can wait, Mira. And *you'll* wait too. No more sneaking out. It's my job to protect you, even if it's from yourself."

I didn't argue, not with that steel in her voice, but I couldn't let the matter go so easily. She was wrong. My news couldn't wait until morning, not when I knew for sure Abraham Miller would be away tonight. But how could I get it to Grant any sooner?

Adelaide was on break too. I sat beside her, glad to rest my ankle. We recapped our nights and then fell into weary silence, simply content to watch the buzzing crowd. The Glittering Court might be the most dazzling guests here, but plenty of Cape Triumph's leading citizens drew the eye in their own elaborately embellished and colored finery. They made a fascinating display as they moved about the room in dances and conversations, and I took a moment to appreciate what a truly incredible world I'd somehow ended up in. Then, amidst all that brightness, I caught sight of a dark spot. A laborer, stooped and clad in a dull, oversized coat, was pushing chairs out through the back door we'd used for our entrance. I couldn't believe it.

"What is it?" asked Adelaide, seeing me stand up.

"I . . . it's nothing. But I need . . . I need to check something. I'll be right back."

I darted down the steps, feeling horrible for leaving her without a real explanation. But I had to know why Grant was here.

It took some time to work my way through the packed room. A few guests regarded me with interest, but it was Aiana and the Thorns I needed to dodge. They were the ones who maintained my schedule here, and they'd know slipping out the back door wasn't part of the agenda.

I managed it unnoticed and found myself back in the holding room, which was mostly deserted, except for a couple of other laborers bringing in barrels of ale and wine. None of them was Grant, and I wondered where he'd gone.

"Here she is, the sensation of the night."

I spun around and found Grant standing right behind me. He was in the disguise he'd worn at our first meeting but spoke to me in his regular voice. "What are you doing here? Checking up on me?"

"Checking up on everyone." The fleeting, upbeat Grant was gone. He was on the hunt again, focused and to the point. "You and your friends might be the alleged attraction, but this is the type of event that throws the rich and powerful together. It's a great chance to watch and see who's chummy with who."

"Whom," I said. "Who's chummy with *whom*."

"Don't correct me on your second language."

"Isn't it your second language too?"

"I've been speaking it longer."

"Well, I've been studying its grammar longer. Look, it doesn't matter. And I can tell you two people who are chummy. Cornelius Chambers and Abraham Miller."

"I already know that. They run in the same circles."

"Did you know Cornelius is having a poker game after the ball?"

"People like me don't make those kinds of guest lists."

"Abraham Miller does. He'll be there. Late. And his town house will be all alone."

Understanding flashed across his face. "Mirabel . . ."

"You can thank me later. Stop moving chairs, and get over there."

He sighed, hope fading. "If only. That's a two-person job, and Silas is still away. You did good work, though."

"Then let me do more," I blurted out. "Take me along." Aiana's disapproving face flitted through my mind, and I promptly disregarded it.

"No."

"When are you going to get an opportunity this good? And you know I can handle myself."

"Handle yourself? Sneaking into Cape Triumph isn't the same as breaking and entering."

"I did it on the ship. Remember? When I effortlessly uncovered all your secrets?"

"Don't even start." He looked me over, and I could almost see his thoughts spinning. This *was* a good opportunity, one he desperately wanted. "You're a little overdressed. Or maybe underdressed? That bodice looks . . ."

"Distracting?" I suggested.

"Cold."

"Don't worry, I'll change so that you can focus on the job."

"As if I'd— Look, this is serious. Miller lives in an upscale part of the city. His building is guarded, and the militia tends to patrol there more than other places. They're bribed to. We've got to be careful."

"Then we'd better make the most of our time. I'll sneak out of the house like I did before." I reconsidered, thinking about the long trip to and from Wisteria Hollow. "Actually . . . I'll just save us the time and slip away as soon as this wraps up."

"You don't think they'll notice they're one girl short? They watch your every move. I've seen it tonight. Aiana never takes her eyes off you or the other two she's in charge of."

"Well, she obviously did for me to get back here. I'm telling you, don't worry. I'll find a way to change and sneak out. That's not your problem. *And* I'll leave her a note. Just so she doesn't worry or report me missing."

He gave an exasperated sigh, but I knew he'd already caved. "Great. Then I'm the one Aiana comes after and yells at tomorrow. There are a lot of words for 'idiot' and 'bastard' in our language, and she knows them all. I even think she invented some."

"That," I said, "*is* your problem."

CHAPTER 14

THE END OF THE BALL WAS CHAOTIC—WHICH WAS PERFECT
for me. Once the official dance schedule ended, brazen suitors tried
to catch our girls' attention for a quick, last-minute conversation or
compliment. I managed to obtain a scrap of paper and scrawled *G.E.*
on it. Aiana was tied up with a group of men all trying to talk to her
at once. Some complained about their dance cards, and others wanted
to schedule future meetings. All the chaperones were in similar situa-
tions. I got someone to deliver my note to her, and then I darted out of
the main hall. She would understand the meaning, but I doubted she'd
be able to break free fast enough to stop me. I was also certain she'd
cover for me—but wouldn't be happy about it.

The back room was empty, but the door had been propped open, revealing lingering mercenaries and the arrival of our coaches. Mistress
Culpepper had had extra boxes of dresses and accessories brought
along, just in case, and I was relieved to see they hadn't been loaded
up yet. It was going to get very busy back here, very quickly, and I
immediately began rummaging through the boxes' contents. Finding a
blonde wig similar to my last one was easy. But inconspicuous clothes
were harder to locate. I finally stripped off my elaborate overdress and
decided to just wear the opaque black chemise underneath. I managed
to locate gloves and a velvet mask but no suitable cloak. Desperate
and pressed for time, I snatched up a wide, burlap tarp and draped it
over my head and body like a cloak, pinning it with a spare broach. I
rolled up the overdress into a big satin bundle that I carried under my

arm. I tried not to think about the wrinkles.

The mercenaries weren't on alert yet, and once I made it past them, it was easy to walk through town to the address Grant had given me. It was a second-floor loft space like Silas's, except above a bakery instead of a tailor. The entrance was on the building's side, away from the main thoroughfare. All the better to conduct clandestine business, I supposed.

"This is yours?" I asked when he let me in. Grant's new lodging smelled like fresh bread. The space consisted of a tiny living area and, from what I could see through a half-open door, an even smaller bedroom that was completely taken over by the bed. It was also the only piece of furniture he had. There was no kitchen either, and I wondered how he ate. "You should get some furniture or decorations. Right now, it looks like a ghost lives here."

"I've been a ghost for a long time. I don't mind it. And look, you're wrong about decorations. I've got a mirror over by the door."

"Yeah, but that's not for aesthetics. It's to put on your disguises. When are we going out?"

He peered at my burlap cloak. "As soon as I figure out what exactly it is you're wearing."

"I didn't have a lot of options," I said defensively, trying to smooth out the tarp.

He tossed me a bundle that had been sitting on the floor. "Good thing one of us has access to a supply store."

I unrolled the clothes and found pants and a real cloak made of drab but rugged fabric. There was also a plain, button-up shirt cut for a man but small enough for me. I changed in the bedroom, impressed that he had guessed my size correctly. "No boots that little," he said later, nodding toward the black dance slippers on my feet. "You going to be able to walk in those?"

"I've been doing it all night." I certainly wasn't going to tell him how much my leg was hurting.

Abraham Miller lived just outside the bustle of Cape Triumph's heart, not far from the town green, which I had yet to see. Here, stately homes and town houses lined quiet streets free from the heavy foot traffic that businesses attracted. Grant—still in his earlier disguise—led me toward a group of identical white town houses. We stopped in the shadows of a cluster of newly planted saplings and watched as a man paced the block in front of us, pausing once to light a pipe.

"A lot of single rich men live here—ones who are too good to stay in a boardinghouse but haven't yet settled down enough to buy a home," Grant explained. "Miller's place is at that end, on the top floor."

"And him?" I asked, pointing at the man with the pipe.

"Watchman. Lots of these houses have them. He's too lazy to go around back, but he'll keep an eye on the front doors, which is—unfortunately—where we need to go."

"How do we get past him?"

"That's where you come in. Assuming you haven't used up all your charm for the night." The way he said "charm" made it sound like he questioned if I ever had any at all.

"Is that what Silas would do if he was helping you?"

"He'd distract in a different way. Maybe flash some credentials and claim he was chasing a criminal."

"That sounds a lot more dignified than what I have to do."

"We all work with the gifts we have," said Grant. "Mine is picking locks. Go talk to him. Keep him facing away from the doors. Once I'm in, finish up and go around to the back of the building. I'll meet you there."

Mystified as to how that part would work, I doggedly set out on my task and headed toward the watchman. He straightened up, startled at my approach, but relaxed when he got a better look in one of the streetlamps. Probably because he thought I was some meek, unthreatening woman.

"Excuse me, sir," I said. I used a lower-class accent, similar to Tamsin's natural one. "Do you know where Benjamin Pierce lives?"

The man, middle aged with a crooked nose, scratched his forehead.

Behind him, I saw Grant creep toward the door at the end of the building, keeping to the shadows as much as possible. "Never heard of him."

That was because I'd made Benjamin Pierce up. "They said this was the place. Corner of Pine and West. White house."

"You must've got it wrong." He eyed me suspiciously. "And what business does a girl like you have visiting a man this late at night?"

I put on an affronted look. "Honest work. His housekeeper's out of town and hired me to come tidy up his place."

Grant was still working on the lock. So much for gifts.

"This late?"

"He doesn't like to be around when it's cleaned and had me come while he's at some fancy party," I replied bitterly. "You think I want to be out this late for one stupid copper? But a girl's got to survive."

"We all do," the watchman said sympathetically. "But you shouldn't be out on your own. Never know who's lurking in the dark."

I knew Grant was in the dark, still unable to open the door.

"My pa's out helping down at the wharf. He would've taken me if he could."

"Well, I'll take you over to East and Pine," said the man. "You probably mixed them up."

Panic hit me. I needed to stay around here, not head off to some other part of town. "Couldn't let you, sir. What if one of your masters came by and you weren't here? You'd lose your job."

His hesitation told me that was true. And at that moment, I saw Grant open the door and slip inside.

"I'll be careful," I told the watchman. "I know how to stay out of sight—a girl's got to do that too. You're probably right, and I just mixed up the streets. Thanks for your help."

I hurried away and walked down Pine until I couldn't see him. Circling around, I made my way to the back of Miller's town house, which faced another building and created a narrow alley in between. The windows at street level were barred, but the upper ones weren't.

"Took you long enough," a voice said from above. Looking up, I saw Grant watching me from a second-story window, arms crossed on the sill as though he'd been lounging there all night.

"*I'm* the one who took a long time? You should've let me pick the lock while you asked for directions."

Grant's response was to toss down a rope. I'd climbed plenty of times on my family's farm and easily made my way up. Two small candles were lit inside, and he handed me one. "Only light we can use without being seen. Search everything, no matter how unlikely. If he's got something here, it's not going to be anywhere obvious."

We still examined the expected places: desk and bookshelves. There were papers and ledgers, but all were clearly marked accounts of army transactions. From there, it was odder locations, like drawers and bureaus. Finally, under Miller's mattress, I found a single piece of paper.

"Got something," I called. "More accounting. But no clear explanation."

Grant came up behind me and peered over my shoulder. "That first column is ship names. Those dates go back to last summer, probably when they came into port. I'm sure customs records will confirm Miller was the agent who did the inspections."

"Five yards oilcloth, ten pounds tin . . ." I tapped the column next to the dates. "Cargo?"

"Stolen cargo. Small amounts, siphoned off the top, probably not significant enough for their owners to notice or protest. It'd be easy for Miller to make that happen, especially with any shipments that sat in the customs houses for a while." Grant's eyes narrowed. "I bet someone noticed, though. Probably figured their goods were stolen by sailors, not a customs inspector. We'll have to go through the official records for any filed complaints."

"Look at the names next to those. Craft is listed five times."

Grant nodded along. "Because he's one of the couriers who carries off the contraband. Those were his assignments."

"Do you know the others?" Four other names were listed multiple times, presumably other couriers who'd transported the cargo Miller helped steal for the traitors. Madisin, Bush, Skarbrow, and Cortmansh.

"Bush. Not the others—at least I don't think so. I know a Madison with *on*, not *in*; Miller might just be a terrible speller. Regardless, men rarely keep honest records hidden under their mattresses. It's not the bed's purpose."

"You mean sleep?"

"Oh, Mirabel. You're such an innocent." Grant took out pen and paper from inside his coat and began copying the records. "It's like you don't even understand men sometimes."

"I understand them well enough. There was this one I met on a ship. I got him to do a big favor for me."

"Not that big. And you know, I've been thinking about that time."

"Oh, have you?" I asked archly.

He paused and looked up, a rueful expression obvious even in the candlelight. "The falling sleeve. Real or faked?"

"Real."

"No."

"Yes."

He returned to his work with a sigh. "That makes it even worse."

"What?"

"Forget it."

When he finished, he returned the ledger to its original hiding spot, and we planned the complicated task of making our exit. We didn't want to leave any sign of our visit, so we couldn't just climb down the rope and leave the window open.

"I'll go down," Grant explained. "You'll untie the rope, step down onto that ledge, close the window, and jump."

He said it so reasonably, so easily, that I had to replay it in my mind several times, just to make sure I hadn't missed the part where it actually made sense. I peered out the window. "Ledge" was a bit of stretch. It was really a type of ornamental molding that wrapped all around the building between the two floors. There was a flat surface on top of it, probably just wide enough for my feet to fit. Certainly not his.

"That's a big jump," I said at last.

"Not really. These stories aren't that tall—not like the place you're staying. Besides, I'll catch you. If you're okay with that."

"As opposed to you missing?"

"You've been in men's arms all night. I figured you might be tired of that."

"I can handle one more set—assuming I land in them. I'll probably knock you over."

"Then I'll break your fall. The risk is on me. Now, come *on*."

I was skeptical of who was really taking the greater risk, especially as I watched him easily climb down the rope and then beckon for me to follow. He was right that this was a much shorter building. It was classy but not meant to impress the way Wisteria Hollow did with its vaulted ceilings and gables. And the ground, at least, was packed dirt. I had to imagine cobblestone would hurt more.

Come on, Mira, I told myself. *Father would do this. Lonzo would do this.*

I untied the rope and let it fall. Gingerly, I stepped onto the narrow molding one foot at a time. It seemed almost laughable now, thinking the climb out of Wisteria Hollow's back window was dangerous. The sill jutted out, and I held on to it firmly with one hand while using my other to slide the window shut. With that complete, I painstakingly turned myself around so that I now faced Grant and not the building. The ground seemed a lot farther away than it had the last time I looked.

Grant held out his arms. "Would it make you feel better to know Aiana's going to kill me if anything happens to you?"

"Not really."

But I tensed, ignoring the pain in my calf, and then launched myself up. In the split second that my feet lifted from the ledge, a shout sounded from far down the alley. "Oy! What do you think you're doing?"

The watchman. It threw both of us off. My jump was clumsy, and I completely forgot about aiming at Grant. He too was startled and looked away for a moment toward the sound, just as I plummeted toward him. The result was that he did, in fact, break my fall, and we both tumbled into the ground.

Grant made it to his feet first and jerked me up. "Run," he said, steering me in the opposite direction of the rapidly approaching watchman. "We're younger and in better shape. He can't catch us."

The watchman's whistle pierced the night. "Thieves! Thieves! Help!"

"Let's hope whoever he summons isn't younger and in better shape than us," I grunted as we cleared the alley. I was keeping pace with Grant so far, but pain shot through my leg with each step.

"Which way did they go?" a new voice barked.

"There—down that alley!" yelled the watchman. The sounds of boots—more than one set—pounded on the ground, one street over at most.

"By the governor's authority, stop and surrender!"

"Of all the damned luck, the militia would be out tonight," growled Grant. "This way. We'll lose them downtown."

We rounded a corner and found ourselves back on the edge of Cape Triumph's nightlife. A giant tavern and inn took up almost the entire block in front of us. Music spilled out of it, and the golden windows revealed crowds of people inside. Other clusters lingered out on the porch, men smoking and women strutting in scanty dresses, despite the cold. Glancing back at the direction we'd come from, I could hear shouts and just barely see silhouettes of running men about three blocks away.

"Take off the wig," Grant ordered as he began tearing at his own and the beard. I pulled mine off, wincing as hairpins snagged at my real hair. He stuffed both wigs into yet another pocket of his giant coat and then grabbed my hand, leading us toward the establishment's door.

Inside, the noise was even more intense. The piano sang with a jaunty tune far removed from anything I'd learned at Blue Spring, and patrons laughed and yelled around us. Some played poker, slamming cards and coins on the table. Deft servers slipped through the crowds with drinks and food. Smoke and the scent of sweat hung heavy in the air. More barely dressed women sauntered around the room—some doing more than sauntering. I stared in disbelief as one couple kissed in a doorway, oblivious to those around them. Another woman had climbed to the center of a table of men, teasing and laughing with them as they tried to lift the edge of her skirt. I became very conscious of my missing wig, with only a mask to shield me.

"I can't be recognized in a place like this!" I shouted to Grant.

"Better here than jail," he called back. "Look—a table opened up by the bar."

We pushed our way through the mob, snatching the two chairs before anyone else could. We sat so close to the bar that Grant only had to stand and call out to the bartender for wine. Moments later, a decanter and cups appeared on the table.

"We're just having a nice drink. A pleasant time." Grant's gaze, anything but pleasant, remained fixed on the door as he spoke. "If the militia does think to look in here, they won't recognize us from whatever descriptions they got."

My hands shaking, I filled the cups with wine but didn't touch mine. "So much for the watchman being too lazy to patrol the other side of the building."

Grant shot me a withering look. "How bad is your leg?"

"Before or after I fell out a window?"

He grimaced. "You should've told me it was still bothering you. I'll take a look when we get back to—" His focus shifted behind me, and I knew what had happened.

"The militia's here."

"Just one. Don't turn around. Drink your wine. Smile."

I couldn't manage the smile but brought the cup to my lips without drinking. A man stormed up to the counter beside us. "I'm looking for a couple of thieves," he told the bartender importantly. "A man and a woman."

The bartender didn't blink. "We've got plenty of them. Take your pick."

"Young blonde girl. Older man."

"Take your pick," the bartender repeated, gesturing to the crowded room behind us. "I didn't notice anyone like that, but then, your description's a little vague."

The militiaman scowled and scanned the room, his eyes passing over Grant and me. "Hey," he yelled, waving at the door. "Come here, and tell him anything else you saw."

Grant's fake smile grew even stiffer. "It's the watchman. He's walking over."

I met Grant's eyes in alarm. I'd been face-to-face with the watchman. Even without the wig, he might recognize me. I averted my gaze as he stomped up to the militiaman and sputtered out what he'd seen.

"I didn't get a good look at him. But I think he had a beard. Gray. The girl was blonde. Pretty. Had a mask."

"Search around if you want," said the bartender, more weary than concerned about housing thieves.

"Let's split up," said the militiaman.

I didn't hear what they said next. All I knew was that I couldn't let them see my face. I couldn't be caught, not after everything I'd done to get to Adoria. My heartbeat roaring in my ears, I climbed over to Grant's lap without any warning and kissed him, angling my body and face away from the bar. His shock lasted only a second, and then he put his hands on my hips, fingers curling tightly into me. His mouth opened against mine, and the taste of his tongue and his lips flooded my senses as my earlier panic melted away. I wrapped my arms around his neck, and one of his hands slid up my back, entangling itself in my hair. His other hand pushed my mask up, and I opened my eyes, meeting his for the space of a breath before our mouths were on each other again. His teeth grazed my lips, and every part of my body tensed, eager for . . . something.

A man cleared his throat loudly behind us, and it took my addled brain several moments to even register it. I quickly shoved my mask down and broke from Grant. We both looked up and saw the scowling bartender standing over us with crossed arms. The watchman and militiaman were nowhere in sight.

"I don't care if she isn't one of our girls," the bartender said. "You want to do that, you take her upstairs and pay for a room like everyone else."

Grant blinked a few times and then gently pushed me back to my chair. "I'll take her to my place. Er, that is, we're leaving." He stood up and tossed a few coins on the table, though his eyes scanned the tavern as he did. A quick nod at me said we were in the clear, and the two of us walked to the tavern door. Or, well, I limped. We paused once more at the porch, double-checking for our pursuers, but they'd moved on.

We made our way slowly down the street, and he offered once to let me lean on him. I shook my head. "It's not so bad," I lied. I was afraid to touch him again. I was afraid to say anything. We walked back to the bakery in silence, and I had to resist the urge to touch my lips and trace where his had been.

"Grant . . ." I found my courage and had to swallow a few times before continuing. "Should we—that is—do we need to talk about—"

"No," he said, staring straight ahead.

"No? You don't have *anything* to say?"

"No." His voice held its usual flippancy, but it felt fragile. Like it was a struggle to maintain it. "Is there something you *want* me to say?"

Lots of things. Like why he hadn't been faking. He was an exceptional actor, but he hadn't kissed me like he was putting on a show. He'd kissed me like he wanted to consume me. And he pulled me to him like . . . well, like he just wanted me, pure and simple.

What do *you want him to say? Why* are *you searching for something complicated?* I demanded of myself. I sought shelter in a cocky attitude. "Mostly I just want to hear you acknowledge that I was a better choice than Silas tonight."

"Well, certainly in some—" He looked ahead, toward his building, and groaned. "Wonderful."

I followed his gaze. "What?"

Aiana stood in front of the bakery below his loft, a horse tethered nearby. She was leaning against a post and snapped to attention when she saw us, her face a thundercloud. Immediately, she began yelling at Grant in Balanquan. He kept his calm when he answered back in the same language, but it only seemed to make her angrier.

She was in the middle of another tirade when I said, "Wait, wait. This isn't his fault. I volunteered. And if it helps, he protested."

Aiana switched to Osfridian. "Well, apparently not enough! Come on, we're going home. It's a miracle no one noticed you were gone in the ball's aftermath. Well, I'm sure Adelaide noticed."

"It was a one-time thing," Grant said. "It was my fault."

Aiana turned on him. "Of course it was your fault! You should've never gotten her involved with any of this."

"She can make her own decisions. She got herself involved with this."

"With *your* prompting! Don't drag her into your reckless lifestyle. Don't make her like you! She has a good chance here. A chance for stability and happiness, maybe even love."

Grant's calm and collected air disintegrated into angry disbelief. "With an arranged marriage to the highest bidder? How'd that work out for you with Mishi, Aiana? And where was your love and happiness when you were slinking in and out of that midwife's bed? You should've learned your lesson from her, but I'm sure you've fallen in with some other disastrous lover while I've been gone."

Aiana looked as though he'd slapped her. "At least I learn my lovers' names," she said quietly. "And at least I try for human connection. Maybe I fail, but I try."

Icy silence descended as they stared each other down, and I had an unwelcome flashback to Adelaide and Tamsin fighting. The heat I'd felt in the tavern was gone. All I wanted was for these two to make peace.

Grant yielded first, the challenge fading from his eyes. "Sekem, I didn't—"

Aiana held up a hand and moved toward the horse. "Don't. She *is* already like you. Maybe she always was. And I'm going to assume from now on, she'll just come and go when she wants. I'll cover when I can, but if anything happens to her, it's on you. I hope all your dreams and glory are worth that. Let's go, Mira."

CHAPTER 15

I FELL ASLEEP AS SOON AS I WAS BACK IN MY BED, AND morning came far too quickly. I opened my bleary eyes to find Adelaide standing over me, dressed for the day and full of questions.

"I'm sorry," I said. "I didn't mean to scare you. Thank you for not telling anyone."

I could see she was waiting for more detail, perhaps an explanation or simply where I'd been. I stayed silent, mostly to avoid lying to her. At last, she asked cautiously, "Were you out exploring the city?"

"Yes." That, at least, I could say truthfully. "Foolish, I know."

"Something could've happened to you! Promise me you won't do it again. It's not safe for a woman alone."

"The world never is," I remarked ruefully. It was the story of my life.

She gave me a sharp look. "You didn't promise."

"Because I can't."

"Mira—"

"Adelaide. You have to trust that I wouldn't do anything— dangerous or otherwise—without a good reason. But . . . well . . ."

I looked away, suddenly faced with a part of this subterfuge I hadn't had to deal with before. On the ship, Adelaide had been too distracted to notice much of my goings-on. And until recently, my biggest fear of detection had been by those who dictated my future, like the Thorns. None of my work for Grant was supposed to have affected her. Technically, it still didn't, but now that she *had* noticed my behavior, I had to choose how to address it.

"We all have our secrets," I said, looking back up at her. "I know you do too, and I respect that."

Adelaide had a hard time arguing against that, no doubt recalling that I'd never pushed for details on her erratic performance back at Blue Spring. Still, I couldn't blame her for worrying. She was all I had left after Tamsin, and I was protective of her. I should've known Tamsin's loss would make Adelaide protective of me too.

She backed off on her interrogation and even gave me an easy smile as she left the room, but I knew I hadn't totally erased her fears. As I finished pinning up my hair, I tried to imagine telling her the truth. What would she say if she knew that I'd been breaking into the home of a respected citizen last night? That I'd kissed a man inside a tavern of ill repute? That said man was a spy with a dangerous past and an infuriating personality?

I stood in the doorway to my bedroom, closing my eyes for just a moment before following her downstairs. Against my better judgment, I let myself savor the memory of kissing Grant. Of being wrapped up with him. I opened my eyes and took a deep breath.

Stop this. Grant is a distraction, that stern inner voice reminded me as I walked down the stairs. *He's just a means to helping Lonzo.*

At the breakfast table, Mistress Culpepper was already announcing today's schedule. The Thorns made sure no one stayed idle. Some, like Adelaide, had had all sorts of requests for meetings, and she spent her day entertaining one caller after another at the house. Those who weren't occupied with individual appointments were sent off on group visits for tea or other activities that would get us exposure. I actually had a couple of callers of my own. One of them was making the rounds to all the girls. The other seemed legitimately curious about me, which was flattering, but nothing about him otherwise left an impression.

Our most important events took place in the evenings. Those dinners and parties drew in the most prestigious suitors and gave us a chance to assess the homes and resources of those who were courting us. Adelaide, Amelia, and I attended our first private party at the home of an esteemed merchant. Despite our host's obvious wealth, the party felt casual compared to the pomp and excess of the ball. We were still made up to perfection and still on our best behavior among Cape Triumph's elite, but at least there weren't so many of them. We also had the freedom to mingle with whomever we chose. There were no set dance cards tonight. Actually, there wasn't much dancing of any kind, which let me give my ankle a rest.

Thinking of my ankle made me think of Grant, and thinking of him made me think of his hands on my leg, and thinking of that . . .

"Are you okay, miss?"

I blinked away from my imagination's treachery and focused on a young man standing before me, his face quizzical. "Sorry?"

"You look so flushed," he said. "I hope the room isn't too hot for you. Should I get you some water?"

"That's very kind, thank you."

I struggled to keep smiling as he flagged down a servant. This was maddening. It had only been one kiss. Well, one kiss and a hiked skirt. When the solicitous man returned with my water, I turned my charm up as high as I could, flirting far more than I had with anyone at the debut ball. If some part of me was intent on experimenting with a transient lover, then surely I could find someone else. Someone less . . . complicated.

But it didn't work. It didn't work with the next man I spoke to either. Or the next. I went out of my way to find the best-looking men at the party and discovered that both Grant and Miss Garrison had been right about my appeal. Some of the men seemed hesitant to initiate conversation with a Sirminican but warmed up once they realized I was a "regular" person. And they needed no warm-up at all when it came to my physical attributes. Even through their masks of gentility, I could see them sizing up my figure. Their interest was palpable, but I felt no stirrings of anything. I didn't want to climb on their laps. I didn't want to feel their lips crushed to mine. I admired their attractiveness, nothing more.

When our group came home to Wisteria Hollow later, we found most of the other girls gathered in the parlor, all eager to talk about their respective parties. Adelaide went to bed early, and I offered to go upstairs with her. She'd been out of sorts today, and I worried the strain of being the diamond was already getting to her. She had the most aggressive schedule of anyone. "Just tired," she said, waving me off. "Stay up if you want to."

I wasn't interested in hearing about everyone's suitors, especially after all the superficial conversations I'd already had to endure. But I did like the other gossip from Cape Triumph. Despite the peace in the central colonies, rumors of Lorandian and Icori threats always circulated. Local scandals and crime were also hot gossip. Hearing the story of a family who'd received no assistance from the militia or soldiers after being robbed on a busy street made me frown, but a switch in topic to the city's enigmatic pirates distracted me. It seemed some of them might have taken to water again.

"This ship just vanished last night," Juliana told us. "The watchmen on the docks never saw anything. Too misty."

"Wasn't anyone on board?" asked Martha.

"Just a skeleton crew, and none of them know what happened," explained Juliana. "They were knocked out, tied up, and left farther up the coast."

I leaned forward, fascinated. "What was on the ship?"

"Mostly sugar. Some spices. They took all the sailors' weapons too. It had just come into port in the afternoon and hadn't been unloaded yet." Juliana sighed. "I hope we can still get sugar for coffee and tea. The gentleman who told me about the ship said those things will be hard to find until spring trade increases from the south. Prices will go up."

Clara ran her hands over her narrow waist. "Just as well. Who needs sweets? You should cut back on those pecan buns at breakfast, you know. You're not engaged yet."

Juliana turned bright red and instinctively wrapped her arms around herself. I tried not to roll my eyes. Honestly, couldn't Clara get through any conversation without finding a way to belittle someone?

"I'm actually surprised you aren't married already," I teased Juliana. "You've had suitors visiting you nonstop. And it sounds like you must have been talking to a well-connected gentleman if he knows so much about commerce."

Juliana brightened. "Oh, yes. Barton Scarborough. He trades all up and down the coast. I danced with him *twice*."

"Ooh, you're lucky," cooed Theresa. "Mister Scarborough is such a fancy dresser! I saw him at the ball but didn't get a chance to dance with him."

"He had silk roses embroidered on his waistcoat tonight." Juliana lifted her chin proudly. "It's because his father—the elder Mister Scarborough—lived in Lorandy years ago. They're a very fashionable family."

I decided it was time to make my exit. I'd restored Juliana's standing and didn't feel particularly compelled to listen to a detailed analysis of men's wardrobes. But when I reached the doorway, I halted. Every time someone said "Scarborough," it tickled a memory—especially when Juliana said it. Like me, she loosened her formal Osfridian in private and would revert to her old accent, a quayside dialect that nearly dropped the second syllable of Scarborough. It sounded like *scar-brow*.

Skarbrow.

That had been a name on the list uncovered at Abraham Miller's. Grant hadn't recognized it because, like some of the other names, Miller had misspelled it. It almost certainly should have been Scarborough. Had Grant made this connection yet? If not, he needed to know. Identifying the customs officials on that list was critical.

A new energy rushed through me. I sprinted up to my room, careful not to wake Adelaide, and wrote out a note in the cipher Grant had taught me. When I came back downstairs, I was just in time to see Aiana at the front door. "Aiana!" I whispered. "Are you leaving?"

"I'm off work now. I don't usually have overnight shifts."

I handed her the paper. "Can you take this to Grant?"

She gave me a look of mock astonishment. "Well, well. I figured you'd just scale down the trellis and do it yourself."

"Hey, I'm really not always looking for danger."

I didn't think she believed that, but she took the note anyway. "I'll stop by on my way home."

"Aiana . . ." She put her hand on the doorknob and paused to glance back. "I'm sorry for last night. For causing you and Grant to fight."

"You didn't cause that."

"But I—"

"I know you played a part in the night's outing, but us fighting wasn't your fault. It's what we do. And we usually forgive pretty quickly. I don't have any brothers, so I suppose this is the gods' way of showing me what one is like."

"It *is* a lot like that. My brother and I fought a lot, but we never held grudges. And there was nothing . . ." I felt my voice start to crack. "There was nothing we wouldn't do for each other."

Aiana's dark eyes brimmed with compassion, but she didn't pry. She just squeezed my hand and said, "I'll see that Grant gets this."

I never heard if she did, and my whirlwind life reset the next day. More suitors, more afternoon excursions. The evening party was held at the home of the governor—the father of Adelaide's most celebrated suitor, Warren Doyle. The gathering would have an exclusive guest list, and I resolved to be watchful around so many prominent citizens. I'd hoped Cedric or Aiana would serve as our chaperone, but Jasper came instead. On the bright side, he rarely paid much attention to me.

Warren didn't either. I wanted to talk to him, not because he was a likely traitor, but because he had the potential to be targeted by them. Supplies for his new colony came into port a few times a week, many of them the basic survival types of items a rebel army would require. I was curious if he'd noticed any shorted cargo.

He monopolized Adelaide most of the time, though, and when she finally stepped away and provided me with an opening, he barely spared me a glance.

"Your family's home is lovely," I told him.

"Hmm? Oh, yes, yes, thank you." His eyes scanned the room, taking in other guests and their activities.

"I know your father's been in Denham a while, but this house was recently built, correct?" When he didn't answer, I prompted, "Mister Doyle? How old is your home?"

"What? Oh. Ah, ten years or so."

Growing impatient, I switched to a more dishonest angle. "You know . . . Adelaide was just telling me she was worried you won't have a house to match this one in Hadisen."

That got his attention, and he swung his gaze back to me. "She did?"

"She likes you very much, but it's a risk—not you, of course, but going off to a new colony. Here, you've got the backing of your father's wealth and prestige. But in Hadisen? Well. That may not be the case."

"I'll be its governor," he exclaimed. "You can't get much more prestigious than that."

"But she's heard there's barely a town there, that supplies are short. And I don't mean luxury items. Even basics."

"Things are rough now," he admitted. "But I'm leading a party there later this month, and we're flush with all sorts of goods that will help boost the economy. And of course, *my* home will want for nothing, no matter how rugged everything else is. Make sure that she knows that."

"I will. What kind of goods are you—"

"Ah, Miss Viana, there you are."

I turned at the new voice, startled, and saw Cornelius Chambers.

"Mister Chambers. I didn't think I'd see you until you hosted that party you'd promised."

He grinned. "I'll still honor that, but you're in luck. The Doyles are great friends of ours, and so Father decided to come out tonight. I can introduce you as soon as you're free."

"Of course, that would be—" I turned and saw Warren had moved on. So much for my investigation. "Well. It looks like I'm free now."

I'd almost forgotten about this bizarre arrangement and allowed Cornelius to lead me over to a corner where a well-dressed elderly gentleman sat in a high-backed chair. Wisps of gray hair escaped from the tail bound at the back of his neck, and a large triangular-shaped hat rested crookedly on his head. He clutched a cane in one hand and was speaking with a younger man in the chair next to him. Seeing us, the young man stood and bowed before excusing himself.

"Father," said Cornelius, "this is Mirabel Viana, the one I told you about. From Sirminica. Miss Viana, my father, Rupert Chambers."

I curtsied politely before accepting the vacant chair they offered. Rupert turned to me, brown eyes kind in his wizened face. "A fair maiden from the tranquil land of poets and philosophers, eh? How did a beauty like you end up in such a primitive place?"

"That land isn't so tranquil anymore, sir," I said.

Cornelius touched both our shoulders. "I'll leave you two to catch up."

"It's a shame," Rupert said, once his son was gone. "What's become of that country. Is it as bad as they say?"

"It depends on what they're saying. Most likely, it's worse."

"A shame," he repeated. His gaze shifted far away. "I'll never forget the first time I gazed upon the ruins of the Palace of Senators. Have you seen it? Where the ancient Ruvans made peace with the western league? Splendid. Splendid and humbling."

I shook my head. "I never traveled that far south. My home was closer to the mountains."

"Ah, yes. Another beautiful place. Tell me, is that part of the country still filled with lemon orchards? I remember how sweet the air was."

I told him what I knew, and for the first time in ages, I saw someone who truly understood the loss of what had happened in the country of my birth. His face filled with sorrow as I spoke but lightened when we discussed Sirminica's past grandeur, how it prevailed as the last bastion of Ruvan culture when the rest of that great empire had fallen away. Talk of my homeland made me think of my father, back when I'd believed all of his glorious victories were achieved by equally glorious means. Sitting at this party made me feel frivolous and useless. An embarrassment to our family name. I'd achieved no victories of any kind.

"You are a delight, young lady," Rupert told me, after a small fit of coughing. "Too good and too cultured for this backwater town. And too young for a relic like me. I don't know why Cornelius got it into his head I should marry—maybe he feels guilty since he's so happy with his new bride. But that's still no reason to inflict me on you."

"You shouldn't say that," I replied, hiding my surprise. Cornelius had said his father had been the one wanting to marry again.

"I'm telling the truth. And, yes, I suppose a rich marriage is appealing, but surely there are other fortunes out there that aren't attached to boring old men."

"Actually, this is one of the most interesting talks I've had at a party," I said sincerely.

He smiled, deepening the wrinkles around his eyes. "And for me. But you've only been in town a handful of weeks. Go out more. Dance. Enjoy your youth. Bask in your admirers. Find some hot-blooded young man who'll give you a brood of children."

"I don't know if I want a brood." I laughed.

"Well, you won't have any at all with me," he said, the subtext clear. "I suppose I can give you good conversation now and then and, of course, your own account. That's about it. Wait a month, and then if you decide you really want to resign yourself to my son's plan, come talk to me again. Actually, come talk to me again regardless. It would be a pleasure."

Cornelius returned, beaming as he looked between his father and me. "Mister Thorn just scolded me for hiding her in a corner, so I must spirit her away. But I hope you had a nice chat."

"Very nice," I said warmly. "I hope to see you again, Mister Chambers."

Cornelius could hardly contain himself as he led me away. "Did you mean that? You'll marry him?"

I flinched, startled by the zeal in his face. Before I could answer, a young woman hurried up to us. "Will she do it? Are they getting married?"

I stared in bewilderment. "I'm sorry, you are . . ."

"My wife," Cornelius said, pressing her hand to his lips. "Lavinia Chambers."

Lavinia was stunning, with silvery blonde hair and cat-like blue eyes. With that kind of natural beauty, it was a shame that she'd weighted herself down with layers of jewelry and a rainbow of silks and velvets that hurt the eye. Her wardrobe competed with her.

"It's nice to meet you," Lavinia said. She sounded as though she'd been born in Osfrid. "Can I expect you to be my mother-in-law soon?"

"I . . . what? No. I mean, I don't know."

Cornelius frowned. "But it looked like you got on so well. And I know he's eager to remarry."

Was he? "He was very charming," I said. "But I still have a lot of my season left."

"He's thinking of moving to one of the family's holdings in North Joyce." Lavinia's voice was hopeful. Impatient. "It's small, but it's on one of the loveliest beaches you've ever seen, just outside Kiersy. That's becoming a very fashionable town."

"I'm sure it's wonderful, but I've still got a lot to think about. A lot of other men to meet." I backed away from their smothering presence.

"And it looks like dinner's being served. We'll have to talk another time."

Mercifully, the entire Chambers family ate at the opposite end of the table, leaving me free to ponder that peculiar episode. The men seated near me made small talk that required little response from me, but one remark snapped me to attention.

"It's about time someone deals with those heretics. I'm glad to hear they're taking action."

I turned to my neighbor. "Heretics?"

He nodded emphatically. "Yes. They're everywhere. Young Mister Doyle and some of the other town leaders are organizing patrols. And recruiting concerned citizens to join them. They intend to root out these heathens hiding among us and see they get the punishment they deserve."

I tried not to wince at that last part or think too hard on the punishments I'd seen in the past. "Which town leaders?"

He and the man next to him threw out a few names, some of whom were suspects of the conspiracy. *Recruiting concerned citizens.* Concerned citizens like respectable shopkeeper Grant Elliott? Grant had said he didn't make elite guest lists, but this might very well be a chance for him to mingle with those who did.

When we'd finished dessert and started to get up, I overheard a woman say, "I'm surprised they don't all have headaches, with the way Jasper Thorn drags them around."

"Is someone sick?" I asked.

The woman pointed across the room at Adelaide, who did indeed look unwell. "They say she's going home early and that—"

I didn't wait to hear the rest. I raced over to Adelaide.

"Are you okay?" She certainly looked pale, and I immediately forgot about heretic patrols and bizarre marriage offers. "Do you want me to come home with you?"

She shook her head. "No, but I do need your help. Answer two questions for me."

"Yes?"

"Do you know where the Alanzans will meet tonight? For their Star Advent?"

I was taken aback. I knew the answer. Cedric kept me informed of Alanzan activity in the city. But I was surprised Adelaide had even remembered that this major holiday of theirs existed. "What's your other question?" I asked uneasily.

"I need to know how you get in and out of the house undetected."

"Those are big questions."

"And I wouldn't be asking them without a good reason."

It was what I'd told her about my own activities. I didn't like having my words used against me. I didn't like the desperation in her eyes either. "You can't tell anyone," I said.

"You know I won't."

"Of course not. I shouldn't have suggested it." I still hesitated, mostly because I feared for her safety, but before I could ask for more clarification, I saw Jasper beckoning to her impatiently from across the room. Time was running out, and I'd just have to trust her. I took a deep breath. "Okay, at the end of our hall is a servants' staircase. If you take it up to the attic, you'll find this window . . ."

CHAPTER 16

I WAS BURSTING WITH THE NEWS ABOUT THE HERETIC patrol, but when I arrived home to Wisteria Hollow later that night, Aiana wasn't there. I was on the verge of going to Grant myself—until I realized Adelaide wasn't back yet either. I stood in our room for a long moment, staring at her empty bed, and then flounced onto my own, suddenly overwhelmed by a terrible, crushing feeling. What if something had happened to her? Why had I let her go alone? I'd already lost one friend. How could I be so careless with another? I should've feigned sickness too. I should've just insisted I accompany her home.

Should I go to the Alanzan meeting? Surely she wouldn't have asked about it if that wasn't her intended destination, right? But then I again felt guilty for being a hypocrite . . . telling her it was okay for me to run around in the night while I wanted her to stay locked away and safe. *Adelaide's not like me, though. She doesn't carry a weapon. She doesn't know how to confront criminals in dark alleys. She could barely style her own hair when she came to the Glittering Court.*

Reluctantly, I decided not to take the news to Grant. I had to wait for Adelaide. I crawled into my bed, only to toss and turn as I constantly chased horrible images from my mind. When Adelaide finally crept into our room, I jerked upright and tried to hide my earlier panic. "Did you get what you needed?"

She paused near her bureau. "I don't know that I ever will."

I couldn't see her expression in the darkness, but the sadness in her voice made my heart ache. "Is there some way I can help you?"

"You already do, Mira. Just by being here. Good night."

She was subdued at breakfast too. Lots of girls were. Daily parties took a toll. Still, Mistress Culpepper pushed us with her usual intensity, laying out the day's social itinerary and reminding us of our duties. I watched Adelaide closely and offered comfort once again, but she just kept reiterating that she was fine.

I found Aiana right before I left for an afternoon tea and asked if she could deliver my message about the heretic patrol today. "It depends on how late I'll be out," she said, her tone brisk. She was on her way to chaperone another group. "I've got jobs all day and then an appointment after dinner. But if I can't make it there tonight, I'll get it to him in the morning."

I hesitated. The revelation I'd had about Scarborough wasn't life-or-death, but I didn't like the uncertainty of her time frame. I'd already sat on this news for one night and was restless to share it. "You have enough going on. I'll just take it."

Aiana made a face. "Don't pretend you're doing me the favor. You *want* to go."

"You said you wouldn't stop me." She was right, though. I wanted to go for the thrill of it. This mission was the closest I had to any sort of heroic deed. And . . . I wanted to see Grant again.

"I won't stop you," she said. "But that doesn't mean I'm going to act like I approve. It's a bad idea."

The anticipation of another clandestine outing in Cape Triumph made the hours drag by. When we finally finished our evening party and returned to Wisteria Hollow, I waited for everyone to go to bed before I donned my wig, mask, and the clothes Grant had given me. Eluding the bodyguards still had to be done very carefully, but once I made it to the woods, I felt like a weight had been lifted off me. No more uncomfortable clothes. No more rules of etiquette. I was free, at least for a little while.

Surprise lit Grant's face when he opened his door. Surprise and . . . something else. Wariness, maybe. Then, his features smoothed, and he was his usual blunt self. "Wisteria Hollow has terrible security."

I stripped off the mask and cloak as soon as he shut the door. He still had no furniture, so I crossed my arms and leaned against the wall. "Aiana was busy, so I figured I'd bring you my news."

"'Busy,' huh? Is that what she told you? No doubt she's off chasing her latest romance." He turned away and paced the empty room. "You're not supposed to come here, you know. This couldn't have waited a day?"

"Maybe . . . but I mean, it's already two-day-old news." The harshness of both his tone and attitude startled me. "Everything else I've brought you has been time sensitive, so I figured you'd jump on this. I didn't expect the attitude. I can go if it's too inconvenient—"

"No." He stopped and ran a hand over his eyes. "Don't go. I'm just tired. Get comfortable, and tell me what you've got."

I studied him a beat, sensing but not quite able to identify something in his words that didn't ring true as he settled down on the floor. "Okay." I sat cross-legged near him, stretching out my stiff back. My scalp itched and sweated from the wig.

As I started to unpin it, he said, "I guess you're really taking the 'get comfortable' part seriously."

I paused. "Are you sure you want me to stay?"

"Do whatever you want." But he looked away as I shook out my real hair, his gaze settling on the darkened window across the room. "So what is it?"

"I was at a dinner party a couple of nights ago and discovered something pretty significant."

"Your future husband?"

"Better. I found a way for you to finally make some friends."

He focused back on me and listened with a raised eyebrow as I explained about the heretic patrols and how he might infiltrate them.

"You wanted to get in with the city's elite," I told him. "If you can't do it by putting on a satin ball gown, then why not by joining a bunch of zealots who want to round up people for their beliefs?"

"I'd rather put on the gown than run around with a lot like that, but it *is* a good opportunity. I heard about some arrests while I was in the shop this morning, but I didn't realize active recruitment was going on." His grimace softened. "That was a smart connection to make."

"I guess it's a good thing I came over, then."

His lips almost edged into a smile. "Yes, yes. I already apologized. Don't rub it in."

"You didn't apologize, actually, but I know you think you did, so that's something." He didn't respond to that as I'd expected, and an uneasy silence fell over us. I wasn't sure what to do now. I didn't usually have to make small talk with Grant. "Why did you shave?"

He automatically rubbed his smooth chin, which I'd noticed as soon as he'd opened the door. "Silas. He thinks being clean cut makes me look more like a respectable shopkeeper. I like keeping some there. Gives me more flexibility with disguises."

"That's why? I always thought you were just lazy."

"So you agree with him?"

I tilted my head so I could better scrutinize him. The shave didn't diminish his looks any. In fact, I found it novel to finally get such a clear view of his face, the enticing shape of his lips, the strong jawline. "I guess I can see where other people might think it's more respectable. But I miss the scruffiness. It was one of the few endearing things you had going for you."

"And you say I've got the attitude tonight."

"You're not the only one who's tired. I've been dancing and smiling all night and then trekked through a marsh to get to you." I stretched out my leg and winced. "It was getting better, but the walk over here undid all the improvement."

He started to reach for my calf and then halted. His hands fell to his lap, and he looked away again. "Just keep trying to stay off it. That'll help."

When the silence returned, I asked, "What's the matter with you tonight?"

"Nothing's the matter."

"But you're . . ." I struggled to articulate it. "You're acting like I really am bothering you. You won't even look at me."

He let out a heavy, exasperated breath. "What else do you want me to do? I already told you the heretic lead was good. And your Scarborough one was too. I even made sure you got full credit for your genius when I passed that one to Silas."

"Did you?"

Something in my tone made him turn back. "Why wouldn't I?"

I bit my lower lip, unwilling to admit to eavesdropping.

"Mirabel?" prompted Grant. "Tell me what you aren't telling me."

"You first."

"What?"

"You said you'd always tell me the truth. But you haven't been."

"That's not true."

"You just lied again."

"I did not— Fine." He pushed aside unruly hair and avoided my eyes yet again. "What do you want to know? Ask a question, I'll answer. Ask two questions. Three. It makes no difference."

"Silas wanted me out that first day. Why didn't you tell me or do what he said?"

That took him aback. "How . . . do you know about that?"

"I listened at the door when you were arguing."

"Of course you did. Look, you want the truth? You're too valuable to this case. I didn't want you out and figured there was no reason to stress you with his grumbling." Grant shook his head, relaxing a little at the opportunity for a quip. "And now I know to always check behind closed doors."

"Don't joke. And look at me. You should have—" I tugged at his hand as I spoke, trying to draw his attention. The touch of his skin sent a jolt racing through my body, every nerve suddenly waking up. He flinched, as though he'd felt it too, and I immediately let go.

And in that agonizing moment, I realized what was wrong. While I'd been fantasizing and wrestling with the throes of lust, he'd had a very different reaction. The opposite, really. That's why he kept averting his eyes. Why he wouldn't touch my leg. Why he hadn't wanted me here at all. I could feel heat flooding my face.

I sprang to my feet. "I'll leave."

I caught only a glimpse of his astonishment before I turned toward the door. I was reaching out to open it when he put his hand on my shoulder. My whole body froze with the realization that he was standing right behind me.

"Mirabel, what's the matter with *you*?"

"I figured you'd just act like it hadn't happened. That's how you are." I kept my words calm and precise. "I didn't expect you to be mad about it."

"Mad about what?" But something in his voice was just off enough to tell me he knew exactly what I meant.

"Us kissing."

"Let's be clear about one thing: *You* kissed me."

"I'm not in the mood for this game." I put my hand on the knob. His grip on my shoulder tightened. I held my breath.

"I'm not mad. It was quick thinking. A good distraction."

I closed my eyes. "Then why won't you look at me? Why have you been trying to get rid of me?"

Silence. Long silence. He shifted, so close now that our bodies touched. His hand dropped, resting lightly on the curve of my waist. "Because it was . . . because you are . . . ugh. *You're* a distraction too."

As I opened my eyes, I realized I'd been wrong about his reaction to the kiss. Slowly, I turned, unable to avoid brushing against his body as I faced him. Our eyes locked, and the tension ramped up in what little space was left between us. Some of it was the usual exasperated kind, but the rest . . . was something more. Electric, I supposed. Electric but underscored with vulnerability.

"I heard something else Silas said to you. A question. That you didn't answer." He went very still, so I pushed forward. "*Do* you want to sleep with me?" When he made no response, I added, "You told me you'd answer three questions."

"You've already gone past three."

I didn't rise to the baiting. "Grant. Answer me."

"Silas would kill me." His eyes drifted away again. "And if you— that is—I can't risk messing this up. I told you, I need this case. And I need you on it."

His body language revealed a lot more than his evasive words did. He was nervous. Nervous because he hadn't read me yet? Because he *couldn't* read me?

"You're still not answering! All you've said was why you can't. Not if you want to."

When he turned his gaze back on me, it was stormy, full of conflict and frustration. He leaned closer. "What do you think, Mirabel? Look at you! You're . . . you. And I'm me. And I'm human."

I went liquid inside. The tension was almost smothering now. It hummed between our bodies. It pulled at us, like a thousand fine, invisible threads. I placed my palm on his chest. "And you don't think I am?" I asked.

I slid my hand upward, and he stopped it with his own. "I think you have other things to worry about." He paused. "And I'm pretty sure you've actually said you don't like me."

When I tried to move my hand again, he pushed it away, pinning it against the door. And as he held it—and me—there, he banished the last fleeting space between us. There was nowhere else for me to go and nowhere I wanted to go. Something was coiled up in my chest, something tight and ready to burst.

"I don't need to like you," I said.

His fingers tightened on my wrist, and our mouths met, frantic and greedy. His other hand returned to my waist, and then a last attempt at caution tugged at him.

"Aiana will kill me too," he said. It wasn't clear who he was making the argument to.

"You think I'm a distraction? *You've* been a bigger distraction. Since the day I saw you on that ship." I barely recognized my own voice. "I don't need to marry you, Grant, but I need to get you out of my system. I need to get this done with so that I *can* worry about other things."

He held me—us—there, suspended on a razor's edge as he searched my face for some answer. At last, he must have found it, because he said, "There's no way I've been the bigger distraction."

And then his lips were on my neck, my cheek, and then back to my mouth, as hungry and demanding as before. We stumbled away from the door and ended up on the floor again, his body over mine. My hands slid under his shirt, and I didn't even realize I was digging my nails into his back until he gave a small grunt of surprise and pulled away. The weight of his gaze pinned me as much as the rest of him. I recognized the familiar, obsessive look. Only this time, it wasn't a clue he wanted to unravel.

His hands and lips moved almost everywhere on me, and in the places they didn't, I guided him there myself. I felt drunk, intoxicated both by what he did to me and the effect I had on him. This was Grant stripped of his cynicism and careful calculation. This was Grant unrestrained, his vigilant nature temporarily blinded by instinct.

I fumbled at the buttons of his shirt, and he took over, shrugging his way out of it. He was much more adept at undoing my buttons, not even needing to look at them as he trailed feather-light kisses along my neck. When he finished with my buttons, he spread the shirt open, his expression eager and expectant. What he found made him pause. "Really?" he asked.

The shirt's thin material showed a little more of me than I liked in certain lighting, so tonight I'd taken the time to put on a jump, a flexible quilted corset with no boning but plenty of laces.

Despite my ragged breathing, I managed to ask, "Would it help if I just gave you my knife?"

He shot me a dry look at that and then started in on the laces with his clever fingers, working his way down as easily as he had with the buttons. Each time he freed a cluster of laces, he'd push the jump open a little more and then continue unwrapping me. I trembled at the newness of it all, of baring myself like this. But that anxiety was fleeting, quashed by an overwhelming eagerness to seize what would happen next.

He'd almost reached the jump's bottom edge, near the waist of my pants, and I ran my hands over his arms, tracing the shape of his muscles. My fingers grazed a spot just below his shoulder where the skin felt rough and uneven. The patch was round, about the size of my fist, and when I lifted my head for a better look, I saw that it was scar, deeper and clearly more traumatic than the little ones I'd already noticed scattered over him.

"What is this?" I murmured, as he pulled out the last lace and tossed the jump across the room.

"Nothing." His eyes raked me over. "An old burn."

He brought his lips to a spot just above the center of my breastbone. I exhaled and started to close my eyes . . . but I couldn't shake that scar from my mind. A wave of emotion, oddly compassionate in such a heated moment, swept me. That wound—that burn—had been no trifle. *What a thing to endure*, I thought. It hit me in a way I didn't expect, and for a few heartbeats, my world centered on *him* rather than what I was doing with him.

I slid my hand to his face and lifted it, cupping his cheek as I looked up into his eyes. "It must have hurt so much," I said softly. "But you pretended it didn't. I know you."

He stopped and stared, looking so consumed by the moment—by me—that I wasn't even sure if he'd heard me. Then, he blinked a few times, like he was trying to wake from a dream, and I could see that razor-sharp mind forcing its way back though the haze of desire. He studied my face with a startling intensity that first seemed incredulous, then confused. A parade of other emotions soon followed: frustration, anger, and—incredibly—fear. They disappeared in a flash, his expression finally settling on coldness. He jerked away and sat back on his heels. For a few stunned moments, the only sound in the room was our labored breathing.

"What's wrong?" I asked. I reached toward him again, and he jumped to his feet.

"This is. It's done. You need to go."

I propped myself up on one elbow, too baffled to feel self-conscious about being sprawled half naked on his floor. "I . . . what? Why?"

"Because it's late." Grant snatched up his shirt and stalked to the other side of the room.

The heat of passion still burned in me, but it was starting to flicker as something icy and terrible seeped into me. I stood as well. "Grant, I didn't mean to—"

"It's late," he repeated, in a harsh tone I knew well. He was closed off again. Back in control. Invulnerable—or at least acting like he was. I watched in bewilderment as he pulled the shirt on and smoothed back his hair, still facing away from me.

"Tell me what's wrong," I insisted.

"This was a terrible— Argh." He'd started to turn, saw me, and looked away. "Can you put your shirt back on?"

I stayed as I was. "Are you actually throwing me out?"

"I'm doing you a favor. And I'll walk you home. Are you covered yet?"

"No." Anger began crowding out the remaining embers of desire. "You threw everything over there."

He stalked over to where my shirt and the jump had ended up. Still averting his eyes, he tossed them back in my direction. The laces sat in a tangled pile at my feet. There was no way the jump would be reassembled anytime soon, and I shoved it into one of the cloak's large pockets. I put just the shirt back on and buttoned it with shaking hands.

"Tell me what's going on! Did asking about the scar bother you that much?"

"Are you decent yet?"

I glanced in the mirror. Hairpins snarled my hair, creating a tangled mess that I struggled to get the wig over. I looked like . . . like a girl who'd just let a man have his way with her on the floor. Except he hadn't.

"Decent enough, considering what just happened."

He dared a tentative glance over his shoulder and turned around fully when he saw me dressed. "Hopefully it was enough to get whatever you needed out of your system. If not, I'm sure there are plenty of other men who'd help you."

"Is that what you think of me? That I'd just fall into bed with anyone?" I demanded.

"No. But you made it pretty clear what you wanted. And it's not that hard to find."

"Well, I wanted it with you!" He winced, though the rest of his expression remained unchanged. "For a moment there, you almost seemed like a—I don't know. Like a normal person. With feelings. Who connects to other people. But it doesn't matter. I'm the fool here. I can't judge you for your character when I just brazenly offered myself up."

He groaned as I stormed to the door. "Mirabel, no. It's not like that at all."

I spun around and met his eyes unblinkingly. "Then help me out, Grant. Tell me what it's like."

He seemed to sag a little. "It's hard to . . . Look, I just can't explain it right now. I don't have the words."

"I guess there's a first time for everything." I yanked the door open.

"Mirabel—"

"Don't come with me. I don't want anything from you anymore."

I slammed the door and didn't look back.

CHAPTER 17

I STOOD OUTSIDE THE DOOR FOR SEVERAL MOMENTS, taking deep breaths of the crisp night air. Fury and heartache warred with the ache of unfulfilled lust. Even in the cold, I still felt flushed remembering what we'd done. If Grant had suddenly burst out and tried to take me back to bed, I might very well have let him—and that made me madder.

What had happened?

I turned that question over and over in my brain as I descended the stairs, trying to understand. Had it all fallen apart because I'd remarked on the scar? I knew he was guarded when it came to discussing his past, but had one small inquiry irritated him enough to halt something he very obviously wanted? Or had I just killed the mood by asking? How would I know? I had no idea what I was doing. And maybe *that* was the problem. Maybe I'd been a disappointment.

I forced myself to put one foot in front of the other. Tears driven by any number of emotions brimmed in my eyes, and the colorful nightlife that usually fascinated me suddenly seemed grating. I took a roundabout path through the lively entertainment district, choosing quieter streets that still kept the safety of public areas in sight.

I wanted my bed. I wanted to close my eyes to darkness and forget this night. I wanted to forget that I'd just tried to give myself to a man—and that I'd been lacking. I'd thought I was bold and alluring, but I was only a girl playing at being a woman.

A cry from the darkness jerked me from my maudlin thoughts. I stopped and spun around. The sound had come from an alley between large tenement buildings, maybe two blocks away. It was where the streets spread out from downtown and turned more residential, with fewer lights and no meandering crowds. In fact, I couldn't see anyone over there at all. The shadows filling the alley gave up no secrets, and I wavered on whether to turn off to investigate. It would mean moving farther away from the safety of the public areas. The cry—a woman's—sounded again. I remembered the stories I'd heard of the militia's haphazard protection of the city. How many out there were helpless? How many felt as though no one could save them?

I made my decision.

I slinked toward the alley and used the shadows for my own cover. When I reached the entrance, a dull streetlamp cast flickering light upon a group of men fighting. Closer scrutiny revealed that three of them had ganged up on one. Unfair odds. And I didn't see a woman anywhere.

After a little more assessment, I realized that the single man was actually doing an amazing job at holding off the others. Maybe it was more of a fair fight than it seemed. But it triggered too many memories of the past, of gangs attacking those they outnumbered, to rob or do worse. That type of crime had occurred nightly in Osfro and was what Lonzo and I used to seek out. I started to charge forward with my knife until I realized how truly pathetic it was. Searching around, I spied a pile of discarded wood and other debris lying nearby. I grabbed a board, about the length of my forearm, that looked like it hadn't rotted yet.

The lone fighter was in a standoff with two of the men while the third attempted to come in from the side. I sneaked up behind him and slammed the board into his back as hard as I could, knocking him to his knees. The unexpected attack made his two companions falter, giving their victim an opportunity to punch one in the jaw. Before any retaliation could take place, the lone man deftly rolled across the ground and sprang neatly to his feet on the alley's far side. As he did, he scooped up a sword lying nearby and pointed it at the others.

The man I'd hit staggered upright and turned toward me, but the swordsman moved faster. He leapt over to us, jabbing his blade into my assailant's shoulder with practiced ease. The man screamed and fell again. Without pause, the sword-wielder moved on to his next adversary, knocking that one down with a blow to the head.

"Want to try your luck?" he asked the third.

That man spoke boldly but backed away nonetheless. "Your crew cheated our boss! Your man had no right to swipe that shipment out from under us."

"Your boss has cheated us plenty of times," the swordsman replied amiably. "And if he had any honor, he wouldn't have ordered an attack like this. Now get out of here while we're all still friends." He glanced between his former assailants. They'd all managed to stand again but hadn't retreated. "And we *are* all still friends, right?" That amiable voice had an edge to it, as sharp and deadly as the sword he held.

"Yeah, we're still friends," said the one I'd hit, not sounding friendly at all. "Come on." He beckoned to his comrades, and they slowly walked away, but not without several backward glances.

When they'd disappeared from sight, the swordsman said, "It's safe now."

I thought he was talking to me until I heard a stirring behind another pile of trash. A woman rose, holding a small child wrapped in blankets to her. "Thank you, Tom. Thank you so much."

"Nothing to thank me for. I thought Abernathy was better than this, but even I'm wrong sometimes. I'll make sure there's no repeat. Let me take you home."

"Oh, no. I can't trouble you anymore. It's just over there. Thank you again. The blessings of the Six upon you."

The woman scurried away, and the man didn't take his eyes off of her until she entered a building down the street. Then he turned to me.

He wore a mask, but it wasn't meant for the elements, like mine.

It was one of the ornamental ones, much as I'd seen among the ear-lier revelers. "And now, my guardian angel, I need to thank you." He sheathed his sword and bowed before me, sweeping his cloak away with a great flourish. "Tom Shortsleeves, at your service."

"It . . . it's nice to meet you, Mister Shortsleeves," I replied, using the Belsian accent again. Even with his sword away, I kept my distance.

He straightened up and tilted his head inquisitively. "You haven't heard of me?"

"No." Sensing this disappointed him, I added, "But I've only just arrived in the city."

"Ah. Then you are forgiven, Miss . . . ?" He shrugged when I didn't answer. "No matter. Angels don't need names to do their deeds. Only brave hearts."

The mask. The sword. The theatrics. "Are you . . ." I paused, grap-pling with a polite way to phrase my next question. "Are you one of the men trying to be a pirate?"

He threw his head back and laughed. "My dear, I am the one *they* are all trying to be."

"Well, like I said, I just got here. There's a lot I don't know."

And one thing I didn't know was if I was in danger. Grant had ex-plained the pirates' bizarre role as law enforcement, but I hadn't really believed it. Yet . . . this pirate—or whatever he was—had just saved a mother and child before my eyes.

"You're pretty skilled with a plank," Tom said. He gestured toward the board I had dropped.

I held out my knife. "It seemed more effective than this."

He leaned closer, but it was only to look. "A pillow would be more effective than that. At least then you could suffocate someone. A proper guardian angel needs a proper sword. But first things first. Let's get in out of the cold and find a drink."

Leave with him? Absolutely not. There was only so much benefit of the doubt I was willing to give. "I'm sorry, I can't. There's somewhere I'm supposed to be."

"Right here, apparently." Tom waved around. "You help saved innocents. Sounds like fate to me."

"Why were those men attacking her?"

"Her husband is one of my associates, and that lot thinks they've been wronged. It was pure and simple revenge."

"So you were the one in the right?"

"Always," he said, chuckling again. "Always."

I didn't know if I believed him, but his smile was infectious. "I'm just glad they're okay. And you. But really, I can't stay." I kept my tone light . . . and my hold on the knife strong.

Tom didn't push any further. "Suit yourself, but I'll feel terrible for the rest of the night, you know. I hate unpaid debts. Here." He made a big show of producing a coin from his pocket and handed it to me. It looked like a standard Osfridian copper, but the side with the king's face had been heated and re-engraved with a feather. On the other side, the seal of Osfrid had been crossed over with "TS."

"Defacement of the king's coin is illegal," I said.

"The king's coin? I don't see his initials on it." Tom closed my fingers around the coin and held my hand in his. "This is my personal token, given out to only a few when I owe a debt. So if you need a favor, come cash this in at the tavern of the Dancing Bull."

"I'll keep that in mind," I said, wondering what favor I could possibly need from him.

"Do." He stepped away and bowed, again making a big show of throwing back his cape, before disappearing into the darkness. "Until next time, angel."

Just when I didn't think my night could get any weirder, I crossed paths with Aiana as I neared the entrance by the fort. She'd seen me in the blonde disguise before but still did a double take. "Mira? Is that you?"

I stopped and hoped the mask would conceal my feelings. "It's me."

She beckoned me toward a building, away from the busy pedestrian thoroughfare. I caught the faint scent of wine on her. "Did you give Grant what he needed?"

"Eh, that's debatable, but I delivered the news I had."

"Then I'll walk you home," she said.

I shook my head. "You're on your way somewhere else. I don't want to delay you."

She nudged me forward. "I was just going to my place. My night is done. Come on."

I didn't think I needed an escort, but tolerating her company was probably easier than arguing with her. And she wasn't Grant.

We walked in companionable silence until we reached the highway. She exhaled. "What a night."

That was an understatement. "Was yours good at least?" I asked.

"No, not at all." Her voice sounded more upbeat than I'd expect for that kind of statement. No, not upbeat. Rueful. "Iyitsi will enjoy telling me all about how he warned me."

I frowned, vaguely recalling Grant's earlier words. "He said . . . he said something about a romance."

Aiana laughed at that. "Did he? I can imagine the way he said it."

"Sorry, it's none of my business."

"It's fine. I just hate that he's always right. It makes him smug—more so than usual." She sighed again, her voice growing sober. "Maybe he's right. Maybe I'm not cut out for love."

"No!" I exclaimed. "You're wonderful. You just haven't met the right person yet. Don't listen to him."

"You're sweet. And he *is* probably the last person I should be getting advice from. I mean, you've been around him enough. He's not that sentimental. Certainly no romantic."

I hesitated, unsure if I really wanted to know the answer to what I asked next. "That one night you two fought . . . you mentioned something to him about how you at least learn your lovers' names . . ."

She groaned. "I shouldn't have said that. It was mean. And to be fair, I'm sure he learns their names first. Though I doubt he remembers them."

"It's hard to picture him, um, having any lovers."

"Well, 'lover' might be too generous a term. Maybe 'partner' is better? I always think a lover is someone you see more than once. Anyway, it doesn't really matter. It's not exactly a common occurrence for him. He doesn't usually have the patience to charm anyone."

"I can't really picture him charming anyone either."

"Oh, he can do it if he really tries." We wound along a trail as she pondered my question. After a few moments, she chuckled. "I remember one time we were traveling up north and stopped at an inn for the night. We were eating in their common room, and they had this lovely barmaid waiting the tables. The most beautiful blue eyes in the world. And he came to life."

Suddenly, I was absolutely certain I didn't want to hear this. "Aiana, you really don't need to—"

"You wouldn't have recognized him. I barely did. Who'd have thought he could be so charming? I suppose it's just another one of Iyitsi's masks. He put everything he had into wooing her—and it seemed to be working. After she finished her shift, she sat at our table all evening. She laughed. She smiled. She was having a good time. He was so proud of himself too. And why not? Since she stayed so long, she must have been interested, right?"

When Aiana paused, I realized I was supposed to say something. "Um, I guess?"

"Oh yes. She was definitely interested. Just not in him." Aiana laughed so loudly that I glanced around uneasily. "You should've seen the look on his face when she went back to *my* room. I almost feel bad about it sometimes. Almost. He had better luck with some other girl the next night, so things worked out for him. Then we were on the road again, and he never looked back. He never does. He doesn't want to be attached to anyone. He doesn't want them to be attached to him."

I was past the point of even trying to carry my half of the conversation. One foot in front of the other. That was all I had to do. We'd reached the marsh, so Wisteria Hollow wasn't much farther.

"So, that's him. But me? I don't know." Aiana's voice continued in the darkness, suddenly more subdued. "A night like that is fun, but it's not what I really want. I want to wake up to the same person every morning. I want to be able to tell her anything. I want honesty and understanding. I want to be dizzy with love and feel it grow more and more each day. But maybe that's too much to ask. Maybe you and Iyitsi have it right after all."

"What?" Was it possible she'd found out?

"I see you at those parties, Mira. You're like him. You aren't looking for attachment either." The lights of Wisteria Hollow peeped through the trees ahead. Her earlier sadness returned. "You stay cool. You don't lose your head. And you know what? You should probably keep doing that—because then you won't lose your heart either."

I stared up at the sky, noting the position of Ariniel's star. "Thanks," I said dully. "I'll try to remember that."

CHAPTER 18

I SPENT ALMOST THE ENTIRE NEXT DAY PROCESSING WHAT had happened with Grant. His rejection filled me with humiliation. I'd brushed off a lot of advances over the years, and as much as I hated to admit it, they had left me with the egotistical assumption that *of course* men wanted me. All I had to do was show up. Discovering that wasn't true still stung.

Aiana's tipsy recounting of Grant's past left me unsettled too—but that was a more complex feeling to understand. Why should I care that he sought impersonal, one-time liaisons? His dislike of attachment had never been a secret. And I'd made my own intentions very clear. I wanted my own shot at passion before being locked into marriage. I'd even gone so far as to say it didn't matter if I liked him or not. So, why had he sent me away? I'd offered him exactly the type of arrangement he liked.

"You look like I feel."

I blinked out of my dreary thoughts to find Cedric leaning against the staircase's bannister. Everyone had returned from the evening's social affairs, and I was the last one to come inside from my group. I stifled a yawn and paused at the bottom of the steps. He was as dashing and impeccably dressed as ever, but an obvious gloom hung over him.

"You look pretty down yourself," I said. "What's your excuse? Too much dancing and small talk? That's what's worn me out."

His expression stayed dark. "I wish that's what it was. Did you hear about the Alanzans who were taken?"

"What? No . . ." But then I remembered Grant mentioning how Warren Doyle's patrols had succeeded in arresting their first batch of heretics. I hadn't known what sect they'd captured. I peered around, verifying we were alone. "Were you there when they came?"

"I got away. I was one of the lucky ones."

"If you were recognized—"

"I wasn't."

I repressed the urge to chastise him about the dangers of worshipping with others of his faith. I'd been around enough Alanzans in my life, however, to realize the futility of that argument. Their principles were too strong. "What will happen to them?"

"They're being held in a city jail right now. Tomorrow, they'll get split up. Some will be locked away at the prison in Archerwood. Others have been sentenced to penal servitude. Do you know what that is?"

"Unfortunately." I felt sickened, thinking of those poor prisoners' fates and the abuses of the system. In my head, those Alanzans wore the faces of Pablo, Fernanda, and countless other friends.

"And there's nothing I can do about it." He gave me a wan smile. "I wish I could be like your father. He wouldn't let them sit there. I wish I had the courage—and skill—to march up there and set them free. But I'd probably just get myself arrested. Or killed."

I patted his arm. "Don't do something reckless or blame yourself. You show your courage in other ways."

He looked skeptical of that and bid me good night. But as he retreated, I felt my heart start to race. Cedric was right about one thing. My father wouldn't let those Alanzans suffer in prison or forced servitude. He wouldn't prance around in jewels and finery while they awaited grim fates. He would take action. He *would* march up there and set the Alanzans free. He would call me selfish for standing to the side. He would call me a coward . . . again.

But I wasn't my father, no matter how much I wanted to be

sometimes. The desire to help the Alanzans burned in my chest. I needed to act, to strike out and save the innocent. But I couldn't break into a jail. I didn't command a network of freedom fighters.

Or did I?

I sprinted to my room and lifted my mattress, retrieving the coin Tom had given me. I squeezed it in my hand. I commanded one freedom fighter. Well, maybe "commanded" wasn't the right word. But he did owe me a favor. What was that favor worth?

It was time to find out.

I made my usual escape, and along the woodsy trail, I noted that the ground was softening even more as the weather warmed. I wore pretty kid leather shoes tonight, which were an upgrade from dance slippers, but they still sank deep in the mud. I'd have to scrub them before Mistress Culpepper saw.

In Cape Triumph proper, I had to ask for directions a few times before locating the Dancing Bull Tavern. Inside, I found it just as packed as the tavern Grant and I had hid in, but it didn't have the same sleazy edge. It was more brightly lit too. Sure, there were made-up women there—women whose intentions were obvious. But they moved about discreetly, with no vulgar public displays. Only two women were roughly dressed, like me. They sat at their tables and drank with hardened eyes, giving the impression that anyone who harassed them would soon regret it.

The rest of the patrons were men. Many wore masks. Some huddled in corners, furtive expressions on their faces. Others, more boisterous, played cards and dice in large groups. Attire ran the full range of common work clothes to the showier looks of the pirates. Some of that pirate attire appeared well-worn, but a number of men displayed the excessively flamboyant, impractical look of pirate pretenders. A man in a white apron scurried around to keep everyone's ale filled, and a woman working the bar made sure there was plenty on hand.

I didn't see Tom anywhere.

Suddenly doubting myself, I lingered just inside the door and contemplated my next move. Tom hadn't provided detailed instructions. A few men eyed me curiously, and I realized I needed to do something decisive before I attracted unwanted attention. I walked over to the bartender.

"Excuse me," I told her in the Belsian accent, "I need to see Tom Shortsleeves."

She was an older woman and didn't look up until she'd finished pouring ale into a wooden mug. When she spoke, her voice was harsh. "You and everyone else. Get in line."

I pulled his coin from my pocket and held it up. "Will this get me to the front of it?"

She grimaced as she studied it and then gave a swift nod. "Jenks," she yelled across the room. "Get over here."

A giant of a man rose from a card table. He wore a mask and had haphazardly shoved it up over his forehead. "Whatcha need?"

"This one's looking for Tom," she said.

A lopsided grin filled his face as he took me in. "Aw, you don't need him, sweetheart. Let me buy you a drink."

The woman gestured impatiently. "Show Jenks what you have."

When I took out the coin, his smiled diminished but not his good humor. "Oh, well, aren't you lucky."

"I need a favor," I explained.

Jenks's eyes glowed. "I always love those favors. Lemme cash out, and I'll track him down."

He disappeared in the crowd, leaving me to wait awkwardly at the bar while the woman continued her work. Casks of ale and bottles of wine filled the shelves behind her, and I noted a gun lying on a lower one. At one point, the man delivering drinks hurried up to her.

"The ones in the corner want a bottle of the Harkford red."

Her displeasure deepened. "That's all the way in the back of the cellar."

He placed a handful of silver and gold coins on the counter. "They're serious about it. I'd go get it, but you know how he is . . ."

"I know, I know." She set down a mug with such force that its contents sloshed out. "I'll take care of it."

The server returned to his work, and I watched as she bent down out of view behind the bar. When she straightened up, she held a key ring. She lifted up a section of the bar that allowed her to step out and walked away without comment to a small, nondescript door in the back. She unlocked it with the key and disappeared. I stared at the closed door, fascinated.

"Well, well, as I live and breathe. My angel has decided to grace me with her presence."

I turned at the sound of the theatrical voice and found Tom striding toward me, Jenks at his side. Here, in the light, I had a better sense of Tom's features. He was older than me, by at least five years or so. His hair was a honeyed blond, pulled back into a tail, though much of it had loosened. The black mask emphasized green eyes. And once his cloak was pushed back, I could see peacock feathers trimming the edges of his elbow-length shirtsleeves.

"Well, I know you hate unpaid debts." I pointed at one of his arms. "Which came first: the sleeves or the name?"

He grinned back. "Does it matter? The one can't exist without the other anymore. It's part of my image."

"It's still pretty cold outside. Is image worth that?"

"Image is everything," he assured me. "Now, Jenks claims you came flashing the coin around. Tell me he's wrong and that you just wanted to see me."

Adelaide's advice from the ship suddenly struck me with perfect clarity. *If you're ever in some situation that needs a crazy solution, just be confident. If you act completely convinced about something, people will go along with it.* This situation was unquestionably crazy, and I knew I had to play up my persona to stay afloat. I smiled slyly.

"Why can't it be both?" I proffered the coin again and lowered my voice. "But it *is* mostly business, I'm afraid. I have some friends who are in trouble—friends currently being held in the militia's jail. They're going to be moved out tomorrow."

"Ah," said Tom. "*Those* prisoners. I never took you for a worshipper. I figured an angel would have her own circle of devotees."

"I'm not Alanzan. But I don't want them held there—or transferred to a worse place. I thought you were someone who could help." I paused, as if reconsidering my decision. "But maybe you can't."

Jenks had been standing a respectful distance away, pretending not to listen, but he let out a great bellow. "She's calling your bluff," he told Tom.

Tom snatched the coin from me. "Nothing to bluff about. Mostly I'm disappointed she didn't ask for something more challenging. How many men do you think they've got on watch there?"

"Two usually." Jenks scratched his head. "Probably double if they're keeping a bigger group of prisoners."

"Easy enough then. Let's go rustle some of the others up." Tom beckoned me to follow as he and Jenks moved back toward the crowd.

I glanced between them. "Right now?"

"Sure," said Tom. "You need it done right away, don't you?"

"Well . . . yes. But I thought there'd be some sort of plan."

"Of course there is. We'll overpower them, get your friends, and be on our way."

I was so used to Grant's calculation and scrutiny that a quick, impulsive act was startling.

As we crossed the room, the crowd's indifferent air shifted dramatically. People stopped what they were doing, shouting out greetings to Tom. He responded in kind, calling many of them by name and making jokes as he did. A few of the pirate pretenders jumped to their feet, hoping to be noticed. They shot me envious looks, and I tried to act like I was completely unimpressed by a den of pirates. Secretly, I was fascinated. I could understand the glamour and intrigue that surrounded them—especially if saving others was a regular practice. But what about their other activities? Stealing? Assault?

Tom kept walking until he reached a table where three masked men played cards. All immediately looked up. "Gentlemen," he announced. "Allow me to present the angel I told you about the other night, the one who rushed bravely into battle, defending me against some of Abernathy's goons."

One of the men guffawed. "I still can't believe you needed help."

"I wouldn't have needed any help if *someone* had told me Abernathy was still angry about that incident last week." Tom looked pointedly at another of the men, a gaunt one in a striped shirt who seemed very young.

"I hadn't heard anything, boss! Honest," cried the man. "And you know me. I've always got an ear to the ground."

Tom smiled, but there was a tightness in his voice. "Well, use both ears from now on."

One of the men, his head shaved and a silver hoop in his ear, stood and shook my hand. "I'm Elijah. That was my wife and boy you helped. You need anything, you ask."

Despite his tough appearance, I heard true emotion in his voice. "I'm glad to have helped," I said.

"Are you from the continent, Miss?" The question came from the man in the striped shirt. "Skarsia?"

"*Lady*," corrected Tom. "One must always address an angel as 'lady.' And anyone who knows anything knows she's from Belsia, not Skarsia. Anders is from Skarsia. Does she sound like him?" Tom's gaze swiveled to me. "But we really must decide on a name for you at some point."

"You can call me whatever you want," I said, "as long as we can help those people."

"She's all business, our angel." Tom nodded at Elijah and the young man. "You two are visiting the jail with us. Peterson, go find Anders and make sure that shipment goes as planned." To me, Tom said, "This isn't really the kind of thing that requires a mastermind to pull off. You don't even have to come along, if you don't want to."

The old thrill of helping Lonzo and my father coursed through me, but I didn't know exactly what Tom was asking. "What would you have me do?"

"Knock a few heads together. Swing a sword." He scrutinized my waist. "Do you even have one? Or just that sad excuse for a knife?"

I pushed back my cloak and remembered I needed to play bold, no matter how embarrassed the blade made me. "It's better than nothing."

"Debatable. Peterson, please assist the lady."

Peterson removed a leather sheath from his belt and handed it over without question. I ran my fingers over the wooden hilt, embellished with bronze and bone, and pulled out a dirk. Its straight steel blade was about seven inches long and had a point so sharp, it probably could have cut my old knife in half. More than a dagger, less than a sword. I hadn't practiced with a weapon like this in years and never with anything so fine. It took my breath away, and I admired it for several more moments before sliding it back into its holder.

"I can't—"

"Hush," interrupted Tom. "And tell me if you're coming with us or not."

I bit my lip and felt like I was standing on the edge of this blade, teetering between two drastic decisions. I'd come to Cape Triumph with simple plans. Settle into comfortable married life, pay off Lonzo's bond. And then I'd become entangled in espionage. I'd sneaked out of Wisteria Hollow's protective circle. I'd robbed a home. I'd interacted with pirates . . . and now I was going to fight alongside them.

"I'll go," I said, fastening on the dirk.

Tom beamed. "You're certain?"

"Positive. I need this."

I needed to remember the principles I'd always held so dear. I needed to remember what it was like to fight for the innocent. And— at least for a night—I needed to forget about Grant Elliott.

CHAPTER 19

CAPE TRIUMPH'S MAIN JAIL WAS OUTSIDE THE ACTIVE city center but close enough to simplify prisoner transfers to the courthouse. "There are smaller holding areas," Tom told me as we traveled in the darkness. "The soldiers have one at the fort. And the militia has a watch of sorts that also maintain a couple. But mostly those places are just to hold petty criminals. Keep drunks confined overnight. The bigger prizes are kept here."

"It all sounds very . . . sloppy," I said. "The city watch in Osfro wasn't always effective, but at least they had a system. Here, there's no real central law enforcement."

"Then they're lucky we're around," Tom said cheerfully. "The burden of justice falls on us."

"Something tells me your justice is selective. And profitable."

"A city watch would get paid. Why not us?"

We stopped about a quarter mile from the jail while Lesser Tom— the young, skinny man—scouted ahead. Since his name was Tom too, the "lesser" designation differentiated them. It wasn't clear to me if Tom or the other men had come up with the addition.

"Jenks was right," Lesser Tom said, trotting back to us. "More than usual. Six."

"Six?" said Tom irritably. "You promised me four, Jenks."

"I didn't promise you nothing. I just said *probably* it'd be double."

Lesser Tom added, "They're militia. Not soldiers."

"Well, that's something," said Tom. "Now. Tell us everything else you saw."

Five minutes later, we had a plan and were all moving toward the jail, keeping off the main road. A lamp near the front door showed us what we needed. The rectangular building was barren and rough, with no windows. Two men stood sentry at the front, and each corner was guarded by one man.

We spread out into the positions Tom had designated for us, and anticipation crackled through me as I moved to a dark patch of trees with Elijah. I'd never gone into a planned altercation. Usually they just happened to me. My grip on the dirk was so tight that I had to keep adjusting it so my fingers wouldn't kink up.

The action started with a gunshot. It was Lesser Tom, firing near one of the guards in the back of the building. Tom had made it very clear he wanted to avoid killing anyone tonight. "The militia is very lenient with us," he'd explained. "And I want to keep it that way."

He'd also warned that because the militia were so inconsistently trained, they were likely to react recklessly. At the crack of the gun, all the guards raced off toward the sound's source—except one. He remained at his post by the front door. Elijah, who was with me, swore. We'd hoped that the guards would all run to the building's back, where our other three companions were waiting.

"Nothing for it," said Elijah. "Let's go. Stay behind me, angled over there. You're the smaller target—he'll go for me, but it's better if you're still out of the way."

The militiaman at the door saw us coming and raised his musket. He fired at Elijah, as predicted, but missed. He'd shot too soon with a gun like that. A few more feet would have given him better accuracy. Elijah and I were on the man before he could reload. Elijah knocked him to the ground and kept him pinned. The guard shouted obscenities as I tied his hands and wrists, and I wished we'd brought gags as well as ropes. Just as I finished, I saw the door open behind Elijah.

"Look out!"

Elijah turned as the barrel of a gun poked out. I leapt up and swung my dirk like a club, knocking the gun off-kilter just enough to miss Elijah when it fired. That gave Elijah the opportunity to pry the door open and grab the gun's owner, another militiaman. Elijah swung him hard into the wall, but the man was stockier and pushed back with his own brute strength. Looking beyond their fight, I spotted yet another guard. Lesser Tom's scouting had only shown us the outside defense. We hadn't known for sure what to expect in here.

That second man hadn't seen me yet. As much as I longed to valiantly wield my dirk, it was Lonzo's training I used. This guard wasn't as muscled as the one Elijah fought, but he was taller than me. I darted forward and took him by surprise, slamming my elbow into his face in a move that put me too close for him to shoot. Instead, he immediately tried to strike back by swinging his gun like I had the dirk. His height worked against him. I wasn't where he expected, which forced him to shift his footing in order to keep his balance as I kept moving erratically. He dropped his weapon and started to go for me with his fists. I used those split seconds to deliver another upward hit, this time to his neck. It lacked precision, but it was efficient. The man let out a small cry and staggered backward. I snatched up the musket and pointed it at him, yelling at him to drop to his knees. I'd never fired a gun before and hoped I could bluff convincingly.

Apparently I could. He obeyed, and I heard a great laugh behind me. "Look at you," said Elijah. "You didn't even need me. No wonder you were able to scare off Abernathy's gang that night." His combatant was lying on the floor, presumably unconscious. Elijah strolled up to my captive and began tying up his wrists.

"I don't know that I did that much scaring. But I'm glad to have helped your family."

Elijah frowned as he finished his work. "They shouldn't have been in that situation. That whole Abernathy mess was Tom's arrog—"

A gunshot sounded from outside, and I looked around in alarm. "Should we do something?"

"No," Elijah said. "That's their job. Let's do ours."

He took the keys from the unconscious man, and we searched the building. It had two corridors splitting off in opposite directions, with ten cells in each. Frightened men and women peered at us through the bars. They'd heard the commotion but had no idea what it meant.

"It's okay," I said, as Elijah unlocked the cells. "We're here to help." As the prisoners hurried past one by one, something occurred to me. "We don't know that they're all Alanzans. We could be freeing hardened criminals."

"Yup," Elijah agreed. "But we don't have time to conduct interviews."

The last of the prisoners ran out the front door, just as Tom and the others strolled in. He grinned. "Looks like everything worked out."

"You should've seen your girl," said Elijah. He pushed the man I'd subdued toward one of the cells. "You didn't tell me she could fight like that."

We locked up all of the militiamen. Tom's crew had a few more cuts and bruises than when this had started, but no one on either side had been shot. The prisoners had long since disappeared into the night when we finally left.

"Thank you," I told Tom as we walked back toward the main city. "I know you'll say you owed me the favor, but still. I appreciate it."

"Happy to." Silence fell for several moments. "Exhilarating, isn't it?"

"What?"

"The rush of battle." He waved his hands around grandly. "The thrill of it. The blood pounding through you. Every part of you on alert. It's hard to come down off the high."

I did feel a rush of sorts. All my senses seemed sharper and clearer. "Yes," I admitted. "And it is hard to come down."

"This isn't the first time you've been in a fight."

"No, but never anything like this." My father had taught me some basic fighting skills but rarely let me go along on any of his raids. I'd been shuffled to the side as pretty bait. Only Lonzo, in our brief time together in Osfro, had treated me as an equal partner and enhanced my training. "It feels good—knowing we saved innocent people from oppression. That's a rush too."

"Well, who can say if they're truly innocent?" Tom asked dryly. "But we did save them from oppression, I suppose. Now. If you've still got a bit of battle lust left in you, I'm sure there are other stops we could make."

I hesitated. "I should really go."

"I can make sure they're noble ones, just for you."

"No. Really, I have to go." I hardened my resolve against the tempting offer. "I shouldn't even be out. But I'm grateful. You more than made up for what I did."

"Ah, well. Maybe next time."

"There isn't going to be a next time."

He pressed a hand to his heart. "You wound me again. Half the men back at the Bull would kill to work for me."

"Work for you? They're welcome to it. And why would you want me anyway? I don't have nearly the experience your other men have." A hollow feeling settled in the pit of my stomach, and I stepped away, suddenly aware of how quiet the streets we'd taken back into the city were. "Look, if you think 'working' for you is going to include something else on the side—"

He scoffed. "You are a pleasure to behold, but no, nothing like that. You held your own tonight, and something tells me you're a fast learner. It'd be worth your while too. Lesser Tom!"

We'd walked far ahead of the others, and Lesser Tom came scurrying to our sides. "Yeah?"

"Show her what I paid you earlier for the visit to Judge Mathers's house."

Lesser Tom reached into his pockets, and I did a double take when he produced two handfuls of silver coins. I counted about twenty. "I spent a few on drinks," he admitted.

Tom waved him aside. "No matter. Thank you."

Lesser Tom put the money away and immediately fell back. Tom shot me a sidelong glance. "You see? I make sure everyone is well compensated. Sometimes they're paid in gold."

Gold? I still felt dazzled by all that silver. "I . . . I didn't do what I did tonight for money. I wouldn't want to. I did it because it was the right thing to do."

"Even an angel's got to eat. But I do like the way you think. Many talk about justice and fighting for change. Few live it. My men are good souls, but most do this for the money. They've got to eat too. I could use someone at my side who truly fights with a noble spirit."

I scrutinized his face in the lamplight, gauging his sincerity. "Do you *really* want nobility? It doesn't seem like you're giving away all your earnings to charity. Those feathers can't be cheap."

"They aren't, but image is important." He fondly stroked the green and blue feathers that adorned one of his sleeves. "I have to keep some for operating expenses. And I freely admit I'm no angel—I like my profit. But I'm also not as selfish as you think. I see the city's downtrodden every day. There's corruption and abuse of power around here, and I have a lot of ideas about how to improve things."

The sincerity in his voice took me by surprise. "Is robbing people improving things?"

"It's not like I'm stealing bread from orphans. I mostly deal in rare and valuable goods, exquisite things that aren't always easy to get ahold of—but pay off well for that difficulty. And trust me, the men we take them from aren't exactly hurting for money."

"They might still be good people, even if they're rich. And I'm sure some get killed when you attack them. Is that fair?"

"No, and neither is the fact that plenty of good people are starving and suffering here. The coin and food I've given away has saved many of them."

"And you . . . you just want me to fight with you?" I asked reluctantly.

"Definitely. Sometimes to 'acquire' goods. Sometimes to issue a warning to those who think they can trample others. I'll try to keep you out of jobs that might go against your angelic principles. And I'd also need you for another task. I aim for luxuries, but plenty of mundane goods fall into my hands that I can't use. Basics, like food and clothing. My workload is going up, and I don't have as much time to distribute that surplus to those in need. Something tells me you'd like that job. And I also think the city would be enchanted by a lovely angel helping them."

"Do you want to use me to boost your image?"

He grinned. "Well, as I said, image is important. But I don't 'use' anyone. The people I work with aren't tools to be pushed around and cast away."

The temptation . . . I could barely hold it back. Gold for Lonzo. Purpose for me. But at what cost? "I can't. I have other commitments."

His eyebrows rose. "Oh. Some husband or lover?"

"No!" My voice gave away too much, and Tom laughed.

"Oh, I see. It's one of those complicated things, eh? All the more reason to make your own way. And I saw your face when Lesser Tom flashed those coins we got from the judge. You have some debts, perhaps?"

The possibility of paying off Lonzo's bond and my own contract suddenly made me heady, but I tried to hide it. "Judge . . . you mentioned Judge Mathers?"

"You know him?" asked Tom, interest clearly piqued.

"Sort of. And I know what he does. The bribes. The shady sentencing of penal workers."

"Then you know he's a bad man who breaks the law."

"*We* just broke the law."

"For the greater good, remember?" Tom's voice hardened. "He sold off a few of our associates recently, to plantation work. Those sentences are far too long for petty theft. No one in my crew, but it's an insult to our brotherhood. He's never punished for what he does."

"What did you do to him?"

"The usual. Let him know we're watching. We stopped by his house, relieved him of a few things, put the fear of the wayward angels into him and his servants. No one died, if that's what you're wondering. I try to avoid friction with the militia if I can help it."

We came to a halt in front of the Dancing Bull, but I didn't follow the other men in. "Tom—"

"No more protests. You need more than money. There's something burning in you. I can see it. You really want to be an avenging angel who rights the wrongs of the world? This is the way. Come back tomorrow night." His face was alight with excitement. "I've got some grain from a job last week I've been meaning to dole out. Come see the other side of what we do."

"I'll think about it," I said at last.

Tom caught my hand and kissed it as I started to move away. "Do more than think, Aviel."

"Aviel?"

"An angel needs a name. Why not the heavenly defender of women and the innocent? Unless you think that's sacrilegious."

I laughed as I began backing away down the street. "After everything else we did tonight? Hardly."

He bid farewell with a grand bow. "Then I'll see you tomorrow, Lady Aviel."

CHAPTER 20

I DID COME BACK. AND IT DIDN'T TAKE LONG FOR ME TO become the hot topic of Wisteria Hollow's nightly gossip. Well, not exactly *me*. Lady Aviel.

In barely a week of working with Tom's crew, the identity he'd given me had blazed through the city. Cape Triumph already had a few female pirates, but they didn't seize the imagination the way I did. Part of that came just by being around Tom. As one of the city's most flamboyant buccaneers, anyone in his company picked up a little glamour. He certainly had an abundance to share. But I was also younger than the other lady pirates, which somehow resulted in stories of incredible—and, in my opinion, exaggerated—beauty. Rolling that up with my angelic identity made me into something larger than life. Something otherworldly. A true angel of justice.

And maybe that was because I really *was* out for justice, not just profit. Not every job was selfless, of course. Tom diligently sought out the city's corrupt officials, but there was no question that his main focus was profit. I was amazed at how hard he worked for those luxuries and at how many he accrued. I was also amazed that, with the kind of prices he sold them for, he didn't just build a palace outside the city and retire.

Tom also kept to his word about having me distribute some of the more ordinary goods that fell into his hands. The people we helped knew I was one of his associates, and my work reflected well on him. But they also realized that the surge in his giving had happened at the same time I'd arrived. And they loved me for it.

As for me? I earned five gold for that week's labor. *Five gold*. Until working with Tom, I'd never even touched one gold coin.

Those busy nights made for exhausting days with the Glittering Court. A handful of girls had already become engaged, and the Thorns were determined to see the rest of us locked into marriage offers as well. We didn't get breaks.

To everyone's amazement, Adelaide wasn't yet among the engaged girls. Warren had maintained his aggressive pursuit, and it seemed as though many men had backed off and conceded to what must be an obvious victory.

"Have you seen Warren recently?" I asked her one night. We stood in front of our bedroom mirror, making last-minute tweaks before heading out to an evening event. "He hasn't been at any of our recent parties."

She smoothed the skirt of her white silk gown. Its silver embroidery sparkled in the candlelight. "I think he's busy preparing for his trip to Hadisen."

"Surely he's not too busy for you," I teased. His courtship left me conflicted. Whenever we did see him, he treated her like a queen—and with his impending governorship, he had the ability to make her one, at least by Adorian standards. On the other hand, it was hard for me to shake his role as an active organizer of the heretic hunters. I knew his opinions on heretics were shared by many residents, but I still wished she had a more open-minded suitor in the running.

I had no idea if Grant had joined the patrols or not. I'd dutifully made note of any useful conversations or observations at the events I went to. I'd picked a couple of drawers in search of evidence. And I'd even gathered a few tips about the city's underworld in my work with Tom. Everything I learned went to Aiana, but she never said how it was received. And Grant sent no message at all.

Tonight's dinner party had particular significance—because it was at the Chambers plantation. Cornelius had continued ardently

pitching his father whenever we ran into each other. I knew he thought
showing off the grandeur of their home would be the ultimate sell, and
as our carriage pulled up to the opulent estate, I had to admit that he
had good reason for pride.

"It's fantastic, isn't it?" he said, almost as soon as I walked in the
door. "There's no way you can doubt our family's standing."

"I never doubted it before," I replied.

He went on and on about their means until another guest pulled
him away. Never once did he mention his father's virtues. I supposed
he figured that, with the age difference, material goods would mean
more to me than the man who possessed them.

I actually liked Rupert quite a bit and purposely sought him out
after dinner. He sat in a plush, overly stuffed chair and surveyed the
festivities with amusement.

"Miss Viana. What a pleasure."

He started to rise, and I waved him down as I pulled up a smaller
chair. "And for me, Mister Chambers. How have you been?"

"Oh, the same. I lead a quiet life, you know. And now Cornelius
insists I ease up on managing our workers. So, lately, my most exciting
days are when new books arrive from Osfrid. I've kept my eyesight,
but the arthritis is getting worse." He opened one of his hands for emphasis and then curled it up again. "I'd had it in my head to write my
life's story, but I don't think these old hands could manage it anymore.
I'd have to dictate to a servant."

"I hope you do. You're an inspiration to everyone who comes to
Adoria for a better life. Look at all you've achieved."

He glanced around the great room but didn't appear that impressed. "There's certainly a bit more to it than there used to be, especially since Lavinia arrived. She has lavish tastes—*very* lavish—and
Cornelius indulges her. But that's young love."

"It's all very grand," I said diplomatically, but I caught his meaning.
Lavish bordered on gaudy. Some thoughtful architect had built the
room with simple but elegant lines, and I could make out remnants

of what must have once been a very dignified aesthetic. Now, it was like someone had covered it up and hadn't known when to stop adding embellishments. Curtains made of brilliant crimson velvet. Vases and sculptures on every surface. Enormous paintings that would have looked lovely, if only *one* of them had been centered on a bare wall. Instead, they sat side by side in a disorienting display. Our earlier dinner had been served with the finest crystal and china I'd ever seen. And everything in the house seemed unnecessarily gilded.

"Lavinia's even very particular about what we drink," Rupert added, his voice wistful. "Only the elitist Evarian wines for her. I miss my rum. It's the spiced kind, from Royal Point. Have you ever had it? Marvelous. But she thinks it's too 'common' and had the audacity to store it away on the pantry's highest shelf. Can you believe that? Out of my reach, like I'm some naughty child. Then she put the fear of the Six into any servant caught fetching it for me."

I studied the crowded room, filled with posh guests who were completely absorbed in their own affairs. I grinned, and suddenly, the party became a lot more interesting. "Would you like *me* to get you some?"

Rupert's complete lack of reaction made me think he hadn't heard the question, but just before I could repeat myself, a low chuckle started in his throat and then grew louder. He slapped his knee. "Oh, I wish you could. Don't tease an old man."

I sprang up. "I'm not. Believe me, a high shelf isn't much of a challenge, compared to half the things I do."

He laughed again. "That I believe, but flattered as I am, I don't want you risking it. Lavinia'll have your head."

I thought about how eager she was for me to marry her father-in-law. "Something tells me she'll forgive me. I'll be right back."

I hurried away amidst his protests and deftly slipped through a door I'd seen servants move in and out of all night. A long corridor extended before me, and I simply followed my nose from there. I passed one servant along the way, and as usual, acting like I knew where I was going got me ignored.

Only one person stood in the vast kitchen, a boy washing dishes with his back to the door. With dinner over, most servants were now out delivering cordials to the guests. I crept to the other end of the kitchen, far from the dishwasher. A cavernous pantry loomed around a corner, filled with enough food to feed a party twice this size. I didn't recognize half the items. High on the top shelf, golden bottles of rum gleamed. As I contemplated my strategy, an uneasy voice said, "I beg your pardon, miss. I . . ."

I turned to see a nervous kitchen maid. "Thank goodness," I exclaimed. "I hope you can help me. I'm trying to do a favor for Mister Chambers—the elder one. It's a, uh, bit of a secret. He was hoping I could find something for him. Something from . . . Royal Point."

I was playing a hunch. After thinking about how Rupert had said Lavinia had threatened the servants, it occurred to me they might not be so fond of their new mistress and her changes. But someone as mild as Rupert? Loyalty to him would likely still run strong, and I might not even have to steal.

Sure enough, the maid's expression softened. "I do know where it's at. And the Six knows he deserves it after such a good long life. But I could lose my job if Mistress Chambers catches me."

"Show me. I'll do it. I'll take responsibility."

"All right then," she said after a moment's deliberation. "There's a ladder right over there."

She brought it to me, and I made the climb in high heels without any difficulty. When I stepped back down with a bottle in hand, the maid handed me an elegant china cup. Catching on, I poured a generous amount of the rum into it.

"Hopefully the mistress will think it's tea if she sees him with it," my conspirator said with a wink.

I replaced the bottle and thanked her. Careful not to spill the cup's contents, I returned to the corridor and slowly made my way back toward the party. Smiling, I wondered if this counted as an act of great justice.

Partway through the hall, I passed a darkened doorway, and a hand suddenly reached out and grabbed my arm. I stared in shock as Grant gestured for me to come inside. I followed him, too stunned to protest.

He shut the door, and we retreated to the far side of the room, to a corner that held what I could barely discern as a piano. I set the cup on top of it. Only a little of the rum had sloshed out. "What are you doing here?" I asked.

"Getting ready to meet Barton Scarborough and some of the others after the party. I'm pretty sure he's using the heretic patrols as a cover to deliver messages and contraband. He sends them out pretty far sometimes."

"Well, then what are you doing in here? The party's not over, and I doubt he told you to come inside." Very faint light edged the curtained windows, a combination of moonlight and outside lanterns. That and a little brightness peeking under the main door gave the room its only illumination. As my eyes adjusted, I saw Grant lean against the piano.

"I was looking for you. I needed to tell you something."

My heart nearly stopped. Despite all the mental arguments I had with myself about why I was better off without him, despite all the excitement of the pirates . . . I was suddenly filled with hope and anticipation. An explanation at last.

"Silas pulled strings over at the customs office," Grant began, completely knocking my hopes down. But before I could feel too frustrated, he continued, "And we found your Lonzo Borges. Sort of."

I gaped. "What? How?"

"His bond was resold to another broker when he arrived, and they all headed south to look for work. That was all we knew, but at least there was a paper trail. You got lucky. That doesn't usually happen. When I found out one of our agents was going to be in that area last week, I had him make a few inquiries. He just got back today."

"And?"

"An engineering firm bought Borges's bond, and there was confirmation he's currently draining swamps outside Williamston. Our man didn't get a chance to go to him in person, but he's headed back tomorrow for another visit. If you get a letter to me by noon, I could have him deliver it."

The world swam around me. *Lonzo.* Was it possible? Had I gotten this lucky so quickly? Williamston was a coastal city at the southernmost part of Osfrid's Adorian holdings. There were no official colony lines drawn there yet, but the territory was firmly in Osfrid's grip. Though rich in resources, most of that region was swampy and rugged. Few wanted to fight for it.

Lonzo is alive.

I wrapped my arms around myself. "I . . . I didn't even know you were looking for him."

"I said I would."

"Thank you. *Thank you.* You don't know what this means to me."

"I'm glad. I was hoping I could do something, seeing as you've been hating me for the last week." I tried to picture the expression on his face as he said that. More sardonic than contrite, I suspected.

"I haven't been hating—" I stopped. "Well. Not all the time."

"I deserved it." And just like that, he actually did sound apologetic. "Hopefully we can just let this go and move on to what's important."

The subtext that I was not important promptly killed any credit he might have gained for that flash of earnestness. "Let it go? Like you let me go?"

He groaned. "Mirabel . . ."

"I realize I did something wrong, and I'm sorry about that, but you could at least—"

"You didn't do anything wrong. It was me, not you."

"Don't dodge this by brushing me off. Obviously, I played some part! I know you're touchy about your past, but if I'd had any idea how much asking about it would kill your interest—"

"Damn it," he interrupted again. "Why is everything such a battle? It wasn't that you asked! It was the way you looked when you—" I recognized one of those rare moments when he got so worked up, he slipped and revealed more than he intended. He caught himself now. "Look, just let it—"

The door slowly creaked open, spilling light into the front part of the room. The darkness still obscured us, but Grant took my hand and we crawled under the piano. We crammed ourselves into the corner behind it—no easy feat in my full dress—and went perfectly still. He didn't let go of me.

Two men entered the room, shutting the door behind them. One lit a small candle, and Grant and I shrank back even farther.

"I got a message from White," the man who'd come in first said. "He wants to know where the shipment is. I'd like to know too. The accounts don't match."

"Everything's fine," said the other. "Sandler got delayed, but he'll bring it to my place just before dawn. The militia stumbled onto their job, so they wanted to lay low a while. I'll take them to Burleigh the day after tomorrow."

"Well, make a count before you go. I don't want to find out they're skimming too."

"Thieves stealing from thieves, eh?" asked the first man. He gave a harsh laugh. "I'll take care of it. You just make sure the money's ready."

"I will. Hey, do you smell rum?"

"I wish. I hate that pretentious port they're serving."

One of them snuffed the candle, and they returned to the party. Grant and I stayed put for a few more minutes until we were certain they wouldn't come back. We let go of each other's hands, and I had to unkink my fingers after how tightly we'd been gripping each other.

"That was Abraham Miller," I murmured. Even alone now, I still felt the need for secrecy. "I don't know the other. I've never heard anyone talk like him."

"That's a North Joyce accent. I'll have to find out who was on the guest list. That was definitely conspiracy talk. If I can identify him, maybe we'll figure out who Sandler is. That's a new player. Now I've got to hurry to get this to Silas and still be back to meet the patrol."

We both started to get up and then realized what a tangle we were in, half sitting on each other and surrounded in the layers of my skirts.

"You and your clothes," he muttered, shifting so that I could pull out a part of my overdress he'd been sitting on. "How can a dress that covers so little have so much to it?"

"It might be low cut, but it still leaves plenty to the imagination." Embarrassment flooded me as I recalled that he didn't have to imagine much. I managed to free myself and get to my feet. As I did, my hand lightly grazed his face.

"You're lazy on your shaving again."

He rose as well, following as I made my way out from behind the piano. We paused in front of it, facing each other in the shadows. "It didn't suit me," he said. "And besides, I hear it's the only endearing thing about me."

"It was until you brought me the news about Lonzo. Thank you again."

"Don't forget the letter." I just barely made out his hand lifting toward me—and then he swiftly returned it to his side. "I need to go. But whatever you're thinking—it's wrong."

"I'm sorry, what?"

"About . . . you know what I'm talking about."

"Then why—"

"Because . . . . well. Just because." He moved to the door, brushing against me as he went by. "Oh, and take your letter to Silas. I don't know when I'll be back."

And then he was gone, leaving me—as usual—bewildered.

I took a minute to collect myself and then picked up the china cup. My hands were steady, so that was something. As I returned to the party, I tried not to think about Grant because that was a puzzle I couldn't solve. Shifting my thoughts to Abraham Miller's conversation didn't provide any answers either. I wished I could discover more, but he'd left the party.

I delivered the rum to Rupert with a bright smile. He took a sip and looked up at me in wonder. "Miss Viana, be careful, or I'll stop encouraging you to marry someone else."

I told him it was my pleasure and then decided to make a sweep of the room in case I might happen upon the man from North Joyce. As I walked toward a cluster of people I hadn't yet met, I saw Cornelius step away from them and wave. I immediately turned off in a different direction, like I'd actually been on my way to see someone else. I had no desire to hear him try to sell poor Rupert to me again. In my haste, I nearly ran into Clara.

"Smart move on your part," she said. "I didn't think you had it in you."

After tonight's series of events, I couldn't even guess what she was referring to. "What?"

"Pursuing old Mister Chambers." Her eyes drifted across the room to him before returning to me. "That's playing the long game. Or maybe not so long. Won't be much fun in the beginning, but he can't have many years left. And then you're a rich widow, free to do as you please."

My jaw dropped. "What? I'm not doing that!"

"Well, you're certainly friendly with him. And word gets around. You've been putting off other men."

She wasn't entirely wrong about that. Over the last week, I'd realized that, once I could be sure Lonzo was taken care of, I had two paths for myself. One was to earn enough money from my work with Grant and Tom to buy my own freedom. That was a long shot. So, if I did have to get married, an open-minded husband like Rupert—who would respect me and give me my space—was preferable to most of the men I'd met. Once I'd settled on those two options, I saw no point in encouraging other suitors. I wasn't rude to anyone—but I also made my indifference clear.

"I'm still considering my choices," I replied.

"Well, I don't care what you do. I think it's brilliant, and he certainly hasn't caught on."

She sauntered off, and my stomach sank. With everything else happening in my whirlwind of a life, I had never considered how choosing an older man might look to others. If I accepted the offer, it would be because it promised an honorable marriage with an interesting companion. I hated the idea of people thinking I was waiting for Rupert to die. I hated the idea of people thinking he was a naïve old man who didn't know he was being used.

Martha waved at me across the room, signaling it was time to go. As guilty as this revelation about Rupert made me, I would have to decide what to do about it later. Too many other matters sat higher on my list of priorities right now.

"What a lovely dinner," Martha said as I joined her. "And such a splendid house! But these shoes are hurting my feet. It'll be nice to get home and rest."

"It will be," I agreed, though I knew there'd be no rest for me. I'd promised to meet Tom for a job, and then I'd have to make sure I took Lonzo's letter to Silas in time.

My night was just beginning.

CHAPTER 21

TOM'S JOB THAT NIGHT WAS A QUICK ONE, DEALING WITH a landlord who had plans to drastically raise rents in one of the city's poorer wharf districts. Most of his tenants couldn't afford the new rates and would be turned out on the streets. Tom knew several of the residents, and one of his own men even lived there. But, as he told me, our task went beyond that: "It's just the right thing to do."

I was inclined to agree when I saw the landlord's opulent home, which was a far cry from the slums he charged so dearly for. We did our usual routine, subduing servants and clearing out as many valuables as we could find in the house. Tom made an abrupt flip from jovial to menacing, warning the landlord that we'd be back if the rents weren't reconsidered.

"Will he listen?" I asked Tom, once we'd left. I always wondered if any of these threats ever actually did any good.

"Maybe. He looked like he took the message to heart. My guess is he'll still raise it but not nearly so much. Saves face, gives him a little extra coin—hopefully keeps us away. And if he doesn't do anything?" Tom shrugged. "We'll find time to visit again."

"It's sort of an . . . erratic system."

"It works, though, doesn't it?"

"Sometimes," I said. We'd returned to the city's heart and were nearing the Dancing Bull. "But we pick and choose who we 'punish.' And there's no consistency in how we deal with these people."

"You don't seem to mind dealing with them."

"I don't. I know they've all done something. But the problem with selective justice is that it's, well, selective." I thought back to Osfro and the bias against Lonzo. "Laws exist to make sure everyone's held to the same standards and treated the same way."

"You know as well as I do that even when you've got an ironclad set of laws, with people to enforce them—which this city doesn't—there will still always be those who slip through the cracks. We deliver justice, my dear. Sometimes you have to operate outside the law for that."

My father had always said the same thing to justify his actions. I often soothed myself that what I did with Tom didn't go to my father's extremes, but there was no question that I was treading in ethically gray areas.

Tom turned even more melodramatic than usual when I didn't respond. "Oh, the agony you cause me. The pain. To suggest paperwork and procedure is preferable to me! You're lucky my faith in you is so unwavering." He handed me a gold coin. "And inconsistent or not, our system pays better."

I pocketed the coin but said, "This technically belongs to some of the tenants he gouged."

"Oh, we'll make sure some of it cycles back to them. But first, we have another good deed to take care of."

The urgency of writing Lonzo's letter had hung over me all evening. "No more jobs. I can't stay tonight."

"It's a deed, not a job."

Most of the crew remained at the tavern, but Lesser Tom joined Tom and me in carrying heavy sacks gathered from the tavern's subterranean storage room. From there, we traveled to a poor neighborhood on the city's west side where I'd made deliveries before. The houses were older and run-down, the people lean and desperate. No one harassed us. Those we passed waved and offered greetings—to all of us.

We knocked on the door of a house belonging to one Mistress Smith. We usually brought our gifts straight to her for distribution.

She knew who needed what in her community and was fair about spreading it around. Not even the most desperate would dare steal from her. She opened the door wearing a thin nightgown and a cap over her wispy curls. Despite the late hour, a smile lit her lined face when she saw us. She'd lived in this neighborhood longer than anyone and was a matriarch of sorts. Her diminutive frame housed a ferocious heart.

"Tom, Tom, and my lady," she said. "Come in, come in. Let me make you some tea."

Tom greeted her with a flourish of the cape. "No time to stay, I'm afraid. We just want to pass on a few gifts."

She exclaimed with delight when she saw what was in the bags: fruit, something scarce and expensive this time of year. The hosts whose parties I attended had the means to pay the current exorbitant prices. I'd been served apple tart just last night. Many of the guests had pushed their dessert away half-eaten, claiming they were full. Thinking of that excess and looking at Mistress Smith now, I no longer felt so guilty about stealing the fruit. Besides, we'd actually taken it from another group of smugglers. *Thieves stealing from thieves.*

"Oh, wait until everyone sees," Mistress Smith said. "The Six's blessings upon you all."

Tom basked in her adoration. He hadn't made many deliveries in person for some time. "It's our pleasure. Lady Aviel doesn't sleep at night if she hasn't given away a bit of my wealth."

Mistress Smith laughed as she watched Lesser Tom pass the sacks of fruit to a sleepy boy inside. "It's good for you. And good of you. Wally, go get the present I made for Lady Aviel."

"What?" I asked, seeing the boy dart away.

"Since you've been coming around, we've eaten better than ever. We all know who's nudging Tom. I wanted to give you something in return."

"It's not necessary. Not at all." These people had so little, I couldn't even imagine taking anything.

"Hush," she scolded. Wally returned and handed her a bundle of cloth. When she held it up, it unfolded into a black cloak with golden stars stitched all over it. I was so surprised that I didn't refuse when she handed it over. The material was a sturdy but very basic wool. Mistress Culpepper would have turned her nose up at its plainness, but the gold thread bore the same quality I regularly saw in the Glittering Court. Tom noted it too.

"Fit for an angel. Where'd you get the thread?"

"Sold one of those jars of honey you brought us," Mistress Smith said. "Bought just enough of a scrap to do up this cloak. I'd thought it'd match your hair."

"Take it," Tom told me. "Yours is battered, and you need to dress up your image anyway. Mistress Smith has obviously put a great deal of work into it."

"I'm honored to wear it," I told her, removing my old cloak and replacing it with the starry one.

"Not many of your lot help us out. And never so generously." Mistress Smith proceeded to tick off names on her fingers as she spoke. "Joanna Steel. Howard Gilly. They come around sometimes. But we never see the likes of Joseph Abernathy or John Gray anymore. Or that new one. Saddler."

"Sandler," corrected Tom. "And that's good to know. Keep me apprised of who else does or doesn't visit."

Sandler! The name Miller and the North Joyce conspirator had mentioned. Could it be the same man?

I could barely contain myself as we walked away. Trying to sound casual, I remarked, "I've never heard of any Sandler."

"New, as she said." Tom grew thoughtful. "He gets some leniency for that, but he needs to learn the system. The veterans can get away with hoarding their loot, but newcomers need to establish goodwill."

"Someone'll raid him," Lesser Tom added. "Just to make a point. I heard he keeps his stash over in that ugly old boardinghouse on Water

Street. Wouldn't be too hard to, ah, stop by." His voice held a hopeful note.

Tom shook his head. "We have better things to do than harass some novice—especially since we may need to hire some extra hands soon. Which reminds me . . . what are you doing the night of the Flower Festival, my lady?"

I was still reeling from the slip about Sandler and took a moment to process the question. "I have some commitments that evening." That was downplaying it a bit. The Glittering Court would be attending a gala second only to our debut ball.

"Well, this would be late, around the usual time you materialize, actually."

"What is it?" I asked, suspicious of the buildup.

"A job, of course. But a big one. I'll need more than my usual team, and I won't lie to you: There's very little that's noble about it. We're just stealing from a merchant who'll be in the wrong place at the right time. It's purely selfish. You may have to get your hands dirty, but I guarantee they'll be filled with gold afterward."

"How dirty?"

"Not at all, if I can help it. You know I try to keep that in check." Seeing my hesitation, he asked, "I assume you still have debts? Make a dent in them."

The need for money had become much more critical, now that I knew where Lonzo was. Slowly, after much deliberation, I gave a nod of assent.

"Excellent." Tom lifted my hand and kissed it, and I wondered what I'd just agreed to. "Find me the night before, and we'll have all the details finalized."

We parted ways, and I headed down a road that would take me to Silas's. Before entering the busier areas, I found a quiet spot to adjust my wardrobe. I swapped my starry cloak for the battered one. A red wig stuffed into the cloak's inner pocket replaced the blonde. I couldn't move freely as Lady Aviel anymore.

I walked a few streets over to the tailor shop and knocked on Silas's door. He didn't look thrilled to see me.

"Aren't you married yet?"

"Grant said to come here because he's out with the patrol."

"I know." Silas shut the door behind me. "He told me about how you two overheard Miller. I didn't even know you were still a part of this."

Ignoring the accusation in his voice, I took off my wig and mask and accepted a plain wooden chair, which seemed luxurious after Grant's sparse loft.

"You've got some kind of letter for me?" Silas asked, arms crossed.

"Er, I actually need to write it here. If that's okay. But before I do . . . I found out something else that might help you. Did you figure out who Sandler was? Grant didn't know the name."

Silas shook his head. "No. But I'll ask some contacts in the morning."

"Well, I think I already know. He's a new pirate. And he keeps his goods at a boardinghouse on Water Street. One that's allegedly ugly and old. That's probably where those supplies will be moved from in the morning."

Both bushy eyebrows rose. "And how in the world do you know that?"

"I have a source. A very reliable one," I added, seeing his eyes narrow in skepticism. "I guarantee this is accurate. Can you get to the boardinghouse in time?"

"Maybe. There are a few boardinghouses over there." Silas sat down at a desk and sifted through stacks of paper until he found what looked like a map of the city. After a quick scan, he rolled it up and tossed it aside. "Not what I need. There's paper and ink over there to write your letter."

I retrieved it and, with no other clear writing surface, sat on the floor. Silas continued rummaging around.

As intimidating as I found him, I couldn't stop myself from asking, "What about the North Joyce man? Could he have been one of the couriers on the list we stole from Abraham Miller?"

"We?" Silas paused in his search. "You were there?"

I squirmed under his gaze. "I thought Grant told you."

"There's a lot he's not telling me, apparently. Ah, this is it." He spread out another map.

I wrote a few lines of the letter, using an old Sirminican code of my father's. Silas made a grunt of what sounded like satisfaction. I looked up. "Did you find the boardinghouse?"

"Likely. There are three on that street. One's new. I've got a hunch on which of the others is 'ugly.' Grant was just over there—he'll know. I expect him any minute."

A sort of excited nervousness fluttered within me at that. His job finished, Silas sat back in his chair with the map, occasionally glancing down at me. Shifting so that I had a better look, I worked up the courage to speak again. "Mister Garrett, may I ask you something?"

"Sure." He stood up and walked over to me. "But I might not answer."

I hadn't expected him to loom over me while I spoke. "Why isn't there any law enforcement in Cape Triumph?"

He did answer, so that was promising. "Well. There's us. And the militia. And the army."

"The militia and the army are two separate groups with two separate ways of operating," I pointed out. "And neither actually works consistently in the city. It's not their main job, and a lot of the militiamen take bribes. As for you—the McGraws—you don't enforce citywide laws. I know you have some authority from the king, but you only use it to serve your cases. There's nothing unified here like there is in Evaria. No central city patrol or watch."

"Forming something like that would be the governor's decision," he said slowly. "Remember that Cape Triumph started off as a few shacks in the woods. Organized city watches weren't really part of any master plan, and the army was enough muscle. Then the militia came along. And even though it's sloppy, it's what has held up here."

"Not from what I've seen. Pirates are enforcing justice."

He snorted. "Then go submit a proposal to Governor Doyle. You're plucky. Maybe you could convince him to organize something."

"I'm Sirminican. And a woman. It's hard to get any credibility at all—let alone permission to form a city watch." I half expected Silas to agree. Instead, he just kept studying me, like this was the first time we'd met. He had a gruff, no-nonsense air and obviously didn't suffer fools. I honestly wondered how Grant—who had his own share of headstrongness—managed to work for an authority figure like this. Or any authority figure, really. Pushing my luck, I asked, "Can I ask something else? About Grant?"

"The less you know, the easier your life will be."

"Please, Mister Garrett. I just want to understand him."

Again, a delay. I kept wondering if Silas was trying to unsettle me or just needed that much time to think over his responses. "You really are ambitious. What's your question?"

"Grant said when he came to Cape Triumph as a child—when he was sent away from the Balanquans—that a couple took him in. Was that you?"

"He told you that too?" That seemed to astonish Silas more than learning I'd helped steal the list. "Yes. It was me. And my wife. She passed a year after he left." He paused again, letting that memory linger. "I tried to talk Grant out of going with him—his father—but Grant didn't want anything to do with me at that point. He went off on his own and had to learn alone."

"But he came back to you. You must have had a bigger impact than you thought."

Silas shrugged. "He didn't come to me right away. He went to the Balanquans first. I don't know what happened there, but he didn't stick around long. Would he have come here after that if he hadn't met Aiana? Hard to say."

That friendship had always been a mystery to me. "Did they meet when he was back there?"

"No. He found her in the northern colonies, on the run from her . . .

wife." Silas didn't sound like he disapproved, so much as he was still getting used to a concept that wasn't openly accepted in Osfrid and Evaria. "The Balanquans were hunting her. She had no idea what to do or where to go. Grant's father might have been a ruthless bastard, but he did teach Grant how to take care of himself. And he took care of Aiana. He needed a fixed place for her to hide, and Cape Triumph was the only one he knew."

"I bet it was more than the city. I bet it was you."

"I don't know. But I didn't waste that second chance. I could tell he would drift away if I didn't tie him down. No one remembered him, so I helped him make a new life. Set him up at the store, had him take charge of teaching Aiana to protect herself. He slipped into new roles so easily that it didn't take long to realize he could do what I do—except he could do it in secret. Everyone knows I run the agency. But they don't know who works for me. And, well, technically, he doesn't. I can only make him an agent-for-hire, so to speak. Sir Ronald can give him a legitimate position—and will, once we stamp out these traitors. Agent or not, Grant can be invisible right now, and that's very, very useful to us."

"Useful for him too," I mused. "He gets to be everyone—and no one. He can move without restraint or commitment. Just the way he likes it." One of Silas's bushy eyebrows rose again. I'd come to realize that was a signal that something had really and truly astonished him. "Except you did tie him down. You gave him something, and here he is."

"But he won't stay." Silas's hard countenance faded, and for the first time in our brief acquaintance, he looked vulnerable.

A loud knock heralded Grant's arrival and ended the conversation. Silas's gruffness returned as he opened the door. Grant entered, dirtier and sweatier than when I'd last seen him. He gave a quick nod to me and focused on Silas.

"We rode all the way up to Hamley. Scarborough had us search around the taverns for signs of itinerant priests while he had a very long talk with a tin merchant about the town's heretic situation."

Silas made a *hrmph*. "Something tells me they discussed more than that. I assume you got his name? We'll get Crenshaw on it. Right now, we've got more pressing problems."

We updated Grant on what I'd learned, and he seemed even more suspicious of how I'd found a "reliable source." But after studying the map with Silas, he confirmed the oldest boardinghouse on Water Street, adding, "Oh, yeah, it's ugly. Horribly maintained. A lot of shifty people go through there. The other one's not quite as old, and that owner's pretty strict about who he lets board."

I listened, ignored, as they plotted strategy. Silas wanted to recruit a few soldiers to follow Sandler when he left with the delivery, arresting him only once they determined his destination and the North Joyce contact.

Silas put a hat on. "I'm going to the fort right now. Wait for me. And let her finish that letter—she's earned it."

I'd been so engrossed in their planning that I'd paused in my writing again. After Silas left, I scrawled the ending and folded the paper up. Grant leaned against the wall, lost in his own thoughts. There was an almost feverish glitter in his eyes from the excitement of the night's developments, but his body looked as though it had been pushed past exhaustion.

"You should get some rest before whatever happens . . . happens."

His dark eyes flicked to me. "It won't be much longer. Just through dawn. Then I'll get a couple hours of sleep before the store opens. Right now? I've got the drive. I can do anything."

I tilted my head. "Are you sure? Can you explain what 'because' meant?"

"Because?"

"In the conservatory. You said I didn't do anything wrong that night. But the only reason you gave for why you stopped was 'because.'"

He straightened up and walked to the other side of the room, angling away from me. "Do we have to talk about this?"

"Well, you're not doing anything else until Silas gets back."

"Would you settle for me saying I did it because I'd hoped to avoid conversations like this? I knew things would get muddled."

"They shouldn't have." My voice cracked a little, and I cleared my throat to sound hard again. "It was all supposed to be simple. I thought we had an understanding."

He was showing all the little signs of agitation I'd learned. Pacing. Raking his hands through his hair. But I knew he wasn't frustrated at me so much as himself, and having to talk about personal things. Finally, he spun around.

"Simple, huh? Okay. Then tell me why you wanted to do it."

I blinked, caught off guard. "What kind of question is that?"

"An easy one. Here, I'll give you a simple answer. I wanted to because you've got a face that could sack Ruva and a body I can't stop staring at. That night we 'met' in the rain? I saw plenty in that wet nightgown, and I've wanted to see the rest for a long time. Those other girls you live with are like dolls. They look like they'll break. But not you."

My mouth went dry, and I had no idea how to respond or even feel. To a certain extent, I'd just been complimented—on my appearance, at least. And wasn't this whole debacle supposed to be circling around physical attraction? Desire and nothing more?

He'd given me a simple answer, but he'd delivered it with almost no expression, no feeling, not even when citing the almost poetic reference to an ancient queen whose beauty had allegedly broken the great peace of Ruva. It sounded so practiced, like he could have been reading from a script.

"No simple answer from you on what should have been a simple matter?" he prompted.

The taunt in his tone sparked me back to life, and I began thinking up a list as impersonal as his. "I don't know what your point is, but yes, it's the same for me, obviously. I like—wanted—your body too! Rosamunde and I were sizing up all the men on the ship on that first day, and I didn't even look at anyone else. You were stronger. Hardened. You had a fighter's stance, and I could tell right away you were more than a shopkeeper. I wanted to touch your face, your arms, your chest . . . and try to figure out if you were some kind of warrior in disguise. You've got this look in your eyes that pierces right through me. It's always hungry. Hungry to tear apart the world and its secrets. And sometimes it's hungry for me, and that . . . does things to me. Even your hair . . . I like it because it's like you. Trying to behave, but ultimately, the unruliness—or maybe it's just defiance?—comes out. And when you didn't shave—"

Grant held up a hand. "Okay, I've heard enough."

Without realizing it, I'd started smiling when talking about his hair, but his pained expression snatched my amusement away. "What? You asked for a simple answer."

"And you didn't give me one." He shoved his hands in his pockets and slumped against the wall. "Seriously, Mirabel. Let go of . . . whatever we stumbled into. Focus on helping with the case and getting your money. Focus on what you worked so hard to get here for: a husband." The word tumbled out harshly, like it left a bad taste in his mouth.

"That's not what I came for," I said after several moments of contemplation.

A small frown creased his forehead. "Isn't it? I can't really believe you sailed across an ocean to help root out traitors."

"No. I came here for my brother." I pointed at the letter and could hardly believe I was telling him what I'd never told anyone. "Lonzo Borges is Lonzo Viana. He got in some, ah, trouble and started using a different name. He sailed here almost two years ago as a bondsman. I lost contact shortly after he arrived—until you found him."

I could see Grant processing this. He rarely learned something he hadn't seen coming. "That's why you want the reward. I wondered if you . . . were trying to buy out your own contract. You've gone through all of this . . . for him?"

"I'd do more. As much as I'd like to buy out my contract, his bond comes first. And if that means finding a rich husband? Well, it's worth it to keep him safe. Why are you looking at me like I'm crazy?"

"I'm not. I'm looking in awe. Whenever I think I know how brave you are, you astound me again."

"I don't feel brave. I just love him, that's all. He's sacrificed for me too." I clenched my hands in front of me and looked down. "He broke with our father because of me."

"Broke?"

"Our father trained us both to be a part of his crusade, but we had very different roles. I was the pretty distraction—even more than I am here. I wanted to go on daring escapades, like the men did, but I believed in my father. I thought he knew best. The cause really was just, and I was born to it." I took a deep breath and almost couldn't go on. "He encouraged me to be friendly with men when it suited his needs. *Very* friendly. I distracted them while my father conducted his secret deeds. Sometimes I coaxed out information. Usually, all I had to do was a kiss or a little touching. Sitting on someone's lap. I didn't like it at first, but after a while . . . well, I just didn't think about it at all. It just became I something I did. I was indifferent to it."

I glanced up. Grant's face gave away nothing, but I could see him hanging on to every word. I had to look away again at the next part of the story.

"One day, he found an informant who could spill all the plans about a massive attack coming against some Alanzans. The man was ready to talk—but he wanted me along with his bribe. He said he'd give my father's faction everything he knew in exchange for a night with me. And my father was ready to make the deal."

Grant jerked upright from his lounging position, face incredulous. "How could anyone make their daughter do that?"

I shrugged. "Fighting injustice was his life's work. And he didn't make me do it, exactly. But he pushed. He told me it was a small sacrifice compared to how the Alanzans suffered. That it'd be over fast and was almost the same as what I'd already done. Except . . . this time, I didn't feel indifferent. I was afraid, but I also felt guilty. I didn't want to disappoint him or betray the cause. And I almost gave in . . ."

"Almost." Grant latched on to the word.

"Then Lonzo found out. He'd always followed our father's way without question too. But this broke him. It broke all of us. My father called me a coward. Lonzo accused my father of selling me like merchandise. We argued all night. I shouted. I cried. And in the morning, Lonzo and I walked away. Our father's way couldn't be ours anymore. He went to Belsia and died shortly after that."

"Mirabel . . . I wish you'd told me that before."

I finally met his eyes and felt a bitter smile on my lips. "Why? Because we're always so forthcoming about our feelings and secrets, Grant? I'm not even sure why I told you now. I guess to explain why I'm here and why I need to free Lonzo from his bond. Although, I suppose I've sort of become a bonded servant myself in the Glittering Court."

"No. You've held true to your family. You *have* family. You bettered your education. You'll move into high society." He stared off but wore the same pained expression he'd had while I'd spoken about my father. "The Balanquans would praise you for raising your status."

"Like . . . prestige?"

"More complex. Status defines your place in society. Your worth." He walked across the room, stopping a few feet in front of me. "Do you know what my Balanquan name is? Not what Aiana calls me— the one I was born with. Agamichi. It means 'without a shadow.'"

"Without a shadow," I repeated. It was ironic since McGraw agents were called shadowmen, but I didn't say so.

"It's one sound off from *akamichi*. That means 'without status.' That similarity's intentional. My uncle named me and thought he was being clever. Among the Balanquans, all social order, all relationships . . . they're all built around status. Not having any is the worst thing that can happen to a person. And a half-breed bastard has very little."

"But we aren't among the Balanquans." A wave of emotion swelled up in my chest, much as it had in the moment I'd discovered his scar. I fought the impulse to reach out to him.

"It doesn't matter. For all intents and purposes, I'm still a ghost. No people, no home, no great deeds. But I've accepted it," he added. "If I don't have anything, then I can't lose it."

"But you have a lot," I exclaimed. Compassion still burned in me, but I couldn't help my shock. "You *do* have a home. You *do* have people. Silas and Aiana love you, and you love them—I've seen it. Creating a family like that is a great deed. So is the work you do. Look how determined you are in breaking up the conspiracy! It seems to me like you're rich in status."

"Because you don't understand status," he said, voice weary.

I moved forward and took his hands. "I understand that you don't see what's right in front of you. And you haven't 'accepted' being a ghost. You've chosen it! Wandering without attachment doesn't free you. It traps you. You need to find your own wayfarers' star and fix your life on something, something with meaning."

He was attempting to keep his temper down. "I'm trying, Mirabel. There are things I'm fighting for, whether you believe it or not."

"I do believe it. But I also believe you're throwing away what you already have. And maybe you're throwing that away on purpose. Is that what you've fixed yourself on? Being unhappy? Is that why you pushed me away? Because some part of you didn't really think you deserved a night where you might actually get something you wanted?"

My anger had flared up again. So had his. Another day, another fight with Grant.

"I wanted something simple." He released my hands and moved away. "And instead I got you."

I stared. Something inside me shattered. Angry tears sprang to my eyes. I shot to the door and was nearly hit by it as Silas returned. "Calhoun and the others are on their way to—" He stopped when he saw me. "Didn't expect you to still be here."

"I was just leaving." I retrieved my things and pointed at the letter. "Please make sure that gets to your agent. It means a lot to me."

CHAPTER 22

THE FLOWER FESTIVAL WAS AN ORDINARY NAME FOR AN extraordinary event. Back in Osfrid, it was a huge, decadent celebration to mark the arrival of spring. The festivities hadn't been quite as extravagant when the holiday first carried over to Adoria, but over time, the New World began to catch up with the Old World. This year, Cape Triumph was embracing a tradition that was wildly popular in Osfro: evening masquerade balls. Mistress Culpepper hadn't liked the unexpected development, but most of the girls in the house were delighted. Not me.

I was tired of masks.

Mine was beautiful, of course. Everything I wore in the Glittering Court was beautiful. It was a half-mask that covered the upper part of my face, much like the one I wore on my nighttime trips. But this one was covered in deep red silk that sparkled with crushed red crystal. It was hardly inconspicuous, though Tom might have approved of that flashiness simply for the sake of his "image is everything" stance.

I was also just tired, period. I was burning the candle at both ends, and sometimes, I wondered how much I had left. I usually made it back to Wisteria Hollow about four hours before our wakeup call. Adrenaline could keep me fueled during those late hours, but in the day, I dragged. I often fell asleep in the coaches when we traveled. Mistress Culpepper began insisting I wear face cream at night because of the dark circles under my eyes. And whatever energy I had left at social events went to searching for intelligence. I avoided dancing as much as possible. Even if I'd wanted to aggressively pursue some man at a party, my exhaustion put a serious damper on my charisma and conversational skills. My suitors fell away—all except one.

"Are you ready to make it official?"

I'd expected Cornelius to find me at the Flower Fest gala, just not so quickly. I accepted his hand for a waltz and put on a bland smile. "I will . . . but not until the end of my season."

Behind his blue velvet mask, Cornelius blinked in surprise. "If you're going to do it, why not take care of it now?"

"I don't want it to reflect badly on your father—or me. You know I like him very much and—"

"That's wonderful! He likes you too," interrupted Cornelius. "So does Lavinia. We all do. See her over there?"

From a refreshment table on the room's far side, Lavinia waved excitedly. She'd scaled down her dress tonight, a lilac velvet creation that almost looked tasteful. Her natural hair, however, had been covered by a towering white wig adorned with a gem-studded gold coronet. That kind of hair accessory wasn't uncommon, but from the way hers picked up the light, I almost wondered if it was real and not costume.

"She's lovely, as always," I said automatically. "But like I was telling you, I've heard gossip saying I'm only interested in your father because of his money, and I'd hate for others to believe I'd think so little of him or that he's naïve enough to be tricked."

Cornelius flinched. "Of course not."

"If we wait until the very end of my season, when I have no other proposals, we can make it look like he was kind enough to take pity on the poor Sirminican girl who couldn't get an offer. I've been dissuading others, you know."

That mollified Cornelius a little, and he agreed to wait, mostly because he had no choice. My explanation wasn't even entirely a lie, but I still clung to the far-fetched hope of buying my freedom. The delay would help.

Adelaide dazzled everyone in the ballroom, and Warren's adoration was clear for all to see. I managed to catch a few words with him and hoped to finally learn if any of the supplies he'd gathered for his new colony had been stolen.

"Will you be leading any heretic patrols later tonight, Mister Doyle?"

"No. No doubt there are all sorts of dark rituals going on, but we all needed a night off. I figured the boys deserved the chance to partake of their own festivities too."

I tried to picture Grant celebrating in a sparkling mask and almost smiled until I remembered our last conversation. "And I'm sure you're busy preparing for your trip to Hadisen. It's in a week, right? Do you have all your necessities?"

His eyes followed Adelaide as she whirled around with another partner. "Nearly. Excuse me, Miss Viana."

I'd warned Aiana I'd be ducking out of the ball a little early. The chaos of these big events made slipping away easy. Aiana had the difficult job because as a chaperone, she was supposed to help do a head count and make sure everyone was accounted for when we returned home. She'd scolded me for being out so much with Grant, and I hoped she wouldn't say anything to him. Neither had any idea that I was really out with Tom.

After trading my glamorous red gown for Lady Aviel's starry cloak and subdued black mask, I made my way to the rendezvous point Tom had given me. Normally, he assembled his crew at the Dancing Bull or one of a handful of other pubs he frequented. Tonight, I'd been told to meet him at a quiet crossroads south of the city limits.

There, I found him and ten other men. All of Tom's regular crew, except Jenks, was there. The rest appeared to have been hired for the night. There was also one woman. I immediately recognized her as Joanna Steel, one of the few renowned female pirates. She didn't work for Tom but was another ally he'd recruited for the night. A bright red kerchief was tied over her iron-gray hair, and she winked when she saw me. Rumor had it that she'd been married to five infamous pirate captains—and that she'd killed them all.

"We're raiding a ship called the *Queen Grace*," Tom told us. "It has a light guard tonight because of the festival, but it has a big cargo. That's why we need so many hands. We need to unload it quickly and get out of there. The crew shouldn't be any trouble. The few who are there are probably put out that they had to work on festival night, and I wouldn't be surprised if they've already hit the rum. We round them up, load our boats, and hopefully still have enough time to attend the festivities ourselves back in the city. Any questions?"

"Should we wait for more fog?" asked Anders, Tom's Skarsian colleague and the one whose dirk I'd inherited.

Tom peered out toward the water. The sky was mostly clear, but mist was starting to roll over the bay. "No, by the time we get there, it should be right where we want it."

Away from the crossroads, down by an uncleared patch of shore, we found five skiffs waiting in a secluded cove. We spread out among them and rowed back toward Cape Triumph's main port, the place where all the commercial ships docked. Tom directed the boats to go wide to avoid detection offshore and then come in behind the large galleys.

"This fog is a lucky break," Tom told me as we sailed. "It'll make this even easier than it already is. Some might say the angels wanted this to happen, so you don't have to have any of your usual moral dilemmas."

"You know I don't like hurting people if we don't have to—especially unlucky sailors who are just doing their jobs."

"Then let's hope they've drank enough to be submissive but not so much that they try something stupid. If it helps, I don't want any shots fired tonight. That sound carries over the water, and the less attention we attract, the better." He scanned the boats with a small frown. "We're down a few more than I'd like. One of my men hasn't checked in for some time. Anders's cousins were going to help, but they've run into some legal trouble, I hear. It is what it is. If luck is with us, this group is all we need."

Tom was right about the mist thickening. By the time we'd reached the port, it was hard to even make the ships out. Tom had to confer with Elijah and another man before determining which one the *Queen Grace* was. When they'd made the identification, the skiffs came up alongside it, and no one spoke. All communication was done by hand signal. Lesser Tom scaled the ship's side with astonishing dexterity and disappeared over the top of the railing. A little while later, a rope ladder came tumbling down, and all but two of us climbed up. The others stayed with the boats.

I was one of the last up, and my comrades had already encountered some of the crew. As I swung over the rail and onto the deck, I saw Elijah disarm one sailor while Joanna held a couple of others at gunpoint.

"Sweep the ship," ordered Tom. "Don't let any of them get a gun."

A few sailors down below hadn't realized what was happening. I went with Elijah and Anders, and the three of us took a group by surprise. One sailor pulled out a knife and looked as though he might rush us. After doing a double take at our blades and guns, he surrendered his weapon.

When all the sailors on the ship were secured, Tom had them locked in the captain's chambers. Then we began the arduous task of hauling out crates from the cargo holds.

"I hope these are filled with gold," one man said with a grunt. "They feel like it."

Each skiff could hold a couple of crates, and once one was loaded, Tom would send it off. I found myself in a boat with Joanna and Lesser Tom. He rowed, and she smiled over at me.

"Easy work, eh?"

"Surprisingly, yes," I admitted. "Tom said it would be, but I didn't really believe him."

"You shouldn't," she said. "Don't trust any man who smiles too

much or gives too many compliments. I keep hearing you're good . . .
but also a little squeamish."

"Not squeamish. I just don't like hurting or taking advantage of
innocent people."

"You're in the wrong business then, little angel. But if you ever
get tired of Tom, come work for me." She kicked at one of the crates.
"Let's see what's in these, shall we?"

"I don't think we're supposed to," said Lesser Tom uneasily.

Joanna ignored him and took out a heavy hunting knife from her
belt. She broke a crate's seal and popped the lid open. Even Lesser Tom
couldn't help his curiosity and leaned in with us to look.

"Cutlery?" asked Joanna in disgust. "It's a good thing we didn't risk
our necks tonight. Would've hated to get shot at for a bunch of forks."

Not just forks. The crate also held spoons, plates, and cups. "Are
they worth anything?" I asked.

"Mostly pewter and horn. The knives are iron, but all of it's plainly
made. Real silver's usually his game." She gazed at the other boats
thoughtfully. "I'll say this, he's certainly got a lot of it. I suppose if he
can sell it all, there's money to be made. But it's not something I'd pick.
Fewer things worth more money are the way to go."

When we arrived back at the cove, the party split up. Tom had had
wagons and horses hidden, and he instructed half of the men to take
the crates to one of his storehouses. The rest of us rode back to Cape
Triumph to collect our pay.

"No Dancing Bull tonight," Elijah said cheerfully. "He doesn't keep
enough money there to cover tonight's work. We're going to Molly's.
She keeps track of his big money."

"I'm sure she doesn't mind," said Joanna. "Then everyone can gam-
ble it away at her place."

Molly's was a nondescript house from the outside, but a gambling den
inside. It was a darker, rougher place than the tavern I'd been to with

Grant. Immediately inside the door, four huge men checked us over and took our weapons.

"Molly trusts no one—not even friends," Tom said. "She moves too much money to take any chances. We won't get any special treatment here, so don't step out of line."

The smell of sweat and smoke that I'd come to associate with these places filled the air, as did the heat of so many people enclosed in one space. But unlike other taverns, this one had a very clear purpose. Some patrons diced or played other games, but poker was the main attraction, and tables filled with a wide range of classes and vocations spread out over the room. There were more of Tom's ilk, but also pirate pretenders, tradesmen, laborers, and all sorts of other citizens hoping to make it big. A number of them wore festival masks and made toasts as they played. Others remained deadly serious. We were regarded with interest by some but not nearly as much as we received in other venues.

A woman, older than me but younger than Joanna, came striding forward. She wore a bright blue satin dress and looked completely unimpressed by us, or anyone really. I was sure part of that strength and confidence came from having henchmen on either side of her. But I also suspected that she, like Mistress Smith, had an inner strength that commanded respect.

"I know that look, Tom," she said. "You must have had a good night and need to pay out. Let's go look at the books."

"Still don't see how it's that big a payout," Joanna said when he was gone. "But you must be happy about it, judging from that big smile."

"Oh, I am," I told her. "I'm also just happy to see another tough woman in this city. I keep finding more and more of them."

Joanna laughed. "Not many of us, but we're out there. We've got to keep pushing. You sure you don't want to work for me?"

When Tom returned, he carried a heavy sack and began doling out gold. He paid each of us ten and kept the rest in reserve for those who'd gone to the safe house. Holding that much money left me momentarily dumbfounded. Then, old instincts from Osfro kicked in. Showing wealth in certain neighborhoods was like an immediate request to be robbed. I quickly spirited the coins away to an inner cloak pocket.

Some men in our group wanted to stay and try their luck, but the rest of us headed for the door. Suddenly, Anders stopped and stared across the room. Incredulity, then anger, filled his face.

"Look who's over there! It's those bastards who think they can call anyone a heretic and beat them up!"

I spun in the direction he indicated and immediately found the table, all the way in the back, that had caught his eye. Ten men sat around it, intent on their cards. A few of them I recognized. At a recent party, I'd caught sight of heretic patrol members coming discreetly to the kitchen's back door to report to Warren. These were some of the "average citizen" members. The patrol's more elite members probably only played cards at the Chambers plantation.

And, of course, I knew one of the players very well. Grant.

Tom put a hand on Anders's shoulder. "Leave them be. They're authorized by the governor."

"You think that matters to me?" Anders shrugged Tom off. "They're the ones that arrested my cousins this week! Broke one's ribs and knocked out some of the other's teeth. And that's only part of it."

"Anders—"

But Anders was already storming away from us, pushing his way through the room and shoving aside anyone who blocked his path.

"Damn it," said Tom, hurrying after Anders. Elijah, Lesser Tom, and I began to follow as well. Joanna caught my arm.

"Don't do it. This is going to be a mess. Leave with me while you can."

"I can't." I left her and caught up with the others.

No one at the table had noticed Anders's approach yet. Grant seemed particularly focused on his hand, which made me think he must actually be here to play and not gather information.

Anders walked over to one of the patrol members, jerked him up by the shirt, and punched him so hard that he flew backward into another table, scattering coins and cards. A hush fell in the room, and the other patrol members—including Grant—jumped to their feet. He recognized me in an instant. Our eyes locked, and even he couldn't conceal his surprise right away.

"What the hell do you think you're doing?" demanded another man from the patrol.

"What you did to my cousins on the east side!" Anders roared.

The man tilted his head. "What, you mean those Skarsian delinq—"

Anders punched him too, and a third patrolman lunged forward. Elijah blocked the attack and grabbed him around the throat.

That was as far as it went because we were all suddenly surrounded by Molly's burly bodyguards. "Out!" she yelled. "All of you! There's none of that here!"

Her men herded my party and the heretic hunters to the front door, some of us—like Anders—more forcibly than others. The bodyguards gave us our weapons back and shoved everyone out to the street.

Anders wasted no time in pulling out his pistol as he strode toward the man who'd spoken to him. "Let's see how you do against men who can actually defend themselves!"

I expected Tom to halt this. He had no qualms with necessary violence in his jobs but usually only engaged in minor scuffles within city limits. Apparently, this was an exception. Things moved so quickly, I could hardly keep up. Joanna and another hired hand from the ship raid had quickly departed. That left six of us and five from the heretic patrol. At most, the patrolmen were armed with knives. They'd only come here for gaming, after all. The pirates, fresh from a job, had guns and swords.

Chaos followed. The pirates descended on the heretic hunters, and Anders promptly shot someone in the leg. As he was trying to reload, another hunter attacked him, and in turn, two pirates attacked *him*. And me, I stood there stupidly, having no idea what to do until someone slammed into me and knocked me to the ground.

Grant.

"What are you doing?" I demanded in a low voice. He held me pinned in the dirty street, as if attacking, while the fray raged behind us.

"What are *you* doing?" he growled back. "Are you okay? Have they hurt you?"

"Me? No! *You're* the one who's outnumbered." He regarded me intently, not satisfied with that answer. "Don't worry about me. Trust me on this."

He hesitated a beat more. "Then keep my cover. I can't get made. Do you understand that? No matter what you see. Don't try to help me out here—"

"Let her go!"

It was Elijah and Lesser Tom coming to my rescue. They ripped Grant away, and I lost track of him in the shadows. I'd just staggered to my feet and took out the dirk when another patrolman tried to grab me. He didn't get very far. Two punches to his jaw sent him stumbling, and then another gunshot sounded. My opponent screamed and put a hand over the left side of his head. It looked like the bullet had only clipped his ear, but it was still a bloody mess. Tom himself came over, shoving his pistol in his belt as he kicked the man in the ribs.

I looked frantically for Grant but couldn't find him. The lighting was too poor, and it had gotten noisy. Along with the grunts and cries of the combatants, half the patrons from Molly's had spilled out to watch the spectacle and offer their own shouts. A couple of heretic hunters were still engaged in active fighting. A couple more were completely down and being beaten further by the pirates. I couldn't tell who was whom.

A voice from the crowd yelled, "The militia! The militia is coming!"

Tom looked up and scowled. "Get out of here!" he shouted. "You know where!"

Between the din and battle lust, I didn't think any of his men would even acknowledge the order. But they all stopped what they were doing and assembled at his side, quickly untying our horses. I was still standing and searching for Grant, but things were becoming even more chaotic in the street.

"Get moving," Tom said, coming to my side. "We need to—"

One of the patrolmen, who apparently wasn't down for the count, had obtained a pistol somehow and was charging toward Tom. Without even thinking, I jumped in front of Tom with my dirk pointing out. The man tried to swerve but stumbled and ran into my blade. It pierced the side of his abdomen, and he crumpled to the ground. I pulled the dirk out and stared at the blood on it, stunned.

"Come on, Aviel!"

Tom practically dragged me to the others, and then he and Elijah roughly lifted me onto a horse. I peered back frantically, still needing to know what had happened to Grant. I was on the verge of actually turning around until Tom slapped my mare, and she took off after her cohorts.

We rode to a town house in a sleepy, middle-class neighborhood that had apparently finished celebrating for the night. The home belonged to some business associate who was away, but Tom had a key. We crowded into the parlor, dirty and bloody, and Tom immediately began issuing orders.

"Everyone lays low for the rest of the night. Elijah, go tomorrow and get some funds from the Bull to pay whoever we're bribing in the militia these days. Lesser Tom, you get word to the men who went to the storehouse. Tell them they'll still get their money for tonight—it's just going to be delayed. And Anders . . ." Tom fixed the Skarsian man with a glare. "As for you, you're going to take your cut back to Molly's tomorrow and give it to her as an 'apology' for the disturbance."

Anders winced, but I wasn't sure if it was because of that punishment or because one of his eyes was almost swollen shut. "Boss, I'm sorry. When I saw them, I just—"

"Yes, yes. I know." Tom sank onto a plush sofa. I'd never seen him look so worn out. "But you caused a hell of a mess tonight. We can't afford to get on Molly's bad side. And, for better or for worse, those men are acting on official orders from the governor. The militia can't ignore that. They'll have to come looking for us, and that's going to be an inconvenience until we get everything settled." He glanced over at Elijah. "You'd better double our standard bribe."

"Well, I can't lay low here," I interjected. "I have to leave. Now."

Tom sighed. "My lady, I know you get distressed about unnecessary violence. I know you don't like endangering the innocent, but those men were *not* innocent. They're more monster than we are. At least we're only in this for profit."

"I'm not distressed," I snapped. "I just have to go."

I stalked out of the parlor, and Tom followed me to the front door. "Wait."

"Are you going to stop me?" I pulled out the dirk. Every second I delayed was a second Grant could be bleeding out in the street. "I won't let you—"

I stopped when I saw the blade, red with blood. Despite all my dreams of sword-wielding glory and the lessons Tom had given me before and after jobs, I'd never stabbed someone like that.

"Have you ever killed anyone?" Tom asked softly, guessing my thoughts.

I couldn't stop staring. "No. But . . . I've wanted to."

"Well, you haven't killed anyone tonight. His wound is going to be ugly, and it's going to hurt, but it wasn't in the right place to kill him. Assuming it doesn't get infected."

"But what about the others? Our guys were beating them when they were down!"

"And I told you, they deserved it—no matter how foolish Anders was to start that madness."

"But did any of them die?"

"I don't know. I had a few other things to keep track of."

Had Grant been kicked and struck while unconscious? My stomach roiled, and I turned the doorknob. "I'm leaving now, Tom."

He put his hand on top of mine. "You're a friend to the Alanzans. I thought you'd be as pleased as Anders at what happened." He tilted his head and studied me. "Did you know them?"

"No. But it's like you said. I don't like unnecessary violence. Please, let me go." I always tried to keep my cool façade around Tom, but I was growing increasingly panicked. Was there any way I could win if I actually had to fight him? Not likely. Especially with the rest of the men just in the other room.

Tom reached into his pocket and handed me one of his favor coins. "For saving me. Not many people get two."

I hesitated as I glanced at my bloody dirk. Then, I sheathed it and pocketed the coin. "Can I go?"

"Turn your cloak inside out. Bind up your hair. I don't know if you'll be targeted, but it's best if you aren't recognized. The only damage you caused was at the end, and you've built up a lot of good-will." He must have been recovering from his earlier consternation because he flashed me one of his charming smiles. "Being an angel might pay off."

I had no time to answer. I was already hurrying down the steps, my heart racing and fear building. Once I was out of his sight, I turned the cloak inside out and then removed the wig completely, stuffing it under my shirt. So many people were masked tonight that I'd blend right in, even with my natural hair.

I ran all the way back to the city's center. When I reached Molly's, panting, the crowd had already dispersed, and all of the heretic hunters were gone. Blood still remained on the road, though. I interrogated a few passersby about what had happened. Some knew nothing. Some knew there had been a fight. Desperate, I actually knocked on Molly's door and faced down the henchman who opened it. My hands were shaking.

"What happened to the heretic patrol?"

He shrugged. "They either left or were dragged away."

"Did any of them die?"

"I don't know."

"Shouldn't you be a little more concerned?" I demanded.

"Not really. If they're dead, Molly gets to keep whatever was in their accounts."

He slammed the door, and I didn't move. I could hardly breathe. A crushing sense of fear began to smother me. Fear that Grant was dead. Fear that I was responsible.

I turned from Molly's and began running toward the bakery.

CHAPTER 23

WHEN I REACHED GRANT'S BUILDING, I TOOK THE STEPS up two at a time, nearly tripping in the process. I pounded on the door and pulled the itchy wig out of my shirt as I waited. When no answer immediately came, I knocked again and gave it a good kick as well.

He's not here. He's lying dead on some street, dragged off by a thief. Or maybe he's not dead but just too injured to make it home, and it's all because—

The door swung open. Grant stood there, holding his shirt. A few dark welts crisscrossed part of his chest, and one side of his face looked a little swollen. The other held a small cut. Otherwise, he seemed okay. He said nothing and simply beckoned me forward, but I saw a glimpse of relief flash through his eyes. After he closed the door, all I could do was stand and stare as I tried to catch my breath.

"You're alive," I finally blurted out.

"I'm hard to kill."

I dropped the wig and removed my dirk. Then I flung myself against him and didn't realize how tightly I held him until he said, "Ow."

I started to move back. "Oh, I'm sorry. I wasn't think—"

"Stop it," he said, keeping one hand on my hip. "I'm not easy to hurt either. Are *you* okay?"

"Yes." I wrapped my arms around his neck and folded myself into him. All the panic, all the uncertainty . . . everything that had built up within me came bursting out. "I thought you were gone. I thought you were dead. And I couldn't handle it—I mean, I didn't know how I'd—and I just—I felt like I would die too—and I—"

"Easy there," he said. His nervous body language contradicted the lightness of his tone. He'd gone rigid in my arms and drew back a little. After a moment's thought, he removed my mask and examined my face. His expression became more troubled as he did, the hand on my hip growing tentative.

My own hold tightened. I needed to cling to him, half afraid he might disappear again if I didn't. That fear of losing him had the same effect as when I'd realized how painful the burn on his arm must have been. The same effect as hearing him talk about being a ghost. Something changed in me during those moments of his vulnerability—because he changed too. He stopped being my adversary, my partner in espionage, or even my object of superficial desire. He was just . . . Grant.

"I'm glad you're okay," I said softly. "Because I actually do like you. And I think . . . maybe you like me too."

He did. I could see it. And I could also see that it terrified him. Keeping his hand there, barely touching me, took more effort than all that fervor on the floor had. Because when you were a man who was resigned to being unfixed to anything, it was easier to tear off the clothes of a transient lover than it was to simply meet the eyes of someone you might care about. And it was beyond comprehension that that person might care back.

"It's fine if you only like me a little," I added.

Despite his unease, a smile began creeping over his face. His grip on me grew stronger, steadier. "Only a little, huh?"

I walked my fingers up his neck and ran them through his hair. "Yes. As little as you want, if it makes you feel better. I don't want you to throw me out again."

"I've never thrown you out. You stormed out."

"I won't this time."

I raised my chin and parted my lips, the invitation clear. He accepted it. His indecision vanished with that kiss, replaced by an intensity that almost felt desperate. Like maybe he thought he'd lost me too. He lifted me up, and I wrapped my legs around his waist as he carried me to his bedroom. The kissing never broke until we fell onto the bed in a tangle. He rolled me to my back and brought his mouth down again, but I stopped him for a moment, resting my hand against the side of his face so that I could just look at him. I smiled, and he smiled back. And even with my body so spun up and restless, I realized I was just as elated to simply be there *with him* as I was to finally let desire run its course. I let my hand drop, and as we kissed again, I sensed a similar revelation in him.

After that, I stopped worrying about whether I was doing everything right. I stopped caring that I still fumbled with clothing while he removed it with such ease. Despite his own eagerness, he took his time and drew out every action in a way that was both glorious and agonizing. He could read my body's cues, and I learned some of his. I also learned that there was a lot I'd never known about going to bed with someone.

And when it was over, when we lay side by side in blissful exhaustion, I discovered another gap in my sexual knowledge. What did you do afterward?

Grant had his hands behind his head and gazed at the ceiling thoughtfully. I sprawled on my side, half-covered in sheets, as I let myself savor all the different sensations still echoing in my body. I felt lazy and liquid. I felt as though I'd been remade.

I looked over at him and couldn't even imagine what he was thinking. He was Grant, after all. But he was so still just then, so at ease for once, instead of constantly fighting his way against the world. I scooted over and rested my head on his chest, cautious of the purpling welts. He'd have bruises for days. He started a little at my movement, but after several moments, he put his arm around my shoulder.

We stayed in that contented closeness for a few precious minutes, and then, in his way, he abruptly said: "I have three questions for you."

That should've immediately set off my alarms, but I was still too languid and dazed to give it much thought. "Okay."

"Your first time?"

"Yes." I hesitated. "Was it obvious?"

"Not right away." His face remained pensive, but there was an appreciative edge to his voice. "You aren't exactly shy about what you want. That threw me off."

A little of my old doubt returned. "Is that a bad thing?"

"No, no, you were fine."

I lifted my head. "Fine?"

He sighed. "You were exquisite. Intense, daring, provocative—more so because you don't even realize it. You make it hard to be patient. Is that better?"

Delight—mixed with a little bit of self-satisfaction—filled my chest. I wondered if this counted as the sort of "sweet and tender things" Florence had spoken of. For Grant, it was probably akin to reciting poetry. "Yes. Is that your second question?"

"You know it isn't." He finally turned his head and looked at me, his expression earnest. "Did I hurt you?"

"No," I said, surprised. "It was . . . I don't know. I'm still reliving it. I don't have the words. It's beyond words."

He looked relieved. "Good. Though I would've settled for 'fine.'" And then, because he excelled at the unexpected: "So. What are you doing running around with Tom Shortsleeves?"

I groaned and rolled away, returning to my back. "Come on, Grant. Do we really have to talk about this now? For once, can't we have a nice moment?"

"I thought we just did. A lot of them. And of course we're going to talk about this now. Mirabel, you were running around with some of the city's most dangerous men! You could've gotten yourself killed."

My body still sang from what we'd done, and I'd even wondered earlier what the odds were tonight of repeating it. Judging from this conversation's trajectory, they weren't good.

"Well, I'm still alive. Don't you have any faith in me?"

"A great deal, which is why, the more I think about it, I should've realized a long time ago who the golden-haired angel that's captivated the city is." He shook his head, expression pained. "When were you going to tell me? Why didn't you already?"

"I don't know. The time never seemed right. Probably because I knew you'd react like this."

He sat up. "Like what? Like being worried about you?"

A glimmer of the old frustration sparked in my chest at his tone. "Like you judging me."

"You should be judging yourself. What happened to your righteous sense of fighting injustice?"

"That's exactly what I'm doing. We give back to the oppressed. We punish the corrupt. It's what I've always wanted to do, and you know it."

"I didn't know you'd do it by becoming a vigilante. *And* a common thief."

"I'm not!" I jerked upright, wrapping a blanket around me. "I don't take any jobs I don't want to. It's earning me money to help pay off Lonzo's bond. *And* it connects me with the pirates you thought the traitors might be buying from. I thought you'd like that."

"Tom Shortsleeves steals art and jewelry, not army supplies. Everyone knows that."

"But Tom knows pirates who *do* steal for the traitors. Like Sandler. Remember the lead I got you?"

He made no acknowledgment of that. "There are better ways for you to earn money."

"And I'm pursuing them all. Marriage, your case, Tom." I waved my hands impatiently. "One way or another, I'll get Lonzo back."

"Marriage is what you list first?"

"I already told you I'll do anything I can to pay the bond. Going through with marriage might not be my preferred plan, but it's the most reliable."

"Going through with . . . wait. Do you have some serious offer?" His eyes widened. "Are you engaged?"

I shifted uncomfortably. "Not exactly. I just have this arrangement. Sort of. If I can't pay off my contract myself or get Lonzo's money any other way, there's this elderly—ah, extremely elderly—gentleman who'll marry me at the last minute. He's very nice," I added quickly. "Very respectable, very generous with his wealth. And he doesn't expect any 'marital duties.'"

I'd never seen Grant so shell-shocked. "I guess you weren't kidding when you said you'd do anything. The other night, you acted like marriage was some distant contingency, but you've got a husband already lined up! Then what is . . . this? What we're doing in bed?"

"I . . ." I averted my eyes, unable to face that outrage. "Having a nice moment?"

"Do I have any place in your life after you're married?"

I turned back incredulously. "Do you want one? Did you change your mind about attachment? I wouldn't know. You aren't exactly expressive when it comes to your feelings."

"Unlike you, overflowing with honesty. Was I supposed to be the illicit lover that you keep on the side while you reign as the pampered queen of your 'extremely elderly' gentleman's estate?"

I ran a hand over my tangled hair, weary and embarrassed. "I don't know, Grant. I didn't really think about us beyond this."

He flinched and stayed silent, which was never a good sign.

"Marriage is my last resort," I insisted. "That's why I never mentioned it. I don't even think about it. I really am hoping to buy freedom for Lonzo and me. I'll either get the money from Tom, or you'll solve your case, and we can all be happy. Me with my reward, you with your official agent promotion."

His furious expression abruptly turned puzzled. "What?"

"Isn't that what you get?" I became equally confused by his reaction. "You've said before you have a lot on the line with this job. And

Silas explained how you're an honorary agent—and that solving this will change things."

"Did he say I'd become an agent?"

"Not exactly . . ." I tried to read his face and figure out what I was missing. "I just assumed it. What else is there?"

Grant lapsed into silence again. Our roles shifted, and now he was on the defensive. "I do get a promotion . . . but not to a run-of-the-mill agent." He took a long, deep breath and exhaled before going on. "Osfrid and the Balanquans have made a deal, in order to ensure relations stay harmonious. The colonies are going to send a delegation—ambassadors and their families—up there to live among them and help with the peace. It's unusual that the Balanquans would allow it—they've become pretty tight with their borders. But as much as Osfrid's king wants a good relationship with them, he also wants insurance. Since I'm trained, I'll be spying on the Balanquans. The whole delegation will, actually, but I'll be in charge of processing all the intelligence. No one will suspect it as long as my cover stays intact. They'll just think I'm there because I know the language."

My whole world came to a standstill. "You're going away. Far away. To the people who treated you like a ghost."

Amusement—dark amusement—crossed his face. "That's the thing. In the Balanquan social hierarchy, ambassadors are treated with extreme honor and indulgence. They acquire a status second only to the league chiefs. I'd be in the sixth branch—that's what the social levels are called. Sixth is well above my family's status, well above my uncle's." Grant pointed to the mysterious scar on his arm. "This was my mark of status before—my citizenship among the Balanquans, born to a third-branch family. When I returned, my uncle made a case that I didn't deserve to be a citizen—both because I was a mixed bastard and because I'd spent so much time away. He argued I was more Osfridian now and had lost my rights to the Empire. The judges agreed. They burned this off and exiled me."

I shuddered. "Grant, I'm so sorry."

"I found out later that my uncle was being elevated to the fourth branch to work in a commander's household. It wouldn't have been possible if he was still related to me. But with this assignment? I'll vastly outrank him. For the first time in my life, he'll actually have to treat me with respect." Grant's eyes glittered darkly, and his words dripped with bitterness.

It was a lot to take in, a lot to process. And I still hadn't recovered from the news he would be leaving. It sat in my stomach like a leaden weight. "So this drive you have to finish the case, this goal you told me you were working for . . . it's not about settling into the agency. It's not about supporting Silas. It's about revenge."

Grant frowned. "There's more to it than that."

"It sounds pretty straightforward to me."

"Mirabel, I'll get my status back." In one of the few times in our acquaintance, he was trying to convince me of something, rather than *telling* me. He was almost beseeching me. "I'll probably get a new name—a real name, not that 'no status' joke my uncle gave me! Everything they took away will be restored—and then some."

"But is it what you want?" I exclaimed. He seemed so indifferent to the world sometimes. This was almost beyond comprehension. "Do you really want to live with people who did that to you? Abandon Silas and Aiana? They're more like family than any of your blood relations."

"It's not just about them. It's the land, too. I thought you of all people would know what it's like to have your homeland ripped away from you."

"I rejected it. It didn't reject me."

"So you're done with it? You're done being Sirminican? You've settled too comfortably into Osfridian high society?"

The questions caught me off guard. "N-no. Of course not."

"Do you want to see Sirminica again?" he pushed.

"Yes. It's still a part of me. But it's not possible to get back anytime soon."

"Well, the Empire's still a part of me too. I feel it inside." He tapped his chest. "I need to see it again, and I *can* get back."

"Yes, but you seem obsessed with doing it in a way that focuses on revenge. Outranking your uncle was the first thing you mentioned—not reuniting with your birthplace."

"You're in no position to lecture me, considering some of *your* current life choices," he warned.

"And you're in no position to lecture me for keeping secrets! When were you going to tell me this? I would've liked to have known before I got into your bed that you were going to head off across the continent afterward!"

"Would that have made a difference?" he asked. "You just said you hadn't thought beyond this."

"I guess I'm not the only one," I snapped. "But why does it matter? You only like me a little, after all." Even as I spoke, I knew I was a hypocrite. I'd made plans without him and then had the audacity to be outraged when he made his own. No one had been betrayed here. There were no promises between us. I knew all of that . . . but it didn't change how hurt and angry I felt. How broken and dismissed.

Grant was clearly upset too, but he faltered for just a moment. He glanced across the room. "Maybe . . . maybe you'd like to see the lands up north."

I pulled the blankets off me and scooted out of the bed to search for my clothes. "I'm not going to be your tagalong, any more than you'll be my secret lover. I have too much self-respect."

He stood up and began pulling on his own pants as I struggled to dress. "Does that involve using an old man for his money? Joining a group of pirates?" Grant gestured angrily around. "Even if you really are picking jobs that let you sleep at night, the rest of your friends aren't so picky. And by supporting them with what you do choose, you're unwittingly furthering them in what you don't. I never thought you were that kind of person, Mirabel."

"I'm not doing this for me!" I cried. "I have to do whatever I can to save Lonzo. And you don't understand that this is the only way to do it!"

"And *you* don't understand that this is the only way I can do what I need to!"

Silence. We stood there staring at each other, eyes locked, both of us raging. All I could think was *Another day, another fight with Grant.*

"I can't keep doing this," I said, my voice hoarse. I nodded toward the bed. "Thank you . . . for that. But I'm done. Done with everything. You should've listened to Silas about me. I'm cutting myself off from your case. I'm sure you'll do just fine alone—you always have."

He crossed his arms. "That's probably for the best. Don't worry— I'll still make sure you get some of the reward. I know how much that means to you. I've got some gold here—"

"No." I held up my palm. "Keep it. I don't want it. I don't want anything from you anymore."

He scoffed. "Of course. Because I'm out of your system now?"

"Yes." Even I was surprised at how cold the word sounded. "And because it's obvious I was never in yours." I readied myself for a biting retort, but it didn't come.

"Mirabel . . ."

He reached out and touched my cheek. I jumped a little, and he quickly pulled his hand back, staring at his wet fingertip like he'd never seen anything like it before. I rubbed my face, embarrassed at those few traitorous tears. I didn't even understand why they were there.

He didn't say anything else and just held that hand up wonderingly. I couldn't handle him seeing me like this anymore. Without another word either, I spun around and rushed out of the bedroom and out the front door. I was afraid he'd try to stop me. And also afraid that he wouldn't.

But he let me go—like he always did—and as I slammed the door, the words of our earlier conversation hit me like a physical blow.

"I've never thrown you out. You stormed out."

"I won't this time."

I ran down the steps. Drunken revelers still staggered down the streets, but I didn't look at anything or anyone until I was outside the city and almost to the marsh path. I stopped to gather myself and was surprised to find myself shaking. There was a terrible ache in my chest, so painful that I didn't know how I could take another step. I wasn't angry anymore. Just sad. And drained. I blinked back more tears and then plunged into the brush.

What had just happened?

I'd been overwhelmed when I found out he was alive, ecstatic when we finally gave in to each other. And now . . . now I just wanted to crawl away and hide myself from the world. His words still smarted, especially because there'd been some truth in them. I wouldn't back down from helping Lonzo, but a shadow of dishonor definitely hung over what I was doing with Tom and Rupert, no matter how much I wanted to convince myself otherwise. I was as bad as my father, using any means I could.

But Grant should've also told me he'd been planning to leave Cape Triumph—and that it wasn't just to wander the colonies, but to settle in an entirely different nation. A nation far from me.

I didn't really think about us beyond this.

I came to a sudden stop on the path as I remembered his face when I'd said those words. I hadn't recognized it at the time, but now, I realized what I'd so briefly seen in his features. Pain. When I'd arrived, bursting with joy and relief to see him alive, he'd told me he wasn't easy to hurt. But it turned out he was—and I'd been the one to do it.

I picked up my pace, getting angrier and more distraught—both at myself and Grant. And the mud. It was growing softer and softer as spring pushed forward. Suddenly, desperately, I wanted to see Adelaide. She was the only person left here I still loved without complication. I knew she'd been distressed recently, but I hadn't probed it because I had so many other things that needed my attention. I'd been a shoddy friend and needed to fix that. I'd find out what was making her sad, and I'd stop holding back from her. I'd tell her ev-erything. She'd be shocked, but she loved me too. And it'd be a relief to finally—

"Mira?"

I'd almost reached the edge of the woods when someone moved ahead of me. I reached for the dirk and then recognized Aiana's voice.

"What are you doing here?" I asked. I could just barely see her peering behind me.

"Is Adelaide with you?"

Something about her tone made my blood run cold. "No, why would she be?"

"I just checked your room—to see if you were back, actually. I wish you'd told me how early you were leaving the gala! Anyway, she wasn't there either or in any of the washrooms."

I pushed my way out to the road. "Well, she must be inside there somewhere. She wouldn't leave . . ."

Wouldn't she? Adelaide had never shown signs of sneaking out again, but I had no idea what the truth might be. It was another mark of my failings as a friend.

Aiana smuggled me inside the sleeping house through a side door she was supposed to be guarding, and I thanked her for saving me a trellis climb. I moved quietly and quickly up the stairs and flung open my bedroom door. No Adelaide. All the panic I'd felt for Grant earlier now returned and shifted onto her. The stark fear of losing her made me tremble as I hurriedly changed out of my dirty clothes and put on a nightgown. I needed to search the house. She couldn't have sneaked out after the gala. She *couldn't* have. She was probably in the kitchen. This was all just a big—

Shouts sounded from out in the hall. I heard people running and doors opening, along with more yelling and frantic voices. I raced out the door and found nearly all the other girls looking out of their own rooms. The bodyguards thundered up the stairs. Jasper, Charles, and Mistress Culpepper followed with Clara right on their heels. They were all running toward the end of the hall, toward the attic door. Toward Adelaide.

She still wore the white satin gown from earlier and clutched her silver mask in one hand. Fear filled her wide blue eyes, like she'd wandered off and now found herself lost and stranded in the wilderness. Cedric stood next to her, but then Jasper pulled him away and started shouting, "What have you done? What have you done?"

I pushed my way through my nightgown-clad housemates and linked my arm through Adelaide's. "It's okay," I told her, not really knowing if it was. "Everything's going to be okay."

Jasper turned toward me, his eyes glittering with rage as he clutched Cedric's arm. "It is not going to be okay! For five years, I've run one of the most prestigious businesses in Cape Triumph, and now it's all going to fall apart when they find out my own son couldn't keep his hands off one of our girls." He fixed his glare first on Cedric, then Adelaide. "These two have ruined us!"

CHAPTER 24

GASPS SOUNDED THROUGHOUT THE HALL. I WAS AS dumbstruck as everyone else, but I forced my confusion aside as I pulled Adelaide closer to me. I had to protect her. "Everything's going to be okay," I repeated. "I'll get you out of here."

"You will do no such thing." Mistress Culpepper strode up to us, fury etched upon her sharp face. She had on the same stiff dress from this morning, and I wondered if she slept in it. "The only place you're going is to your room. *Now*."

Adelaide was still in shock, and I guided her toward our door. Everyone was already whispering and pointing, and I refused to let them see more. Cedric was practically being dragged away by his father and one of the hired men. Seeing them pass us was the only thing that snapped Adelaide out of her daze. "Cedric . . ."

He looked back over his shoulder at her, and then he was gone. I pushed her into our room, and just as I closed the door, I heard Mistress Culpepper say, "I want two of you stationed outside her room all night. No one goes in or out."

Adelaide flounced onto the bed and buried her face in her hands. I moved swiftly to her side and put my arm around her. "What happened?"

She dropped her hands and shook her head. "Oh, Mira. I don't know what to do. I don't know what's going to happen."

"Tell me what *already* happened."

Tears began to roll down her cheeks. She was one of those people who still looked beautiful while crying. "Cedric and I—we—that is— Clara found us—and now . . . I don't know."

It was strange to have poised, eloquent Adelaide so at a loss for words. But even with her lack of coherency, a feeling of dread began to build within me. Was it possible that I wasn't the only one who'd done some scandalous things tonight?

"Adelaide, what did Clara find you and Cedric doing?"

"Nothing!" she exclaimed. "I mean, it was only kissing. Not whatever she's saying. We only kissed. Just like the last time."

"Last time? How many . . . times have there been?"

She wiped at her face. "Only those. I've loved him longer than that, ever since . . . well, I don't know how long. We can't get married, though. But there's no way I can marry anyone else. Not anymore. What are they going to do to Cedric? What are they going to do to me? I'm going to have to go to a workhouse!"

"You absolutely will not. I'll smuggle you out on a ship before that happens. Now, let's get you cleaned up. You'll feel better."

I helped her get out of the elaborate dress and into a nightgown. As I washed the makeup from her face with a cool cloth, my mind raced. I was an even worse friend than I'd thought. Because in looking back, I realized that I should've known a long, long time ago that Adelaide and Cedric were in love. It was so obvious in the way they sought each other out, the way she used to light up whenever he visited Blue Spring. Any friend of theirs would have seen it. Any friend whose head wasn't filled with spies and pirates.

As she grew calmer, I got a slightly clearer version of the story. Apparently, she and Cedric had only recently discovered their love, and they'd tried to ignore it—resulting in both of them being miserable for the last month as Adelaide was trotted out for man after man. Everything had exploded when Clara had walked in on them kissing in the attic tonight.

"What are they going to do to Cedric?" Adelaide asked again. "They can't ignore this. We're all supposed to be protected and virtuous."

I certainly wasn't in the ranks of the virtuous anymore. I felt embarrassed that Adelaide and Cedric—so deeply in love—had managed to restrain themselves. As for me, I'd shamelessly given myself to . . . what? What was Grant to me?

I couldn't unburden myself to Adelaide now. Not anymore. She had too much going on without taking on my problems. She spent most of the night telling me variations of the same story, crying, and worrying about what would happen next. When she dozed a little near sunrise, I stayed awake and watched over her.

Mistress Culpepper came knocking early and told us Adelaide needed to be downstairs in thirty minutes for a meeting with the Thorns in their private office. We were released from our confinement and allowed to clean up in the washrooms, but the bodyguards still hovered in the hallway. Adelaide's hysteria had faded, and she stood ready to face what was to come. There was no sign of last night's tears, and she strode down the stairs with her head high.

The other girls were already up, lingering in the foyer or parlor or anywhere that kept them within sight of the office. Once Adelaide had gone inside it and shut the door, I stood in the hallway opposite it and crossed my arms over my chest.

My defensive stance made the others steer clear of me, though I saw a few eye me curiously, no doubt hoping I had some new piece of the story. I stared straight ahead and stayed silent, even when I heard Clara recounting a very exaggerated, very unflattering version of what had happened last night.

I only broke my silence to ask loudly, "What were you doing in the attic last night anyway, Clara?" When she promptly stopped her story, I suspected I wasn't the only one who had discovered the trellis.

Things got more interesting when Warren Doyle and his mother showed up at the front door, insisting they speak with Charles and Jasper.

"I—I'm sorry," said Mistress Culpepper, more flustered than I'd ever seen. "Mister Charles and Mister Jasper are currently engaged with, ah, Mister Cedric and Miss Bailey."

But after a quick check with the Thorns, the Doyles were admitted to the office. I wondered how they could have found out so soon. Certainly not from us cloistered girls. The bodyguards, I supposed. This was good gossip for a festival night.

"Who in the world is that now?" exclaimed Mistress Culpepper when another knock sounded. "Does everyone in the city know? Answer it, Judith."

When Miss Bradley opened the door, it was obvious those waiting outside weren't from Cape Triumph. Three men and a woman in plainly cut clothing of blue-gray wool stood on the front porch, their expressions solemn. One man looked a little older than me. His companions were middle-aged. I glanced beyond them in astonishment. More people—a *lot* more people—dressed in similar clothing stretched out into the house's yard. Most appeared to be women.

The younger man took off his hat, revealing neatly cut blond hair. "Good morning, Mistress. My name is Gideon Stewart. Can you tell me if this is the household of Mister Charles Th—"

"Winnifred! Joan!"

Martha came tearing across the room, and suddenly, two very pretty girls pushed past the men in the doorway and ran to her. And then more girls came in. And more. All were drably dressed in variants of blue and gray, but as I took in their ages and beauty, I knew who they were. The foyer filled up, and I had to stand on my tiptoes to find who I sought over the crowd—but there she was, all the way in the back of the group, not even inside the house yet.

I felt weak for a moment, like my knees would give out, and then a burst of energy jolted me to life. I couldn't get across the foyer easily, so instead, I ran to the office door and threw it open. Adelaide sat with the Thorns and the Doyles, and all looked up in astonishment at my entrance.

Jasper scowled. "I told you lot not to—"

"They're here!" I cried. "They're here! I don't understand it, but they're here."

"Who?" he demanded.

"The other girls! The other ship." I looked at Adelaide, needing her to understand how crucial this was. "Adelaide, Tamsin's alive!"

Everyone in the room sprang out of their seats and into the packed foyer. Adelaide was right beside me as we sprinted across the room, pushing our way through as we desperately tried to see if the impossible was truly possible. And it wasn't just us. Chaos reigned.

Every time I'd lost someone, the same questions always tormented me. I'd ponder if I could have done anything differently. I'd ask myself if it was fair that I lived while they died. I wondered how I was going to get through without them.

But I'd never asked what would happen if one of these people came back. Because no matter how much their loss hurt me or how much I ruminated over what had happened, I'd always accepted that it *had* happened. It was done and over. No one came back from death.

And yet . . . Tamsin stood right in front of me.

We couldn't stop hugging each other. The three of us laughed, cried, and babbled apologies that none of us heard. We were too consumed with each other, too caught up in the miracle that somehow, against all understanding, we'd been reunited.

"Friends! Friends!" Jasper had climbed on top of a chair and was attempting to be heard over the commotion. "You're witnessing a miracle right before our eyes. Something none of us thought possible. I've just learned that—as you can no doubt tell—the *Gray Gull* wasn't lost at sea! It sustained great damage in the storm and was blown off course—far, far north to the colony of Grashond."

Adelaide's shock mirrored my own. Tamsin's grim nod told us he spoke the truth.

"Who do I have to thank for this?" exclaimed Jasper. "Who do I have to thank for saving my girls?"

The young man who'd first spoken at the door—Gideon Stewart—was singled out and promptly became Jasper's favorite person in the world. Jasper swept him and the other leaders from Grashond away, showering them with gratitude and promises of gifts.

"They won't take anything," said Tamsin. She pulled a white kerchief off her head and shook her fiery hair free. "They saw it as their duty from Uros to bring us here."

She seemed understandably happy to be here, but there was a weariness—both physical and mental—in her that was impossible to miss. "We shouldn't be standing around like this," I said. "Everyone should be resting. And eating too. When was the last time you ate?"

"I don't know," said Tamsin. "Last night, I guess? It's pretty much been all salt fish since we left. They have loads of it up there. It all runs together after a while."

With the initial shock over, Mistress Culpepper had recovered herself and jumped into the organizational and administrative role she excelled at. Along with the returned girls, the Grashond settlers needed accommodations. There were *Gray Gull* sailors there as well, and although she wouldn't dream of letting them stay in the house, she did make sure they were made comfortable until they could settle up business matters with Jasper.

Tamsin was assigned to our room, obviously, and Adelaide and I both badly wanted to know what had happened in her time away. She didn't seem up to any interrogation and simply said that her ordeal had been "not awful," so we let her be and mostly just basked in the joy of having her back.

When Tamsin was cleaning up in the washroom, Adelaide said to me, "If she really is okay like she told us, why won't she talk about it?"

I reflected back on the string of tragedies I'd seen in my own life. "Sometimes, when you go through something like that, it takes a while for you to want to talk about it."

I had no idea what living with the Heirs of Uros must have been like. That sect had settled Grashond years ago in order to build a community focused around the strict and austere principles of their faith. Their religion wasn't heretical since they didn't alter any of the orthodox doctrine, holidays, or texts, but they stripped down anything they thought was indulgent or excessive. They didn't strike me as fun people to be around.

Heloise, who'd become the emerald and now was engaged, gave her clothes to Tamsin. Once clean, fed, and dressed in green, Tamsin was ready to talk. But not about herself.

"I hope you've left some men for the rest of us." She sat on the bed and clasped her hands, looking between Adelaide and me expectantly. "You must have both gotten slews of offers by now."

Where did I even begin to explain what had happened to me? I kept my answer brief and vague. "Not that many in the way of, ah, official ones. But I feel optimistic about my future."

Tamsin's hard gaze swiveled to Adelaide, and I realized I had no idea what had occurred in her meeting. She stammered out a recap of what had happened between her and Cedric, as well as the judgment they'd received.

"Cedric and I can get married, with conditions. His father and uncle won't advance us money to cover my contract—but Warren will. He says he doesn't want someone who doesn't love him in return and would rather cut his losses by recruiting upstanding citizens for his new colony. So we're going with him to Hadisen next week. I'll find a family to board me in exchange for housework and teaching their children. Cedric's going to work a gold claim. He'll get to keep some of the profit, and Warren gets the rest. When the contract's paid off, we can get married and go somewhere else."

Something in her tone made me suspect she was well aware of Cedric's controversial faith and his plans to go to Westhaven Colony.

I didn't know which was more outlandish: accepting help from the man she'd spurned or the thought of dapper Cedric working outside and panning for gold.

Tamsin, as usual, had no shortage of speech. "What were you

thinking? You turned down a future governor for . . . what, an impoverished student?"

Adelaide looked at her feet. We were both beyond ecstatic to have Tamsin back, but feeling the full force of her personality again took a little adjustment. "Well, he dropped out of the university. And he's not impoverished. He's just . . . um, without assets. But I'm sure that will change."

"This would have never happened if I'd been around to look after you." Tamsin turned her chastisement toward me. "Mira, how could you have stood for this?"

"I had no idea," I said honestly.

"You're her roommate! How could you not?"

How indeed. I didn't have a good answer and again berated myself for neglecting my friend. Adelaide looked guilty as well and probably thought it was her fault for not telling me. Between us and Tamsin's reticence to talk, we were a circle full of secrets.

In the week that followed, I saw little of Adelaide. She and Cedric were swamped with preparations for a journey that other settlers had been planning for months. Tamsin, on the other hand, was a nearly constant companion. The arrival of twenty new girls had completely changed the way the Glittering Court functioned. Normally, the social season would be winding down. Instead, it was almost like they had to reset and start all over again.

"We'll have to sponsor another great ball," I overheard Jasper saying to Charles one afternoon. "It'll be an expense we didn't plan for, but we've also got a profit coming in that we'd written off. The sensationalism of this is already spreading. The Lost Girls. Missing at sea, surviving in the wilderness—but still here, beautiful and refined. This'll renew interest from those who passed on the first batch and pull in men who weren't even considering marriage. We should go back over the prices we'd settled for each one and consider raising them."

"Jasper, I recognize the importance of recouping our losses. But by the Six, don't start pushing these girls into parties right away, not after everything they've been through."

"Of course I won't. We need time to plan new events and get them outfitted first. All their original clothes were lost, but we can save money by altering the dresses of all the engaged girls. And," Jasper added, "if any girls *do* want to jump right in, not even you can deny them that."

Tamsin was one of those girls. Two nights after the Flower Festival, Governor Doyle hosted a party celebrating the anniversary of Cape Triumph's settlement. I still had misgivings about the deal Adelaide and Cedric had gotten enmeshed in, made worse by the fact that Cedric—a secret heretic—was locked into a business contract with a self-proclaimed heretic hunter. But Adelaide and Cedric were also desperate. Whatever his beliefs on religion, Warren had given them fair terms in his deal. The two of them remained wary, but as long as they fulfilled their half, everything would hopefully work out.

"I'm so excited," Tamsin told me as we prepared for the Doyle party. She'd required almost no alterations to fit into Heloise's clothes and looked stunning in a celadon silk gown that bared her shoulders. "This must be old to you by now, but being able to wear something like this feels like a dream after those shabby things they put us in."

For me, the dream was still just having her back. I'd often find myself watching her and wondering if I'd suddenly blink and find her gone again. More and more pieces of what had happened to them had leaked out from the other girls. Along with the Grashond settlers, they'd apparently encountered Icori, Lorandian traders, and Balanquans while waiting for warmer weather to travel in. Tamsin occasionally offered up tidbits but otherwise remained reticent about her adventures.

Her return was pretty much the only thing that could distract me from constantly moping over the fallout with Grant. I still did plenty of it, of course. He'd had such a central role in my life, and now, he was gone. And no matter how hard I tried to ignore them, little and unexpected things would remind me of him. Some weren't so subtle, though. It was impossible not to think of him when I choked down a bitter herbal mixture twice a day that I'd "borrowed" from the stash Mistress Culpepper kept around for newly married girls. It was one of a number of concoctions our Female Studies book recommended for preventing pregnancy. It was also, from what I'd heard, the worst tasting, but that was a small price to pay in order to keep my life from becoming even more chaotic.

"You look beautiful, but you don't have to go out so soon," I told Tamsin. "No one would blame you if you wanted to recover after all that hardship."

"The only hardship I've faced is wasting five weeks that could've been spent looking for a husband." She paused to tuck in a minuscule strand of hair that had crept out of her updo. "I could've been married by now. I *should've* been married by now. That's what I came here for—not trekking through a frozen wasteland."

We heard a call outside our room that it was time to go to the coaches. I touched Tamsin's arm before she walked out. "If you ever need to talk about anything, I'm here." It took a great deal of effort for me to say that. I too understood wanting to keep pain locked in—and how it could eat you up.

Her fierce expression melted into a smile. "I know you are. And I'm here too if *you* want to talk. I can tell Adelaide's not the only one with problems." The smile diminished, growing sad now. "I should've been here to keep you both in line. I . . . I never should've gotten on the other ship."

"It's in the past. You're safe, and you're back. Let's go to your first party."

❧

She was right that our social life had become old for me. Seeing her face when we stepped into the Doyle mansion reminded me just how truly indifferent I was now. She asked to be introduced to Warren, and I was happy to oblige. I wanted an excuse to speak with him as well.

Even though I'd cut myself off from the case, it was hard not to pursue leads in the conspiracy. With Adelaide out of the picture, I hoped he'd finally start talking to another girl.

And he did. Tamsin.

To be fair, she was such a powerful force that it was hard for anyone else to steal the scene from her. The two girls she'd tied with had been on the *Gray Gull*, and they too had been eager to jump back into the Glittering Court. They'd immediately honed in on Warren, but Tamsin captured his attention so well, they never stood a chance. That meant I didn't either, but I stayed after they drifted away because there was still information I might glean. He was happy to tell her all about Hadisen, but most of his talk was about its gold. There still seemed to be no indication that any of his supplies had been stolen by the traitors' cause.

The most difficult part of the evening turned out to be avoiding Cornelius and Lavinia Chambers. They'd accepted my decision to wait to marry Rupert but never missed a chance to talk about their amazing family and lifestyle.

"We're redoing the conservatory," Lavinia bragged. "Gorgeous upholstery, straight from Lorandy. And I want to fill it with sculptures from all over the world. It'll be our own little museum, with nothing else in Denham to match it."

Cornelius nodded along eagerly, and I smiled appropriately, relieved when someone else finally called them away. A low, dull ache remained in my ankle, but it was vastly improved compared to what it had once been, and I was able to accept a few dances. But although my body caught every beat perfectly, my mind was far away. Grant sneaked into my thoughts a lot. I replayed much of what had happened in bed—before we started talking, at least—and although I still felt a thrill in remembering each part, its loss didn't bother me nearly so much as the simple loss of Grant.

After breakfast the next morning, Aiana beckoned me over as I left the dining room. I stepped aside and waited for the Grashond visitors to move past me. They were staying on for a while but always dined separately.

"I have to take Adelaide into the city to help outfit her for Hadisen," Aiana told me. "Do you want to come along? Tamsin is. You've all got the afternoon free."

"Sure," I said glumly.

She cocked her head and eyed me. "What's wrong? I thought you'd be overjoyed to have Tamsin back."

"I am, I am. But . . ." I studied her face for any indication that she might know what had happened the night of the Flower Fest. She and Grant were close . . . but how close? He didn't seem like the confiding type. "Have you talked to Grant recently?"

"No, why?"

"We . . . well, I'm not working for him anymore. I've really been cut off. Silas never thought it was a good idea."

Her voice grew compassionate. "Neither did I. I know you liked the adventure of it all, but this is for the best. Look, when we find some time, I'll teach you the Balanquan crossbow. Maybe that'll make your life feel a little more daring."

"That's nice of you," I said automatically. "But I don't know if I'll ever have reason to attack with a ranged weapon."

"We attack however we need to," she returned. "Now. Let's gather the others and go into town. We're actually going to Grant's store."

I tried not to gasp. There were a number of supply stores in town, but of course, Aiana would only go to one place to buy frontier apparel and supplies. And even though Grant had wreaked such havoc with my life, a traitorous part of me wanted to catch a glimpse of him. When combined with an outing among my best friends, the day suddenly became more interesting.

✺

I'd actually never been inside Winslow & Elliott. Shelves and hooks held all sorts of supplies, everything from heavy mining and farming equipment to racks of apparel to horse and wagon gear. Grant worked behind the counter, assisting the store's many customers, but never so much as glanced at me. He was perfectly aware of our entrance, though, and even offered Aiana a brief hello in Balanquan. Tamsin and Adelaide got nods of greeting too. But not me. My elevated mood plummeted.

"Hey, remember Grant Elliott from the ship?" Adelaide whispered to me. "He's working here."

"Who?"

I moved as far away from him as I could and feigned great interest in browsing hardy textiles. Tamsin looked with me until Grant was ready to help Adelaide. I stayed where I was and tried in vain to ignore them as they spoke across the room. He sounded so pleasant in his helpful shopkeeper role, and it bothered me that I couldn't tell if our fight truly hadn't fazed him or if he was just concealing his feelings with another mask.

When we walked out of the store, Aiana slipped me a small piece of paper while Adelaide and Tamsin chatted. "What's this?"

"Grant gave it to me at the store." She shook her head, clearly displeased. "Maybe you aren't cut out after all."

I clutched it in my hand until we got home, my heart beating furiously the whole time. A note for me. A note from Grant. Until that moment, I hadn't realized just how desperately I needed something to fill that chasm between us. Maybe even to bridge it. What did he have to say to me? Was he really just following up on some leftover part of the case? Or was he trying to make peace? Hope began to blossom within me.

I finally unfolded the paper in my room, sitting on my bed and hiding it behind a book so that Tamsin and Adelaide wouldn't notice. My fragile hope nearly crumbled when I saw it wasn't Grant's writing until I realized—

It was Lonzo's.

CHAPTER 25

I FRANTICALLY SPREAD THE PAPER OPEN ON THE PAGES OF THE book. Like me, Lonzo had used the old code of our father's.

Mira,

You have no idea how happy I am to hear that you're safe and sound on this side of the ocean. I've worried night after night about you in the slums of Osfro, and now I found out you'll be the lady of a rich household! I admit, it's hard for me to imagine you settling down as a demure wife. Something tells me you won't actually be all that demure, though, so I hope you've chosen a man who appreciates your wild nature. And please don't waste his money on me. I have sixty gold left on my bond, and I'll pay it off myself in a year. I've volunteered with a crew that's working on levees and drainage in some of the swampier lands. It's dangerous work, but the money is good and far more than I'd make doing common plantation labor. I'm one of the strongest men here, and that's what they need. Keep writing to me about your new life, and I'll come to you once I'm free.

With love,
Lonzo

I was glad my roommates were both busy about their own tasks because my expression probably looked ghastly. I knew about the efforts to tame the boggy areas down in Osfrid's unincorporated territories. I knew a great deal about it, actually. I'd once danced with a man whose cousin was a surveyor, and a lesson in engineering had filled up most of the dance. Drainage *was* dangerous work. Extremely so. Men frequently died, both from accidents and sickness.

Sixty gold. I had to secure sixty gold—and I had to do it quickly. I couldn't risk Lonzo staying there a moment longer. Grant's reward—if it had ever come—would have helped immensely, but that was off the table now. My work with Tom so far had yielded fifteen gold. Getting the rest was possible, but how long would it take? I could marry Rupert now and have the money right away . . . but no matter how nice he was, I still wanted to hold off on that if I could. Except . . . could I really? Even if I made the rest of the bond through Tom's jobs, there was no way I'd earn enough to pay my own contract in time. I'd have to marry Rupert regardless.

I rubbed my eyes, frustrated at my lack of options. Tom, I decided. It would have to be Tom. He'd always hinted at bigger jobs that were morally ambiguous, and I'd loftily turned them down. But now? With Lonzo on the line? How far would I go?

I looked down at the letter and ran my fingers over the familiar handwriting. The pain of missing him filled every part of me. And I was surprised at the effect seeing Sirminican had on me. I spoke Osfridian with such ease now that my native language had almost ceased to exist for me. The words before me, even out of order from the encryption, triggered a flood of memories, and I suddenly longed to see the green foothills near my family's farm and the graceful spires of Santa Luz.

The Empire's part of me. I feel it inside.

A new understanding of Grant's words hit me and, with them, a pang of guilt. No matter what he said, an element of revenge still drove him. It was obvious in how he described his uncle. But I realized now that there really was more to his wanting to return and that I had misjudged it. Was that enough to offset everything else he'd said and done that night? The spark of anger kindling in me said no.

I focused back on the letter and again pondered the question of how far I'd go for Lonzo. The answer came quickly: as far as I needed to.

I sneaked out to the Dancing Bull at my usual time, once the household was asleep. Now I had two roommates to elude, and I didn't know if Tamsin would be so accommodating as Adelaide. Tamsin was a heavy sleeper, though, and I had to hope she'd just never know that I'd left.

I received a slew of greetings when I made it to the tavern, many of the patrons offering to buy me drinks. I waved them all off with a smile and approached the bar, where I could see Tom standing. Just before I opened my mouth to speak, I realized Tom was having more than a casual conversation with the man standing opposite him. After a few moments, recognition hit me. He was one of the militiaman who'd come looking for Grant and me in the inn. I recoiled and nearly ran for the door until I remembered he'd never really seen my face, and the incident had happened weeks ago.

"Allen, you'll make me a poor man," Tom was saying. I recognized the tone—amiable on the surface, irritated at its core. "We've already paid you far more than necessary."

The other man crossed his arms. "That patrol's run by the city's high-and-mighties. We convinced them it was someone else who started that brawl, but they're still on us to find who did. That's a lot of dodging for us."

"I don't have extra coin to spare here. You'll either have to wait or take something else in exchange."

"What do you have?" asked the militiaman, interest piqued.

Tom thought for a moment. "We've still got some of the Belsian cheese. Brass candlesticks. Those bolts of silk. Three clocks left and—"

"Silk?" interrupted the man. "My woman's always fancied a silk dress. What colors?"

"Come back around noon tomorrow, when it's less crowded, and I'll show you."

"Are you still mending things with the militia after the Flower Fest?" I asked, once the man was gone.

"Yes. We had to grease a few—no, a *lot*—of palms, but in the end, gold—and silk, apparently—speaks louder to the militia than the governor's directives. But don't worry about that. Where have you been? We've all missed you."

"I've been busy. But I'm ready to jump into the work again." My words came out a bit too vehemently. The frustration I felt over the fallout with Grant made me crave an altercation.

I could just barely see an eyebrow rise behind the mask. "So it would seem. What's stirred this fire?"

"I need more money."

"Don't we all. But something else has you worked up." He put on an expression of mock astonishment. "Why, Lady Aviel, you aren't letting some man play games with your heart, are you? Nothing but trouble there. Stick to your own path. You might even consider being a true angel and focus on a chaste life."

I scowled. "Do you have a job tonight, or not?"

"We do," he said, still with that mocking smile. "And I could use extra help. Jenks hasn't returned from his last job, so we're short-handed. This is a good one too. Bad men to take down. If it's a fight you want, you'll get it."

He was right about the fight. Our target was a wagon coming from the north, as so many were now that the roads had cleared and opened up trade. This wagon and its cargo had already been stolen, and its new owners had left none of the old ones alive. They apparently had a long and bloody history. Tom had received a tip of where they'd be tonight, and we waited along the sides of a north-south highway, leaping out when the wagon appeared.

Six men immediately jumped down, ringing the wagon with muskets and blades. A shot sounded right beside me, and one of the bandits on the wagons fell, clutching his leg.

"Wait for it," Tom said from my left. Two more shots came from the wagon, missing my comrades in the trees. "There—on the end, while the others are reloading! He's going for the reins!"

Dirk in hand, I raced toward the front of the wagon. One of the men had scrambled to the driver's seat and was trying to flee, now that he'd assessed the odds. I jumped up to the seat and stabbed at the side of his torso. The blade drew blood, even though the worst of its blow was deflected by his ribs. He missed when he swung at me with his own knife, but his forearm managed to hit me and knock me back into the seat. He loomed over me, and I kicked as hard as I could. My boots slammed into his stomach. I charged forward with the dirk while he stumbled back to the wagon's edge. I landed another sharp kick to the stomach, and he fell to the ground.

Behind me, in the wagon itself, Elijah and Lesser Tom were fighting other bandits. There were only three of them left up here now. Those on the ground had engaged with Tom and Anders. I moved to help Elijah and Lesser Tom, and then I spotted one of the fallen men rear up from the road and aim at Elijah. I leapt forward as the gun went off, knocking Elijah down.

"Go!" yelled Tom from the darkness.

Lesser Tom pushed the last man over the edge and moved to the driver's seat. He seized the reins and urged the nervous horses on. I knelt in the rumbling wagon's hold with Elijah and tried to help him sit up. The bullet had grazed his arm.

"I've had worse," he told me, seeing my concern. He dabbed at the bloody sleeve with his cloak. "But you should've let me be and taken care of yourself. You could've been killed."

"He was out of range. I probably wasn't in that much danger." I patted Elijah's good arm. "Besides, we're friends."

He looked a little startled at that declaration and then began to smile. "I suppose we are."

I grinned back and clung to the wagon's side as we thundered forward. After about a mile, Lesser Tom drew to a halt, and we waited in the darkness. Minutes later, I heard more hooves pounding on the road, and Tom and Anders came riding up with our horses in tow. Tom immediately dismounted and climbed up into the wagon, his eyes fixed eagerly on the three sealed crates we sat around. Anders was right behind him, carrying a crowbar. He opened the crates while Lesser Tom lit a lantern. We all leaned in.

Elijah grunted in approval. "Balanquan trade goods. The north only just thawed out. Someone was eager to get these down here and get a jump on the sales." He lifted an elegant sculpture of a woman riding a deer. At first, it looked like the stone was black, but then I could see a silver sheen on the smooth surface as he rotated it in the light.

"We can't make anything like these. It'll fetch a good price with the right buyers," said Tom. He nodded to another crate. "That silk over there will too. I guess that means I can replenish what Allen fleeces out of me. I don't suppose you'd like a silk dress, my lady? No? Well, I'm sure this other crate will please you. More fruit, fresh from the lovely Balanquan coast. Mistress Smith will adore you even more than she already does."

We headed back for the city in triumph. Tom and Anders led our party, discussing the best ways to sell the sculptures and silk. I rode near the back with Elijah, who always readily explained things to me. He'd already held me in high regard for saving his family, and helping him tonight only furthered my standing. He seemed to think of me as a younger sister. "The stone in those Balanquan statues—I've never seen anything like it before," I remarked.

"They have a lot of it up there. We don't, so it's a good deal for them. Rich collectors get excited by it and think they've gotten a hold of some lost relic. What we've actually got is just regular art they'd use in any home. But like I said, it's worth a lot here."

"How do you know that? Have you ever been to their empire?" This was actually more information than I usually got from Aiana or Grant. They spoke little about the Balanquans. I was curious about the land Grant was willing to risk so much for.

"When I was younger, my pa was a trader, so we were up there a lot. We even lived there for a time. They're pretty closed off now, but the trade still flows from the borders."

"What's it like there?"

Elijah grew reflective. "Pretty. But different. It's so different from here that it didn't even seem like a real place, you know? Even though it's so far north, the eastern coast is warm—something about the sea currents. They've been in Adoria a lot longer than us, so all the homes and businesses . . . they're not new and thrown together like in the colonies. All the wood and stone are carved. I loved it as a kid. Stare at some home, and you'd always find something new in the woodwork. Animals. Leaves."

"What are the people like?"

"Different from us." He shrugged. "But also the same."

We took the goods back to the Dancing Bull, and Tom directed his men to take them down to the storeroom. Once he was satisfied, Tom relaxed with a mug of ale and eyed me shrewdly. "So. What's this about you needing more money?"

I grimaced. "There've been some unexpected developments—new debts I need to pay."

"I hope you're not shelling out to this man of yours."

"There is no man!" I insisted. "This is for family."

"Ah. That certainly ups the stakes, doesn't it? Lucky for you, I might have an opportunity that could work out quite nicely—assuming fifty gold would be of any use."

"Fifty?" More than triple what I'd already earned. Combined, I'd have enough for Lonzo's bond. "In just one job? What kind of job?"

"I have another big haul coming up in a couple of weeks—similar to what we did with the *Queen Grace*. Sneak onto a ship, sailors—hopefully—detained not killed, and then off we go with the cargo."

Suspicion dampened my enthusiasm. "If it's so easy, why does it pay so much more than the last one?"

"Because the cargo is worth more."

"Who are you stealing from?" I asked. "Is this another just for-profit job from some poor merchant trying to make ends meet?"

"It's for profit, but I can say with absolutely honesty the man who owns the cargo is most certainly *not* poor and makes his living by the deaths of countless people. And I hope you know that I value life, just as you do. As always, we'll try to do this with as little harm to the crew as possible. The Six know I can't afford any more bribes."

I was growing tired, now that the thrill of the fight had faded. And I knew it would be best if I didn't go near any kind of job that even Tom admitted wasn't noble. Lady Aviel's original purpose had become clouded, and there was no black and white anymore, the further I became involved with Tom. I was lost in gray.

But fifty gold. For one night's work. And Lonzo's freedom.

I never thought you were that kind of person, Mirabel.

I ignored Grant's voice in my head. After everything he'd put me through, defiance suddenly felt as good as what I could do for my brother.

"I'm in."

Tom gave me the details about when and where the job would occur, and then I made my exit. I returned to Wisteria Hollow and found both Tamsin and Adelaide sleeping soundly. I slinked into my own bed, falling asleep almost as soon as I closed my eyes.

It made for another exhausting day, but I was cheered by the thought of earning Lonzo's bond so quickly. Just like every recent day, however, every lift in my mood ended in a horrific crash.

Adelaide was leaving tomorrow.

I'd known it was coming. I'd even helped with the shopping. But the reality of it, that she'd be gone the next day, off into a new frontier . . . hit me in a new way. I'd just gotten Tamsin back. I wanted them both with me now, safely together in the security of our room. But the world had other plans. Adelaide left early to pursue more preparations, so I couldn't even have the day with her. Tamsin was off to a fancy tea, and me? I actually had no engagements until nighttime.

That was a rarity around here, but the Thorns had been giving most social opportunities to the *Gray Gull* girls. Jasper knew of Rupert's interest—and that it'd likely be my only resort after I'd put off any other potential husbands. So, Jasper wasn't wasting resources to show me off anymore.

"Good news," Aiana said, intercepting me again after breakfast in that way of hers. Sometimes I thought she actually lurked outside the dining room. "I have the day off too. We can work on some crossbow lessons and put a smile back on your face."

"Somehow, I don't think Jasper or even Charles will agree to that."

"Well, they won't know, of course." Her eyes sparkled with mischief. "I'm authorized to chaperone you for walks. We'll go off into the wooded patch to the west and get some target practice in."

I was still lukewarm about learning the crossbow, but getting outside—freely—was a precious opportunity. "Okay. Let's do it."

Aiana looked pleased at my acceptance and reached into her coat. "But first, this. For someone who's supposed to be 'out,' you're certainly getting a lot of messages."

I took the letter, angry at myself for again hoping it might be from Grant. *Stop it, Mira*, I scolded myself. *You're letting him ruin your life. Tom was right. Follow your own path.*

But then, what else was this? Who else would be sending me letters via Aiana? Lonzo again?

A sudden fear that he'd been injured or killed seized me, and I nearly tore the paper as I opened it. When I saw who the message was from, my jaw nearly hit the floor. I had to read it twice.

"Everything okay?" Aiana asked, noting my reaction.

I slowly dragged my gaze up. "I'm not sure. It's from Silas. And . . . he wants me to do a job for him."

CHAPTER 26

SILAS SEEMED EQUALLY ASTONISHED TO BE ASKING.

*I've never approved of you being involved in this,
but a situation has come up that only you may be
able to help us with. Governor Ryan of Paxton is in
town, and my other spies have learned he's a major
player in the conspiracy. He's in Denham to deliver a
letter to another courier, and we need to get it before
he disappears. While here, he's staying at Governor
Doyle's. Word has it you'll be there tonight. I don't
like asking you to risk yourself, but if there's anything
you can do to locate the letter, we could potentially
crack this mess wide open. The choice is yours.*

I lowered the letter and saw Aiana's eyes narrowed with suspicion.
"Something tells me I won't like what that says."

"It could be worse," I replied, tucking it into a pocket. "Now teach
me how to use a crossbow."

No one questioned her as she escorted me outside on what seemed
to be a simple stroll. The sun shone brightly for a change, but the letter preoccupied me so much that I couldn't appreciate the day. What
should I do? The fact that Silas would actually ask me underscored
the job's importance. But he hadn't given me a lot to go on: one letter

somewhere in a giant estate. What if I was caught snooping in the governor's house? *We could potentially crack this mess wide open.* I didn't want to be involved in anything Grant was even distantly connected to . . . but I couldn't ignore what was at stake.

"Get your head out of the clouds, Banle," Aiana told me. We'd reached the edge of Wisteria Hollow's property, and she produced a small, sleek crossbow from the cover of a scrubby bush. "You need to focus on this."

"What did you call me?"

"Banle." She crooked me a smile. "It's like a baby bird. One still in the nest who wants to fly."

"You just gave me a close name." I couldn't help smiling back, though I wasn't sure if I should be flattered or not. "Banle."

"No, Bahn-lay."

"That's what I said."

"You just said the word for boiled potatoes."

"They sound the same."

"No—listen."

She repeated them, and I could just barely pick up a slight pitch difference on the first syllable. "Balanquan uses intonation!" I exclaimed. "I read about it in my linguistic studies, but no Evarian language uses it."

"I don't know what it's called. It's just the way it is. Maybe it's why your people have so much trouble learning our language."

I would've rather learned Balanquan than the crossbow, but Aiana was insistent. She started with basics, how to load the bolts and gauge my range. The crossbow was beautiful, decorated with that silvery black stone I'd seen on the raid. The trigger, irons, and other parts conveyed a fine workmanship I didn't even think was possible in Evaria. Its beauty and petite size were deceptive. It still required a lot of strength and made my arm hurt at the end. But she was right that I'd enjoyed it.

"It felt more like a target game than a weapon," I told her as we walked back. I couldn't remember the last time I'd played anything.

She *tsk*ed in disapproval. "It's not a game where I come from. In darker times, a woman might be left alone with her children. A crossbow like this could help her defend her home. It's unlikely you'll ever be in that situation, but the more ways a woman knows to protect herself, the better."

"Have you been out in the woods?" Tamsin asked me when I got back to my room.

I looked down and saw dirt and leaves stuck to the hem of my dress. "I wanted to get out and walk, and Aiana supervised."

"You'll get too much sun," she scolded. "But we've got other things to worry about now. What should I wear to Warren's going-away party tonight?" She paced in front of her closet, occasionally pulling a dress out and shaking her head. "I've got to leave a good impression on him. *And* his parents."

I frowned. Tamsin had astonished us all with the way she'd charmed Warren in so short of a time. Of course, she was Tamsin. Who could stand against her? But he troubled me now as much as when he'd pursued Adelaide.

"He hunts heretics, you know," I said.

She let go of a dress and turned to face me. "What are you implying?"

I shrugged. "I don't know. It just bothers me to see people persecuted for their beliefs when they aren't hurting anyone. Doesn't it bother you?" We'd never really discussed religion. For all I knew, she hated heretics too.

But something flashed through her eyes. Doubt, maybe. It vanished quickly as her normal resolve took over. She clenched her hands. "He's an intelligent man. If something's wrong . . . well, I'm sure he'll reconsider. Don't look at me like that, Mira! He's a governor. No one can give me the kind of life he can. He's anxious to have a wife once he's set up there. And I'm anxious to be one."

"I just want you to be happy, that's all."

"If this works out, I will be." She stared off for several moments, caught in her own thoughts. "Well, that's enough about that. Let's get back to figuring out what I'm going to wear. *And* what you're going to wear. We'll get you a husband yet."

But it wasn't a husband I was after that night. All sorts of wealthy and important people packed the manor, many more than had come to the anniversary party earlier that week. A number of guests had even traveled from other colonies. A governor's son becoming the governor of a new colony was a huge event. A crowd like that offered pros and cons. More people meant more eyes. More people also meant it was easier to blend in.

I found Governor Ryan easily. He was a large, gregarious man who loved his wine and, from the conversations I overheard, gambling as well. His eyes fell on me once, his expression first puzzled and then disapproving. He returned to his companions and never looked at me again. It had been a while since I'd received such blatant condescension. Not all of Cape Triumph's elite accepted me, but most had at least become used to seeing me at social events.

I didn't need the governor. I needed his letter. If he had it on his person, I was defeated. I'd pickpocketed before, but only in private. Governor Ryan was constantly surrounded by people, and there was no way I'd penetrate that circle. If the letter was somewhere in the house, then my task was only slightly less impossible.

"But, Father, think of the money we'll save!"

"No. Our fortune wasn't built on human lives, and that's not going to change."

I just barely caught the familiar voices above the room's buzz. After a quick scan, I spied Rupert Chambers resting in a small alcove, with a visibly agitated Cornelius standing over him. I started to retreat, but Cornelius caught sight of me at the last second. He dashed over and practically dragged me to his father.

"Miss Viana! What a delight. Father, aren't you happy to see her?"

Rupert gave his son a sharp look. "Don't try to distract me with that poor girl. Not that I'm displeased to see you, dear."

Cornelius tugged me to a chair. "Sit, sit. Your feet must be tired."

I normally wouldn't mind visiting with Rupert, but other matters demanded my attention. "I'd love to, but—"

"Just a small break," insisted Cornelius.

"Let her go," exclaimed Rupert, in a roar of a voice I'd never expected to hear from him. "By the Six, leave her alone and let her go dance with men her own age."

Cornelius balked at the tone in his father's voice and dropped my hand. I curtsied to Rupert. "I don't want to interrupt your conversation, Mister Chambers. I'll catch up with you later."

I hurried off before Cornelius could stop me. What had *that* been about? Nothing should surprise me about the Chambers family by now, but they still managed it.

I weaved through the chattering guests, getting a sense of how the estate was laid out. I'd been here a few times but never before needed to know the floor plan. I watched which corridors servants and family went through. Finally, after much scrutiny, I gambled on which way would lead me to the residential wing and hovered near that doorway. I waited until I was confident no one was looking in my direction and then made my move.

At first, I thought I'd guessed wrong. I walked past a study, a closet, a parlor, and rooms that didn't even seem to be in use. So much excess. But at long last, a bend led me into a hall of closed doors. I opened the first and found a tidy bedroom that showed no signs of occupancy. It was a start, though.

Door after door revealed a few more guest rooms, as well as Governor and Mistress Doyle's massive master bedroom. Not far from it, another large bedroom was filled with trunks and crates. Warren's, no doubt, ready for travel. Two doors after that came a guest room with a rumpled bed and a small trunk. I slipped inside and lit a small lamp.

The trunk was locked, and I let it be while I searched the usual places: the desk, the bed, the bureau. Nothing. If it was here, it'd be in the trunk. I knelt down and pulled out my pick kit. The lock popped open with little effort. Inside, I found ordinary traveler's items. No letter. I tilted my head, gauging the trunk's height. Running my hands around the trunk's interior, I found a small catch. I couldn't help a laugh. It was Grant's cabin all over again. And to think he'd said I wouldn't need those skills in this case.

I opened the second lock and lifted the trunk's bottom. There it was, a sealed envelope. I broke the wax and pulled out a single piece of paper filled with gibberish. Well, not gibberish, but a string of Lorandian words that made no sense. It had to be a code.

I put the trunk back in order, snuffed the lantern, and headed back to the hallway. I'd learned enough to know I couldn't just take it. I stopped by the study I'd passed earlier and lit another lamp. As hoped, paper and pen sat neatly on the desk, and I quickly began to copy the strange note. I couldn't let Governor Ryan know what had happened. From there, it was back to his bedroom to return the letter. I waved the original over the lantern, somewhat melting the seal back together. Hopefully he'd think it was crushed in transit.

No one had been looking for me back at the party. The Chambers men still appeared to be having a heated discussion, and Tamsin stood close to Warren across the room, laughing at something he told her. I watched them a few seconds, still unsure about that match. Old words of hers replayed in my head, words that felt as though they'd been spoken a lifetime ago: *You're right that I'll choose success over anything else, but I hope I don't have to. I hope I'll love him—or learn to.*

Adelaide was asleep when Tamsin and I returned home, much to my dismay. I'd wanted to spend time with her before she and Cedric left in the morning. I paused near her bed, studying her lovely features and sprawling hair. A lump formed in my throat, and Tamsin slipped her arm around me, guiding me away.

"She'll be okay," Tamsin murmured. "She's tougher than you think."

Tamsin fell asleep quickly, no doubt exhausted by her work on Warren, and I left for Silas's office shortly thereafter. He looked me over when he opened the door and nodded in satisfaction. "You found it."

We leaned over the desk as he spread it out. "Hmphf," he said. "I don't suppose you speak Lorandian?"

"Some. I looked at it earlier, but it doesn't make sense."

"I'll be the judge of that. What's it say?"

I touched the words of the first line. "I don't know what the second one means, but the rest is 'my map rabbit short to dance to stop.' Is that a code you know?"

"No," he admitted. "Maybe that word you didn't know is key."

"What I can read of the rest doesn't make much sense either. Just words in no logical order. No consistency with verb conjugation. I have a Lorandian dictionary back at the house. Maybe it'll make more sense once I translate the whole thing. Maybe words just need to be moved around."

He didn't answer and instead pulled a wooden box out of one of the desk's drawers. When he opened the box, I saw a dozen small vials. After a little more thought, he selected one and dipped a small brush into it. The liquid in the bottle had a metallic smell, and he dabbed a little of it between the first two lines. Nothing happened. He tried a second bottle and then a third.

"You think there's an invisible letter in there?" I asked.

"It's not looking like it. None of the common reagents are working. People are always coming up with their own, but that takes a fair amount of chemistry. I don't know if the conspirators have those resources." He tapped the words. "They could certainly come up with their own code, though."

"Can you figure it out?"

"I've got a few resources to consult." He hesitated. "How fast can you translate it all?"

"Tomorrow," I said promptly.

Silas glanced over at me and grew thoughtful. "Why are you even doing this? Grant said you didn't want to do it anymore and backed out."

"Did he?" I asked casually.

"He wouldn't talk much about it. Was pretty worked up. The only other thing he said was that it was for the best you were gone and never crossed our paths again."

I flinched, and he noticed. "Well. I've got a lot to worry about with the Glittering Court. And didn't you want me out anyway?"

To my amazement, Silas looked abashed. "I did—back in the beginning. I thought you'd be a distraction and do more harm than good."

I lifted my chin. "And now?"

"I think you do more good than harm." He smiled at my indignation. "For the case, that is."

"Let's make a copy, and I'll get to work back at the house."

He hovered over me as I worked, brows knit as he studied the words, as though some revelation might hit. When I finished, he sighed in irritation and stepped back. "So close," he muttered. "We'll get there. Thank you."

"I'm glad to help."

He walked me to the door but didn't open it. After clearing his throat, he said gruffly, "Grant's south with the patrol for a couple of days. He hates those damn zealots, but it's keeping his cover. Anyway. Is there . . . is there any message you want me to give him?"

I had a sudden fluttering in my chest as all the memories from the night of the Flower Fest seemed to whirl through my mind at once.

And then I thought about our encounter at the store, in which he'd refused to acknowledge my existence.

The only other thing he said was that it was for the best you were gone and never crossed our paths again.

"No," I told Silas. "No message."

CHAPTER 27

ADELAIDE'S DEPARTURE HIT ME HARD THE NEXT MORNING. No matter how busy our lives had been in Adoria, I'd always had the comfort of knowing I'd see her back at Wisteria Hollow. That wasn't the case anymore. Her future was off in the foothills of western Hadisen now, away from Tamsin and me. She was going to a dangerous land with dangerous people, and that scared me. I wouldn't be able to keep track of her anymore. Adelaide was on her own.

Well, not entirely on her own. Cedric was with her. And despite the mess they were caught up in, both of them looked radiantly happy at the Hadisen party's send-off. The expedition west was huge, comprised of wagons, animals, and almost two hundred people. Some were going to find gold, others were going to farm. Some people just wanted any kind of work at all.

Adelaide's happy because she's free, I thought, watching her wave at us from a wagon. Maybe she wasn't free of her contract yet, but it was within grasping distance for her and Cedric now. And if nothing else, she was free of deception. I envied her that.

Warren Doyle gallantly rode at the front of the caravan, ready to lead them to a better life. He looked very dashing atop his stallion, but his role in organizing the heretic patrols still bothered me. It had been bad enough when he had his eye on all of Denham and parts of neighboring colonies. Now his focus was narrowed in on this group, his new citizens. And Cedric—the man who had both taken the woman Warren wanted and practiced an illicit faith—would be locked into that group as they made the ten-day trip to Hadisen. My gaze fell back on Cedric and Adelaide, and I prayed they'd never let their guards down.

"I wouldn't want that life," Tamsin told me after the party departed. "But she's in love. I guess that helps offset moving to the wilderness."

"I thought you wanted to move to the wilderness," I teased. "Isn't that the whole point of chasing Warren?"

"I want to move into the governor's newly built house that's in the wilderness. There's a difference."

Before Adelaide had left, we'd learned that Tamsin's full-scale "attack" on Warren this week had been pretty successful. She'd been right that he wanted to start his new governorship with a wife, and he'd quickly recognized her strengths. He'd asked that she not accept any offers of engagement until he returned.

"Do you have any appointments today?" I asked when we were back in our bedroom later. Although she'd promised Warren she wouldn't accept any offers in his absence, she'd made it clear that she'd still be meeting with other suitors. It was either a way to force his hand or keep her own options open. Maybe both.

"Yes, of course." She'd finished writing one of her daily letters and now sat on her bed with a book. "I'm just taking a short break. I've got tea with Melvin Yates in an hour and then that dinner party at the Waverly house tonight."

I settled on my own bed with the Lorandian dictionary and the coded letter. I did a double take when I noticed her book's cover. "Are you reading *A Testament of Angels*?"

"Huh?" She glanced down at the book, which was a standard church text. "Oh, yes. I started it in Grashond. There wasn't a lot of reading material there, and I figured I might as well see it through. And I need something to pass the time now. Warren's coming back by water after they make it to Hadisen, but it'll still probably be two weeks before I see him." She gave a dramatic sigh and leaned back against the headboard. "These days are going to drag."

My day didn't seem to have enough hours in it as I hurried to finish my translation. The letter wasn't long, but I couldn't do a word-for-word replacement. I had to take tense and conjugation into consideration, as well as words with multiple meanings. At least I had nothing else to distract me, thanks to my thin social schedule.

When I finished a couple of hours later and set my Lorandian dictionary aside, the words before me still didn't make sense. There was no sentence structure at all or any attempt to follow the language's grammatical rules. If there was a message there, it was beyond me. I made my own copy of the translation and gave Aiana the first one to relay to Silas when she went into town later.

I didn't hear anything back until she gave me a small note a week later, during one of our crossbow lessons. It was from Silas: *Thanks for the translation. Still no luck breaking it.*

The hope that my efforts had provided some revelation faded away. Silas and his network had had to go to incredible lengths to even learn about the letter's existence, and then I'd done the work of obtaining it. All for nothing.

I lined up a shot with the crossbow and tried to keep my tone light as I asked, "Silas gave you the note? Or was it Grant?"

She crossed her arms and checked my form. "Silas. I've hardly seen Iyitsi at all. He's too caught up in this case."

I let the bolt fly, and she grunted in approval. "He told me how important it is to him. How it'll get him back to his people. Is there . . . is there any other way he could do it?" I'd been troubled by this, the more I thought about Sirminica. I understood more of his reasons but was still bothered by the idea of him holding a grudge for so long.

"Nothing he'd get anytime soon. And certainly nothing with this kind of a status and legitimacy. It really is a rare opportunity to go home. There have been Balanquan ambassadors in the colonies before, but no reciprocal offers until now. My guess is that this 'bonding' isn't so much about friendship as it is giving the Balanquans a direct line of communication to what's happening down here."

"Is the status Grant will get as important to him as going back?"

"*As* important? I don't know. But certainly important. His uncle dismissed him as nothing. I'd want to confront him too. And I understand the call to reclaim his birthright. Our family branches are ingrained into us. It becomes part of our identity. Having that taken away—or walking away from it—is hard." Aiana stared off at the trees for several moments, her eyes darkened by troubling memories.

"Will you visit him?" I asked as I loaded another bolt.

Her lips turned up in a bitter smile. "No. No one can. He's trying to get there; I'm trying to stay away. The arrangement is strict. Only the ambassadors and their families are allowed—wives and children, people like that. No friends or well-wishers. Not even servants or bodyguards. My people have strong beliefs about protecting ambassadors, though. That's part of why they're given such a high status."

I lowered the crossbow. "Won't you miss him?"

"Of course. I wish he'd stay. But maybe he'll have something to hold on to, instead of going through life wearing mask after mask. Maybe it's better he's gone. I'm wanted by my people, and if they ever found me and tried to take me back, Iyitsi would get himself killed trying to stop them."

"I didn't know that—about you, I mean." I mulled over the last part of what she'd said. "I'm not surprised he'd do that for you. You're his friend. He's gone on about how dangerous attachments are, but I've seen how he cares about you."

"Oh, yes." Her eyes sparkled both with amusement and affection. "Don't be fooled by that gruffness. When the time comes for hard choices, he always does the right thing."

Not long after that day, word came to us that Warren had returned to Cape Triumph by water after a successful land journey. I breathed a sigh of relief knowing Adelaide and Cedric had made it safely. Tamsin was glad too, but her fixation soon shifted to her uncertain future with Warren. She paced anxiously around the house and constantly watched the front door for any couriers. When someone finally came, it was Warren himself. Tamsin had been watching from the top of the stairs and ran back to our room.

"It's him, Mira." She clutched my sleeve and looked like she might hyperventilate. "In person. He asked to talk to Jasper. Do you know what that means? He's going to make an offer! This could be it! What I've been waiting for."

I didn't know what to say. I wanted her to be happy and fulfill her dreams, but was Warren the right person?

Not long after his arrival, Tamsin was summoned to the office as well. She came back to our room an hour later, elated. "We're not engaged," she announced.

"You . . . aren't? Then why are you so happy?"

"Because I'm going to Hadisen! Warren says he doesn't want to lock me in until I've seen exactly what I'll be facing. So I'm going back with him in two days by boat. The wife of one of his associates will come stay with me in Warren's house while I'm there, so it'll all be very proper. We worked out the details with Jasper."

"Two days."

She was too excited to know just how hard those words struck me. First Adelaide, now Tamsin. I was going to be alone again, just like I'd been in Osfro after Lonzo left. Grant was . . . out of the picture. I had no one, except Aiana, I supposed. And the looming potential of becoming Rupert Chambers's bride.

If I stopped delaying, I could marry Rupert now and have a whole new world open up to me. Freedom from Mistress Culpepper's rules. Lonzo back in my life. The ability to visit Tamsin and Adelaide in Hadisen. What was I waiting for?

Who was I waiting for?

Tamsin left on the hottest day we'd had since coming to Adoria. The air hung thick and heavy with humidity, and Mistress Culpepper was at her wit's end trying to keep us doused in powder and relatively sweat-free. Tamsin was supposed to have sailed in the afternoon, but some delay on Warren's part pushed them into an evening departure.

"I'm sorry," he said, when he finally arrived. Two of his associates accompanied him and loaded her luggage into a carriage. "We'll have to make part of our trip in the dark, but we'll still arrive tonight. I hope it's not too exhausting."

"No need to worry. Our Tamsin can handle anything," said Jasper, eager for the prospective deal.

Tamsin hugged me, and just like that, I was alone. Both of my roommates were gone, off to glorious futures with the men they wanted. I went upstairs and gazed at my friends' beds. It was selfish to feel sorry for myself. After all, they were alive and happy. But I couldn't help it. The room seemed ten times bigger than it had before, and I felt very small.

It might have been lucky, then, that I had Tom's fifty-gold job that night to distract me. I had no social engagements at all (though Jasper had told me he could arrange a visit to the Chambers house anytime), so I was able to sneak out earlier than usual once darkness fell.

I rendezvoused with Tom's men in the same spot as last time. There were a lot more people present this time—but not Tom himself.

Elijah smiled warmly at me as he leaned against a tree. "Don't worry, he'll be here."

"Is everything okay?" I asked.

"Oh, yeah. He had to go oversee something in person. We've got a regular who buys a lot of our fancy stuff, but he was trying to change the price at the last minute. So, Tom went to see him and our, ah, sales associate."

"Do you mean fence?" I teased.

"Hey, I'm trying to be genteel for you." His smile faded as he stared off over the bay. Even at night, the heat was still oppressive. The air stood perfectly still, with no hint of a breeze, and everyone's clothes were sticky with sweat. I wished Lady Aviel's image didn't require so many itchy and heavy accoutrements.

Tom came trotting up soon, with Lesser Tom at his side. "Glad to see you didn't leave without me," Tom called, earning a few chuckles from the men milling around. "But we'd best get on with it."

Elijah straightened up from his lounging position. "I don't think we should do it."

"Why not?" asked Tom. His tone was light, but I knew he didn't like being questioned in public. Or ever.

"This weather, for one thing. It's going to turn on us."

Tom shrugged. "I'm aware, and that's what we'd hoped for. Those eastern clouds will help us."

Elijah looked skeptical. "Well, that's not all. I saw two naval ships in port when I was in town."

That drew everyone's attention, but Tom's expression didn't change. "Yes, I already know that too, but we have no reason to cross paths. They've just arrived and will restock before moving on to patrol the coast. It'll be dark. We'll get to the *Sun's Promise* without being seen and make sure no one raises an alarm. Now. Let's not waste any more time."

A few men looked uneasy, and I couldn't blame them. Facing armed sailors defending their ship was risky enough. But detection by the royal navy? Their entire purpose was to hunt down pirates and any hostile ships from other countries. We were exactly the kind of group they wanted to seize.

"My lady." Tom tipped his hat upon noticing me. "Come ride in my boat. I need someone cheerful to counteract Elijah's doom and gloom."

Elijah made no comment, but once our group set out on the water, I couldn't help glancing over at his skiff. His face was still dark and troubled.

Tom noticed my stare. "It really will be fine," he told me. "Elijah is making a big deal out of nothing. I've had much closer calls with the navy, and I wouldn't lead any of my people into something that was stupidly dangerous. No matter the profit at stake, I always look out for my own. I value those who follow me more than any agenda."

As our party approached the harbor, I admired the way Cape Triumph's lights hugged the coast. The port was full of ships of all sizes, now that the crossing from Evaria and Osfrid was safer.

"I see the *Sun's Promise*," a man in our boat said. I'd never met him. Tom had hired a lot of additional help for this.

Tom nodded in approval. "Bring us in then."

The skiffs glided forward, dark shapes on dark water. A few strands of hair tickled my cheek, and I brushed them aside. "Finally, some breeze."

The temperature had dropped abruptly since we'd left, and I suddenly found myself thinking of the day the storm had hit aboard the *Good Hope*. I'd been studying Grant's hair then, how still it had been when we first stepped outside, and before I knew it, it had been back to its unruly state as the wind rapidly picked up.

I turned back to Elijah. His head was tipped up as he studied the sky. I looked up as well and saw the dark clouds Tom had mentioned earlier—the ones that would help give us cover. There were more of them now, stretching almost entirely across the sky. Ariniel's star was gone. All the stars were.

The *Sun's Promise* was bigger than the *Queen's Grace*—but not the biggest ship I'd ever seen. That honor went to the two naval ships farther down the harbor, which loomed over the smaller boats like sentinels. I could just barely make out the lines of gun holes, whose lids concealed cannons. As I watched, both of them began to trim their sails. Above us, the *Sun's Promise* started to as well.

"Excellent," said Tom. "They're all going to be busy with ballast and bringing in sail."

Elijah's boat floated right next to ours. "Of course they're bringing in sail!" he exclaimed. "Every bloody ship out here is—"

"Enough." I'd never heard Tom speak so fiercely to Elijah. "If you don't want to do this, then swim back. You lot—get up there."

Five men made the short swim to the hull. Our cluster of skiffs wasn't up against the side this time. We held position farther away, at an angle to the stern that made us harder to see. Tom's men were skilled swimmers and moved swiftly through the choppy water. They climbed up the ship's side and slipped in through a small round window about midway up the hull. Then we waited as our own boats began to bob more violently on the water.

Tom stared unblinkingly at the ship's deck, his tension tangible. Thunder rumbled, and I wondered what the men were doing inside. When a ladder unfurled over the hull, Tom relaxed. "Excellent. Let's go."

We brought our skiffs in closer and boarded the ship. The five scouts had already subdued the topside crew, and the rest of us spread throughout the ship to search for other crewmen. Tom once more warned against using guns. There were more sailors here than on the *Queen Grace*, but their busy storm preparation had given us an advantage. After only a handful of scuffles, we were able to round them up and confine them to the brig.

"Move," Tom ordered us, once the brig was locked. "The storm's helping us right now but won't for long."

We had a lot more cargo to transport this time, and it was heavier too. As I climbed down to a lower deck and heard the wind howl outside the rocking ship, I once more had that disorienting feeling of being on *Good Hope* again, tossed around by the elements, not knowing if I'd live or die.

Elijah nudged me. "You okay?"

"Fine." I kept moving. "Just thinking about another storm I was in. It was worse."

"This is going to get worse, and Tom knows it. He hasn't been away from the sea that long, but he wants this—badly."

Lowering the heavy, bulky crates down to the waiting boats took time and had to be done carefully. It created a bottleneck. That was the disadvantage of raiding a ship that was anchored instead of docked. Sneaking aboard might be easier, but getting everything off wasn't.

Lightning tore apart the sky, and soon the rain came. One of the hired men and I carried a crate together and set it down near an expanding pile by the edge. I started to return below when I heard shouting: Tom and Elijah arguing.

"Even if we get it all off, the skiffs won't make it back in this chop!" yelled Elijah over the thunder.

After a little more back and forth, Tom grudgingly yielded. "Get everyone back here," he called to us. "We're going to load what we've got and—"

A bright flash near the stern made him stop. A hanging lantern had been knocked off by the wind and smashed to the deck. I knew from crossing the Sunset Sea that most lanterns were doused during storms, but these sailors hadn't had time to finish their preparations. Flames started to spread over the deck, and sparks blew up onto some of the rigging. The rope ignited too quickly for the rain to put out, and the fire jumped up to a loose sail that also hadn't had a chance to be properly brought in. That sail whipped into another sail, and I watched in horror as the blaze expanded and expanded. I looked at Tom and saw him wrestle with indecision. He glanced at the remaining cargo and finally shook his head.

"Everyone, off! This'll bring the navy."

He didn't have to repeat himself. Everyone raced to the edge, lining up to scramble down the ladder. Anders threw a second one over. I started to join the line and then stared back at one of the doors leading below.

"Tom," I called. "What about the crew?"

"There's no time, Aviel. The wind's feeding the fire, and this ship is gone when the cargo lights up. Go!"

I couldn't. Not when I thought of all those sailors locked in the brig, burning to death. "I can get down to them! I won't take long."

"There's no time! Don't be stupid!"

"I'm going!"

"Aviel—"

I'd already turned around. As I started to run, I just barely heard Elijah say to Tom, "Get the others off and away. I'll stay back with a boat and wait for her. She can make it before the ship blows."

"The longer we wait, the more the cargo we've taken is at stake."

"You shouldn't have brought skiffs out in—"

I didn't hear the rest as I climbed below and ran to the brig, trying to keep my footing as the ship heaved violently back and forth. When I finally made it, I grabbed the key off a hook in the hall and unlocked the brig's door with shaking hands.

"The ship's on fire!" I shouted to the men inside. "You have to get off!"

I raced back down the hall and was soon overtaken as sailors thundered past, shoving me out of the way. I saw no fire below yet, but I could smell smoke. We emerged into the tempest, and I fought my way over to the rope ladders so that I could climb overboard.

But there were no boats down below. Lightning flashed, and I just barely caught sight of the skiffs bobbing on the waves—well away from the *Sun's Promise*. I turned around and stared. Nearly half the deck was burning now, and wet ash blew at me along with the rain.

Someone grabbed my arm. "Lady, come on! Follow me!"

It was one of the ship's sailors, an older man with dark hair slicked back from the rain. He tugged me over to where the rest of his fellow sailors were frantically untying and lowering dinghies into the water.

"Give me a knife," one of them yelled. "This rope is stuck."

Before anyone else could act, I handed over my dirk. The sailor used it to chop the rope, and as he was giving it back, a burst of wind hit me from the side. I grabbed hold of the rail to keep myself steady, but in doing so, the dirk slipped from my hand and fell into the dark sea below.

Sixteen of us scrambled into three dinghies being tossed around on the sea. As soon as we were all in, sailors began to row us away. Through the flares of lightning, I could make out one of the naval ships slowly parting from its mate. The other two dinghies rowed toward it, but mine headed in a different direction.

"Where are we going?" I called to the sailor who'd led me here.

"That man-of-war's coming to look for survivors. Don't worry, we won't let them pick you up."

"You should go to them—they're closer!"

"And they'll lock you up. We know who you are, Lady Aviel."

"We'll get to the south dock," said another sailor. "No one'll notice what's going on. And it's not much farther."

But it was farther than the warship, and more than once, I thought we would capsize. It was a wonder any of these tiny boats were still above water. "Why would you do that for me?"

"You saved us," the first sailor said. "And we know what you do. Ellen Smith is my sister."

Mistress Smith. The matriarch we'd given supplies to. Before I could respond, a deafening boom—far more monstrous than the thunder—sounded behind us. Ears ringing, I turned and saw the *Sun's Promise* engulfed in a ball of flame.

"There she goes," said another sailor. "No surprise."

There's no time, Aviel. The wind's feeding the fire, and this ship is gone when the cargo lights up.

Tom had known the ship would explode. "What was in the cargo?" I called to the sailors.

"Ammunition," said Mistress Smith's brother. "Gunpowder. Bullets." Another explosion sounded, as remaining cargo ignited.

Chaos reigned when we reached the south dock, crowded with other small boats. The wind and rain made moving on land almost as difficult as at sea, and debris blew all around us. One warehouse's roof had been torn off. The old sailor nodded a goodbye.

"May the Six keep you safe, Lady."

"And you as well. Thank you."

As I made my way through the city, I saw that much of Cape Triumph had hunkered down against the storm. Shutters and boards covered glass windows, and only a handful of people struggled through the tempest, often stopping to cling to a lamppost or building. Wisteria Hollow suddenly seemed as great a journey as sailing from Osfrid to Adoria. Spying a solidly built blacksmith's shop, I hurried to it and crouched under the door's overhang, holding tightly to a post as rain and wind beat against me. I closed my eyes and waited. And waited.

After what felt like days, the wind and rain began to slacken. The calm didn't fool me. I remembered it from the storm at sea, but I took advantage of the lull and started running. I took the long way via the highway, rather than risking the wooded path by the marsh. Fallen branches littered this road as it was, and I tripped multiple times. The old pain in my ankle flared up.

The storm began to resume just as Wisteria Hollow came into sight. I picked up my speed and was relieved to see the trellis still standing. The wind shook it violently as I made my way up and fought against the storm shutters. At last, I got the window opened and tumbled inside.

Back in my room, I peeled off my soaked clothes and was astonished to see the wig was still in place. It was a testament to my hairpin skills. I bundled up in a flannel nightgown, took a few extra blankets from Adelaide's bed, and then dove into mine, wondering if I'd ever feel warm again.

I'd pushed myself past exhaustion, and even the raging storm couldn't keep me from falling asleep. But as I drifted off, one thought kept replaying through my head.

Tom had left me behind.

He'd left me behind, knowing I'd probably die. He'd left those sailors behind to die too. Elijah had gauged the ship's explosion correctly, but Tom hadn't wanted to risk his cargo.

No matter the profit at stake, I always look out for my own.

A loud, rapid pounding sound startled me out of sleep. I jerked upright, wondering if I'd dreamed it, and then it boomed out again. The front door. I glanced out the window and saw the lavender sky of sunrise.

More knocking.

I pulled on my robe and made my way to the top of the stairs. A couple of other sleepy girls followed me. Mistress Culpepper, fully dressed, hurried through the foyer and opened the door. An annoyed Jasper joined her.

I didn't recognize the two men outside. They wore suits and long coats, but the fabric was cheap. They weren't potential suitors.

"I'm sorry to disturb you," one said, his eyes wide. "But Mister Doyle wanted us to come right away."

A few more curious girls emerged from their rooms, and Charles and the Grashond party entered the foyer.

"Mister Doyle?" asked Jasper. "Isn't he in Hadisen?"

The man who'd spoken hesitated. "He is. But . . . your girl . . . Miss Wright. She's not here, is she?"

"Miss Wright is supposed to be in Hadisen." Jasper looked between the two men, and both averted their gazes. "Why would you come here asking for her?"

The second man jerked his hat off his head and clutched it to his chest. "I—I'm so sorry, sir. We lost her in the storm last night."

CHAPTER 28

"WHAT DO YOU MEAN . . . LOST?"

Jasper's voice was very low, very cold. The two men shuffled their feet, each seeming to hope the other would do the talking. The first one gave in and explained. "It happened when we were about to sail last night—you see, we were all on board, ready to go. Then that storm started blowing in. And your girl, she just . . . just . . ."

"She panicked, sir," supplied the second man. "She said she wouldn't do it. She was hysterical. Jumped overboard, waded to shore, and disappeared into the woods."

"And nobody went after her?" exclaimed Jasper.

"We did, sir! But it was dark. We don't know how she got away so fast. We searched as much as we could. Then the captain said they had to sail right then or they couldn't go at all because of the weather. Mister Doyle left us behind to keep looking."

"Mister Doyle left without her?" asked Charles. Even he was incredulous.

"He didn't want to, sir, but he had to get to Hadisen on time. Important business today. He thought we'd be able to find her. He thought for sure she'd come back here."

"When the storm got so bad that we couldn't search anymore, we headed back to town ourselves," added the other man. "But we stopped at any house along the way, in case she'd begged for shelter. No one saw her. We thought . . . hoped she'd be here."

I didn't realize my knees had buckled until Rosamunde's arm slipped around me. "Easy, Mira," she murmured.

I felt weightless. Black stars sparkled in my vision.

"Well, she's not here!" yelled Jasper. "And you shouldn't be here either! You shouldn't have stopped looking. Doyle shouldn't have left!"

The two men cringed. "We w-would've kept looking, sir," one said. "Honest. But you—you saw the storm. We could barely find our way through it, and it wasn't safe for us to be in the woods, not with trees blowing over."

I grabbed the rail again and pulled myself up. "Do you think it was safe for her?" I screamed down. "Do you think she was able to find her way through it when you couldn't?"

Everyone looked up at me in surprise, but no one chastised me. Jasper fixed his glare back on the men. "Well, it's safe now, and you're going to keep looking. Everyone is. Charles, we have to go to town and get the militia to start searching those woods."

The household sprang into action, but I stayed still. I couldn't move from that spot. I kept waiting to wake up, but it didn't happen. This wasn't some dream brought on by the exhaustion of last night's peril. This was the same horror that kept happening over and over in my life: my loved ones, snatched away. Except Tamsin had been returned to me. She wasn't supposed to leave again.

I sat down on the top step and said to no one in particular: "Why would Tamsin do that? She wanted to go with Warren more than anything."

An answer came, unexpectedly, from Winnifred. I didn't know her well, but she'd been on board the *Gray Gull* with Tamsin. "I can't speak for her. She never seemed as afraid as the rest of us, but I have a hard time getting on any boat now. We took a river skiff part of the way from Grashond, and it just about killed me. If someone tried to put me on a boat during another storm, I might run too."

I studied her. Before Adelaide had become the diamond, that title had been Winnifred's. She was poised and beautiful and liked to flaunt her superiority, but her face was deadly earnest now. If she had been so affected, why not Tamsin?

Because Tamsin never once uttered a word about a fear of boats. When she'd say anything about their time in the northern colonies, Tamsin would mention her dislike of the weather, the rough lodging, the strange customs of the Heirs. But boats hadn't made her list of complaints, not even when she'd referenced that river trip.

Rosamunde tried to tug me up again. "Mira, come back to your room. You should rest."

"Rest? How can I rest?" I jumped to my feet. "My best friend is out there in the woods, cold and scared! Maybe injured!"

"You only assume your friend is alive." The woman from Grashond stood at the bottom of the stairs, staring up at us with pale, cruel eyes. "She was a prideful, unrepentant girl who reached too far. She didn't heed the first warning Uros sent, and now she's been dealt her final punishment."

Both Rosamunde and Winnifred had to stop me from running down the stairs. In the foyer, Gideon took his companion's arm and steered her away. "Come along, Dinah."

The fury she ignited smothered my shock and sorrow. I was wide awake now. My focus grew sharp and clear. I wouldn't sit around and lose myself to my own despair. I would act. I would find Tamsin. She had survived one storm and could survive another.

Getting anyone to let me help was difficult, though. Jasper and Charles mobilized quickly but didn't expect us girls to have any part of the search. The Glittering Court was supposed to go on as usual, though most of the day's events had been cancelled in the wake of the storm. Other lost people had been caught unaware last night, and many places had suffered damage—especially the poorer areas, where they didn't have the means to brace against these seasonal storms. Lowlands had flooded. A few fires had broken out, and I even heard one brief mention of the *Sun's Promise*. The militia and army were in high demand, but Jasper secured some of them for a search, along with other civilian volunteers.

"Let's go," Aiana told me around noon. I hadn't seen her at all that day, but she must have either guessed or heard that I'd want to help—and that I'd been denied.

After having my offers of help constantly rejected, I didn't even pause for a coat or cloak when she spoke. But as we headed for the front door, I asked, "Won't I get in trouble? Won't you?"

She walked along briskly, her expression grim. "Not enough to matter. There are too many other things going on."

The coasting ships that ran between Cape Triumph and the far sides of Denham Bay left from a small quay on the city's edge. It was south of the main commercial port I'd been in last night—the one that received the bulk of incoming and outgoing ocean vessels. The quay was easily accessible via a well-traveled dirt highway, but the land surrounding the road and wharves had seen little clearing and soon gave way to even denser forest to the west. I could understand how anyone wandering off the main road could easily get lost in those woods, especially in last night's conditions.

And Warren's men hadn't been wrong about the dangers. I'd faced plenty myself last night. Now, in day's full light, I could see fallen trees and all sorts of debris littering the road. The woods themselves were worse, barely traversable in some places.

The militia had put together a relatively organized search. They had a map of the area and had portioned it off, assigning teams to systematically scour each region. Aiana and I earned a few strange looks, but the militiaman in charge still went ahead and assigned us a team. It was too much to hope that I could have worn pants, but I hiked my skirts up to mid-calf and would deal with any of Mistress Culpepper's wrath later.

It felt good to be doing something—far better than when I could only sit around helplessly after the *Gray Gull*'s disappearance. As the day went on, my spirits began to flag. I clung to my burning hope—insistence—that Tamsin was alive. But as we fought through over-growth and fallen limbs, I began to imagine how easy it would be for someone to get crushed or trapped. I'd even heard that winds from these storms had been known to carry people off.

No one reported finding Tamsin's body. No one reported finding any trace of her at all. And as dinnertime neared, many of the volunteers left with muttered apologies, and some of the militiamen were assigned to other duties. We weren't the only ones who needed help.

"I've got to bring you back now," Aiana told me. "We can't push it much further, and there's a dinner I'm chaperoning that's still on for tonight."

"But we haven't found her," I protested. "How can we go?"

"We've covered a huge amount of area, miss." That was one of the organizers, and he showed us a map. Parts that had been searched and cleared were marked off, and that included a radius of a few miles around the quay.

I could feel my frustrated tears returning. "Maybe she made it a long way."

"Possibly." The militiaman didn't sound very confident. "We'll search some of those far areas. And a squad of bloody rangers even showed up. They're going to spread farther out and recheck a few of the other spots." He nodded toward two men heading off into the trees. They wore rough woodsmen's attire, but military insignia stood out on the breasts of their coats.

"What are rangers doing here?" asked Aiana wonderingly.

"Dunno," the militiaman said. "They just came here and said they were joining the hunt. Not my place to ask questions."

"Who are they?" I asked.

"Part of the royal army, but they specialize in woodlands and other rough terrains," Aiana said. "My understanding is they do a lot of scouting and ambushes in times of war."

The militiaman nodded. "Did a lot in the campaigns against the Icori. They know every stick in Adoria and can track down anything. They'll cover ground faster than we can and even work at night. If your girl's out there, they'll find her."

My spirits lifted fractionally. I'd been certain darkness would put an end to the searching, but hope wasn't lost yet. Maybe these rangers could do what the rest of us couldn't.

If your girl's out there, they'll find her.

If. But how could she not be?

Other searchers left as we did, and I caught sight of Warren's two men. I waved them over. "Will you be returning to Hadisen soon?" I asked.

"In the morning," one said. "Mister Doyle will be anxious to hear what happened."

If he's so anxious, why didn't he stay and search as well?

Instead, I asked, "Would you be able to bring a letter over when you go?"

"Of course, miss. Get it to the governor's house by ten, and we'll bring it with us."

I spent the rest of the evening working on the letter. It took me three tries. How could I explain to Adelaide what had happened? How could I put the horror of this event into writing? But I had to. She had to hear it from me, not someone else. After stopping multiple times to wipe away tears, I finally finished and sealed the letter. When I went downstairs, I was surprised to see how late it was. Nearly everyone was asleep. I'd never even thought about dinner.

Mistress Culpepper kept a tray near the door for outgoing mail that a courier picked up twice a day. I dropped the letter in to go out with the early morning batch and felt a lump form in my throat when I thought about Adelaide reading my words. As I turned to go upstairs, I heard a voice on the other side of the foyer whisper, "Miss Viana?"

It was one of the hired bodyguards, Alan. They were all discouraged from interacting with us, and he glanced nervously around the empty foyer. "Yes?"

"I shouldn't . . . I shouldn't do this, but . . . well, there's a man at the kitchen door asking for you. It's . . . one of the royal rangers. I'm not sure what to do . . ."

The rangers must really have a fierce reputation if they could make Alan waver from keeping us away from strange men. "It's okay," I said, mystified. "Take me to him, and then disappear. I'll be fine, and I won't say anything about you if I'm caught."

I had no idea why a ranger would ask for me specifically, but I quivered with excitement as I hurried to the kitchen. A ranger, here! I'd hoped all night a messenger would come to Jasper with miraculous news about Tamsin. Maybe it was coming to me directly.

The man at the door was unshaven and wore a fur-trimmed hat. His leather coat had seen rough times, but there was no mistaking the lion of Osfrid stitched into it in green and gold. He touched his brow in greeting but didn't take off the hat.

"I'm sorry for the late hour, but I was told to talk to you discreetly. I'm Lieutenant Kenmore, fifth rangers' division."

I nodded, not trusting myself to speak.

"We've been scouring the woods all night and finally just called it quits. And . . . I hate to say it, but we couldn't find Miss Wright. Not even a trace."

There went another piece of my heart.

Mira, you will never lose me. No matter what else happens or where we go in this world, I will always be there for you.

"Th-thank you for telling me," I managed to say. "I'm sure it must have been difficult."

"It was. And I'm sure the storm wiped away plenty, but I'm surprised we didn't find anything. Not a scrap of dress or a blurred footprint. But we looked. We really did."

"Will you continue searching tomorrow?"

He shook his head. "There isn't much more to search. We doubled the field, and I can't believe she got farther than that in the storm."

"But then, what happened to her?"

"I don't know. Maybe she'll turn up in some impossible place. Maybe she made it back to town and is hiding. Stranger things have happened. I wish we could do more, but we've got to report to Armsfield at first light. How we even ended up here is beyond me."

I tried to push my despair aside for a moment. "Weren't you dispatched here?"

He frowned. "Eh . . . yes. And no. Our commander got a requisition this morning asking us to assist in the search and then unofficially let you know the results." Lieutenant Kenmore took a rumpled piece of paper out of his coat pocket. "Signed by Silas Garrett of the McGraws."

Silas had told me himself the McGraws had a lot of power to throw around when they needed it. Most royal resources were obligated to help him if called.

"I'm surprised he'd do this for me," I admitted.

Kenmore scratched at his beard as he collected his thoughts. "Well, I'm not sure he did."

"You just said he did."

"I said we got a requisition signed by him. But the thing is, I know Silas Garrett. Good guy. I also know that he's not in Cape Triumph right now—which is where this was sent from. I checked the requisition against some other documents he'd signed. The signature's a perfect match."

"So . . . what are you saying?"

"That someone else sent this, pretending to be him. Someone who can do a damned good match of his signature—pardon my language."

I held my expression and didn't dare to even blink for fear of giving anything away. "If you knew it was a forgery, why didn't you say anything?"

"We were nearby. Maybe it's an abuse of resources, but I had no problem searching for that girl. I certainly wouldn't get in trouble." He held up the piece of paper. "But whoever wrote this? That's another story."

"W-what do you mean?" My head was swimming.

"Well, I'm not going to tell anyone, but forging Silas Garrett's signature and requisitioning part of the royal army? That's ten kinds of treason if you get caught. That's a death sentence back in Osfrid." He looked me over with such scrutiny, I could fully believe he was a master tracker. "You must have someone who thinks very highly of you to take a risk like this. Good luck with everything, Miss Viana. I hope that girl turns up."

When he'd left, I shut the door and leaned my back against it, closing my eyes. There was no question in my mind about which person knew Silas well enough to forge his signature. But I'd become unsure if that person cared if I lived or died.

I opened my eyes, took a deep breath, and returned upstairs with renewed purpose. My heart felt too big for my chest as I grabbed a new wig and made the attic climb. The path by the marsh was patched with standing water from the storm, but I barely even noticed the mud or branches whipping against me. My steps felt light, and the stars above me seemed to burn more brightly than ever, with Ariniel's star the most radiant of them all.

Signs of the storm still marked Cape Triumph, but it was otherwise business as usual. I turned down the familiar streets and then hesitated—only for a moment—at the bottom of Grant's staircase. After another deep breath, I made my way up and knocked.

The door slowly opened, and Grant peered out, not looking entirely surprised to see me. He leaned against the doorway and waited.

My whole body trembled with nervous energy. "Why did you do it? You could've lost everything! Not just your cover and chance with the Balanquans. You put your life on the line! Why, Grant? Why would you risk all that?"

"Because it was for you," he said simply. "And I like you."

"But only a little."

He shook his head. "A lot."

I studied him intently, drinking in all those features I felt like I hadn't seen in years. The lines of his body, the shape of his face, the unruly hair. But it was his eyes I finally settled on. "If you like me so much, then why haven't you asked me inside?"

He arched an eyebrow. "Do you *want* to come inside?"

"I want to kiss you. And I'll do it out here if I have to."

"Oh, well. In that case . . ."

His arm snaked around my waist, and he pulled me to him, kissing me as we stumbled inside. He managed to kick the door closed with one foot and then pressed me against it. Reluctantly, breathlessly, he broke the kiss but leaned so close that our foreheads touched. He cupped my face with his hands.

"Promise me you won't storm out again."

"I won't, if you give me a reason to stay."

He kissed me again and then scooped me up in his arms. "I'll give you a lot of them."

CHAPTER 29

"Some things were the same," I remarked. "But some things were different."

Grant shifted closer to me in the bed and draped an arm around my waist, which was an astonishingly intimate action for him. "Thank you for that specific feedback. I'll be sure to make note of it."

"Don't worry." I shifted to my side, and he curled up at my back. "It was still fine."

His response to that was a small grunt of amusement, and then he kissed my shoulder before resting his cheek against it. He knew perfectly well that it had been more than "fine." It was still wondrous to me that I could feel so many things. And it was almost more extraordinary to have any space of time when the world simplified to just me and him. No machinations. No half-truths. No arguing. Of course, there was also no acknowledgment of what would happen with us in the future. Through some unspoken agreement, we were ignoring that detail.

We let ourselves stay entangled in that contentment for a while until Grant finally asked, "Are you okay?"

"You're still worried about that? Do I really need to elaborate on 'fine'?"

"No, not that. Tamsin."

Her name cut through the spell that had wrapped around me, and I felt a sudden pain in my chest. What right did I have to this warmth and security when Tamsin was . . . what? What was she? Where was she? Cold? Alone? Still in this world?

"I'm sorry," he said when I didn't answer. The words were for my loss, I realized, not for bringing her up.

"She's not dead," I said vehemently. I rolled over and saw the skepticism in his eyes. "She's *not*! She's a survivor. She's somewhere . . . I don't know where . . . but not dead!"

"Okay, okay. Then what happened to her?"

"I don't know," I admitted. "But the whole story is so strange. She wouldn't have panicked and run away. And those rangers didn't find any trace of her at all. Even with the storm, there should have been *something*."

Who was I trying to convince? Me or him? He didn't push the issue anymore, but I knew he still had his doubts. And no matter how much I tried to convince myself otherwise, some of my own gnawed at me too. The storm had wreaked destruction everywhere. I had to acknowledge the very real possibility that fate hadn't spared her a second time.

Silence fell over us, but I didn't expect it to last. Grant couldn't help himself. Even happy and at peace in a moment like this, his mind couldn't stop spinning.

"Are you engaged yet?" His face and tone were forcibly neutral.

"No. But I don't know how long that'll last. I don't have enough to pay off the contract myself. I can't even pay off Lonzo's bond yet."

"How much has your alter ego earned?"

"Fifteen. And there won't be any more. That's done." I could tell Grant wanted some elaboration, but I stayed tight-lipped. "And I really should've told you about that. About all of it. Rupert Chambers and Lady Aviel."

"No," Grant said after waiting a beat. "Not if you weren't ready. And I shouldn't have attacked you for it." He let that hang between us a moment more. "So. Money. You'll have fifty from the case."

I had to retrain myself to keep up with his abrupt topic changes. "I'm not part of the case anymore."

"You're part of it," he said firmly.

"Well, it doesn't look like it's getting wrapped up anytime soon."

He didn't deny it. "I can give you twenty-five."

"Twenty-five?" I studied his face for some sign of a joke. "What happened to not having five to your name?"

"I wasn't at Molly Siegel's because I liked spending extra time with the patrol."

I sat up in shock. "You risked what money you did have on a poker game?"

He looked ridiculously smug. "Lots of poker games, actually— well, until I got banned after the Flower Fest. Twenty-five would go a long way for you."

"I'd almost have Lonzo's bond. Not enough for my own contract, though." Still, a surge of excitement shot through me. Forty gold. So close to Lonzo's freedom. But then . . . "No, I can't. I can't accept that. It's yours. Don't worry about me. Just focus on figuring out this conspiracy. I still get the money that way, and you can go back to the Balanquans."

Grant shifted away, onto his back, and stared upward. "I should've told you about that before . . . everything."

"Not if you weren't ready." He smiled at his words being echoed back. "And I was so worked up, I didn't really hear what you were saying. I heard, but I didn't understand. I do now, and . . . I think you should do it. You need to reclaim that piece of you that was lost. It's just that . . . I'll miss you."

Even just in profile, I could see the astonishment in his face. He kept his eyes trained upward. "The eastern part of the Empire is beautiful. It's where all the cities are, all the art and culture. The ambassadors will visit there, but I've heard they'll spend most of their time in the west. It's less settled out there. Colder, wilder. But still beautiful. You'd like it."

Another quiet stretch, both of us lost in thought, until I finally managed to say, "I think . . . I think I'd maybe like to see that someday. The lands up north." It took as much effort for me to reference the passing offer he'd made the last time we were in bed, the one I'd dismissed in anger. I was no better than he was at admitting certain things.

Grant slowly turned his head and regarded me with something almost like apprehension. "Would you?"

"Yes, but . . ." Now I averted my eyes and stared off at the flame of a small candle. "I have to . . ."

"Your brother."

I nodded, still unable to look at him. He sat up beside me and turned my face toward his. He kissed me. Long. Deeply. I wrapped my arms around his neck and wished the world could just be this simple.

"Can I come back tomorrow?" I asked, when I was finally able to draw away.

He ran a hand through my hair. "*Bas agiba kor; kalichi hanek.*"

"What does it mean?"

"'The dam has burst; make way for the river.'"

I couldn't stop the grin that spread over my face. "Well, well, you do recite poetry in bed."

He smiled back, but there was an uneasiness to it. "It's more of a warning than anything sentimental. It's a proverb for when there's no going back."

I moved with a lightness in my step when I left. It was hard not to, with my body still humming and content. But it was countered by the darkness of all the uncertainty that hung over me. Uncertainty about what exactly was between us. Uncertainty about saving Lonzo. Uncertainty about my own future.

And Tamsin.

She's alive, she's alive, I told myself. *There's just more to this than we know yet.*

I reached the crossroads where I'd normally turn to reach the city's main gate, but I stopped instead—so abruptly that a group of men stumbled into me. I stared down the street that led to the Dancing Bull and made a decision.

My Aviel wig had been irrevocably ruined in the storm. The one I wore now was a deeper gold, and I'd braided it back to further conceal me. Now, as I walked, I shook it all out. The color was close enough. I'd worn the mask out of habit, even though the warming weather no longer required it. And even without the starry cloak, the rest of my clothes would make me recognizable.

Sure enough, the tavern came to a standstill when I entered. Tom and his regulars sat at their usual table, and a couple of the men stood up. One of them was Elijah. "You're alive!" he said, relief visible on his rough face.

Tom remained sitting, with no change in expression. He brought a mug to his lips and drank deeply. "I told you she was."

"I'm surprised you gave me any thought at all," I said icily. "You certainly didn't last night."

Tom grimaced and set his mug down with a *thump*. "Excuse me, gentlemen. This is a conversation best done in private, I think."

He led me to the door in the back, the one where all the goods and supplies came and went from. Stepping through it, I found myself on a landing next to a stairwell that led underground, into darkness. Tom shut the door and faced me.

"I'm so thrilled to see you, my dear," he said. "Though, as I said, I wasn't worried about your safety. Not when I heard that the crew of the *Sun's Promise* miraculously made it off. I knew exactly which agent of divinity had helped with that."

I crossed my arms. "Were you so certain of miracles when you left me and those sailors to die?"

"I didn't want any of you to die! You have to know that."

"Then why did you leave? You only had to wait a few minutes." I held up a hand. "No, don't answer because I already know why. You wanted to get your gunpowder back to land before the storm got worse. You needed your profit because, as it turns out, you really do value your agenda more than your followers."

"Aviel, it was a tense situation. I had to make an ugly decision, right then and there. Everyone's scrambling for ammunition these days. I don't know what's going on, but it's worth a fortune."

"I hope you got it then. Because I've come for my pay—unless you're betraying me on that."

"Of course not." He reached into a pocket and took out two crown coins, each worth twenty-five gold. "And I swear, we won't do anything next time that—"

"Next time? Are you serious?" I studied his face. He was. "Tom, there isn't going to be a next time. I'm done with all of this."

Now he doubted that I was serious. "Whatever for? You've done so well."

"At boosting your image. That's why you want to keep me."

"Not true. We've done all sorts of great things together. If you want more pay—"

"I want to be done with this," I interrupted, trying to keep my cool. "And I hope you aren't going to try and stop me."

He rolled his eyes behind the mask. "Of course not. But you're being completely unreasonable! Look at the gold you've made. Look at the good you've done! Look at the poor you've helped. Look at the corrupt you've brought in line."

"Through selfish, immoral, and illegal means."

"Sometimes justice has a cost. Sometimes it requires sacrifice and unpleasant deeds. But the greater good justifies those tough choices."

Tough choices. I stared, at a loss for words, suddenly having the surreal sensation that I could have been standing in front of my father. And that, I realized, was exactly how I'd been behaving. I'd hated what my father had asked me to do. But I'd always felt guilty for walking away when I could have possibly done something to help others. Tom had provided a redemption, a chance to strike out against those who'd take advantage of others. I'd believed I was fighting for justice in a new way. A better way. But at its heart, it was the same: a crusade that made its own rules and, no matter how extreme, found a way to justify them—even at the expense of others. Tom was as blind as my father had been.

"Thank you," I said softly. "Thank you for helping me realize that this has never been my path, that I have to find a new one and stop repeating the past."

His eyebrows knit in confusion. "You're not making any sense."

"I want to make the world safe. I want to protect others. But not this way. Not by picking and choosing rules. Not by making a profit on the side. I appreciate what you've done for me, but I really am finished here. And I don't plan on ever seeing you again."

I could tell Tom didn't quite know how to react. He was used to being admired and fawned over. He didn't get dismissed. "You're making a mistake! What we do here is bigger than you realize. You have the chance to be part of something great. Others would kill for the chance I'm offering you."

"Then let them. I'm sure they'll be happy to hear you've got an opening."

Tom thrust the coins into my hand and jerked the door open. "Go," he said, pointing. "Enjoy your money. You earned it. I'm glad your high morals don't interfere with you reaping the rewards of 'picking and choosing rules.'"

His words and smug expression felt like a slap to the face. I stared down at the coins. Fifty gold. The rest of Lonzo's bond. But it was fifty gold stolen from someone else's pocket. Fifty gold that nearly cost a ship full of sailors their lives. And what kind of men was that dangerous cargo being sold to?

Lonzo, forgive me. But I know you wouldn't want it this way.

I turned my hands and let the coins clatter to the floor.

"Farewell, Tom."

I left the Dancing Bull with my head held high, keeping my expression imperious and detached. Inside, I still couldn't believe I'd let the money go when Lonzo was still tied to a dangerous job. Did it really matter how he got the money? Yes. Yes, it did. I had any number of other ways to get the rest. Rupert. Grant. After all, I was a girl who made her own options when no others were there.

I went back to Grant the next night. And the night after that. And the night after that.

The only night I didn't go to him was when he had a patrol, and I was surprised at how keenly I missed . . . what? What was it I missed? What we did in bed? Or did I maybe just miss him?

Cornelius Chambers invited me to tea that afternoon, and I endured his and Lavinia's not-so-subtle suggestions about how my contract would be coming due soon and how amazing their southern beach house was. Rupert listened with amusement and told me as I was departing, "Don't let them bully you, my dear. Fight until the end."

I held those words in my heart on the ride back home. They emboldened me—at least until dinner at Wisteria Hollow, when Jasper casually said to Charles, "Good news at last. I received a message from Warren Doyle today. He feels terrible about the incident and has offered to make up the loss to us by paying Tamsin's marriage price."

The fork dropped out of my hand and hit the plate with a clang. Everyone turned and stared. "I . . . excuse me." I shoved my chair back and jumped to my feet. "I don't feel well."

I hurried upstairs and covered my mouth to keep from screaming. I wanted to go back downstairs and rip Jasper Thorn apart, just as my heart had been. *He feels terrible about the incident and has offered to make up the loss to us by paying Tamsin's marriage price.* There was no price in this world that could make up for her loss! But why should I be surprised Jasper wouldn't see it that way? He hadn't even been willing to lend Cedric any money to marry Adelaide. Why should one girl matter more than his own son?

The next night, I nearly ran to Grant's. He hardly got a greeting out when I entered. I pushed him onto the bed and surprised myself with the feverish way I went after him. I couldn't get enough of him. I couldn't touch him enough. I couldn't get close enough.

Later, as we lay together in stillness, he said in that dry way of his: "So. That's what happens when we take a night off."

I didn't know how to explain how I felt, that Jasper's words and those empty beds had driven home how alone I was. That Lonzo was far away. Grant was all I had left, and the thought of losing him terrified me. But I would. One way or another, it was going to happen. He'd leave, I'd leave. I didn't know. Because although we often talked about all sorts of other topics in bed, our future—if there even was one—never came up. Even the far-fetched idea of going north together had been voiced cautiously. And it had never been mentioned again.

My face must have betrayed all the emotion churning inside me. I saw it startle him. I saw it scare him. He didn't mind unbound passion in bed, but he was still skittish at the thought of anyone caring about him too much.

I braced myself, ready for him to close himself off or even get up. Instead, he ran his fingers through the long strands of my hair and asked, "Why me?" It almost sounded like one of those world-weary "*Why me?*" exclamations people make when they're burdened with woes. "Maybe you didn't know any better the first time. Maybe not even the second, but you should by now. You could have your pick of other men. Nicer men. Less complicated men."

He spoke as he often did: light and flippant. But the hand that touched me trembled. I reached out and put my own over it as I studied him. Flyaway black hair. Scars. Square jaw. Questionable shaving. I thought about his brusqueness and biting humor. His courage in the face of danger. The loyalty he swore he didn't have.

"Because I wanted something simple. Instead I got you." I tightened my hold on his hand. "And it turns out, that was what I needed."

He shook his head. I could sense his guard coming up, but I didn't regret my words. "Mirabel—"

A rap at the door caused him to jerk away. He leapt off the bed and managed to tug on his pants as he hurried toward the other room. "Stay here," he warned. He shut the bedroom door, but it didn't catch.

I scrambled out of bed and pulled on my chemise, peering out through the small gap between door and wall. Grant picked up his gun and went to the front door, asking who was there. He'd grown even more cautious since we'd become lovers. I think he expected Jasper or Cornelius to show up one day.

I didn't hear the answer on the other side of the door, but he opened it and Aiana hurried in. She immediately began speaking in Balanquan, and a tense conversation ensued. I couldn't understand it—their language was still a puzzle to me—but two words came through very clearly: *Adelaide* and *Cedric*.

I pushed open the bedroom door and rushed forward. "What's going on? What's wrong?"

Aiana stopped mid-sentence. She looked at Grant, she looked at me, and then she looked back at him. Her face darkened, and she barked something to him that didn't sound complimentary. He answered back, and I interrupted before she could respond.

"Enough! Fight later. Tell me what's happened to Adelaide and Cedric. And speak Osfridian."

Aiana kept her eyes on Grant for several more seconds and then slowly turned to me. She spoke stiffly at first and then fell into the urgency of her story. "Something happened in Hadisen. Silas is back— and he brought Warren Doyle and some of his men. They're being held at the jail, and Cedric will join them once he's well enough to travel. Silas found them in the middle of a fight and took everyone into custody. Cedric and Warren each claim they were attacked by the other."

"Why wouldn't Cedric be well enough to travel?" I demanded.

"They don't know who started the fight, but they know who finished it. Cedric was outnumbered and took a beating, but he'll be okay. And Adelaide's fine . . . but . . ."

"But what? More than this?" I exclaimed. I wanted to go demand a boat take me over the bay right now.

"Did you know . . ." Aiana considered her words carefully. "Did you know about Adelaide's background?"

"She was a maid for some grand lady."

"Well, they're saying, *she* is—or was—the grand lady. A noble. Does the name Witmore or Rothford mean anything to you?"

"The Rothford earldom is one of the oldest, and it's held by the Witmore family," I said, reciting my history instructor's words. "But there's absolutely no way—" I groaned and walked away, putting a hand to my forehead. I was an idiot. "Of course. Of course she is." Adelaide had come to us knowing how to use seven different forks, but she hadn't been able to brush her own hair. The amazing turnaround in her grades hadn't been a turnaround at all. She'd been faking until then.

Grant leaned against the wall, arms folded across his chest. "Well, I didn't see that coming, but does it change anything?"

"It has people's attention. I guess we'll see what that's worth when she gets back with Cedric. Silas expects them to come by water in a couple of days. I'm surprised he hasn't stopped by yet." Aiana glanced around, as though she expected Silas to materialize out of thin air. "You'd better watch out—he's not going to take all of this as well as I did."

"Really? That was taking it well?" asked Grant. "I'd hate to see when you don't. I didn't even hear a *manasta* when you came in."

I rested against the wall too, close to Grant but not touching. "Warren's up to something. First Tamsin and then . . ." I lost track of what I'd been about to say. My mind had jumped somewhere else, clutching at a fragile thread. "*Manasta*."

"*Manasta*," Grant and Aiana both repeated at the same time, correcting my pronunciation.

I went to the bedroom and returned with a Lorandian version of the letter. Grant and I didn't read poetry in bed, but sometimes we tried to puzzle this code. "*Manasta* means 'greetings,' right?" I pointed at the letter's first line. "*Ma nahz taback*. Do you hear it? *Manasta* is in there. Wouldn't you open a letter that way? I mean, it's not a perfect match. The *back* syllable is still there, and—"

"What's the next word after that?" interrupted Grant.

"*Dapine*. It means 'rabbit.'"

"Forget the meaning," he said. "Read those words again. Use your best Lorandian pronunciation."

"*Ma nahz taback dapine*."

"*Bakda*," said Aiana. She looked at Grant. "Or *bakda*?" There was a very slight shift in her tone the second time.

"*Bakda*," he said, with a third tone. "*Manasta, bakda*."

"What is that?" I asked.

"'Greetings, friend.'" He had that light in his eyes, the one that said he was about to go on the hunt again. "Mirabel, you've broken the code."

CHAPTER 30

TRANSLATING THE LETTER WAS PAINSTAKING WORK. Grant and Aiana had to sit apart from me and listen as I read, focusing strictly on the sounds and how they could be strung together into Balanquan words. Equally complicated was that there was no word-for-word substitution. One Lorandian word might contain all the sounds for two Balanquan words. Or maybe one Lorandian word contained half a Balanquan word that was continued in the next Lorandian word. On top of it all, we had to take the Balanquan tonal and stress differences into account. So, even when Grant and Aiana were certain they'd parsed a Balanquan word, they had to puzzle out which meaning it had.

We were bleary-eyed by the time we finished, and even then, the letter still had holes we couldn't decipher. People's names had been swapped with numbers, and Grant said the traitors probably had a key that listed them all. The writer also hadn't focused much on grammar or style, so I tried my best to clean it up and add punctuation.

> *Greetings, friend. We have had occasional detection.*
> *17 is replacing lost goods and still sending gold. He*
> *will supervise usual transfer so that you can deliver to*
> *green mountain.*
> *How long until your _____ sees more gold?*
> *We need additional supplies and _____ start soldier*
> *payroll. Important to stay on schedule. First attack*

must be autumn. 34 is creating final schedule and will
send out with _____ seekers on healing night. Send
your gold to bay land if you can. If _____ then we will
come to you in gold land.

    Send response by 17.

I slumped back against the wall and yawned. The three of us sat on the floor, all worn out after the long hours. Well, Grant didn't seem worn out. He burned with restless energy and leaned forward to study the translation sitting between us.

"An autumn attack," he mused. "If they can act that soon, then they've got more in place than we realized. Or at least, they think they will by then. It sounds like they're scrambling. Autumn's a smart time. The land is still passable, but sea travel will shut down and limit Osfridian help. Discovering that part of the plan is huge. Osfrid can start sending backup now. I'd love to get my hands on whatever thirty-four's schedule is—we need to figure out who those seekers are. And I'll bet you anything that 'bay land' is Denham, which would probably mean 'gold land' is Hadisen. Whoever this was meant for is sending money—"

"Iyitsi, enough." Aiana rubbed at her eyes. "You've got your translation. Stay up all night with it if you want, but we need to get back to Wisteria Hollow."

"Wait just a little longer." Grant's eyes stayed fixed on the letter. "This needs to go to Silas right now. It's already two weeks old. Come with me in case he has any questions, then you can leave."

Aiana nudged me. "Can you hang in there a little longer, Banle?"

I answered with a nod and a yawn, and Grant finally glanced up. "Banle? Really?"

"No worse than Sekem," she shot back. "But maybe not a good match anymore. The fledgling's already left the nest, apparently."

Grant pointedly looked back down at the letter.

                                                ∽

Silas took a long time to answer the door, and I understood why when I saw him. Exhaustion had etched new lines in his face, and his glazed eyes didn't seem to recognize us at first. He'd been traveling all day, and even the water route between here and Hadisen was taxing. But after a few blinks, his gaze grew sharper, and the familiar shrewdness appeared.

"It can't be good if all three of you are here in the middle of the night," he grumbled.

"It *is* good, actually." Grant strolled in without invitation and beckoned for Aiana and me to follow. He laid the papers out on the desk and explained about our breakthrough. Silas was fully awake now and rewarded me with one of those raised-eyebrow glances when he heard about my role.

"We need these," he said, tapping the blanks. "That schedule could change everything. And I'd like to know where that green mountain is."

Aiana leaned closer. "I think we got *entwa* wrong. It's *entwa*. Bend, not mountain." As usual, the two Balanquan pronunciations sounded identical to my ear.

Grant scrutinized the words and nodded. "You're right. It's a city. Green Bend."

"Up in Alma," said Silas. "We've had our eye on someone there for a while, and he may be the one inventorying all the supplies as they come in. I've got a man there right now I can get to check on it."

I was studying the line about the schedule that both Silas and Grant found so critical. *34 is creating final schedule and will send out with _____ seekers on healing night.*

The words Aiana and Grant had brainstormed to the corresponding Lorandian sounds were written by the blank: disbelief, serpent, hazy, and wet. I went through them as I had before, placing them in context.

"What's the Balanquan word for 'heretic'?" I asked.

"There isn't one," said Grant.

"We don't even have the concept," added Aiana. "No one should dictate another person's worship."

"Then, for this code, they'd have to substitute something—like the way they use 'bay land' for Denham." My certainty grew. "Could 'disbelief seekers' be a way to say 'heretic patrol' then? Heretic hunters? You said you ride all over."

"Yes," said Grant. I could almost see his thoughts spinning faster and faster as he stared at the words. "And we sometimes deliver messages. There were a few people the patrol checked in with regularly when we made our rounds—people I suspected were more than citizens concerned with corrupt religions. If I had anything else to go on, where this person was, when the patrol will be there . . ."

"Assuming they haven't already come and gone," muttered Silas. "You better pray all your work wasn't wasted."

"*Pray.*" I tried to remember the date. My days were running together lately. "Tomorrow night. It's Ramiel's Day. That's the healing night they're talking about."

Grant frowned. "I thought Ramiel was the angel of peace and mercy."

"Healing's rolled into that. She's the patron of doctors too." Silas swung around so he could meet Grant face to face. "Tell me you know where the patrol's going to be then. *Tell me.*"

"Bakerston." Grant clenched and unclenched one of his fists, as though he was already grasping the case's conclusion. "I'm not on duty, but I know who the patrol's contact is up there. I know who thirty-four has to be."

Silas let out a grateful sigh having a burden lifted and then immediately straightened up. "Then you'd better make damn sure you see that message before they carry it off."

"I'll go now," said Grant.

"Morning," corrected Silas. "Get a few hours of sleep. I want you sharp. You'll need to search his house for anything else. Might be better to wait until after you copy that mystery schedule. Lay low until everyone's asleep."

"I know, I know. I can handle this."

"Don't get overconfident. You may be younger and a *little* faster, but I've done this longer. Be smart. Don't be impulsive. If you lose your cover, you lose the rest."

"I know." Grant speculatively ran his fingertips over the letter. "Warren Doyle started the patrols. If they're being used as couriers for the conspiracy, it seems like there's a good chance he might be part of it. And the letter mentions Hadisen."

Silas's face twisted into a scowl. "I thought about that. Hadisen turns out a lot of gold, too. Sir Ronald was certain their big financer was a Lorandian noble, but we're going to have to look into Doyle now."

Warren Doyle, a conspirator. It certainly fit with the villainous image of him I was building.

"Don't go the usual way to Bakerston," Silas added, rummaging through his papers. "You can't risk crossing paths with the patrol if they head up early. This road here . . ."

He took out a map, and Aiana tugged at my arm. "*Now* I'm taking her home. She's proved her worth. She deserves some sleep."

Silas lifted his head from the map and fixed me with a piercing look. "You've more than proved your worth, Miss Viana. And you've also proven—again—that I was a fool for wanting to get rid of you."

"Uh, thank you." Compliments from Silas threw me off almost as much as Grant's.

Aiana was already at the door. "Good luck, Iyitsi."

I followed reluctantly, needing to say more to Grant but knowing I couldn't. And even if others hadn't been around, he wouldn't have given me an emotional, heartfelt farewell anyway. It wasn't his way.

Aiana walked outside, but I stopped in the doorway to look back at Grant. Despite his and Silas's brusque attitudes, I knew how dangerous this was. Grant was penetrating the heart of the conspiracy. "Be careful," I told him. "I—we want you to come back."

Silas snorted and stalked off into his bedroom, apparently searching for something. "Don't worry. I'll still make sure you get your reward even if he doesn't."

"Glad to know you'll be so torn up about it," Grant called. Turning to me, he pitched his voice low. "I'll be back. No need to find some other man's bed yet."

"You think I'm that kind of woman?"

"I think someone as brave and beautiful as you could find other company if she wanted to. Oh, and brilliant too. You were brilliant tonight."

The earnestness in his voice took me aback almost as much as the words themselves. I grasped for a witty response but ended up blurting out: "I don't want you back for your bed. I want you back . . . for you. It's just that simple."

Grant faltered a moment, as discomfited as I'd been. "This has never been simple."

"Mira!"

Aiana sounded impatient, and Silas was returning from the bedroom. I gave Grant one last look of farewell and then scurried off after her.

~

We didn't speak much as we walked back. The brief high of the discovery at Silas's faded, and the effects of so little sleep slammed into me. It took a lot of effort just to put one foot in front of the other. Still, I managed to tentatively ask, "Are you . . . mad? About . . . you know."

"Mad? No. Not exactly. Worried for both of you. And surprised. You never seemed interested in anything like that."

"I'm interested in it with him." As soon as I said those words, I felt my face heat up and was grateful for the darkness. "And it's . . . I mean . . . it's better than I thought it would be. A lot better. It's also easier than I expected. Well, *in* bed, at least. Outside of it, things are more . . . complicated."

She laughed loudly at that. "That's the way it always is. And I imagine it's doubly true with Iyitsi. You probably never know which face is going to show up."

Her words hit harder than she realized, and I thought back to the moments before she'd arrived. "What did you say to him when you walked in?"

"Oh, I called him a few names. Maybe more than a few." The mirth vanished. "And I told him he was leading you into things you aren't ready for."

"And what did he say?"

"That you were doing the same to him."

It was another of those nights when I felt like I hadn't even had a chance to close my eyes before waking. And when I stepped outside of my room, the whole house was buzzing about what had happened in Hadisen.

"Did you know?" Sylvia kept asking me. "Did you know Adelaide was the Countess of Rothford?"

But that wasn't even what they found most shocking. Apparently during his arrest, Cedric had been caught possessing Alanzan artifacts—which increased the stakes for him. No one thought to ask if I'd known about that, but they speculated on everything else. The chatter was grating.

"No one knows for sure what he was caught with. And even if he did have something, that doesn't mean he's one of them."

"Why else would you have something Alanzan?"

"Do you think Jasper and Charles knew?"

"I don't think so. Jasper won't even come out of his office."

"Yeah, but if he did know beforehand, of course he'd pretend he didn't."

The gossip persisted in the days that followed, and I stayed away in my room as much as possible. The delay caused by Cedric's recovery in Hadisen only fueled the excited speculation. Everyone was eager for Adelaide's return, simply to hear more of the drama. I wanted her back so that I could see with my own eyes that she was safe and sound. Her continued absence gnawed at me, as did Grant's. I had no idea what had happened on Ramiel's Day. Silas, reported Aiana, didn't either. It worried her too, and she continued with the crossbow lessons when time allowed. She needed the distraction as much as I did. What I really longed to do was don Lady Aviel's mask and strike out into the city. When my housemates could drag themselves away from gossiping about Adelaide, they had plenty of tales of danger and intrigue they'd heard about in Cape Triumph. Petty robberies, assaults. The militia could only follow up on so many—and the ones they did usually only involved influential citizens. The injustice of it made me restless, and I longed to stand up for the downtrodden. But I held myself back, both to avoid being the type of vigilante I'd lectured Tom about and because I didn't want to cross paths with him.

I *almost* wished I had the backing of Tom's crew again so that I could go see Warren Doyle in jail and . . . what? I wasn't actually sure what I'd do. Even though he was locked away, I heard that he was well treated and even allowed fine food and clothing from his father. It incensed me to think of him enjoying those luxuries while Cedric healed from his beating. And there was Tamsin, of course. Warren knew more than he'd revealed, and I wanted to shake the answers out of him. I wanted him to pay for the way he'd made my friends suffer, but the law would have to decide that, not me..

To my surprise, a few social events crept into my schedule. Jasper and Charles were making a last, desperate effort to throw me in the path of eligible men, but it was to no avail. I didn't even have to try to dissuade any would-be suitors. My mind was full of Grant, and I hardly spoke to anyone.

A little less than a week after he'd left, I found myself at a party honoring some visiting delegates from Williamston. There'd been no further communication between Lonzo and me, and I made an attempt to be charming tonight, in the hopes of learning more about the territories he worked in. But partway through the event, Aiana slipped into the elegant drawing room. She wasn't assigned here tonight, and I stopped mid-sentence in a conversation I'd been having. Her eyes quickly scanned the crowd, and she hurried over to where Charles chatted with a few merchants. She pulled him to the side and said something in his ear. He looked across the room and, after spotting me, gave Aiana a nod.

She cut through the guests—who were more than a little startled to see a casually dressed Balanquan among them—and took my arm. "We have to go."

Her face held a rare urgency, and all I could think was that something had happened to Grant. "Why? What's the matter?"

"Adelaide is back."

CHAPTER 31

CEDRIC HAD GONE STRAIGHT TO THE JAIL UPON arriving in the city. Jasper had refused to let Adelaide come back to Wisteria Hollow, so Aiana had offered up her home. She had another of those second-floor lofts, one as large as Silas's. When we walked in and I saw Adelaide, I rushed across the room and dropped the secondhand clothes we'd acquired for her. Aiana retreated to give us privacy, and all I could do at first was take in the sight of Adelaide, alive and well. Her hair was damp, and she wore a robe. Tears glittered in her eyes.

"Mira—how did this—Tamsin—"

I hugged her closer. Aiana had warned me that Adelaide had only learned about Tamsin today. My letter had never reached her. "I don't know. I couldn't believe it when I heard."

I recounted what I knew—what was publicly known—and how strange the circumstances were. I withheld any speculation about Warren since Silas and Grant didn't have their hard proof yet.

"I can't lose her again," Adelaide said.

"I know. I feel the same way." I had a lump in my throat and had to fight to stay in control. Tamsin would have to wait. Adelaide was the one who needed me right now, and I tried to give her a brave smile. "But you have to put that grief aside for now. We'll cry for her later—a lot."

Adelaide told me her backstory in Hadisen, explaining how Warren and his men had tried to kill Cedric and make it look like an accident.

Warren denied it, and the words of a new governor earned more respect than those of a suspected heretic—even one involved with a no-
blewoman of considerable standing. Studying her as she spoke, I felt
increasingly foolish for not having suspected her secret sooner. There
was something powerful in the way she behaved and talked, even when
she played a scattered student or looked as disheveled as she did now.

A knock interrupted a conversation about Jasper. In a flash, Aiana
was at the door. Alert and dangerous, she placed one hand on the knob
and held a knife as long as her forearm in her other. She reminded me
of Grant, the night she'd discovered our affair.

"Who's there?" Aiana yelled.

"Walter Higgins," came the muffled response. "I'm looking for Adelaide Bailey—Cedric Thorn's partner."

"That's Cedric's agent!" exclaimed Adelaide. "Let him in."

A svelte young man entered, his eyes scrutinizing every detail
around him. I'd had no idea Cedric had an agent of any kind. Adelaide explained to us how Cedric had been trying to buy his stake
to Westhaven Colony by selling a forged Myrikosi painting. After a
lot of searching, Walter had finally found a buyer for him—one who
wanted authentication from anyone who might have knowledge about
Myrikosi art. That wasn't an easy request around here.

"Sirminicans look a lot like Myrikosi," Walter told Adelaide, giving
me a quick glance.

Adelaide immediately latched on to the idea. "You can do a
Myrikosi accent. I used to hear you do it back at Blue Spring. All you
have to do is meet this guy and tell him the painting he's interested in
is an authentic piece from one of Myrikos's greatest masters."

It turned out "this guy" lived an hour north of the city, but I couldn't
refuse her. If Cedric had a stake in Westhaven, Denham would have
to grant him immunity for his religion. With the trial beginning in the
morning, the odds of getting everything together in time seemed slim.
But, as Aiana bluntly pointed out to Adelaide: "You need to accept
that there's a chance Cedric may not get out of this. And if he doesn't,

you're going to need your own resources to escape."

I later left Adelaide with assurances that everything would be okay, just as I had the night she and Cedric had been found out. I hoped my words would end up being true now—because I really wasn't sure they had back then.

A throng of hopeful spectators had formed outside the courthouse when we arrived. Aiana managed to slip away from her duties long enough to lead me out of sight and direct me down a small road canopied with oak trees.

Everyone was up early the next morning to see the trial that would determine Warren's and Cedric's fates. Aiana had to help chaperone girls at the courthouse, and our hope was that no one would notice my temporary absence amidst all the drama and activity. I put on a deep burgundy riding dress that was far too elegant for a day in court, but no one paid any attention to it.

A throng of hopeful spectators had formed outside the courthouse when we arrived. Aiana managed to slip away from her duties long enough to lead me out of sight and direct me down a small road canopied with oak trees.

"I arranged for Silas to go with you," she told me. "I'm sure you'll say you'd be fine on your own, but a fancy Myrikosi lady wouldn't be traveling alone."

"Silas . . . not Grant?" There'd been no word from Grant, and he'd left almost a week ago.

Aiana shook her head. "Still not back."

My heart heavy, I turned down the rough road and found Silas easily. He wore a wide-brimmed hat, tipped down to shield him from the morning sun, and sat atop a deep brown mare. A gray one stood nearby.

"A sidesaddle?" I asked, not bothering to hide my disdain.

He lifted the hat's brim to examine me. "Only way you're going to ride in that dress. Or convince whoever it is you're trying to fool that you're some aristocrat. Aiana didn't really give me the whole story."

"Do you want to know it?"

"No."

We set off down the quiet road. Sunlight shone through the trees in dappled patterns, already making the heavy riding dress itchy and smothering.

"Aiana said Grant's not back."

"No, but I did finally receive a message last night. He got what he went after, but it needed some follow-up. He had to chase down a few more people, seize some more evidence. Even had the army arrest a couple of men to question. We're starting to dismantle this."

"And Grant's okay? Not hurt?"

Silas shot me a sidelong look. "Yes."

We rode in silence until our little road joined a larger one. Unsettled woodland flanked it, but the size and packed dirt suggested it saw a lot of travel. Silas cleared his throat a few times and finally asked, "So. Do you still want to fix the lawlessness in Cape Triumph?"

For a moment, I thought he knew about my work with Tom, and then I recalled the conversation in which I'd asked about the city's haphazard justice. "Well, I'd like to see it fixed. I don't think I said I wanted to do it myself."

"You didn't. I said you should bring it up with the governor. You said he wouldn't listen to a Sirminican woman."

"I still don't think he would."

He shrugged. "Well, he listened to me when I went and talked to him—before this whole Hadisen mess broke out."

"I . . . don't know what you're getting at."

"He agreed the city needs an official watch and went ahead and authorized the formation of one. The paperwork's back in my office, detailing a few operating procedures, as well as how much money he'll allot."

"That's wonderful!" It was probably the only purely good news I'd heard in a long time.

"I'm glad you think so," Silas said. "Because you're the one who's going to put it together."

"What?" I repeated his words in my head. "But you just said that *you'd* talked to him—"

"I got the paperwork and permission to get it started, but that's it. You think I want to take that kind of job on, along with everything else I juggle? Organizing patrols? Hiring watchmen? I'm not that crazy. But I think you might be."

All those dreams of valor, all the stories I'd idolized . . . even my attempts at justice as Lady Aviel. None of them had anything to do with reality. But this . . .

The light that had surged in me at his words abruptly darkened. "I can't do anything like that. I'm still bound to my contract with the Thorns."

"Well, that's the other thing." Silas scratched one of his ears and stared off down the road. "We've got a budget. That's meant to cover your pay and anyone you hire. Work the numbers, and you could take an advance against your pay. Deal with the fee that way."

My head swam with the possibilities—and complications. *If* this freedom was even possible, it would be hard earned. "But how could I hire anyone? Most would be men. They'd never accept me. They'd never respect me."

"Then you make them respect you. You fight and stand strong until you've won. You survived through Sirminica, Osfro, here. You think you can't whip a few patrolmen into shape? Plus, you'd be paying them. Holding the purse strings goes a long way."

I swallowed. "Speaking of purse strings . . . could I . . . could I get an advance on a little more than my fee?"

Silas snorted. "Depends on your definition of 'a little,' I suppose. Borrow too much, and you won't have any watch at all."

"I know. But, my brother . . ." I took a deep breath. It still felt strange talking about Lonzo. "My brother's a bondsman down in—"

"Yes, yes," Silas interrupted. "Williamston. I thought that was all taken care of."

I gaped. "You . . . know?"

"Of course. I'm the one who passed the money on to one of our agents headed that way."

"What money?"

"The sixty Grant gave me a couple of weeks ago." Silas rolled his eyes. "I don't even want to know how many card games it took to get that. Last I heard, the paperwork's finalized, but your brother's been delayed because of some injury."

My hand flew to my chest. "What?"

"Something with his knee, I think. I just heard yesterday that he'll be okay and should be here within the month."

Lonzo. Free. And coming here. Soon. I half expected to wake up in my bed at any moment. It was the only way to explain this increasingly astonishing day.

"You okay?" Silas peered more closely at me. I had no idea how long I'd been silent.

"I . . . yes. I just didn't know. Grant never said anything." I focused back on Silas. "Why wouldn't he tell me?"

"I don't know. My guess is he didn't want to worry you until he knew the full story about the injury. But that's just a guess. I have no idea what goes on in Grant's head or what goes on between you two." Silas cut me a look. "Actually, I do have a few ideas about what goes on between you, and if you were my daughter— Well. It doesn't matter. Right now, at least. Let's focus on the job offer. Do you want it? I'm not going to lie to you. It *will* be hard. I meant it when I said I think you can win, but you'll be battling more than the men who work for you. A lot of this town doesn't want any law. But the rest of it, the ordinary folk, they need that law."

Since coming to Adoria, I'd imagined and adapted to countless scenarios. An opportunity like this never crossed my mind. It had never even crossed my dreams. Independence. The chance to really and truly help others in a fair way. I could give Lonzo a job when he arrived. "It's amazing, Mister Garrett. Really. I'm flattered you even considered me. And yes . . . I do want it. I just hope you're right about paying off my contract."

"Eh, I've faced worse problems. And if we really are on the verge of closing in on the traitors, you'll get that absurdly high reward that Grant promised without consulting me."

"My reward," I reiterated. And Grant would get his too. My brilliant, exciting career suddenly felt hollow as I accepted that it'd be without him. He'd be off with the Balanquans, away from me, away from everyone here. He liked working alone, though. Or did he?

Maybe . . . maybe you'd like to see the lands up north.

My breath caught in my throat as Grant's words came rushing back to me with a sudden, impossible revelation. Beside me, Silas said something about us being on the outskirts of Crawford, but I barely heard him. My mind flew far from this sunny road. I was back in Grant's dark bedroom when he'd nervously hinted that I might go with him to the Balanquans.

I'd been too mad at him that night to even consider it. When Aiana had later explained the deal's strict conditions on who could go with him, the implications of Grant's offer hadn't hit me. And even when I'd admitted to him that I *would* like to travel with him, I still hadn't thought about my role. I just wanted to be with him—at least, I did until my priorities with Lonzo had dragged me back to reality.

Only the ambassadors and their families are allowed—wives and children, people like that. No friends or well-wishers. Not even servants or bodyguards.

Wives.

What had Grant been asking of me? Had he even known what he was saying? He'd been so hesitant each time the topic came up, as though he couldn't acknowledge even to himself what he was doing.

Had he—in his bizarre, complicated way—been proposing marriage?

The rest of the morning passed in a daze. I put on a good performance for the potential buyer—an older man who reminded me a lot of Rupert—and convinced him I'd grown up around all sorts of fine art in Myrikos before falling in love with an Osfridian merchant who'd brought me here. If I'd had the painting on me, he would've handed over the money then and there.

But even as I smiled and chatted, all I kept thinking was: *What had Grant meant?*

Silas and I made good time back to Cape Triumph, and he left me almost immediately. "I'm testifying just before lunch and need to be on hand at the trial. If you don't want anyone to notice that you've been gone, wait until the recess when you can blend in with the crowd."

I made myself comfortable in a grassy clearing just off the lane, my mind still full of the day's developments. When I heard the sound of voices growing in the distance, I hurried to the courthouse. I slipped in easily among the lunch-seeking crowd and was just in time to see the prisoners being led away. I almost looked right past Cedric. His arm was in a sling, and bruises shadowed his face. He wore rumpled and worn-out clothes, whereas Warren and his men were clean and smartly dressed. I thought about the day I'd met with Cedric in the church, when he'd been so stylishly dressed and hadn't had a hair out of place. I never would have recognized that man as the one who walked by me now.

Adelaide and Aiana met me at the door. Adelaide's face was pale and drawn, and I slipped my arm around her as we left to eat. "Everything's going to be okay," I said automatically.

"It was awful, Mira. Awful."

The biased tribunal hadn't allowed Cedric to fully tell his story, and the line of questioning had assumed he was already guilty. They'd accused Adelaide of deceit and loose morals when she testified. Warren, however, had been met with sympathy. He'd had time to polish his story, and his men had backed it up.

The afternoon session proceeded as the morning one had. When the trial ended for the day, only a few witnesses were left to testify. They'd have to do it first thing in the morning, which disappointed the crowd. Governor Doyle had said he'd see the sentence carried out immediately, and many had hoped to see an execution today.

When Aiana and I returned to Wisteria Hollow, I was in no mood to hear gossip. I slipped into my room and stayed until after midnight. Only then did I creep out in search of food. I hadn't had an appetite for most of the day but was ravenous for the stale tarts I discovered. A shadow appeared in the kitchen doorway, and I jumped.

It was Gideon Prescott, the young man from Grashond. He and the other Heirs of Uros had lingered to wrap up some trade in town and kept saying they'd be leaving soon, but there was always some new delay. "I'm sorry," he told me. "I didn't mean to startle you."

"Did you just get in? There's some food over there."

"Thank you." He accepted a tart. "I was in town later than I expected to be. I . . . I think I helped your friend. Miss Bailey. At least, I hope I did. I'm not sure."

I set my food down. "What do you mean?"

"I approached her tonight, offering to help. I was friends with Tamsin—Miss Wright, and I just felt like it was something she'd want me to do." He looked away for a moment before continuing. "Anyway. I suggested Mister Thorn buy a share in a new colony called Westhaven—"

"I already know about it. How he'd get amnesty in Denham."

"Miss Bailey knew too. What she didn't know was that there are some representatives of the Westhaven charter in Cape Triumph right now."

"But she doesn't have the money for it yet."

"She seemed to think she could get it."

"Well, yes, there's a deal in place, but there's no time to—" My breath caught. "Mister Stewart, what was she doing when you left?"

"Getting the money, I think. She said she was going on a short ride. I gave her my horse."

A short ride! She was going to get the painting and try to close the deal. Walter Higgins, scrupulous with forged art, had stashed the painting in a village south of Cape Triumph. Adelaide would have to go there first and then back up to Crawford. She'd be on horseback all night.

"Was anyone with her?"

"No. She was alone."

Adelaide. Alone. Riding in the dark.

"When did she leave?"

"I . . . let's see. I'd say three hours ago. Almost four."

"Thank you, Mister Stewart," I said, rushing past him.

"What are you going to do?"

I didn't answer. I ran up the stairs to my room and began looking for the starry cloak.

CHAPTER 32

"LADY AVIEL," TOM SAID COOLLY. "I THOUGHT YOU retired."

I stormed through the Dancing Bull and slammed the coin he'd given me down on the table. "I'm calling in my second favor. Now."

The other men seated around him fell silent, their eyes wide at my tone. I'd run the entire way from Wisteria Hollow and hoped my exhaustion didn't show as I glared at Tom. "I'd forgotten you had that," he remarked. "In retrospect, I'm not sure that scuffle during the Flower Fest really warranted it. I think I was just caught up in the moment."

"Don't play games with her." Two seats away, Elijah got to his feet. "What do you need? I'll help you."

"You certainly will not," snapped Tom. "Sit down, and finish the assignments for tomorrow. I'll deal with this."

For a few seconds, the two men were locked in a silent showdown that made the others shift uncomfortably. I recalled how upset Elijah had been about Tom's actions the night of the storm, but I'd assumed that had all faded. Elijah was one of Tom's longtime followers. When Elijah did finally return to his chair, his expression stayed vigilant and wary.

Tom let some suspenseful silence drag out before standing up. "Let's speak in private, my lady."

"We can do it outside," I told him, as we walked from the table. I nodded at the door. "All I need is a horse."

"That's all? Once again, you've asked for a boring favor. The coin's wasted on you. Come along, then."

He led me out to the tavern stables, and I was pleased to see my favorite horse there. "Are you asking to keep her?" he asked.

I began saddling her. "Only borrowing."

"Boring."

"I don't need her for long. I'm just riding out to Crawford and back."

Tom cocked his head speculatively. "You aren't by chance pursuing the much-talked-about Lady Witmore, are you?"

I paused in my work. "Why would you say that?"

"Because this is the second time I've heard that little town brought up tonight, and I can't think it's a coincidence. There's a man who frequents the Bull—a man of ill repute, not like the rest of us—who came running in not too long ago and gathered up some of his cronies. He said he'd seen Lady Witmore riding north on the border highway. You know there's a reward for her, right? Put out by her family?"

I did know that. It was why Adelaide had worked so hard to hide her true identity. If she was riding north already, she'd made good time. She must have the painting, but that was irrelevant if she had brigands in pursuit. I worked more quickly.

"And," Tom added, "saving a tragic, romantic figure like her is exactly your style."

"I have to go now." I climbed up and took the reins. "Get out of my way."

Tom sighed. "Wait a moment, and I'll go with you."

"Get out of my way," I repeated. "I don't want your help."

"Yes, but you need it. There are five of them. You're good, but you can't take them alone." He glanced at my belt. "Especially not with that ridiculous knife. Did you get rid of the dirk out of spite?"

"I lost it in the storm when you abandoned me. Now move!" I growled. "So help me, I *will* run you down."

Tom grabbed a saddle and started working on his destrier. "I'm going. And we'll grab another dirk on our way out."

We left the city under a gibbous moon and thundered up the border highway. Fury boiled inside me, and I was glad our pace didn't allow for conversation. I didn't want his prattle. I didn't want anything from him.

But I wanted Adelaide safe.

For that, I'd swallow my pride. Tom was right about the numbers and my knife. If having him along bettered my odds, so be it.

"We have to move faster!" I shouted at one point. "We have to overtake them!"

"We will," he called back. "I've seen their horses. They're adequate but nothing like these. They can't maintain this kind of gallop."

Maybe not, but it still seemed like they had too big of a lead. I berated myself for not having thought to finish the painting deal myself. I could've done it all in one day, but we hadn't known about the Westhaven representatives in town.

Tom slowed, and I started to chastise him when I caught sight of a light ahead of us. A lantern sat on the road, illuminating a cluster of men and horses.

"Told you," he said.

We raced forward, and the men turned at the sound of our horses' hooves. Just behind them, I spied Adelaide standing in the road. She looked unharmed, and a man near her clutched his calf in pain.

Our presence set the brigands into disarray.

"Pirates!"

"Tom Shortsleeves!"

"And Lady Aviel!"

Tom and I drew our blades. "You have something we want," he said. "Leave Lady Witmore with us, and go."

Two of the men actually started to run away, abandoning the horses they'd dismounted. Maybe image really was everything. A broad, burly man—less intimidated by us—strode forward, a knife in his hand. "She and her reward belong to us. Get out of here before we—"

Tom slammed his sword's pommel into the man's head. I charged forward into another of the brigands and stabbed his shoulder with the dirk. He grunted and reached into his coat for something. A gun? A knife?

I jumped off the horse and jabbed at his stomach. He made a lot more noise this time and pressed one hand to where I'd hit. His other hand still kept moving and produced a gun from the coat. I struck his arm with the dirk, and a kick to the knee brought him down. A follow-up kick to the head made sure he stayed down.

I spun around, searching for someone else to hit, but only Tom stood there. He regarded my fallen foe with interest. "Well, well, it looks like you have a dark side after all."

"Where is she?" I demanded. "Where did she go?"

"Not far. She got on her horse during the fight and went north."

The remaining brigands were either unconscious or wounded. Tom slapped their horses, sending the animals back toward Cape Triumph. "Just to make things a little more difficult."

He and I rode on and came upon Adelaide pretty quickly. Her horse was hobbling. "You don't need to worry about those men anymore," Tom told her.

"Dead?" Her posture and voice were both filled with distrust.

I averted my face and made sure my Belsian accent was strong. "Maybe. Or they ran."

"Well, it doesn't matter. I wasn't going with them, and I'm not going with you." Her defiance made me proud.

Tom mostly seemed amused. "We don't want to take you away. Wherever you're going, we'll help you get there safely. We're your escorts for the night."

"Why?" she demanded. "What do you want?"

"Nothing that you need to worry about. Our interests are our own. All you need to know is that you're safe with us." He tilted his head to get a better look. "Your horse is lame?"

"Not yet," she said. "But she threw a shoe."

"Then we'll have to take you on ours," Tom said.

After looking between us and her hobbled horse, Adelaide reluc-tantly agreed. She tied Gideon's horse to a tree, and I was forced to ride with Tom so that she could share the mare with her painting. After one more uneasy glance at us, she gave a nod, and the three of us set off toward Crawford at a brisk pace.

When we reached the village's outskirts, we all agreed that Adelaide should go on alone while Tom and I waited by the road. Masked strangers skulking in the night could be taken the wrong way.

As soon as she was out of sight, I jumped down and paced. "Am I that bad?" Tom asked after a while.

I turned my back to him. "Just stretching my legs."

"Aviel, I wish you didn't hold such a grudge."

"Stop talking. I didn't even want you here tonight."

His voice grew uncharacteristically serious. "I've always meant it when I said you have potential. I really wish you'd reconsider. We all miss you. So much is about to happen, and you should really be a part of it. In fact, I've actually got—" The sound of hooves cut off whatever he was about to say, and he turned to watch Adelaide ride up. "All done? Then let's get you back. Dawn is coming."

The tired horses managed an aggressive speed to Cape Triumph. The eastern sky was already lightening to purple, and the trial would be resuming soon. Adelaide still had to complete the transaction with the Westhaven representatives.

We left her near Cape Triumph's main entrance. "Thank you for your help," she said as she dismounted. "I couldn't have done this without you. Either of you."

"Our pleasure." Tom made as much of a bow as he could from atop the horse and made up for the lack of cape flourish by sending her off with an old Lorandian farewell that Osfridians and Sirminicans often used. It meant, "May Ariniel guard you." Even though I knew Tom was showing off, I repeated the words in my head and hoped the angel was listening. Adelaide had a strength I'd underestimated, but she still looked small and alone as she walked away.

I returned the new dirk to Tom, turning down his insistence I keep it. "This is Lady Aviel's last outing," I told him. "I mean it this time."

"Then be someone else if you want, because I've got one more job for you."

"Tom—"

"Just listen. No stealing, no attacking. Defensive, not offensive. *I'm* the one moving goods this time, and I need able-bodied men—and women—for protection. I've got several wagons heading out to Alma today. You'd be assigned to one, and if all goes well, the worst you'll experience is a boring ride there and back. If things don't go well— that is, someone takes an interest in our cargo—then you'll help send them on their way. It's easy."

"You always say that, and it's never true! And Alma's three days away."

"Eh, closer to two. We're barely going over the border."

"It doesn't matter. Even if I had that kind of time, I'm not doing any more work for you."

He nodded his head toward the gate. "If you're worried about Lady Witmore, you can wait and see how the verdict turns out. I plan to. It'll be easy catching up to the others."

"No."

"The money—"

"*No*, Tom. For the last time, stop asking."

His green eyes weighed me for long moments. Here, in sunlight, they reminded me of the sea along Sirminica's western coast. "Whatever you're caught up in is something foolish and sentimental, isn't it? Such a waste of talent." He urged his horse forward and led the one I'd ridden. "I won't ask anymore, but I hope we meet again. Farewell, angel."

A cloud lifted from me as he rode off toward one of the city's more discreet entrances. Life would be easier without Tom Shortsleeves—and Lady Aviel—in it. I flipped my cloak inside out and took off the wig and mask before entering the city, but I needed something better. Pants were a rarity for any woman, let alone one in the Glittering Court. I had to find something else to wear before going to the courthouse.

No one answered Aiana's door, so I picked the lock and hoped she wouldn't mind. Inside, the lingering smell of tea told me I'd probably just missed her before she'd headed off to work at Wisteria Hollow. I helped myself to breakfast and found one of the dresses we'd procured for Adelaide. The fit wasn't great, but it was better than nothing. I finished the last of the bread and prepared to head over to the trial. Hopefully, I could just slip in with the other girls before anyone noticed that—

A rap at the door made me jump up. I glanced around frantically for one of Aiana's knives, but all I could spot was her crossbow. Then, a familiar voice called, "*Sekem! Ta qi.*"

I flung open the door and found a very bedraggled—and surprised—Grant standing outside. "What are you doing here? Where's Aiana?"

"Where have you been?" I exclaimed, pounding my fist against his chest. "Do you know how much I've worried?"

And then we were all over each other, kissing our way into the room—which seemed to be something we did a lot. I couldn't get close enough to him. I needed to hold on to him and feel that he was real.

He broke the kissing with some reluctance, keeping one hand tangled in my hair and the other on my waist. "Look, any other time you want to attack me in a dress that's too small for you, you can go right ahead. But we don't have the time." He glanced down. "Really too small. Why are you wearing this?"

I put my hands on the sides of his face and turned his gaze back up. I was still stunned that he'd just walked through the door. "Grant . . . I've been so worried about you." My voice started to crack as all the anxiety and terrible imaginings that had tormented me this week came

crashing down. "I didn't know if . . . that is, if something had happened to you . . ."

That sardonic humor vanished as he met my eyes. He didn't move
away, but he suddenly felt tentative in my arms. "No," he groaned.
"Don't look at me that way."

"What way?"

"*That* way. The way you looked when you asked about the scar.
The way you looked when you thought I was dead. The way you
looked when you were supposed to be giving a shallow explanation
for wanting to sleep with me. The look that says . . . you like me."

I stared at him for a long moment. "I don't like you, Grant. I love
you."

He pulled away and began pacing, so I knew I'd struck something.
He wasn't mad, but he was clearly at a loss. "No, no, don't say that.
Mirabel, I don't know how to—that is—argh."

The words had been waiting inside of me for so long that they'd
slipped out before I could stop them. I wanted to say more, to make
him face them, but then my gaze fell on a bundle of papers he'd
dropped when we'd grabbed each other. The weight of what was at
stake today returned, and so I gave Grant the escape he wanted.

"What are these?" I asked, crouching down to retrieve the papers.

He took a few seconds to collect himself, and then his business face
slid into place. "We've identified most of the ring and started arresting
some," he said, more comfortable grasping facts than feelings. "One
man gave a great confession, and the paper evidence just keeps growing and growing. I was coming to ask Aiana to give these to you to
check something."

We leaned together as he unrolled the papers. He looked up at me
as we touched, his gaze furtively searching my face before he quickly
looked back down.

"We've got a lot of evidence implicating Warren Doyle, including one of the confessions. But this letter's in Lorandian, and I didn't
have time to find a translator." He flipped through the pages, and I

saw familiar names—the ones Abraham Miller had misspelled. This writer had corrected Skarbrow to Scarborough, Madisin to Madison, and Cortmansh to Courtemanche. Grant settled on the last page and pointed. "Here. What's this say about Warren Doyle?"

The letter was actually in Lorandian—not Balanquan disguised as Lorandian—and I was able to parse the paragraphs after a bit of puzzling. "It says Warren will be sending his next shipment of gold in late summer when . . ." I paused. "I think that's 'settlers.' Yes, when his settlers have paid their taxes. He'll deliver the promised . . . eh, cut of them to a Lorandian messenger. Or proportion of them. Something like that."

Grant slapped the paper and stalked away in triumph. "That's it! That's it, Mirabel. Exactly what I was hoping you'd say. Embezzling from his own colony. The last piece in the cage that's about to slam down on Warren Doyle. We've got him."

Excitement burned in me, along with some well-deserved fury for Warren. He'd made my friends suffer, but now, as a confirmed traitor, he'd be the one paying. "Is he the big financial backer?"

Grant's victorious air wavered a little. "No. He's *a* backer. Looks like Courtemanche is the one with deep pockets, but we probably won't get him. Word's already been getting around about the ring unraveling, and a bunch have fled. Wish I knew which Balanquan helped him decipher that code. It's not Aiana or me, so there must—"

Sudden shouts drew us both to the window. Below, people gathered in excited clusters and started hurrying down the street. Grant pushed the glass open a little, and we could better hear what had everyone so worked up.

"They're going to hang the heretic!"

"Hurry, or we won't get a spot!"

"Damn it," Grant said, backing up with a scowl. "I knew they'd have a verdict early, but I thought there'd be time for Silas to bring all the evidence beforehand. Don't worry—there's no way they'll carry out the sentence so soon."

"They will! You saw those people. And I heard yesterday that Governor Doyle intended to act right away." I clutched his hand. "Grant, we have to—"

"Okay. Okay. Don't worry. We can still do something. It takes time to set up a proper gallows. I'm sorry," he added, seeing me flinch. "But it's not too late. I'll get Silas so he can go to the courthouse. He's got enough clout with the governor to delay things."

"Why isn't he there already?"

"He escorted some of the arrested traitors to the fort. He didn't want them in the city's jail with all the other madness going on."

"Why delay? Can't *you* just go straight to the governor?" A flash of guilt on his face answered me. "You don't want to expose your cover."

"We've got the time," he insisted. "You have to know I wouldn't let someone innocent die for my own gain. And this'll have more impact coming from Silas anyway. No, wait."

He put his hand on my arm as I moved toward the door, and I shrugged away from him. "They want to hang Cedric! I have to be there for Adelaide."

"You will be. But first, I need you to go to Silas's." Grant fished a key from his pocket. "The Balanquan letter and all the other documents are there. If the verdict's in, we'll save time if Silas and I can go straight to the courthouse and you meet us there with the evidence."

"But I have to stop them if you can't!" I wanted to scream in frustration. "Grant—"

"Mirabel. Brave, beautiful Mirabel." He took my hands and kissed my forehead. "I know you want to lash out at the monsters of the world, but this isn't the time for swords and heroics. Information is real power, remember? These pages are how we stop Doyle."

I swallowed back my rage, knowing he was right. Cedric's and Warren's fates were mired in legal intricacies. Words, not weapons, were what we needed. I tried not to think of Adelaide, alone, fearing the man she loved was about to be executed . . .

"I'll go, but Grant, you can't let them hang Cedric! You can't. He doesn't deserve it . . . and it'll destroy her! Whatever happens with Warren, just don't let Cedric die. Not after everything we've all been through." I squeezed his hands and met his eyes without blinking. "Promise me. Promise me you'll save him. You have to."

Grant leaned close and brushed a kiss against my lips. "Mirabel, I will do everything in my power to make sure he stays alive. I promise. He'll get out of this. We all will."

I let out a long breath. "Then let's finish this."

We split off in opposite directions outside, with only one last look as a goodbye. I'd just barely gotten him back after a long week of worry, and now we were parting again. *I don't like you, Grant. I love you.*

I moved toward Silas's at a brisk pace, my heart ready to burst. A momentary panic seized me when I stepped into his office and saw that messy desk, but the papers I needed were stacked neatly and prominently on top. My translated letter was first, followed by a map and an array of documents that Grant must have been gathering over the last week. Some were coded and marked up with translations. Others bore the acrid smell of reagents. He really had been busy.

And then it was back to the streets of Cape Triumph. Snatches of conversation about heretics and hangings reached me as I hurried past, and I hoped Grant was right about having enough time. Otherwise, this would all—

"Miss Viana?"

I came to a halt and turned around at the unexpected sound of Rupert Chambers's voice. He strolled forward, leaning on his cane, and gave me one of his gentle smiles. Beside him, two servants and a very subdued Cornelius carried bundles and crates.

"Mister Chambers. I didn't expect to run into you here. It's a delight, as always."

He bobbed his head. "Likewise. And it's lucky. I'd been hoping to catch a word with you."

I shifted from foot to foot. The papers itched in my hands. "I'd like that very much, but I really can't spare the time right now."

"I understand. But before you go, I want to see Cornelius apologize to you." Rupert's features hardened as he glared at his son.

Cornelius seemed to shrink in upon himself. "I-I'm very sorry for all the pressure I've put on you recently."

His father gave an exasperated sigh. "That's the best you can do? Well, nonetheless, I'm sorry too, my dear."

Despite my impatience, curiosity held me a moment. "For . . . what?"

"For you getting caught up in this scheme of his and Lavinia's. They've been burning through my money to support her ridiculous lifestyle and wanted to send me off with a distracting new bride so that they'd be able to manage the assets here. Since I still legally control everything, I've put an end to this, and Cornelius is being very accommodating about returning some of their garish nonsense. Mostly because he's afraid I'll cut him out of the will." Rupert sighed again. "Most of it can't be returned because he bought it on the black market, so now we have to sell it. The wretches he bought it from don't want it back. They're only dealing in gold."

"Well, there's been no harm done, so . . ." My words trailed off as I saw the cloth slip off from Cornelius's burden. Silvery black stone shone in the early sunlight. "That's a Balanquan sculpture."

Cornelius turned hopeful. "You want to buy it off us?"

"No. Where'd you get it?" But of course I already knew.

"I don't know exactly where it comes from. I mean, it's the same person I buy from, but I always deal with his go-between. He's always turning up rare and beautiful things. Those of us in the know are always ready to jump at anything he gets. His goods are pricey—but almost impossible to get anywhere else."

"Don't talk about him like he's an art connoisseur," scolded Rupert. "He's just some common thief."

It was another unexpected twist in the weird world that was my life lately. But it was a twist to be marveled at some other day. "I wish you the best of luck in rectifying everything, but I have to go." I began backing away, hoping the message was clear.

"Oh, we'll fix it all," said Rupert. "And I'm not broke yet. Which is why, when you do have time, we'll talk about paying off your contract. Not for marriage. We've always known I'm too old for you. It's just something I'd like to do as a gift and an apology—"

I stopped walking again, but not because of those extraordinary, impossible words. It was a series of shouts and screams that froze me up. People were running toward us, the *opposite* direction they'd headed earlier for the hanging. *It's over*, I thought frantically. *I should've run to Silas's. I should've ignored Rupert's greeting. The execution is over. Cedric is dead.*

But no. This wasn't an enthusiastic crowd. They weren't high off the drama of watching a heretic die. These people were afraid. They were fleeing for their lives.

"There's an Icori army coming! They're invading the city!"

CHAPTER 33

THE ICORI?

That wasn't possible. Not in Denham. The Icori still shared uneasy borders with the outer colonies, but they'd been pushed out of this region for some time. The treaties created with Denham and its neighboring colonies had held peacefully. And anyway, how could an Icori army have made it all the way to Cape Triumph without anyone noticing until now?

Improbable or not, the panic ramping up around us was very real. Without another word to the Chambers men, I took off at a run, moving against the flow of the frantic crowd. It gave me an eerie flashback to Sirminica, when I'd seen the same kind of hysteria seize mobs who became obsessed only with their own self-preservation. I fought my way through the crush of bodies, often getting shoved and bumped. At one point, I stumbled into a man who helped keep me from falling. He and a few others were running in the same direction as I was. "Where are the Icori?" I called, keeping pace with them.

One glanced over at me. "Over by the northwest highway."

The northwest highway. After the entrance by the fort, that highway was the next most common way into the city. It was also near the courthouse. Near my friends.

I took note of my companions' guns and knives. "Do you have an extra weapon?"

"Don't be foolish, girl," one barked back.

I split off from them when we reached Aiana's block and nearly tripped over my skirts while sprinting up the stairs to her loft. Inside, I grabbed the crossbow from its spot on the wall and wavered on whether to burn time searching for weapons I felt more comfortable with. No. Better to go into a fight with this than to miss the fight altogether.

And I was ready for a fight, ready to do whatever it took to protect my friends. Whether it was Warren Doyle's machinations or an invading army, I would face it. As I returned toward the door, I noticed a small leather bag with a long strap. I snatched it up too and hung it over me, across my chest. It gave me a place to store the precious papers while leaving my hands free for the crossbow.

Out in the street, a few others had rallied and taken up arms to face the Icori. I joined a small group and charged forward, determination obliterating all traces of my sleepless night. But when the courthouse finally came into view, that fierce resolve faltered, and I staggered to a halt. Those beside me did too.

The scene before us looked more like some elaborate theatrical production than real life. The gallows sat atop a high platform that allowed for a good view, except the audience was no longer made of Denham residents. They'd fled. Instead, a mass of riders filled the space. Icori riders.

I'd never actually seen Icori before, outside of sketches in Osfridian books. They all wore cloaks and wraps of brightly patterned plaid and stripes, a custom they'd maintained long after being driven out of Osfrid and over the sea two hundred years ago. All that color made it difficult to gauge numbers, as did the fact that most of them had blond and red hair. Maybe forty or fifty? From where I was standing, I couldn't get an accurate view.

But I could see their weapons clearly and sense the tension crackling through them and the danger they presented, even though they made no threatening moves. No one attacked them either, but really, who could? Part of Cape Triumph's regiment had recently been called to the outer borders, and the fort held only a skeleton regiment. The present militia were outnumbered, and a few looked ready to bolt.

Only one thing could draw my attention from this strange spectacle. Cedric, Adelaide, and a lawyer they knew stood at the end of the gallows platform. Warren Doyle did as well, and he had a gun pointed at my friends. Governor Doyle stood farther down from them and seemed to be in conversation with the Icori. He either didn't notice or care about his son's actions just then. Maybe he thought he had bigger problems.

He probably did, but my sights were on Adelaide, Cedric, and that gun. Warren had a desperate, almost crazed look on his face, and I wanted to run right up there and do something, anything, to stop him. Too many people blocked my way, and I didn't know what Warren would do if he suddenly felt threatened.

"You've had no wrongs done to you," the governor was saying. "We've all agreed to the treaties. We've all obeyed them. You have your land, we have ours."

A deep male voice responded from the Icori, somewhere near the front. His Osfridian was good, even with the heavy brogue that still lingered in the far reaches of Osfrid. "Soldiers are moving into our land and attacking our villages—soldiers from the place you call Lorandy," he said. "And your own people are aiding them and letting them cross your territories."

"Impossible!" the governor exclaimed. "Lorandians moving into your lands means they would flank ours. No man among us would allow such a thing."

"Your own son would."

For one moment, my world froze. That response came from a woman. And I would've recognized her voice anywhere.

I pushed forward through a wall of petrified bystanders and tried to get a better vantage. It was Tamsin, it had to be, but she was too obscured for me to see. A handful of militiamen had hunkered down behind an overturned wagon, and I scrambled to its top, ignoring their protest.

"Your son and other traitors are working with the Lorandians to stir up discord and draw Osfrid's army out of the central colonies—so that Hadisen and others can rebel against the crown," Tamsin continued.

Tamsin. Alive and well. With the Icori.

"It's a lie, Father!" Warren turned to the governor, moving the gun away from my friends. "There's no telling what they've brainwashed this girl into believing. What proof does she have for this absurdity?"

"The proof of being thrown off a boat in the middle of a storm when I discovered your plans," Tamsin shot back.

"Lies! This girl is delusional!" Warren swung the gun uncertainly toward the audience and then back toward Adelaide and Cedric.

I knew that kind of panic could make a man rash and unpredictable. I stood up and prepped a bolt in the crossbow, uncertain if I could make the shot. Even though I was in range, Warren made a small target from this distance and wasn't standing still. My hands shook. I'd only had half a dozen lessons with Aiana.

Suddenly, a man jumped onto the platform's stairs and made his way to the gallows. He came to a stop by Adelaide and Cedric, but his focus was on Governor Doyle. I could feel those piercing eyes even from this far away.

Grant.

"She's telling the truth," he said. He wasn't the wry Grant or the tender Grant, not even the eager Grant chasing clues. This was Grant at his fiercest, hard-edged and unwavering in a volatile situation. "There are stacks of correspondence. Witnesses who'll testify."

Warren stared at Grant with wide eyes. "Elliott? What the hell are you talking about?"

"I think you know." Grant's attention shifted to Warren. "About Courtemanche. About the heretic couriers."

Warren also knew his situation was deteriorating. It was written in his face and body language. After a quick threat assessment, he turned the gun on Grant. I aimed the crossbow but wasn't fast enough. Adelaide hurled herself at Grant just as Warren fired. Her save knocked her and Grant out of the bullet's path, but Warren's gun was one that held two shots. He immediately aimed at her.

I didn't even think as I pulled back and released. The bolt sprang from the crossbow with a *thwack*, and I momentarily lost sight of it as it sped through the air. A second later, I saw it again. Sticking out of Warren's leg.

He shrieked and collapsed, and Grant was on him in seconds. Confusion and terror doubled in the crowd. Heads turned, trying to figure out what had just happened. More people ran. The Icori looked a little confused at seeing their dramatic confrontation upstaged. Adelaide's eyes scanned the area and rested on me. Her face filled with shock, and then slowly, she began to smile.

I jumped down and wound my way past the lingering militia. Moments later, I was up the platform stairs and in Adelaide's arms. Cedric, smiling, watched us from nearby, and I pulled him into the hug.

"I'm so glad you're all right," I said. I couldn't keep the emotion in. Tears pricked my eyes. "Both of you. You're safe now."

At those words, Cedric and Adelaide turned. Farther down the platform, a flabbergasted Governor Doyle stood with Grant. Warren lay between them, tied up. "Who are you? Why do you think you have any right to seize my son?"

"Because we have a mountain of evidence indicting him for treason. We've been collecting it for months."

"What 'we' are you talking about?" demanded the governor.

"The McGraw Agency. I work for them." Grant didn't falter or lose that collected air. His face was still hard and tough. But I saw something fade in his eyes, the destruction of a dream he'd fought for for such a long time. My heart broke for him.

Grant had been made.

I took a hesitant step toward him, and then Adelaide exclaimed, "Tamsin!"

Spinning around, I saw Tamsin climbing up the rickety stairs. I

immediately ran toward her. Adelaide was right with me, and we practically knocked Tamsin over the platform's edge with our hugs.

"What happened?" cried Adelaide.

I clutched at Tamsin's sleeve and couldn't stop the tears now. "I
thought we'd lost you again."

"No," she told me. "But I'm never getting in a blasted boat again."
Tears of her own brimmed in her brown eyes. She was a wonder to
look at in all that bright tartan, with her shining hair wound into
elaborate plaits.

We talked over each other, laughing and asking questions and simply marveling that we were there at all. Silas's sharp voice jolted us
from the bubble of our reunion. "Thorn. A word."

I looked up and saw that both Warren and Grant were gone now.
Silas stood near Governor Doyle, who was speaking with a commander from the fort. Several other soldiers had arrived and were
spread in a loose but watchful ring around the Icori. Cedric separated
from us, Adelaide right behind him.

Tamsin and I held hands and watched as the three of them spoke in
hushed tones. "What's going on?" she asked. "I didn't expect to come
back to this. Whatever it is."

"It's a long story," I said.

"And that?" She nodded at the crossbow tucked under my arm.

"Also a long story. Probably not as long as yours."

Adelaide's face was alight when she returned. "Mister Garrett said
there's enough shift in the evidence to rescind the verdict! There's still
a lot to go over before Cedric's entirely clear, but for now—"

"Mira!"

I looked over the platform's edge and saw Aiana standing below,
her face somber. "I'll be right back," I told my friends. I darted down
the stairs.

"You have to find Grant," Aiana immediately said.

I glanced quizzically up at the platform. "I thought he must've
taken Warren away when Silas showed up."

"Yes, but once he has, I'm worried he'll disappear. If he hasn't already."

All that earlier joy drained from me. "Disappear how?"

"It was his backup plan—if the mission didn't work out or if his identity was discovered. Get out of Cape Triumph immediately before he's easily remembered. Take on another name in another place, get work in some trading company in the hopes of eventually going up there with a party granted access to the border or even just over the border."

I gaped. Grant had never discussed a contingency. "That would get him in?"

"Maybe. It could take a long time. And there's no certainty of traders getting through, which is why he wanted to avoid this. If he was reckless enough, he could sneak in and try bribing his way to amnesty for the illegal crossing, but that could just as easily get him killed." She rested her hand on my shoulder. "Look, that's for later. Right now, you need to talk him out of it before we lose him. I think you're the only one who can."

I thought back to our parting. Grant had balked when I told him I loved him, but he'd also sworn to me he'd save my friends at any cost. That cost had been his cover and nearly his life. The look in his eyes when he'd announced himself haunted me.

"I don't know if I can talk him into anything."

"You have to try, Banle," Aiana insisted. She handed me a key. "Hurry. If you're lucky, he stopped by his place to pack."

I bit my lip and glanced around. Adelaide still stood above me with Cedric, but Tamsin had come down and now spoke with a mixed group of Icori and soldiers. *I'm worried he'll disappear.*

Grant disappearing. Wandering off to be a ghost again, with a new life and a new mask. It was all he knew how to do, probably the only chance he could see to return to the Balanquans—even if it was dangerous. I couldn't let him do that to himself. I couldn't lose him.

I gave Aiana the crossbow and took off through the crowd.

Traveling free and alone no longer mattered. The Glittering Court was nowhere in sight; they'd probably scattered when the Icori arrived. I didn't care if I got in trouble with the Thorns anymore, especially when it seemed I'd be free of my contract soon—one way or another.

Grant wasn't in his loft, and it wasn't obvious in that empty place if he'd been there recently. His trunk was still there, and clothes still hung on their hooks. But I thought there might be less of them than before.

I locked the door when I left, and as I started to tuck the key away, I remembered I had another in my pocket. Silas's. Could Grant have gone there? He spent as much time at his mentor's and the store's as he did his own home.

But Silas's place was empty too. Heavy hearted, I started to leave for the store and then remembered the papers in the bag slung over me. Amidst all the surprises, I'd forgotten to give them to Silas. He apparently had enough to free Cedric and hold Warren for the time being but would need these eventually. I took them out and placed them back on the desk, not sure I could count on him still being at the courthouse.

Seeing notes scrawled in Grant's heavy handwriting triggered a pang of despair in my chest, as though I'd already lost him. As my gaze passed over the coded letter, I couldn't help but automatically read some of what he'd written. A few new additions stood out, like the name of the man who'd had the schedule in Bakerston. *Recipient is Cortmansh* had been written at the top and underlined three times. And then beside it, underlined four times: *How is he translating Balanquan?* The new corrections we'd discovered were there too, like the heretic patrols and Green.

My eyes suddenly jerked back to the top. Cortmansh. Grant had written that before seeing the Lorandian letter I'd translated earlier, which had corrected some of Abraham Miller's misspelled names. Cortmansh had become Courtemanche, which made more sense if he was Lorandian. We'd always used a harsh Osfridian pronunciation because of Miller's writing. But it wasn't an Osfridian name.

"Courtemanche," I said, using the lilting Lorandian pronunciation. It added another syllable, dropped some consonants, and revealed the words within: *Courte* for short, and *manche* for sleeve.

I've got several wagons heading out to Alma today . . . we're barely going over the border.

I glanced farther down the page and reread our corrected line: *He will supervise usual transfer so that you can deliver to Green Bend.* I pushed the letter aside to look at the map I'd noticed earlier in the stack. It showed all the Osfridian colonies and had been marked up by both Grant and Silas. There was Green Bend, the first major city just inside Alma Colony when coming from Cape Triumph.

I closed my eyes and put a hand on the desk to steady myself as I strung all the pieces together. Tom Shortsleeves—Courtemanche, the traitors' chief Lorandian financial supplier—was transporting wagons of valuables to other conspirators in Green Bend. Most of those valuables probably consisted of pure gold currency. Tom never kept anything else around for long—except goods that might be useful to an army, like ammunition and camp silverware. He gave away common items to Mistress Smith and sold his luxuries to people like Cornelius Chambers, rich collectors who eagerly handed over large sums of gold in exchange for rare Balanquan art . . .

I opened my eyes. Elijah had been the one to tell me about those sculptures, Elijah who'd spent his childhood with a trading group in the Balanquan Empire. Tom wasn't the one translating the Balanquan portion of the code.

I could scarcely breathe. With shaking hands, I jotted out a quick note to Silas: *Courtemanche is Tom Shortsleeves. He may still be in the city. I'm going to the Dancing Bull to try and find him.*

There was no time to explain my deductions, no time to even get Silas. The courthouse was out of the way from the Dancing Bull, and Silas could be off with the governor or the army. And Grant . . .

I slowed for just a moment as I descended the stairs back to the street. Grant. Was he at his store? Checking would delay me from getting to the tavern. If he was there, he wouldn't be for long. I would miss him if I didn't go now. But Tom was leaving—or had left—the city too. He'd said he was going right after the verdict, and Warren's outing as a conspirator would probably have hastened that departure.

My steps quickened again. I wanted Grant. I wanted to find him before he disappeared behind another mask. But I couldn't let the traitors' greatest source of gold get away, not when he had the potential and wealth to resurrect another plot. This was a sacrifice for the greater good that I couldn't refuse. I had to try to protect Adoria from the blood and destruction of war that still engulfed Sirminica.

Ignoring the ache in my chest, I pushed Grant from my thoughts and ran to the Dancing Bull. No one in the city gave me a second glance, not in a day filled with so much tumult. In fact, when I burst breathlessly into the tavern, my ankle hurting once again, it seemed as though no one had the time to sit down for a drink either. The common room was empty, aside from a sallow-faced bartender I didn't recognize. I was never here during the day. He stopped polishing a mug when he saw me.

"Where's Tom?" I demanded.

The shock on his face smoothed to neutrality. "Tom who?"

"You know who!" I stormed forward. "Is he still here?"

The bartender set down the mug and fixed me with a cool gaze. "Miss, I don't know what you think you're— Argh!"

I climbed over the bar and kicked him in the chest, doing it much less skillfully in a dress than I would have in Lady Aviel's pants. But it was so completely unexpected that the surprise gave me an advantage. I pushed him back with a knee jab to the stomach, trapping him in the small space. Another hit from my knee made him double over, and I forced him down by sitting on his back. I weighed less, but he didn't have room to maneuver. I grabbed a length of rope sitting near an ale cask and bound the man's hands with knot skills learned from my father.

"Where's Tom?" I repeated.

The bartender glared up at me defiantly, and I resisted the urge to slap the answer out of him. I had no time for torture or interrogation. If Tom was here, there was only one place he could be. If he wasn't here, he was probably out of my reach anyway. I located the back-room key, and a widening of the man's eyes made me think I might not be too late after all. On my way out from behind the bar, I spied the pistol kept on the shelf. I wasn't familiar with its style, but at least it was a close-range weapon. I fit the gun into my skirt's pocket as best I could and headed for the back-room door.

Beyond it, I found the stairwell that I'd seen the night Tom and I had argued. This time, the steps were illuminated from lanterns below. With a deep breath, I began my descent. The wooden stairs creaked beneath me, killing any chance at subtlety. But I didn't need it, not if I could pull off the plan I'd formulated on my way here.

"Barnaby? Has Elijah come back?" called a familiar voice.

I reached the bottom and found myself in an enormous storage area. Marks on the dusty floor showed that a huge number of crates had once filled the room. All were gone now, except for a few in the corner. One had its lid off, and Tom knelt before it, carefully putting in burlap bags that clinked when they bumped each other.

"Barnaby?" Tom glanced over his shoulder and jumped to his feet when he saw me. He tilted his head and looked me over, cautious but not threatened. "Well. You're certainly prettier than Barnaby. And maybe cleverer, if you made it down here. How may I be of assistance, fascinating creature?"

"I'm here to help you." I switched to the Belsian accent. "If you still want it."

Tom stared, speechless for a change, and then a huge grin spread over his face. "Lady Aviel! Is this the real angel at last? In a dress? And here I thought this was turning out to be a terrible day."

"Things not going your way?" I asked, returning to my regular voice.

He shrugged. "Just a lot of surprises. You're a good one, though. I can't believe I didn't catch on sooner. You do that Belsian accent flawlessly. But you're Sirminican, yes? Exquisite. And of course I want your help. Looks like we'll have to get you something a little more durable to wear to Alma, but we can worry about that once we're out of town. No wig, though. I won't allow it. It'd be a crime now that I've seen your real hair. I'm not even sure about a mask, though I suppose you'll want to—"

"Stop." He'd been inching nearer, mostly out of curiosity. I retrieved the gun from my skirt without him realizing it and pointed it at his chest. "Not a step closer."

"Really?" His eyes narrowed behind the mask as he studied me. He didn't look frightened in the least. "Is this about the wig? You can wear it if you want."

"It's about you and your operations, Mister Courtemanche. Get on your knees."

He obeyed, grinning. "And she speaks Lorandian too."

"Not as well as you," I said, recalling his farewell to Adelaide this morning. "And I can't hear a trace of it in your Osfridian."

"As well you shouldn't. I've been in or around the colonies for most of my life. My family came from Lorandy years ago, and I support my homeland's vision for Adoria."

"By funding a bloody revolution so that Lorandy can get its hands on the colonies' resources?"

"I *have* done a remarkable job," he said with false modesty. "If I'd only worked this hard in my youth, I'd be living like a king by now."

"The Osfridian authorities actually think you're a nobleman—that it's the only way you'd have so much gold." I nodded toward the bags in the crates.

He brightened even more, still far too at ease considering his current position. "Well, that is high praise indeed."

"It's over now. Lie down and put your hands behind your back." Some of the gold bags were tied with rope. It was a narrower type than what I'd used upstairs, but I was certain I could get it to secure his wrists—so long as I could do it while holding the gun.

But he didn't move. "Aviel, I really can't say enough how much I'm loving this. Not just seeing your real face. I mean: seeing this side of you. It really has improved my day—which makes it that much sadder that I have to be the one to tell you that gun isn't loaded."

I didn't blink. "You're lying."

"I'd never really leave a loaded gun that accessible. I keep it on display to make drunken customers think twice about harassing the bartender. And if they don't, my men can deal with any altercation."

"I don't believe you." But I was less confident now. Since I didn't know this type of pistol, I couldn't use its weight to tell me if it was loaded or not.

Tom got to his feet and brazenly moved forward, putting the barrel back to his chest. "Then fire and find out." When I did nothing, he chuckled softly. "Even if it was loaded, I wouldn't be afraid. I know you won't hurt me."

"You don't think I have the nerve?"

His smile broadened. "Oh, no. You're no coward, Aviel. You were brave to come here. I used to tease you about not getting your hands dirty, but now I know that's not true. It's just your last resort. You'd rather appeal to man's better nature. That kind of idealism will only hobble you, my dear. Because if you're trying to get ahead, if you're trying to further a cause, you have to shrug off honor and sentiment. If you really wanted to stop my actions, you would've tried to shoot me the instant you walked in. Instead, you decided to take the honorable path, to bring me in and see justice served through the fair channels everyone else faces. Thinking like that is why people fail. Why they get killed. Attachment to people, to principles, is a waste of your time. You need to be ready to sacrifice them."

"My father used to say the same thing."

"Smart man."

I pulled the trigger. It clicked. Nothing more.

My hands shook, as though the hopelessness of my situation had cowed me. I turned the gun to its side and made motions to surrender it—and then I swung upward and slammed the grip into Tom's face. He managed to grab my hair as I leapt for the stairs, jerking me back. I fell with a yelp, and moments later, he had me pinned on my back. He pressed a more familiar gun's barrel to my forehead, and I knew it was loaded. It was the one he often wore.

"I like you, Aviel," he said, with none of his usual levity. "And I wish you'd stuck with us. Lorandy's going to do great things in Adoria—far better than Osfrid could have. But your chance is over, and I can't leave loose ends. I, you see, have no problem making the tough decisions."

"Neither do I," said a welcome voice. "Pull that trigger, and I pull mine."

Still keeping the gun on me, Tom glanced over his shoulder, toward the stairs. He blocked my view, but I knew who stood there. "Mister Elliott, right? Spy and alleged shopkeeper. Until my lady showed up here, I would've said you're the best-kept secret in Cape Triumph."

"Lower your gun and stand up," said Grant.

"How are you giving commands? Are you really ready to sacrifice some innocent girl for the McGraws?" When Grant didn't answer, Tom *tsk*ed. "Well, Aviel, there you have it. Someone not afraid to get his hands dirty."

"Worry about yourself," said Grant. "If you shoot her, I shoot you. If you surrender, you can live. Those are your choices. I walk out of here either way. It makes no difference to me."

"Oh, stop. Of course it makes a difference. If I live, you get the glory of bringing me in for interrogation."

My mind raced. Tom was behaving too casually again, just as he had when he'd known my gun wasn't loaded. True, he was in a deadlock with Grant right now, but Tom wasn't the type to just sit still when a situation showed no obvious solution.

"Grant, someone else is coming! He's just wasting time!"

Tom still had one arm draped over my chest, letting him lean his body weight into me, but he kept his head and neck twisted to watch Grant. It couldn't be comfortable, but Tom also couldn't risk an unseen attack. "Are you on a first-name basis with him? No wonder you always seemed to have such romantic troubles. Never fall in love with someone who wears two faces, Aviel. And, Mister Elliott, I'm guessing you actually aren't so indifferent to—"

There. It was what I'd been braced for. I'd known Tom would have to shift eventually. He couldn't maintain that awkward position. And although he didn't release me, that slight rearrangement of his body gave me the only chance I'd get at fighting back. In the few seconds that his arm moved, I bucked up and jabbed his face with my shoulder as best I could. He immediately fired, but I'd maneuvered over just enough to escape the barrel. The gun went off right next to my head, though, and its blast sent a shock wave of pain through my ear. The world suddenly muted, and all I could hear on that side was a ringing.

Grant wasted no time either and was across the room in an instant, pulling Tom away from me. The two of them grappled on the floor, each trying to position his gun for a killing shot. They were too close and couldn't clearly aim with all the jostling. Tom had one bullet left and had to make sure his shot counted. Even with two bullets, Grant had to be cautious too. I glanced around for any weapons, but all I saw was the empty gun Tom had knocked out of my hand. Picking it back up, I moved over to the two men.

A brief opening let me slam the gun against Tom's head. He cursed and fumbled for just a moment, enough that Grant fired. Tom had squirmed away at the last possible moment and rather than continuing with Grant, he grabbed my bad ankle. I lost my balance and fell onto them, putting us into a momentary tangle of limbs and confusion. Tom managed to sit up and aimed at me, his clearest target, ready to use his last shot. Grant shoved me aside just as the gun discharged, and I saw his body jerk when the bullet struck. I screamed and dove for the gun he'd dropped. Tom was faster.

"Not an inch more, Aviel," he said, clamoring to his feet. I could barely make out the words with my ear still ringing. His mask was crooked, some of his feathers rumpled. But aside from a few red blotches on his face, he stood unharmed as he trained the pistol on me.

I looked over at Grant lying beside me. A crimson stain blossomed along the side of his shirt, spreading farther and farther. His eyes stared upward, and although his chest rose and fell, those breaths were shallow and ragged. I was too shocked to feel grief or anger or anything at all. This was too unreal to even process. I clutched Grant's hand and turned resignedly back to Tom, back to the gun's barrel. There was no mirth or cockiness on his hardened features.

"I really am sorr—"

A blast sounded behind me, and Tom fell. I looked back and saw Elijah standing at the base of the stairs. He stalked forward, attention solely on Tom's fallen body. It didn't move. After a few more seconds of scrutiny, Elijah lowered his gun and swiftly knelt by my side.

"Help us," I told him, leaning over Grant. I ran a hand over his sweaty forehead and started to reach for the wound. I pulled my hand back, unsure what to do.

Elijah pulled his coat off and handed it to me. "Use it to put pressure on the wound. Lean into it. I've got to get someone else to help lift him out of here."

He ran up the stairs, and I followed his orders with the coat, pressing it into Grant's side. He flinched but didn't cry out. Those shrewd dark eyes that normally never missed a detail stared up in a daze. Now that my stunned state had passed, I had too many emotions flooding me, the foremost being terror. I tried to swallow it back, knowing I needed a clear head.

"Hold on, hold on," I said, my voice cracking. "Don't leave. Don't become a ghost for real."

After a few blinks, his glazed eyes managed to focus on my face. He said something in Balanquan and then frowned, like he'd realized what he'd done but couldn't change it. At last, he managed some Osfridian, but it was so soft, I couldn't make it all out with my ringing ear. ". . . don't worry . . . I can't wander far . . . not when . . . my Saasa is here . . . I . . ." He switched to Balanquan and then trailed off into silence, his face blanching as the pain reared up.

A tear ran down my cheek, but I had no free hand to wipe it away. I gazed at the stairs, willing Elijah to appear, even though it had only been a couple of minutes. I turned back to Grant and found myself rambling. "You shouldn't have come. You're not supposed to be here. You were supposed to go chase your obsession."

He closed his eyes, but his mouth looked like it wanted to smile. He wet his lips a few times, and I leaned closer to hear his next raspy words." . . . I'm kind of obsessed with you."

Something moved in my periphery. Elijah. He was back so quickly, I wondered if he'd just decided to give up. A moment later, an ashen-faced Silas darted down the stairs.

And then I let the tears come.

CHAPTER 34

CAPE TRIUMPH WAS UPENDED IN THE DAYS THAT followed. Governor Doyle had known nothing of his son's treachery but had to deal with its aftermath, working with other colonial leaders and the McGraw Agency. The Icori had been given permission to camp on the city's outskirts and addressed their grievances in diplomatic talks that Tamsin helped facilitate.

Elijah, as I'd suspected, had been the one coding and decoding Balanquan for Tom. Elijah had only discovered the full extent of the conspiracy recently. That knowledge had come on the tails of increasing uneasiness with Tom's work, but fear of retribution on his family had kept Elijah from breaking away. Now, free, he bought amnesty for himself by telling all he knew. Seeing Tom about to kill me had been the catalyst to finally shake Elijah up. He'd grown too disillusioned with Tom and too fond of me, thus proving Tom wrong. Closeness, attachment, and treating others as humans, not pawns, weren't a weakness after all.

And Grant? Well, Grant wasn't easy to kill.

A doctor removed the bullet and said nothing vital had been struck, but the threat of infection or too much blood loss still loomed over us that first day. I spent those hours in agony while Grant spent them heavily sedated under painkillers at Silas's. The doctor finally an-nounced that Grant would make a full recovery, and as he gradually came off the painkillers, he proved to be an unruly patient. He hated being restricted. He especially hated being waited on. It made him grouchier than usual, but Silas, Aiana, and I didn't mind as we took turns keeping him company.

When I wasn't with him, I had plenty of other things to preoccupy me. I had both Adelaide and Tamsin back in my life, and despite their own obligations, we managed to spend time together every day. I loved having all of us together again, though it wasn't the same as our easier days at Blue Spring. We all felt so much older now.

Incredibly, Rupert insisted on paying off my contract, no matter how much I tried to tell him I could borrow for it. Only the Thorns and Silas knew. Cornelius had done so many embarrassing things that Rupert wanted his business affairs righted before making what he'd done public. But even if others didn't know right away, *I* knew. When Jasper had given me a copy of my fully executed contract, I couldn't stop staring at it. I was free. I'd made it to Adoria and bought a life for Lonzo and me. His knee was well enough for travel, and I expected him any day, thanks to Grant's generosity. I'd given Lady Aviel's earnings to charity.

My involvement in forming a city watch was kept under wraps too, though I jumped right into its planning with Silas. His experience was reassuring, but I wouldn't have it for long. He was scheduled to escort Warren and a few other traitors back to Osfrid personally, and I had to accept the daunting reality of soon being completely in charge.

I think Silas was relieved when Grant moved back to his own place. Grant might have felt like a son, but he was a grating son. Once he was home, I spent so much time at his loft that I might as well have been living there too. The Thorns let me stay at Wisteria Hollow a little longer but could no longer dictate my actions. I was still at the house a lot, and amidst all the other chaos in the world, no one really kept close track of my whereabouts.

"We shouldn't be doing this," I told Grant one morning. It was a luxury to wake up with him instead of scurrying off in the middle of the night.

He rolled over and wrapped his arms around me. "Sleep in?"

"*No*. You know what. You shouldn't be . . . exerting yourself." I gently traced the edge of the bandage that still covered his side. "You're recovering."

"Recovering isn't the same as dead. The doctor says I'm fine, and anyway, you're a little late in expressing your concern."

"I expressed it two days ago."

He kissed the side of my neck. "And yet here you are."

"I can't stay. Neither can you. Silas wants to meet with us this morning." I wriggled away and sat up. Before getting out of bed, I asked hesitantly, "Are you leaving?"

He put his hands behind his head. "Not today."

My question wasn't about him going to Silas's. It was part of the same exchange we had every day since he'd become lucid again. Each morning, I'd ask if he was leaving—really leaving. *Not today*, he would say. And we'd go on with our lives until I had to ask again. We didn't talk about us or the future. I couldn't even get him to talk about how he felt about losing the ambassadorial opportunity. When I'd brought it up, he had just shrugged and said, "It's over. No point getting caught up in it."

Today, though, I didn't go on with my life. I stayed where I was, perched on the side of the bed in a thin chemise, and asked, "Are you happy?"

The change in our morning dialogue caught him by surprise. "Why would you ask that?"

"Because I'm tired of asking if you're leaving every day. I'm tired of being afraid that one day, I'll come over here, and you'll be gone."

"You think I'd go without telling you?"

"I don't know, Grant. I really don't know much of anything, except that I love you and keep coming back to you each night."

He no longer panicked when I told him I loved him, but he always got a quizzical look on his face. "What else do you want?" His question didn't come across as confrontational or sarcastic. He seemed sincere, like he really wasn't sure of the answer.

"I'd like to know what you're going to do. I'd like to know if you're going to search for another way to go to the Balanquans. I'd like to know if you're going to stay . . . with me."

He fixed his gaze on the bright window for a long time before finally turning back to me. "I don't know how to be with you, Mirabel. Here—in bed—that's never been a problem for us. But I don't know what to do outside of it. Whenever I've had someone or someplace I thought was good and real and lasting, it disintegrated. I don't want that to happen with you."

"And so you'd just rather live day by day, too afraid to go past this? Grant, I don't really know any more than you do. I mean, look at me. I came in thinking I could sleep with you without liking you."

"Turns out you could," he said, unable to resist himself.

"No, I always liked you." I paused. "Most of the time. Look, we'll probably make some mistakes, but we can figure it out together. If you want to."

I sounded very sure of myself, like maybe I actually did know something about relationships. Inside, I was terrified. A perpetual knot of tension in my chest tightened as I waited for his response. What if this was the moment I lost him? Maybe I should have let us go on forever in that undecided state, where we could keep ignoring uncomfortable topics.

"I want to." He sat up and reached out to brush hair from my face. His hand trembled. "I can't leave you, Mirabel."

The knot in me eased. I took his hand and brought it to my lips. "Then I can stop asking if you'll leave?"

"Yes, but I can't guarantee you won't want to throw me out one day."

"We'll be okay. And I can't really throw you out of your place anyway. I told you, we've just got to be in this together. We've got to make sure we talk—really talk. Not all snips and banter."

"Wait, wait. You didn't mention that before. We *can* still banter, right?"

His recovering state saved him from getting elbowed. "Yes. We can even designate exclusive times for it, if that makes you feel better."

"It does. And as for throwing me out . . ." He gestured around us. "I don't know how much longer this will be my place if I can't pay the bills. I'm done with the store; it was just a cover. And I don't get along with the agent who'll fill in here while Silas is in Osfrid. So probably no McGraw freelance work either. I may have to rely on the Lady of the Watch's charity until I figure out what nonwandering job I'm cut out for."

I smiled back. "Well, the Lady of the Watch happily extends her charity. But maybe . . . maybe you'd like to work for her too."

"Are you offering me a job?" He sounded more amused than interested.

"Sure. I've got to hire people—people I can trust. And I think it is the kind of job you'd be good at. You're observant. You don't mind running into a fight. In fact, you seem to have an easier time doing that than talking about your feelings."

"Who's snipping now? And I've been pouring out my heart here, you know." He grew more serious as he contemplated my offer. "I'd do this—the watch. But . . . what goes on between us isn't going to stay a secret. I don't want it to undermine your position."

"Why would it?"

"Because—since you know I tell you the truth—there are going to be people who have a hard time accepting a woman in charge. You may—you will—get resistance to your orders. Not from me, of course. I'm already used to following your orders. But some people will try to use you being involved with an employee as an excuse to attack you. Can you handle that? If memory serves, one of the first times we met, you were threatening someone with a knife over slander."

Thinking about what I knew of human nature, I suspected he was right. "I can handle it. Can *you*?"

"Handle attacks on you? Not peacefully. But on me? I don't care. They can say whatever they want. They can call me Mister Viana."

I laughed. "Would that be a problem?"

"No. I collect names. But . . . maybe . . ." He had to glance away and steel himself before meeting my eyes again. "Maybe you'd want to be Mistress Elliott."

It was another of those moments I had to puzzle over what he'd said to understand what he'd *really* said. And then: "Did you just . . . propose?"

With the effort of that task over, he slipped into his familiar cockiness. "Well, I've done it before."

"Have you? To me?"

He cut me a look. "*Yes*. When we talked about you going with me to the Balanquans."

"That wasn't a proposal. Neither was this." I reached back into my memories to when he'd mentioned traveling north. "They were more like passive suggestions. Proposals usually involve . . . well, a little more. I would at least expect an actual question."

He feigned shock at that. "Whoa, hey, you knew what you were getting into here. If you want hours of flowery speeches, you'd better go find out if Cedric Thorn has a brother."

I laughed. "No, I just want you, despite how impossible and complicated you are. Maybe because of it."

"And I want you because . . ." The humor on his face faded as he studied me, and I suddenly understood what he meant when he talked about "that look" I gave him in emotional moments. I was pretty sure he was giving me his equivalent. And it was overwhelming. "I want you because you're you, Mirabel. Because I don't want to wander when I'm with you. And because I love you." He said that last part so fast that I nearly missed it. And then he kissed my cheek and got out of bed. "But don't let it go to your head."

When we went to Silas's later, I expected another meeting about city watch logistics. Instead we found both Silas and Aiana standing there with their arms crossed, waiting for us. Grant looked between them suspiciously.

"What is this?"

"We need to settle some things before I sail," said Silas sternly. "Are you leaving, boy? Give me an answer, once and for all."

Grant's tension melted. "Wow, this is really my day. Yes, I'm staying. Yes, I'll be here when you get back."

Silas kept his expression hard, but I saw relief flow through him. "So you're fine with Aiana's offer. You'll wait for it."

"Yes." Grant fixed a sharp eye on her. "Even though I told her there's no need."

"It's my choice, Iyitsi," she returned evenly. "Take advantage of it."

They'd lost me. "What offer?"

Aiana met Grant's challenging look with defiance a few moments more before answering. "I violated my marriage by running away from my wife—that's a great offense in the upper branches. There are serious punishments for that if I'm caught. It's why I hide out here. But if we're apart for five years, the marriage is dissolved, and I'm free of the repercussions. I just need to stay away for about a year and a half more. Then I can safely visit—and bring Grant with me. He can petition for his citizenship back."

"You don't have to go back at all," Grant insisted. "They'll make you finalize paperwork and see her again."

Aiana dismissed him with a wave of her hand. "I'm not afraid of her anymore."

I turned to Grant in wonder. As happy as I'd been to hear he'd stay here, I'd felt a nagging guilt about him being denied his homeland after all he'd done. "Then . . . you can go back. Not quite the way you wanted or as soon, but . . ."

"But he can wait," finished Silas. "What can't wait is you two. You can't keep carrying on like this."

"Carrying on like what?" I asked innocently.

"Don't play coy. I know where you sleep." His gaze swiveled to Grant. "Stop it or go make this official on paper."

Grant didn't flinch. "See, Mirabel? Compared to him, I'm a

fountain of romance." To Silas, he said, "Relax, we're planning on getting married."

"Are you?" asked Aiana, startled. She looked at me for confirmation.

"Yes. Apparently Grant proposed to me. A couple of times. I think." I thought back to our discussion of proposals this morning and realized there never really had been a question or answer.

"*Yes*, I did." Grant shot me a pointed look. "It was a beautiful moment."

Aiana seemed more surprised by that than him actually proposing. "Really?"

"Why are you so shocked, Sekem? I'm not completely insensitive. I know how proposals work."

"That's right," I added slyly. "He took my hand and asked . . . what was it?" I glanced over at him expectantly.

He recognized the trap. His face was angled from Silas and Aiana, and the look he gave me said, *How could you do this to me?* I just smiled even more, and after clearing his throat, he said, "Well. I don't remember the exact wording, but I'm pretty sure I asked if she'd do me the great honor—an honor I know I'm not worthy of—of becoming my wife. I told her she's incomparable among women and is the brightest, truest thing I've ever had in my life—*unlike my friends*, who are currently staring at me as though they've never seen me before. And I also said I'd be slightly less cynical and do everything in my power to make sure her days and nights were unbelievable. Unbelievably happy, I mean." He paused. "Oh, and it was definitely an actual question. To which she replied . . . ?"

I received the expectant look now, and I said, "Yes. Definitely yes."

I think I answered a little more seriously than he expected. He faltered a moment, and I probably had "that look." Recovering his composure, he turned to the others and said, "Are you satisfied now?"

Their speechlessness answered for them.

Later, while Aiana and Silas discussed a favor he'd asked of her, I pulled Grant aside. "Did you decide to stay with me before or after Aiana offered to go back with you?"

"Are you doubting me?" He angled his head to peer more closely at my face. "I can't tell if this is designated serious time or bantering time."

"I'm starting to think it's all the same. And I believe you . . . except you didn't actually answer."

"I figured the profound sincerity in my face answered for me. Look, the whole reason I found the note in Silas's office after the trial was because I'd decided to stay. If I'd intended to leave that day, I would've been gone. I knew how I felt about you a long time ago, way before she offered. I just had a lot of things to figure out. Like how to acknowledge I had feelings. Obviously, I excel at that now, after that incredible speech I gave. Did you hear it?"

"I heard it." I took his hand and laced our fingers together. "I'm actually still kind of stunned. I don't need Cedric Thorn's brother."

"Well . . . I also needed to get you to say 'yes' in front of witnesses. In case you changed your mind."

"Now you doubt me?" I laughed.

"Just a precaution. I wouldn't have given you a close name if I doubted you."

I took a step back. "You did not."

"I did." He wore the same self-satisfied look that he'd had when revealing the truth about his monk costume. "Even on my deathbed, I was a hopeless romantic."

"Deathbed . . ." I wracked my brain for every detail of the last week, scouring anything that could connect. "The cellar."

"So you were paying attention." He still had that smug grin. "But apparently not enough to remember. If you only knew, you'd never doubt me again."

"I already said I don't doubt you! I was half deaf back then. And I was a little distracted by you bleeding to death in front of me." The memory was fuzzy and not just because of my hearing. There'd been too much adrenaline, too many raging emotions.

I can't wander far . . . not when . . . my Saasa is here . . .

"Saasa?" I asked. "What does it mean? Do I have it right?"

"I'll tell you tonight in bed. During designated bantering time."

I paused in scrutinizing my memories. "That's designated bantering time?"

"Eh, I hear it's all the same." He put his hand behind my neck and pulled me to him, kissing me far more intensely than I would've expected with Silas and Aiana across the room. He drew back from the kiss but kept me close a few moments longer. "See you later, Mirabel."

He left to take care of an errand Silas had asked him about previously, and I later found myself walking back to Wisteria Hollow with Aiana.

"Hey," I asked her. "What does *Saasa* mean?"

"*Saasa?*"

"It was something Grant said. After he'd been shot and we were waiting for help."

Aiana studied the road ahead as she thought. "It means axe. Also bubbly. Oh, wait. *Saasa?* Is that what you mean?"

"Isn't that what I said?"

"You said *Saasa.*"

"They sound the same! What's that one mean?"

"It's a path made out of rocks. People use them in front of their homes."

I shook my head. "Never mind. Sometimes your language is more annoying than fascinating."

"Weren't you deaf then?" she asked.

"Only partially." I thought back to Grant's face at Silas's. "I've got it right. Or, well, I'm close."

After several minutes of quiet walking, Aiana suddenly said, "There's also *Saasa.*"

I withheld a sigh. It sounded like all the other variations. "What does it mean?"

"It's like, oh, I can't think of which of your angels it's named for."

She gestured in front of her, like she might grasp the meaning from the air. "The star that doesn't move. The wayfarers' star."

I stopped walking. "Ariniel's star."

"Right. That's the one."

For Balanquans, Ariniel's star is the wayfarers' star—the star that always brings you home, no matter how lost you are. The only thing a wanderer can count on.

A smile began to creep over my face.

I can't wander far . . . not when . . . my Saasa is here . . .

Aiana studied me curiously. "Do you think that's it?"

"Without a doubt," I said.

IN A VILLAGE WITHOUT SOUND,
ONE GIRL HEARS A CALL TO ACTION

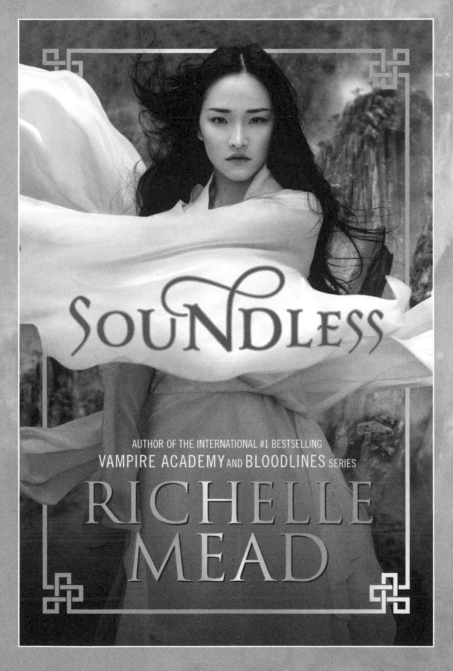

SOUNDLESS

AUTHOR OF THE INTERNATIONAL #1 BESTSELLING
VAMPIRE ACADEMY AND BLOODLINES SERIES

RICHELLE
MEAD

"Fans of Rose Hathaway and Sydney Sage will flock to
this impressive stand-alone novel."
—*Booklist*